I0783797

Wendelton
Press

A LIGHT from the NETHER

A LIGHT FROM THE NETHER

MOLLY DOWD SULLIVAN

First edition: June 2025

Library of Congress Catalog Number: 2025901364
ISBN: 979-8-9877136-8-6

Published by Wendelton Press, LLC
www.wendeltonpress.com

Stay up to date on new book releases at www.mollydowdsullivan.com

Content Warnings for A Light From the Nether:
Contains spousal, sibling, animal, and parental abuse, suicidal ideation, self-harm, hoarding, disordered eating, schizophrenia, substance misuse, violence, homophobia, depression, anxiety, insanity, insomnia, imprisonment, religious extremism, drowning, and animal corpses.

There are graphic depictions of physical injuries, ailments, and parasitic infections. Contains instances of questionable consent or a lack of consent regarding bodily autonomy, though not in a sexual context. There is no sexual abuse. Expect frequent swearing.

This is a love story.

For my mom

And my dad

And all the lights who guided me out of the Nether.

You did not meet me then
You would not meet me now

SECRET HIDEOUT
The Letterbox
RABBITS
N
W
E
S

GLOSSARY

The Nether: A plane composed of trauma and memory. It is an inverted dreamscape of our Waking World—a quilt of horrible fragments of time, sewn together by a sloppy hand. In a way, it is sentient. This is where Flukes reside.

Fissure: A tear in the fabric separating the inner world of human minds from the Nether. Flukes are drawn to Fissures by human soul energy—their source of food.

Flukes: Parasites that live in the Nether and feed on human soul energy and trauma.

The Fluke Types and the Five Baits that attract each of them:

- Red Fluke - Vice
- Yellow Fluke - Neglect
- White Fluke - Subjugation
- Violet Fluke - Violence
- Blue Fluke - Despair

Phren/Mindscape: The landscape of a person's mind.

Sophont: An individual who can travel into peoples' Phrens.

Teletravel: The act of entering another person's Phren.

Wedge: A Sophont employed to seal Fissures.

Patch: A lesser, local Wedge. Can teletravel but usually does not have the ability to exterminate anything more powerful than a minor Fluke (such as Red or maybe Yellow). Typically works in smaller towns that are less likely to have serious Fluke attacks.

Splint: A Sophont psychotherapist assigned as the partner of a Wedge. They assist in Fissure scenes and counsel Fissure victims in the process.

Host: The victim of a Fissure/Fluke attack.

Husk: A Host or Sophont whose soul has either been separated from their Phren or devoured by a Fluke.

Wick: A soul in the Nether which has been mutilated by Flukes.

Hitch: A type of Wick that is linked to a living soul. It can inhabit or possess the mind of the individual to which it is tied.

Pelt: A person under the control or influence of a powerful Sophont.

Paraphrenologist: One who studies Fissures, Flukes, The Nether, Sophonts, Wicks, Hitches, and Phrens.

Paraphrenology: The study of Fissures, Flukes, The Nether, Sophonts, Wicks, Hitches, and Phrens.

The Waking World: The plane of consciousness of the living.

Nether prison: A personalized cell of memory and trauma inflicted by a Trypanon with the ability to manipulate the Nether.

The Other: The theoretical opposite of the Nether, where human souls naturally go after death. Like all concepts of heaven, it is only a theory.

Tryp/Trypanon: An extremely rare individual who can travel between the Nether, Phrens, and the Waking World. They possess the ability to open and close Fissures. There are only seven known Trypanons in the world. They are immune to Fluke attacks.

Trypanism: A spirituality that worships Tryps as divine links to God/Gods and their holy judgement. The belief is that people die from Fissures/Flukes because of their sins and weakness.

FUSE/Fissure Unit for Security and Extermination: A branch of the Federal government responsible for sealing Fissures and exterminating Flukes.

The National Academy for the Paraphrenically Gifted—Northeast, Southeast, Midwest, Northwest, Southwest: A mandatory federal boarding school for all Sophonts. Education begins at age twelve and continues until eighteen. Most children present abilities before age twelve. It is very rare that they present after age fourteen.

PROLOGUE
Chicago, January 2018

LIAM IS SICK of the wind. It shoves at him like a bully, stuffing his nose with sewer stink. He zips his hoodie up to his throat. Frigid air slips down his back in an unwelcome caress.

"No winter coat tonight, I see," Makoto says without looking at him. A police car careens by, its siren scraping against the edges of Liam's hangover. Shades of blue and red light chisel the landscape of Makoto's deliberately blank face. It's annoying.

"I'm fine."

"You're shivering."

Liam stuffs his hands in his sweatshirt pockets. He sidesteps a dead pigeon, belly up with its legs in the air and eyes frozen white.

"According to you, I'm too 'self-destructive' to dress for the weather," Liam says.

"Surely, you can't be that bad."

"Your diagnosis, not mine."

"I can still be optimistic."

"I'd rather you be quiet."

They round a corner. Webs of caution tape come into view. A swarm of police officers huddle at the mouth of an alleyway. Liam grabs Makoto by the sleeve.

"Why the fuck are there this many cops?"

"My assumption is they found out you'd be here."

Gossip is unavoidable, but Liam still manages to be surprised by how fast it spreads. The last thing he needs is a bunch of cops breathing down his neck. Not that there's anything he can do to stop them. When his fourth scene in a row was contaminated by too many officers trying to catch a peek, Liam went to his boss, Archer, to get something done about it. After cringing through three cups of herbal tea and calling in every favor she owed him, she promised to help. Apparently, she'd been too busy reading her horoscope to follow through.

It wasn't that he had an issue with cops in general. They served a purpose. But they also tended to mishandle a Fluke victim until a simple extermination became a master class in fuckery. There was a good reason an independent sector existed to handle Fluke attacks. It nerfed liability, and, theoretically, kept people out of Liam's way. That is, if his colleagues were on time for anything in their damn lives.

"Where the hell is our team? How long did Archer say it would take FUSE to get here?"

"She didn't."

Of course she didn't.

FUSE stood for Fissure Unit for Security and Extermination. Liam liked to call them "Fuck Ups Serving Egomaniacs." Makoto didn't find it funny. Or maybe he did. Liam couldn't tell.

Someone calls out, "He's here!" and everyone looks at them.

Strangers' eyes have always followed Liam like pilot fish, eager to feed. He'll never get used to it. He halts, grinding his fingernails into his palms. Mouths gape open. He's reminded of cats trying to drink up a scent. His throat tightens.

A pulse of calm—not his own—brushes against his mind and takes the edge off. He shoots Makoto a glance, grateful, even if he is just doing his job. There's a reason Makoto is the one Splint, or personal telepathic shrink, capable of counseling Liam. Makoto's mind is a lake beneath a mountain, glassy and clean. It's a fitting counter to Liam's, which Makoto once described as "a storm on a sea." Liam thinks "fire in a dumpster" is more accurate.

Before Makoto, Liam had gone through Splints faster than Archer could assign them. Normally, a Splint's job was to pull a Wedge back from the brink when the job got messy, using their power to inject calm and order into a mind. The problem was that Liam was never at the brink; he was over it. That's what made him exceptional and damn impossible to pair with anyone. Except Makoto. Where other Splints fumbled, doing more to irritate Liam than to calm him, Makoto was a lifeline.

And he somehow kept from punching Liam in the throat, which was a superpower several of the other Splints certainly failed to master.

A prickling static grows stronger as they approach the scene. The air crackles and steams with it—makes the hairs on his neck itch. It's distracting. Liam almost doesn't notice when the chief steps into their path.

"Good evening, Chief Hamley. It's nice to see you again." Makoto is nothing if not polite. The same cannot be said of Hamley.

"Took you fucks long enough to get here." Spit mists out of her mouth. Her jowls dent with a smirk. "Too busy writing fan-porn about yourselves to do your jobs?" She looks to her comrades for support, which they obediently provide like their jobs depend on it (which they do).

"We were delayed," says Makoto. "Delayed" is a fancy word for "Liam couldn't get his ass out of bed." Liam sends a pinch of amusement Makoto's way and feels a sprig of satisfaction when his eyebrow twitches. Getting a reaction out of Makoto is Liam's favorite, if most challenging, hobby.

A cadet at Hamley's flank comes forward, eyes sparkling at Liam. His uniform is too new, his hair stiff with white-flaked gel. A pimple throbs on his chin. "I can't believe you're really *Calico*. It's an honor, sir." He takes a step closer. Liam's hit with a waft of caustic body spray. "May I ask you some questions?"

"I—"

"Is it true that your hair changes every time you seal a Fissure? Like, you get a new patch of color? Or do you just dye it that way? If you do, that's cool. It looks so good on you."

The cadet frowns at Liam's baseball cap, like it's barring him from playing with a new toy. Liam hates it, hates his stupid hair. He'd shave his whole damn head if it didn't make him look like a neo-Nazi. Makoto doesn't understand why he bothers dyeing it every other week, since the color changes keep happening anyway. But Liam has waged a Sisyphean battle with the nickname "Calico" since college. Giving up now would make the whole effort feel like a waste.

"But what does your hair matter, right? I mean, you're a *Wedge*. It just blows my mind. I always wondered how you do it. Tell me, what do they look like—the Fissures? I read online that they look like a door. How do you close one up? And what's it like going inside someone's mind? Can you do it without them noticing? Wait, are you in my mind right now? Can you hear my thoughts?" His eyes are big as traffic lights. Drool glistens on his lip.

Liam is spared from responding by Hamley, not that she's trying to help him.

"Get a date on your own time, Barston."

Barston flushes between his freckles and his shoulders bunch. The audience they've accrued starts to snicker.

"S-sorry."

"You're fine," Liam says. He takes the kid's damp hand in a shake. "It's nice to meet you too. No, I'm not reading your mind. Yes, a Fissure is like a door." That's a lie. The truth is that a Fissure is closer to a tear and Liam is the seamstress who sews it back up. But that sounds far less sexy and Liam isn't interested in wasting time on questions.

Barston stumbles on half-formed words, settling on either "you too" or "I love you." Liam turns back to Hamley before he finds out which. He shoves his hands back in his hoodie, subtly wiping them off on the fabric.

"What have we got?" He injects a note of command into his tone, honed through years of navigating red tape and obstinance. He adds a touch of psychic influence. A sprinkle. Faint enough that no one outside of Makoto would notice. It's not strictly ethical, but who's going to stop him?

Liam stares until Hamley grunts and goes on.

"Homeless lady named Samantha Munn. Black. Early seventies. No criminal record. Her husband died a couple decades ago from a stroke and that's when everything went to shit. One of her hobo buddies found her and called it in." Her voice rises, ensuring an audience. "I knew she had a Fluke in her the moment I saw her. I can practically smell it."

She looks to Barston, seeking the same naked admiration he's leveling at Liam, and comes up empty. Liam holds back the urge to correct her. While Hamley might guess a Fissure victim from a catatonic meth head on her better days, she'd never be able to sense a Fluke. Only Sophonts like Liam and Makoto can do that.

It's too early for Liam to tell if there's a Fluke. All he feels is the Fissure, spewing out energy like a crack in a dam, fed by the dark world contained on the other side. If a Fluke has crept through the crack, even Liam won't know without a closer look. A Fluke is an interloper—a fiend. They're good at hiding.

Liam doesn't understand people like Hamley. He's met a lot of her kind—those with a desperate wish to be a Sophont—to be special, gifted, a paraphrenic mind walker. Their envy is a foreign smell, cloying and baffling. All they see is the power. Fucking fools. The power is an illusion. Liam doesn't want any of this, and what he wants doesn't matter. A Sophont's wants never matter.

"Any idea how long she's had the Fissure open?" he asks.

"She hasn't frozen to death yet, so not that long." Hamley scratches a mole on her chin. A hair curls out of it like a worm. Liam wants to pluck it.

"Where is she?"

"Down the alley, third shit pile on the right."

"And you didn't move the Host like you did last time, correct?" Hamley had taken it upon herself to drag the poor man—some kind of politician—back to the police station so she could showboat. Liam was not kind when he'd arrived and found the Host dribbling, his mind mauled to bits by a Red Fluke. For scolding her in front of the whole precinct, Liam has a vague memory of being called "a jumped-up little shit with a drinking problem." Which was both fair and irrelevant.

"I dunno', pretty boy, what do you think?"

As it happens, Liam thinks many things. Makoto responds before he can share them:

"Thank you for your help. Our crew is on their way, but we have authorization from Archer to begin now."

"If you could keep the perimeter secure, we'd appreciate it," Liam adds. "From *everyone*. We can't have any distractions." Makoto side-eyes him. With a sigh, Liam grumbles, "please."

Hamley bristles. A headache spikes behind Liam's eyes, and the Fissure jabs at him, demanding attention. He'd give anything to be back at his apartment, curled in bed where he can wallow in peace with a bottle of scotch and some cheese fries.

"My officers have a right to be here. Chances are they're going to encounter a Fissure scene at some point, and some of them haven't even met Sophonts before. They need to learn what to do, and it's your fucking responsibility to teach them. We're the ones on the ground while you waltz in smelling like a bar bathroom, do your magic tricks, and leave. We all deserve to see the job done." She puffs out her chest. "That is, unless you're worried you can't do it. Wouldn't be the first time you made a mess of a Fissure sealing. Best Wedge in the world, my whole ass."

The last of Liam's patience dries up.

"This isn't a show, ham sandwich. I'm not your fucking teacher and this isn't your jurisdiction. The only thing your officers need to learn is to stay out of the way and let us do our job."

A low murmur sweeps across the lot. Hamley mouths soundlessly. Liam ducks under the caution tape before she finds her way to a retort. Or an arrest warrant. He holds the tape up for Makoto.

"You called her a ham sandwich," Makoto says once they're out of earshot.

"And?"

"You used to be clever. And polite."

"I'm tired."

"You're hungover." It's not that kind of tired and Makoto knows it. The hangover is a symptom, not a cause. "She may have had a point," he adds, twisting the knife.

"Jesus, bite your fucking tongue. I'm doing my best."

"I am aware."

They're a few strides into the alley when Liam's smacked with the stench of a Fluke. His fingers snap to his temple, jostling his glasses. He tries to blink the acrid taste of it from his eyes. A cat wails nearby. Makoto puts a hand on his shoulder.

"How bad?"

"The synesthesia or the Fissure?"

"Both."

Liam sniffs, rubs his cheeks. Makoto hands him a tissue to blow his nose. It doesn't help. His senses scramble.

"I can taste the piss behind that trash can and smell that goddamn cat screaming in my ears. There is a Fluke. Probably a Yellow."

"You detest Yellows."

Liam tosses the tissue into a sewer grate.

"I detest everything. Well, except you, Mak Attack."

Makoto sighs. He hates that nickname, which is entirely the point.

"I suppose I should be grateful you didn't call me a sandwich."

"Wish I could have a sandwich."

"Later."

The alley is a canyon, funneling Fissure aura and wind. He shivers as they move past cardboard box houses and stray shopping carts.

"You should have worn a coat," Makoto says.

"Mind your fucking business, you grandma—"

He stops. His awareness sharpens, his senses dilate. Lips parting, he tastes the texture of his surroundings: the dead dog lying in rigor on a soggy blanket, the crunch of feasting cockroaches in a trash bag. He feels the Host before he sees her.

"Ah, shit," he sighs.

Samantha Munn sits against the brick with her head tilted back, staring at the sky in a silent scream. Most of her teeth have fallen out—her mouth looks like the wet burrow of a rodent. A patchy wool coat cocoons her, and her bare legs sprawl on a cake of newspapers. She is a weak, gray creature. Un-human. Liam imagines she's made from paper-mache.

"Definitely a Yellow," Liam says.

"I agree."

Liam's skin prickles with the sense that he's being watched. He glances behind them. Hungry silhouettes stare back, their badges catching the light.

Makoto nudges him. "Ignore them."

"I hate an audience."

"Pretend it's only you and me."

"Like a date?"

"No."

Liam takes a breath; shakes out his hands.

"Here goes nothing. Fuck, I hate doing this."

"I know."

With a hard swallow and twitch, he makes his perception blur and shift—as a lizard blinks a third eyelid—and sees what Hamley never could: the true form of Samantha Munn. This is why he detests Yellow Flukes.

Samantha's skin is dotted with holes, as if her pores are dilated. From them, small, black heads peek out like grubs in fruit. They squeak and click. Opalescent pus leaks from her nose and ears, crusting where it dries. But the worst thing, as always, is the smell. Neglect is a stagnant thing, sickly and sad—thick as spores in the air. It's not the worst he's ever seen.

The thought shakes the cage of a memory—the small village he'd been sent to heal in Haiti after a massive Fissure Event. He can still smell the Hosts, convulsing in their scrap metal huts, mad with Fluke. A teenager had lurched out and bit Liam on the ankle. The wound had festered, and he'd almost gone septic. There are two smile-shaped scars on each side of his Achilles. He dry heaves whenever he looks at it.

Fingertips touch his wrist, startling him back into the moment.

"Alright?" Makoto frowns at him.

"Yeah. Shit. No, not really. My Phren is a mess."

"May I?"

Liam nods.

A door opens in Liam's mind and Makoto slides through it, his presence cool as well water. He's the only Sophont Liam allows to do this—to enter his mind. Makoto always asks permission, not that he could waltz in without Liam's consent; Liam is too powerful for anyone to break into his Phren. Still, the gesture is appreciated more than Liam admits. Though, he supposes, he doesn't have to admit anything; they share almost everything like this.

The walls of a living room rise around them in Liam's mind. Makoto walks the perimeter as if he hasn't been here hundreds of times, eyeing the couch and the fireplace, the cobwebs in the ceiling corners. Without looking at Liam he says,

"Thinking of Haiti again?"

Liam stuffs the memory away into the cellar, kicking the door shut behind him.

"Not by fucking choice."

Makoto steps up next to him. He watches Samantha through Liam's eyes. Makoto's form is different here. Soft wrinkles credit emotions never expressed in the physical world. He looks older. Tired. It's the honest version of him.

"This is an unpleasant one."

"Yeah," Liam says. "Fucking Yellows. I really don't want to do this."

"So you've said. Technically, you don't have to."

"Bullshit."

Back in the alley, in their bodies, Makoto squeezes his wrist. Liam feels the touch even as Makoto's form in his mind doesn't move. Makoto won't let go of him until they're done. If asked, he would claim it's easier to maintain their mental link when they're touching, but Liam doesn't buy it. Makoto has monitored Liam's pulse during Fluke exterminations ever since Liam fainted and cracked his skull on a vintage Nintendo 64 two years prior (the console was fine). Five stitches later, and Liam gets his hand held like a kindergartner.

"Ready?"

Makoto nods.

Liam sucks in a breath. With a shudder, he dislodges his consciousness from his body on an exhale, like sliding off a dock into dark water. Makoto follows.

They quickly secure a mental thread between them, tying them to their bodies and to each other. He can still hear Archer's lecture at the Academy, back when she was his teacher and not yet his boss; "This is the most important lesson anyone will ever teach you! Tie the thread!"

Together, Makoto and Liam breech Samantha's mind.

It shifts into focus, pulling them in, locking the door behind them.

"Not the worst we've had," Makoto says, looking around.

"Not even close."

Samantha's Phren is like any other: predictable. The word "Phren" always seemed too pretentious. "Mindscape" was more palatable. It's the human mind, manifested. And it isn't some grandiose, artful thing; it's an exhibition of home and nostalgia, usually a house or school. Boring. If Liam is lucky he'll get a garden, though his particular favorite was a theatre. But what really makes each Phren unique is the furniture: adornments of memory, given form. His own Phren is no exception; it's his grandparents' big old house in New England. He likes it simple. When he was younger, he experimented with all sorts of designs: castles, old ships, even an amusement park. It was too easy to lose memories or make a mess. When the house took shape on its own one day, he never found a good reason to change it.

Samantha Munn's Phren is an apartment. Liam and Makoto stand in the entryway.

Though Fluke infection coats the air like batter, it's clear that Samantha's Phren wasn't always unpleasant. The light is warm, and the wallpaper is floral. As Liam takes a few slow steps down the hall with Makoto close to his side, he clocks the family photos of fishing trips and picnics. Carnivals. The living images call like sirens, seductive with strong memory. If Liam looked too long, he'd be able to creep inside them. He doesn't because he's not a fucking rookie. Or an idiot. Most of the time.

"Is the Fissure in the living room?" Makoto asks as they approach an open door.

"Doubt it."

It's a cozy, calm space, less contaminated than the rest of the Phren. A newspaper declaring the end of the Vietnam War holds a place of honor on the mantel. Echoes of music and secret dances are soaked in the floorboards. There's a pile of love-worn books in the corner: Woolf, King, Camus. On top of a record player, *Bookends* by Simon & Garfunkel. It's been played too many times (never enough). Happy memories.

"Lots of material here," Liam says. "Not gonna have trouble weeding out a Neglect Fluke. Looks like the bait didn't happen 'til somewhat recently."

That was good. Fresh neglect wasn't pervasive. It was the Hosts with childhood neglect that he had to worry about.

"And the Fissure?" Makoto sounds impatient. Liam can't blame him. Being inside a Fissure victim's Phren is like touring a hoarder den—uncomfortable and fascinating and embarrassingly intimate.

"I'd bet my first born it's in the bedroom."

"You told me you don't want children."

"Oh my God, not the point, Mak."

As they move deeper, the apartment mutates around them. Where there were vases of flowers and Christmas decorations, now are piles of discarded memories: a rusted Winchester rifle, a dusty mound of pill bottles, an argument never resolved. Everywhere the stains of lovely expectations, gone sour; striations of disappointment woven in the sheetrock. Neglect soaks it all.

"Christ, I can see why she attracted a Yellow. There's bait everywhere."

"Yes. This should not happen."

A door appears.

"There. I can hear it," Liam says.

"I can as well. Ready, then?"

"For a drink? Yes. But I guess we can do this shit first."

"I will buy."

"You better."

Liam pushes the door open.

Against the far wall, Samantha Munn kneels beside a double bed. Her forehead is pressed into the quilt, her fists clenching on nothing. A prayer circle of IV poles surrounds her, casting long shadows. A cross on the wall above the bedframe is crooked

There's a human-shaped dent on the mattress with a tear down its center. It emits a glowing hum.

"There," Liam says. "That tear. That's the Fissure."

Liam knows by the way it kneads at him. He feels it before it forms. There's pain—an itch. A wound that's festering. The Nether's fetid energy oozes like pus.

Movement. Liam flinches when the Fluke flickers into focus. The sight jars him as it always does. From the Fissure, scabbed fronds unfurl. Their tips latch onto Samantha's head and neck. He can hear the suck and pull as they drink. Liam is reminded of wading out to sand-bars as a child. He'd poke at mounds of sandworms with driftwood sticks. "Quit messing around with those," his grandmother would squawk. "They'll bite your fingers off."

Yet, in every way they are like sandworms, they are also different, as Flukes are in everything. Earlier in his career, Liam made valiant efforts to articulate what Flukes and Fissures look like to non-Sophonts. It's all an impression, he'd say. A *feeling* more than an image. An unfathomable dream. But no matter how well he described the sickly sweet or the worms that were not worms or the inhuman sentience, nothing sufficed. You had to be a Sophont or, if you were unlucky, a Host, to understand.

The Yellow Fluke jerks at Samantha like a nursing piglet.

Though they aren't fun to look at, Yellows are easy to starve out. Neglect takes a long time to settle in. It doesn't take much to clean it out. He just needs the right tools.

He approaches Samantha slowly. The last thing he needs is to startle a soul he's trying to help. Makoto projects calm around them—the trickle of a gentle stream, a warm breeze carrying fresh cut grass. He's bailed Liam out with this technique more times than he can count.

Squatting down, Liam touches his fingers to Samantha's nape. This is the worst part. In forming a connection, he feels what she feels—crawls into her skin to wear the years of loss and pain. For most Sophonts, this part is too much. They fail to separate their lives from the Host's and get lost. Only a handful of unlucky fools have the fortitude to work in the field. Liam wouldn't say he's good at it, but he is used to it.

He begins.

Drawing from what he saw in the halls of her Phren, Liam conjures the flowers of a past well-loved. He hands them to Samantha's soul like sweets; a Simon & Garfunkel song—he plays it for her—and the sway of white satin, the smile in his eyes. He offers the smell of a steak dinner, just for two. A spring of joy when he came home. She had been tinkering on an Impala engine, a smudge of grease on her cheek. It had smeared into his uniform when she hugged him.

God, I missed you. His voice was rougher than she remembered.

I didn't notice you were gone.

Then why are you crying?

I'd forgotten how ugly you are.

I think you look beautiful.

Liam glances at the Fluke. It writhes and shrivels, mouths popping as they dislodge. Veins blacken in its limbs, a sign that Liam's poison is working. One more strong, good memory should weed it out.

He takes a risk.

It was one of her husband's last days. Liam sees it carved into the walls of their bedroom. Samantha had held his hand and kissed his wedding band. Somehow, despite the pain of it all, she'd made a joke. It doesn't matter what it was. He'd laughed. Even in the worst of it, she had made him laugh. It chimes like holy bells; a final gift. Liam hears it like it's made for him. It's not. He's never known something like that.

The Fluke recedes into the Fissure. Liam starts to pull away, ready to seal it.

"That wasn't so bad," he says.

But then Samantha, caught like a fish on a hook, is yanked toward the Fissure.

"What the hell?" Liam grabs her by the shoulders. He catches sight of a silver string tied around her finger before its pulled into the Fissure.

"What's happening?" Makoto asks.

"I don't know. Shit, I can't hold her."

"Can you seal the Fissure instead?"

"Not without damaging the Host."

He thinks fast. It's a rush job, but Liam manages to conjure ropes. It's not easy to manifest an object in someone else's Phren. Well, not easy for other Wedges. He wills them to wrap around Samantha's waist, securing her to the bedpost. It's silly, but the mind is powerful in its own realm. Samantha's mind believes the ropes exist, that they do what ropes do, so for now they work. But the Fluke has been feeding for a while, and she's not as strong as she used to be.

"That's not gonna hold. I have to go in."

"Liam, I don't think—"

"I don't have a choice."

He doesn't wait for Makoto to fire off the myriad of reasons why he shouldn't do this. He climbs up onto the mattress, crossing his arms against his chest, and with a deep breath, a hop, and a sudden plunge, he tumbles into the maw of the Fissure …

And lands hard on his knees. The ground is damp and gummy with dirt. It's dark. He wipes his palms on his jeans.

For a moment, he falls for the trick. He's certain he's back in the alleyway. Then the delusion dies. He knows this place too well to be swindled. It may look like reality, but gravity is stronger here. It pulls heavy in his chest and crackles on his body hair like he's covered in little wires.

This is the realm of Flukes, of warped spirits and fragments of trauma stuck in time. It's a tapestry of memory, spawned by the worst of the Waking World. This is the Nether.

He takes it in.

A crippled horse-drawn carriage stands a few feet away. Blood drips from the hub and long, red hairs twist around the axel. From a window above, the muffled rhythm of disco and a fist hitting flesh. He startles at a scuffling sound. It's Samantha's Fluke, slithering into an old milk crate, dragging its body like a soldier with shattered legs. Liam can afford to ignore it as it is now.

It wasn't always possible to ignore things in the Nether, especially in a place as traumatized as Chicago. When he was in college and first moved to the city, he engaged with things he'd never touch now (the echoes of H.H. Holmes will stay with him forever). He isn't certain how much damage he did to himself in those days, when he was too stupid to suppress curiosity. When Makoto asked him to describe the Nether once, he told him it's like one of those I Spy drawings where every inch is cluttered with the detritus of the past. If he didn't train himself to focus on what he was looking for and ignore the rest, he'd never find what he needed. Or find a way out.

Turning, Liam looks back at the Fissure. It's a crack in a brick wall. Samantha's hand sprouts out of it, the silver thread still wrapped around her finger, pulled taut. When Liam tries to touch it, he's hit with a shock that shakes the walls around him.

"The hell?"

Liam? Makoto sounds like he's speaking at the other end of
a tin can telephone. *Are you alright? Can you hear me?*
*Yeah. Still haven't found out what it is pulling her in, but I have a
theory. I'll make it quick. Try to keep her out of the Fissure.*
Please be careful.
I'm always careful.

He wishes briefly that Makoto was beside him, taking his jokes too seriously. But Makoto isn't Liam. Like everyone else, Makoto can't go into the Nether and come back alive. It would be a one-way door. The idea of him trapped in here is too barbed to touch. Liam shakes it off.

He follows the string, suspended at waistline level. Everything flickers, unstable. The Nether is ever-changing and unpredictable. A crevice appears in front of him, and he barely avoids tripping on it. He often gets the sense that the Nether is taunting him. It has a mischievous, cruel sentience. It knows him, hates him, is infatuated with him. The feeling is mutual.

The path of the string leads him around a corner, down a narrow street. A strange door takes shape at the end, with the string closed in its hinges. Glossy red and fresh, the door is an aberration. It's offensive as a ball gown in a soup kitchen. Beyond—a faint, dull buzz.

Liam gathers himself. Fear chills the air. He longs for the drink he'll get to share with Makoto after this is done. Soon, this will be nothing but another memory he can try to forget. He just needs to finish it. He's done worse for much less.

He pushes the door open.

A force hits him hard, knocking him down. His shoulder collides with a sewer grate, his ears flood with a scream of fear as sickness burns in his eyes. It's a soul, and Liam recognizes it. Its essence had been so clear in Samantha's Phren.

Like this, Samantha's husband is contorted far beyond himself. Nothing remains of steak dinner dates or slow dances or a joke to spite death. The Nether ate those memories long ago, leaving only a hungry shadow. And he's powerful. His aura pounds at Liam, biting; consuming. This is not like the hunger of a Fluke, or of a fan who wants something from him. This is an appetite without direction, without taste or limits. This is a soul; corrupted. This is a Wick.

It beats on him, incessant, and Liam is tired. The Wick's rage and anguish leak into him. Everything is so pointless, so devoid of pleasure. The point of fighting is foggy. He can't remember what he has worth going back to, or who. Liam has no memories like Samantha's, no sweet flowers of connection—only isolation. Loneliness. A gaping void, a constant sense he's missing something he can never find. What is the purpose of him? He grasps for something, anything, and his hands are empty. He's empty. He closes his eyes.

Then Makoto yells in his head. Not with words. It's a feeling—a command. It hits him with purpose. This is all wrong. He must escape. Not for himself, but for the hassle his death would be for Makoto. He'd probably blame himself. Liam won't do that to him.

Using every bit of his power, Liam slashes out at the mangled soul, aiming for the string. It's not a power he uses lightly. Shame rises. This is the darkest part of him. It makes him feel like he's a part of the Nether—like it's formed by his hand. Makoto doesn't know he can do this.

But he has no choice. He reaches deep. Grabs. Detonates.

Mr. Munn is thrown off him in a discord of static and sent reeling back behind the door. Liam slams it shut, sealing him inside. He conjures a few deadbolts for good measure. After a couple desperate pounds on the door, silence.

It's a while before Liam catches his breath and buttons up the panic. He's threadbare; hollow. It's not the first time he's faced a mangled soul in the Nether, but he doesn't have the strength (or the will) he once did.

Staggering to his feet, he stumbles back out into the alley.

William O'Connor, Makoto booms. Liam winces.

Jesus, I'm coming. How's the Seam?

She appears safe. Please get back here.

I said I'm coming, for fuck's sake.

Liam rubs at his shoulder as he shuffles back to the Fissure. He's not looking forward to seeing the bruise bloom on his body when he gets back. He'll have to hide it from Makoto.

He pauses.

There's a presence at his back. A smell oils against him—salt and sundried crab shells, seaweed dredged in silt. It's familiar.

He looks over his shoulder.

There, behind him, is something Liam has seen many times before:

Black, pure, hideous nothing. And in it, a wisp—one solitary golden light, longing for something fathomless. It knows him. This is not like any Fluke or Wick he's encountered. It feels created just for him, or worse, *by* him. A specter from his nightmares given form in the Nether.

Liam breaks into a run.

He throws himself forward, bending time and space to speed his way, back to the Fissure. But the Nether doesn't want him to leave. It grows thicker around him, tacky like a spider's egg sac. The light follows, desperate; only getting closer.

Heat wets Liam's neck. Walls crumble around him. Eyes glow behind windows, drawn out to spectate. Liam shouts. Then he sees it: the Fissure. His way out. With a lurching dash, he hurls himself into it, toward the sound of Makoto's voice.

He falls back into Samantha Munn's Phren, tumbling off the bed and hitting the floor hard. The light—the wisp—wails behind him. He can't let it through. Makoto tries to touch him, and Liam shoves him off. Using the last of his strength, he seals the Fissure like a deckhand packs a joint with oakum. He catches one last glimmer of light before the seal is done.

Now Makoto's fingers are all over his face, as if he's checking for something.

"Cut it out, I'm fine." Liam jerks away before Makoto can discover the bruises.

Makoto sighs. "What happened?"

"I'll tell you after."

Liam's attention shifts to Samantha. She blinks back, eyes wide.

"Mrs. Munn," he says. His voice shakes only a little. He offers Samantha a gentle touch to her shoulder, noting with a glance that her left hand is gray and lifeless. She'll never be able to use it again. Not in her Phren, not in the Waking World.

Nothing alive can survive the Nether, except people like Liam.

"My name is Liam O'Connor. I'm a Wedge. That means I seal Fissures and exterminate Flukes. You had a nasty one just now, but we took care of it. It's nice to meet you."

Samantha's eyes narrow.

"Why am I tied to my bed?"

"How's my hair?" Liam lifts his hat to the side, attempting to lighten the mood, as they make their way out of the alley. He gives Makoto a weak smile and gets a blank stare in return.

"You have a new patch of red near the front and a large white spot in the back." There's an unspoken *we'll talk about this later.* Usually, Makoto severs their telepathic link as soon as they're done with the Host, but Liam can still feel him in his Phren. Either he is very concerned, or royally pissed off.

FUSE moves around them. Good. They can deal with Samantha's aftercare now that Liam's finished doing all the fucking work. He's gasping for a drink to chase Makoto's inevitable scolding.

Someone from FUSE slams into his sore shoulder. He hisses through his teeth.

"Better watch where you're going, Calico."

"Go fuck yourself, McClellan."

"Aww, what's the matter? Not enough cadets suck your dick today?" she cackles. "And what are you—a bitchy teenager? Get a fucking coat." She saunters away like she won something.

"I hate her."

"She is teasing you to hide her feelings for you," Makoto says. Sometimes his empathic senses are useful. Sometimes they make Liam want a lobotomy.

"Never say that to me again."

"I was trying to help."

No, you weren't. You're punishing me for going into the Nether.

Makoto's silence is loud. Message received.

The easy exit from the scene that Liam is hoping for is not forthcoming. Cops crowd them when they pass the yellow tape.

"Excellent job, sir," a bright-eyed woman tells him. "My grandma is a big fan."

"Let us watch next time, will ya'?" another says, clapping him on his bad shoulder.

Liam glimpses Hamley standing off to the side, ignoring him. She looks like Liam just canceled International Donut Day.

By the time they reach the perimeter, Liam's breath is shallow and thin. He's raw from the Fissure. His senses are too sharp. It's suffocating. He sweats despite the cold. This is why he hates wearing coats. He wishes he could take his hat off.

Then he sees his least favorite thing in the world.

Oh fuck, no. He shoots Makoto a desperate look, hoping he's not too annoyed to help.

I will handle it.

Makoto intercepts the reporters while Liam pulls out his phone and orders an Uber. Though it's not strictly legal, he can tell Makoto is subtly nudging the reporters toward distraction. If FUSE had any inkling of the extent of Makoto's abilities, they'd never let him function in polite society. It's a good thing Makoto happens to be the most moral man Liam knows. He just bends the rules sometimes, and he's subtle about it.

"Liam?" someone says, coming to stand in front of him. Reluctant, Liam looks up from his phone. It's Barston. Liam swallows back a groan. "That was incredible." Barston steps so close Liam feels his breath. "Everyone says you're the best Wedge in the world, but to actually see it …"

Liam edges back. His headache whines.

"It was just a Yellow."

"Have you ever seen a Blue?"

It's his least favorite question.

"No one has seen a Blue."

"But the news said you did. I mean, you must have. You're a *Trypanon*."

Barston's lips chisel the shape of the word, and the sweat freezes on Liam's skin.

"That's enough for today," Makoto interrupts, stepping in between them. "We need to be going." A threat reverberates off Makoto. Liam watches it hit Barston like a challenge. The kid flinches back, blinking in confusion. Liam almost feels sorry for him.

When their car pulls up, Liam collapses into it. His shoulder throbs dully. He's trembling. Outside, it starts to snow.

You should ice your shoulder tonight.

I can take care of myself, thanks.

The lie is so comically obvious, Makoto doesn't need to call it out.

Shadows of buildings pass. Liam's vision blurs. The engine rumbles a gentle rhythm. It's a while before Makoto asks the inevitable question.

Are you going to tell me what you saw?

Buy me that drink before you ask me to put out.

Their usual bar is horrible, and Liam likes it that way. The chances of running into a coworker or adoring fan are nil since no one is scummy enough to go there. A bowling tournament plays on the TV as Liam picks at initials carved into the bar top. He breathes in the stale scent of spilled beer and disinfected barf, familiar as a migraine.

"It was a Hitch," he says.

Makoto stops drinking mid-sip. He slowly puts down his wine glass.

"Hitches are very rare."

"No shit."

"Was it her husband?"

"Yeah. His soul was at the other end of that string on Samantha's finger. I thought he was just a Wick at first—he'd been chewed to a pulp by a Fluke. Guess that means he died from a Fluke attack, not a stroke. They probably misdiagnosed him. Christ, I bet he'd been following Samantha for years, tying her to the Nether and fucking with her mind. Probably set her up for that Fluke attack. Maybe he even ripped open her Fissure somehow. No real way to know. Anyway, he attacked me, and I almost died. A regular Wick could never be that strong. He had to be drawing power from a Hitch link."

Makoto stares at him. It takes Liam a moment to sift through what he said.

"I mean … I would have been fine."

Makoto's glare sharpens.

Liam scrapes a hand through his hair. "Alright, let me have it, then. I know you're itching to."

"You told me you would avoid going into the Nether again at all costs."

"And I didn't break that promise. The Host would have died. And I had to go in if I wanted to sever the Hitch from her." That may not be strictly true, but no one knows enough about Hitches to deny it. Most of the scholarship on the Nether was written by Liam.

"And what if you couldn't fight it off? As you said, you could have died. Or worse."

Liam manages to hold back the "who cares," but Makoto is still in his Phren. They both go still.

"Liam."

Liam glances at Makoto, then away again. He can't face him when he looks like that.

"I'm fine."

"You're not. You're exhausted."

"The whole 'not sleeping' thing might have something to do with that." It's not like his insomnia is new. The dark smudges under his eyes have made more than one person ask who punched him in the face.

"Are you not sleeping because of the dreams or because Claire left you?"

"Jesus, Mak."

Makoto shrugs. Liam supposes he deserves that one. At least they're tabling the Nether for the moment.

"Both?" Liam admits.

"Has she contacted you?"

"She's tried. I'm not interested in her pity." Liam downs the rest of his whiskey and wipes his mouth with the back of his hand. He signals for another. He still can't look at Makoto.

"She is concerned about you."

"Not concerned enough to stay."

A pause. Liam feels Makoto weigh the risk of his next words.

"*I* am concerned about you."

"Then what the hell do you want me to do about it, huh? Quit? You know they'd never let me."

"Technically, they cannot force you to stay."

Liam rolls his eyes. Makoto can be oddly naïve about random things, but usually not about FUSE.

"Yeah, *technically*."

"If you did not want to do this anymore, I would advocate for you. I would make sure it happened."

"I'm just shy of thirty. As far as they're concerned, they got another twenty years left in their investment. You can't bamboozle the whole department with a few paraphrenic nudges—not without being caught. But thanks anyway."

"If you were passionate about leaving, FUSE would let you. Archer would force them."

"The hell she would. They don't let people like me out into society without a leash and you know it."

Makoto shrugs. "The question is: would you allow yourself to leave?"

"What's that supposed to mean?"

Liam regrets asking as soon as the words are out. He unclenches his fists. Half-moons, flecked with blood, dent his palms.

"Perhaps your sense of responsibility for the lives of strangers is crippling you."

"Funny, I thought that's what made me a good person."

"Not if it comes at the expense of your own well-being. I don't have to be a Sophont to sense what this job is doing to you. Are you still seeing the Nether around you even when you don't try?"

The bartender slides Liam a tumbler of whiskey. Liam chugs it in one gulp and doesn't answer. In the corner of his vision, the wall bursts into flames that aren't really there. He's starting to get used to fire in Chicago. The Nether is full of it. He doesn't bother asking if Makoto can see it too.

"You told me it gets worse every time you enter the Nether," Makoto persists.

"Last time I tell you shit."

The drink is a hot swell in his chest. He welcomes the first tingle of a buzz and decides it's a good night to get drunk. Makoto takes a deep breath, a sign that he's gearing up for a psychoanalysis. He better not. Liam is one "how does that make you feel?" away from walking out.

"Human minds, even Sophont Phrens, were not meant to enter the Nether. It is a world of trauma and apathy, and you soak yourself in it when you go in there. You're different every time you come out—I can tell. And not just because you get a new patch of color in your hair. You take some of the Nether back with you, and it takes some of you. What if you go so deep that you can never come back? What if you do come back and you're not yourself anymore? I don't want to see that happen."

"Is this your professional opinion?"

Makoto pauses.

"I am your friend."

"You're my federally assigned shrink. Thanks for not letting me forget it."

Silence snaps like a bowstring. Makoto's Phren recedes, leaving Liam's mind. The abrupt emptiness is startling. Cold rises between them.

Makoto's phone rings. It's the ringtone assigned for FUSE. They look at each other and pass a silent confirmation: something is wrong.

"Makoto Mori," Makoto answers. Liam watches his eyes sharpen at the muffled voice on the line. "We're coming." He hangs up; their eyes meet. "Samantha Munn's Fissure has reopened."

"That's impossible. My seals never reopen."

"I know."

Liam hates hospitals. His senses chafe at the blend of bleach and bed sweat— the wear of loss. It reminds him of the Nether. Impending stress radiates off every Phren in the building, patient and employee alike. With the addition of a crackling Fissure, it's inundating.

As they rush down the hall, a FUSE escort at their flank, Liam begins to realize that Samantha's Fissure is different than before. Neglect is a distinct scent, and its absence is stark.

They reach the doorway to Samantha's room, and Liam's feet stick to the floor. Makoto runs into his back.

"What is it?" he says.

"Get back in my Phren."

"That bad?" Liam doesn't respond until Makoto has slipped into his mind again.

It's like Iris.

It's a word Liam never says aloud, and certainly not to anyone but Makoto.

> *You cannot go into the Nether, Liam. Please.*

Liam doesn't respond. He steps up to Samantha's bed.

"When did it reopen?" he asks the room.

"About half an hour ago." It's McClellan. "I was here when it—" her words catch. "When it happened. Liam, it … it feels weird."

Liam's known McClellan since they were in school at the Academy. She was never strong enough to make it as a Wedge or a Splint, but she had the fortitude (stubbornness) for some field work. He's never seen her shaken before.

"I need everyone out of here," he says.

When Liam was younger, this request would have been met with resistance. The benefit of his reputation is that people generally do what he says without question now. Even McClellan.

Once they're alone, Makoto's fingers find his wrist.

> *Your pulse rate is high.*
>
> *Can't imagine why.*

Makoto squeezes.

> *Promise me you won't go in the Nether.*
>
> *No.*
>
> *Liam.*

He jerks out of Makoto's grasp.

> *Let me do my fucking job.*

Makoto is wise enough not to push back. Guilt wells up. None of this is Makoto's fault. It doesn't change the circumstances.

He makes his perception switch.

There are no holes on Samantha's skin now. No worms. No crusted pus or stench of neglect. Her body is a black pool, reflecting nothing. Liam stares at it. It stares back. He catches the faintest spark of light.

> *Liam. I don't.*

Makoto's thought dies. Liam feels the stutter, the fear gumming up his Phren. Makoto tries again.

> *I don't think we should go in there. It's … it's as if her entire Phren*
> > *is a Fissure.*
>
> *Then stay behind. I can handle it alone.*

Makoto grabs his wrist again, clenching so hard that Liam feels his heartbeat in his fingertips. There was never a chance Makoto would let him go alone. Still, Liam would hate himself if he didn't try.

The tether is secured between their souls and their bodies. Liam has never crafted one so strong.

Makoto looks at him. His eyes are a secret for Liam alone.

It's a Blue, isn't it, he says.

They dive in …

To a ruin.

The walls of Samantha's apartment are barren and crumbling. There are no decorations, no memories. Only shadow. Chunks of sheetrock whisper into dust around them. The door to her bedroom hums. Blackness pools out from the base of it like blood in moonlight. Liam looks at Makoto.

"I have to go in. I can't seal this one unless I do," Liam says. "I don't want you to come with me."

Makoto's head snaps to him. His eyes narrow. "We don't need to go in there at all. Samantha is gone. I can tell a Husk as well as you can. There is nothing we can do for her now."

"Nothing *you* can do."

Makoto gapes at him. "If her soul is in the Nether, she's gone, Liam."

"And if I don't seal that Fissure, that Blue Fluke will spread as soon as it's done with her. We're in a goddamn hospital; there's bait everywhere. It'll feast until I can't stop it. It's not like a regular Fluke. Blues can hop. I've seen it. You haven't."

That stops Makoto short. Liam was alone when Iris happened. It's the only other time Liam has encountered a Blue (shit, it's the only time *any* living Wedge has). He'd hoped it was the last.

"I'm going. You stay here."

"Liam, no."

Makoto grabs his arm. His Phren tries to take hold of Liam's, but he's not strong enough. Liam falls out of his grip.

"You promised me."

His words stab; the tone—so rare from Makoto—is poison on the blade.

"I have no choice."

Using the full power of his Phren, Liam locks Makoto to the floor of Samantha's dead mind. It's a violation of all they've built together. Liam hates himself even as he ties the final knot. Makoto says nothing—just stares in shock. It's worse than words.

Liam gives him the courtesy of eye contact. He knows it's the final time. This was always inevitable for someone like him.

"I'm sorry."

Liam strides toward the bedroom door without looking back. He shoves it open without touching it, and slams it shut behind him.

And is hit with a force so absent that for one, scalding moment he is wiped clean. A purge. A baptism. He scrambles to gather the pieces of himself and reassemble. It's harder than the last time.

Then he looks into the eye of the Fissure.

The light. It's been waiting for him. Always. He'd seen it in the Nether. He's seen it in his dreams every night since he was twelve. Its pull is stronger than ever, and Liam is too blank to resist. He's drawn like a widow to a grave. Makoto is screaming in his Phren. The sound is in the past.

There is only the scent of sand and tidal grass, the taste of water briny as tears.

William.

He floats into the Nether, is welcomed into its arms. It's been waiting. The light is close. Ever closer. It knows him so well. It bleeds into him, filling a void that once gasped and starved. Finally. They can finally be together. There's no point in running anymore.

He loses himself.

Then firm hands take him by the arms, yanking and spinning him away. The light cries out in anguish. Liam blinks back into himself.

And sees the worst thing he has ever seen, in all the horrible sights of his life: Makoto in the Nether.

"No." The word is a breath, spoken from every pore. All the pieces that make Liam crack and invert, rewritten by unfathomable horror.

"Don't." Makoto shoves Liam back through the Fissure. An agony unlike any he's ever known blooms from the last place they will ever touch. Liam tries to speak. To move. To stop him. He can only watch as Makoto is swallowed by pure dark.

Then, Makoto seals the Fissure, separating them and locking himself away forever.

When Liam returns to his body, he chokes. Makoto is lifeless on the floor, his eyes vacant and skin gray. A final breath parts his lips.

And Liam screams and screams, until he has no voice left.

And then he doesn't speak for long time.

DUST AND SILT

Shoalport, New Hampshire. June.

THE DOOR YAWNS open. Flakes of dust puff up from the ground like gnats, catching the light.

"And here it is. Welcome home, Calico!"

Liam blinks. His eyes burn. The word "home" sounds like a joke. Liam doesn't laugh anymore.

"That's not my name." He's already corrected her once. Liam had spoken to Maggie on the phone before he'd left Chicago. In person, she is far worse than he'd imagined. Her hair is an offensive shade of carrot, frizzy and kinked, her cheeks shining greasy. Her arms hang from her sleeveless sweater like dented white dough. She didn't believe him when he said he didn't have a Facebook account.

"Of course it is, with that hair. I wish you'd take that hat off." She reaches up and he jerks back.

"The house," he snaps.

She juts her lip out in a pout. "So serious. Have it your way. So, three large bedrooms, two and a half baths. The kitchen is vintage but that has its charm, right? You've got a total of four fireplaces. *Four!* Though, I wouldn't light a fire until you get them cleaned. They'll be full of nests and dead squirrels. Plumbing and electricity could use some updating, but how about that wraparound porch? And the tower, too? Can't find that just anywhere these days. Your grandparents kept things in great shape. Too bad no one came to take care of the place when God took them to heaven. Mind, they were Catholic, but nobody's perfect. Well, what do you think of your new house?"

Liam looks around the entryway, at the decaying staircase and tired wallpaper, the tall ceilings. The air is stagnant, laced with a thread of familiarity. He sees it through a fog. "It's old."

"And how! It dates back to the early 1800s. Of course, we have older homes in Shoalport. We are very proud of our history here. This is one of the oldest towns in New England."

"Okay."

Liam doesn't give a shit about the house or the town. He'd have moved into a shack in a Walmart parking lot if it meant getting out of Chicago. This just happened to be free.

"You have some of the original furniture, passed down through your family. The rest were Peter and Deb's, God rest them. Your grandparents were good, God-fearing people. You must have been so devastated when they died. I don't think I caught you or your parents at their funerals, though." She arches a threadbare eyebrow and fondles her cross. Liam counts the spider veins on her nose.

"Yeah."

Maggie's smile twitches. Her eyes spark with an aggressive (futile) demand for him to be more interesting. She sucks on her gums before shifting tactics. "This is an awful big house for one man. Will a young lady be joining you? The online forums couldn't work out if you were single or not. Wouldn't want you stuck in such a big house all alone with no one to cook and clean for you. This is no place for a bachelor. Do you at least have a pet?"

Liam side-steps her and escapes to the living room. White sheets shroud the furniture. The fireplace whistles with wind in its clogged throat. Memory comes. He sees a young version of himself running past to the kitchen, his grandmother yelling that he'd better not have sand on his feet.

"I have a rabbit," he says without thinking, and regrets it immediately.

"You do? That's adorable! Whoever heard of a grown man having a rabbit?" She giggles until she snorts. "What's his name?"

Liam sighs. "Kermit."

"But that's a frog's name, silly! You can't name a rabbit after a frog."

Liam remembers the day Makoto brought Kermit home. He'd been shocked to see Makoto take on any pet, let alone a small, black rabbit. When he'd asked why, Makoto had frowned for a few moments and said, simply: *"Kawaii."*

"What the hell does that mean?" Liam had said.

"It means I am allowed to have something cute."

"I'm cute." Liam had winked. Makoto hadn't responded.

"You know, you're something of a celebrity here," Maggie says, invading his reverie and dragging him back to the present. He resents her for it, wanting to be left alone with his memories.

He closes his eyes and prays hopelessly that she'll burn out.

"Everyone in town still talks about what you did when you were a kid," she continues. "My church group will be just buzzing over you finally coming back."

"I came here to get away from all that."

"That's right—you quit, didn't you. You must have a lot of money saved, huh? How much does Wedge work pay, anyway? Do you get endorsement deals?" She stares at him expectantly, and he's reminded of a reporter digging for a story. The press had been kicked into a frenzy after the Samantha Munn case, hounding him wherever he went. He couldn't leave his apartment without being accosted.

"Is it true you saw a Blue Fluke?"

"What were Makoto Mori's last words?"

"What will you do now?"

Their words are loud—too real.

"I don't know."

Liam strides into the kitchen like he can run from the voices in his head. Maggie trails on his heels, muttering something under her breath.

He pretends to examine the rusted stove, as if he will ever use it. Maggie's heterosexist dig about his cooking was annoyingly accurate. Claire had made some noble attempts to get him to expand his culinary prowess and received snotty eggs for the effort. Yet another improvement he'd failed to make for her.

He scratches at the corner of a tall white cabinet. A chunk of paint falls off and shatters on the counter. Maggie bristles like he did it just to slight her.

"Calico—"

"Liam."

"It's been a couple years since your grandparents died. My agency did its best to keep the place nice for you out of the goodness of our hearts." Liam could interject that this "goodness" came with a hefty price tag and little to show for it, but he doesn't care enough to bother. "There's only so much we can do since you never came to check on it—"

"It's fine. Let me see the upstairs."

Maggie looks close to stomping her foot. She spins on her heels, jerking her head. A drop of sweat flies off the back of her neck and lands on Liam's shoe.

The rest of Maggie's tour circles them through the dining room—where a squirrel has amassed a pile of dead leaves in the corner—and back into the foyer. The stairwell moans as they climb it. Mice scurry beneath the boards.

"You must have lots of memories of being here as a kid. Your grandparents were always so excited to have you. I'd love to hear a few of your favorite memories."

"I don't have any."

As if to admonish him for lying, memories, laced with stale emotion, unlock as they move down the upstairs hall: fear when the house twisted in a late summer storm, and intrigue when he snuck into the tower after his grandmother ordered him to stay out. He'd been fantasizing that he was a prince in a castle, until a trapped yellow jacket stung him in the neck. His grandfather had given him a bag of frozen peas for the swelling. His grandmother had told him he got what he deserved.

Liam didn't know what else they expected him to do all day. He was an only child, and the secrets of the house were damn irresistible. He was always finding new hidden treasures—an old note or a suspicious stain, a drawer full of rusted keys. Maybe it's fitting that one day he'd come to use the blueprints of this house to build his Phren. Or perhaps it was an act of defiance. He could go wherever he wanted in the stupid house now.

"And here's the primary bedroom," Maggie says at the end of the hall. She's less cheerful now. The top right edge of her lip keeps twitching, revealing a silver-capped tooth.

The room is smaller than Liam remembers. He feels a curl of rebellious satisfaction as he enters it. He'd never been allowed in here unless his grandmother was supervising. Even then, he'd be ordered to stand by the door and keep his grubby hands to himself. His grandparents had committed to the two-point-five kids, white picket fence age. Separate beds. Boiled meat. Dining sets. Privacy above all else. Cocktails at five o'clock sharp.

He surveys the room like an auctioneer, but there's not much to appraise. There are no ceramic rabbits or music boxes. No doilies as yellowed as his grandmother's toenails. He vaguely recalls that his mother had hired someone to clean and sell anything valuable of his grandmother's stuff after she died. Maybe a younger version of Liam would have regretted the family heirlooms he'd lost. Maybe not.

"When did you say your movers are getting here?"

"Soon."

"Hope you brought a new bed. Looks like someone died on that one, dear."

Liam waits for the shame to fall over Maggie's features, since his grandmother had, in fact, died on that bed, just a few months after his grandfather. When it doesn't come, he thinks briefly that she may not know. Then he sees the curl in her smile.

Of course she knows.

A sick feeling turns in his chest when he meets her beady eyes, pupils like barnacle mouths. He hears the buzz of the yellow jacket in the tower. His forehead itches, raw from the hat. He still won't take the hat off.

"I'm not staying in this room," he says. She clucks a few eager questions about his reasoning, which he ignores in favor of turning his back on her, walking down the hall past the stairwell, and into his childhood room. It's the same as he left it, though his perspective has changed. There are wooden toys and faded board games stacked on a small table below the window. His old dresser has a familiar collection of books on top of it: *The Chronicles of Narnia* and *Prydain*, a few by Roald Dahl and Shel Silverstein, and some anthologies on Egyptology, pirates, and the Celts. Beyond that, however, there's not much to indicate that a child occupied this room. His grandmother had viewed anything childlike as a forfeiting of masculine tradition and an affront to her own humorless upbringing. It was an "if I couldn't have it, I'll be damned if he can," form of familial affection.

"I assume you're picking this room for the ensuite bathroom? Or perhaps nostalgia? Those toys must have belonged to you, right? Oh, you had to be the most adorable child! Must have been a troublemaker though. And popular with the little ladies."

Turning away, he looks for any excuse not to meet her eyes and finds it in the window. He makes a show of taking in the view. The yard below borders an expanse of tidal river. It's calm today. The tide is high. His gaze skims across the water to an island breaking from the surface. The shores are rocky and garmented with seaweed. Beyond—a hill. Overgrown manes of grass part in the ghost of a path. His eyes follow it, drawn. And there, at the top, is a house.

He pauses.

"That house looks just like mine. Is it the only one on that island?"

For a moment he doesn't think Maggie heard him.

"Yes," she whispers, slinking up to his side. He flinches when her hot arm grazes his. "That's the Knox House. Don't you remember it?"

"Not really."

This time he's not lying. He stares at the house, almost identical to his own, its siding painted slate gray while his own is white. It has the same wraparound porch, the same tower and tall windows. A hint of recognition prods in the back of his mind. The house stares back at him with a bored challenge from its private island and river-like a moat.

"It was made by the same architect as your house. That's why they match. Creepy, isn't it?" Maggie leans in, too close.

"Who lives there?"

"Oh, no one has lived there for years."

"Hard to get to your house when it's on an island."

"That's not why, though. Plenty of people around here live on islands. No. It's because there's a lot of *dark superstition* surrounding it. I really am surprised you don't know. *Everyone* around here knows."

Liam fights to keep from rolling his eyes.

"I could tell you all about it," Maggie says, eyes sparking. "I'm something of a town chronicle, you see. There's a legend about that house that involves the O'Connors, actually—"

"I'm good, thanks."

Maggie's nostrils flare.

"You don't care at all about your heritage? Don't you feel a responsibility to know your hometown's history? To preserve it and pass it on. It's God's calling for you."

"If God's calling me, I'm not picking up."

Maggie clutches the cross, strung too tight around her thick neck. The sick feeling rises. Liam wants her to leave.

"Calico—"

"Yes, *Marge?*"

Maggie's mask falls away. Her beady eyes flare as spittle foams on the corners of her mouth. Liam catches stale liquor and rotting calcium on her breath. A phantom of the Nether appears in the corner of his vision—shattered glass, spilled whiskey, righteous anger, the faint keen of a little girl crying.

"Now you listen to me. Everyone was curious when I said I was meeting with you. They want to know what I think of you. I'm very influential around here. Important. Nothing happens around here without me knowing about it. You don't want to start off on the wrong foot. My blog has *lots* of readers."

"I don't give a shit."

Maggie's eyes bulge. The Nether growls at Liam's senses. His constant headache spikes.

"Just because your Splint died doesn't mean you—"

"Hey." Liam's voice cracks low in the room, calm yet loud at once. He doesn't recognize it. "It's time for you to get out of my house."

A strange stasis passes over Maggie. Liam watches her brain do a hard reboot. She mouths soundlessly. A vein pulses in her forehead. With a sharp squawk, she stomps out of the room.

The front door slams behind her just as the movers pull in. Liam rubs at his face, the stubble scratching his fingers. He has a feeling he's going to pay for that later. It doesn't matter. He doesn't want to talk to anyone, especially Maggie. If she ruins his reputation—fine. Maybe it will keep people away from him. He indulges one last look at the Knox House, isolated on the island, and wishes he'd inherited it instead.

The movers leave as the sun sinks low, bruising the sky purple and orange. Liam downs three glasses of scotch, takes a swig from the bottle, and refills his tumbler. The burn is dulling; welcome. He ambles out to his back porch.

The tide is low, and smells like it—silt and dried seaweed and something dead. It reminds him of the smell that follows him in the Nether. And yet, somehow, it's comforting. He kicks off his shoes and steps down from his porch onto the overgrown grass. A baby rabbit ducks under a bush.

The scent of salt water grows stronger as he shuffles to his small beach, bordered by a stone wall. He plops down on the sand, spilling scotch onto his hand. A shell digs into his ass.

For the first time in weeks, he allows himself a slow, deep breath. It punches out on a whine, involuntary. He sniffs back the ache in his throat and takes a drink. It strikes him that he hasn't slept in two days. Or five months.

He blinks, trying to ground himself in the present. The river is calm, stretching far to a graveyard on the other side. Small islands break the water's surface. Most are composed of just a few large rocks, though some boast a dead tree or some beach roses. There's one close by that he might be able to walk to if he tried, while the tide is low. He feels the Knox House staring at him in his periphery. He looks—

To find a light in the window.

He blinks again and it's gone. A trick of the sunset, or a bit of the Nether peeking through. He's having trouble trusting the things he sees these days. Makoto had always been his lens when reality got fuzzy. Without it, he's as alone as that house.

He yanks off his glasses and drops them into the sand. Covering his eyes, he rubs hard—bites his lip to punish it for quivering. He pulls off his hat and scratches at the heat rash on his forehead.

There's not a moment when he doesn't think of Makoto. That's why he'd fled from Chicago: every facet of his life reminded him of what he'd lost. His favorite dive bar, his living room, his job, his entire fucking city. There was nothing for him but to run.

Liam drifts. It's dark and the whisky is long gone by the time he realizes he should go inside. He knocks his shin on a rock on his way back and swears loud enough to traumatize a nearby seagull.

The inside of the house is a jungle of boxes and bubble-wrapped furniture. He can barely squeeze by it to get into the kitchen. There's no food beyond a few cans of long-expired beans, a bushel of parsley, and the Cheetos he'd bought on his drive. He's not hungry anyway.

In the living room, Kermit jumps to attention when he draws near with parsley in hand. He tosses it into the pen and enjoys the simple pleasure of watching a rabbit eat. Though he may not take care of himself, he'll be damned if he doesn't spoil that animal rotten.

He has no idea where his sheets are packed, so he digs out his old sleeping bag and climbs the stairs to his room. His shin throbs and his joints ache. A sense of stepping backward grips him as he crosses the threshold into his old bedroom. After everything, after all his accolades and achievements and experiences, he's back where he started. The utter meaninglessness of his life folds over him, curling his shoulders like a shepherd's crook. He spreads the sleeping bag haphazardly over his mattress, which, thankfully, no one has died on yet.

His big accomplishment for the night is brushing his teeth. There were weeks when he couldn't even do that.

Though he's exhausted, sleep evades him. His mind churns over thoughts of Makoto, obsessing over little things Liam did wrong over the fifteen-plus years of their friendship. It feels like torture. He deserves it.

When sleep does come, his dreams are haunted by Makoto's face in the Nether, and by that light in the dark, waiting for him. It's never felt closer. The smell of low tide fills the room.

He wakes up more tired than the day before.

CHAPTER TWO
THE SALT CELLAR

A WEEK PASSES and Liam drifts. Each day bleeds into the next. Sometimes every minute is a century. Sometimes a day passes into night without Liam noticing the sun.

One morning, he wakes hungry for the first time in a long time. He makes his way to the kitchen, shuffling between the maze of boxes and bubble-wrapped furniture that he's still failed to unpack. He rationalizes that he has nowhere to put his stuff anyway; the closets and basement are full of crap that his mother couldn't sell. Turns out his grandmother was a bit of a hoarder. Hardly the O'Connor's darkest secret.

He makes his way to the kitchen. His shirt hangs limp, too big for him now. It's his favorite *Star Wars* tee, given to him by Makoto when they were first assigned together. It smells pretty damn rank, but he's too afraid of ruining it to wash it. Not that the washing machine is hooked up anyway.

He stares into his fridge with one eye open. Unless he wants to dig into Kermit's carrot tops, there isn't much for him besides the coffee in the pantry. He gets it brewing, and wonders if that's the biggest task he'll manage today.

There's no good reason he decides to turn on his phone for the first time in weeks. He's half asleep, and some impulse he can't recall led him to charge it the night before. A barrage of messages ping when it boots up. He doesn't read any of them.

He's on his second cup of too-strong coffee when a call comes through. It's Claire.

His first instinct is to toss the phone in the garbage. She was the one who said they shouldn't talk anymore to "make things easier" (on her). She doesn't get to change her mind now. And yet, something makes him pause. Maybe it's an old habit. Maybe it's because he hasn't spoken to another person in a week, and there's enough humanity still left in him to crave contact. Regardless, he wishes he hadn't answered the instant he hears her voice.

"Liam!? Holy fuck—you actually picked up."

He sighs. "Hi Claire."

"Jesus, you sound awful."

"Thanks. Why are you calling me?"

"Are you kidding? Why am I calling you?"

"That's what I said."

"Because no one's heard from you in weeks and I'm worried about you, dumbass. I've been so damn stressed out because of you. Where have you been? Are you okay? You can't just disappear like that; I don't care what happened. I've had a bunch of people calling me because they're looking for you. Reporters, FUSE goons. Even your bartender. What the hell are you thinking?"

He can see her expression so clearly in his mind. She always had a talent for excoriating him with a look, not that she needed one. Her words more than sufficed.

The thought of people looking for him, of going through Claire of all people to find him, justifies every fear that led him to move. It's violating. It makes him want to run all over again.

"I'm thinking I'm going to hang up now."

"Wait—"

Liam's finger hovers over *end call.*

"Li, wait. I'm sorry. You know me." She huffs a laugh like this is a private joke. Neither of them finds it funny. "Are you okay?"

"I'm fine."

"You don't sound fine."

"Why ask me, then, if you already know?"

"I'm relentless." That, at least, they could agree on. "Will you tell me where you are?"

"I'd rather not get into specifics."

"Please."

He sighs. " … I moved to New England—"

"*New England?* What the hell is in New England besides leaf-peeping and lobster rolls?"

"Me. And I don't like lobster."

"Don't they burn you at the stake for that over there?"

"I dunno."

The line falls silent. In a different time, he would have had a snarky retort for her—a joke that she'd never laugh at, something equal parts self-deprecating and flirtatious. The absence of his humor is stark, and he knows she notices, and he hates her for it. He wishes he was fucking flourishing without her, could prove her wrong for once.

"Liam. I'm worried about you."

"*Bullshit,*" he doesn't have the balls to say.

"Are you taking care of yourself?" He feels her gearing up for a familiar diatribe, not likely to stop now no matter what he says. Hot shame wrenches in his chest. "I know how difficult all this has been for you, but you can't just abandon your life. People need you. You need to do something with yourself. And you need help. I mean, how are you living now, alone, with no one checking in on you? Are you eating? What about clean clothes? I bet you haven't even unpacked. When was the last time you left the house?"

Liam's face heats up. He tugs on his shirt collar. A few threads break.

"It's not healthy, Li. You gotta come back to Chicago. You're still one of my best friends and I can help you get on your feet. I've talked to Ken, and I know it sounds weird, but he says you can move in with us if you—"

"No. I'm fine. Please don't call me again."

He hangs up and mutes his phone.

And paces.

He's struck by his own anger. It fills him from the bottom up. And he harnesses it, thirsty to feel something besides despair for the first time in months. Her words revolve in his head, whipping the ire inside him to a blaze. It's obscene for Claire of all people to call him out for struggling, as if she didn't have a hand in sculpting the mess he's become. She wasn't there. For the scourge of his life, for the great rewriting of his entire being by grief, he was alone. She had abandoned him for an untarnished, easy accountant with a dumb name like *Ken.* A fucking Barbie doll. She gets easy, and he gets this. The injustice of it is baffling.

And yet, the absolute worst part is … she's right. Everything she said is fucking true, as always. He shoots a glare to the towers of boxes and rubs hard at his stubble as if that will make it go away. He's lost weight, lost days. The time on his phone says 2:08 p.m. It occurs to him that he hasn't seen a morning since he drove all night from Chicago. He's pathetic. He's dirty. He can't take care of himself.

How could anyone want him like this? How could he want himself. He doesn't want to live like this, die like this.

He does something about it before he loses momentum.

Downtown Shoalport isn't how Liam remembers it. The architecture is the same: stuck in time, pretty, and smug about it. Quaint shops and restaurants line narrow streets, with ivy climbing brick. Colonial homes stand preserved as museums and galleries, open to the discerning few who appreciate pewter table settings and oil paintings of boats. He can smell the sea and waffle cones.

When Liam was a kid, Shoalport was still a secret. There was always a vacationing class, but for the most part locals ran the scene. Now, the place is overrun with weekenders, sporting L.L.Bean flare fresh from the outlet. There's an air of entitlement that's different from an old man who's claimed the same barstool for two decades. These are retired adults who have temper tantrums at minimum wage service workers when their coleslaw needs more mayonnaise.

He can't use the sidewalk without his shoulder bumping someone too busy enjoying disposable income to look where they're going. The sun is too bright. Car horns are too loud. It isn't until smoke starts billowing from a window overhead, unacknowledged by anyone but him, that he realizes what's happening.

His sense of sound sparks. The nape of his neck prickles. Shards of the Nether itch in his periphery, potent with the age of the town. A horse-drawn carriage turns onto his street and Liam isn't sure if it's real. He tries to block it out, to shove the Nether back where it belongs, but he can't. There are too many people, too many sounds.

He breaks into a run, dodging tourists like he's going for a touchdown.

"Watch where you're going, young man," someone says.

"No one has any manners anymore!" bleats another. He hears something about "avocado toast." His throat burns.

"Fiddleheads for sale! Two pence a barrel or have me a trade!"

"Able-bodied men wanted for the fourth regiment! Ten-dollar bounty will be allowed! Down with the rebellion!"

He ducks into an alley.

Spots dance in his vision. He blinks them away. Thankfully, his hideout is empty. The Nether has spilled into his vision before, but not like this. This is loud. This is real. Sweat drips down his temples. It's too hot for the hat, but he won't take it off. He's already exposed. He leans back against brick—breathes. The alley around him winds like a canyon. It feels old, almost European. The

Nether tries to weasel in again. This time, he holds it back.

Then a realization hits, unbidden:

The last time I was in an alley was the day I lost my best friend.

He can't stay still. He moves, but he'll be damned if he goes back into the street. He strides deeper into the alley. The path curves, and the Nether licks at his heels. He sees the dead dog on the blanket, hears the cockroaches crunching in the garbage bin. He's certain Samantha is waiting for him around the bend, her mouth stuck in a black, gaping scream.

He stops. A door seems to materialize. A worn sign with gold lettering hangs above it, reading The Salt Cellar Pub. He eyes it skeptically, unsure if it's real. But there's nothing pleasant in the Nether, and this feels warm—welcoming. The orange glow beyond the glass calls to him, offering an escape hatch. Surely the tourists won't know about a place like this. Maybe he should go inside. A beer would be damn near celestial.

He pulls open the heavy door and a dark, worn staircase leads him down. The scent of stale beer and fried potatoes wafts up, curling in familiar notes, spiced with a hint of mildew and old wood.

When he reaches the bottom and heaves open another door, all eyes swing to him. There aren't many people, and it's evident that Liam is an intruder—an interloper in a secret underground club. He makes his way to the bar, canting his head down to hide his face. Distrust bears down from all angles, like he's violating consecrated ground. He wants to turn and leave, but somehow that feels more offensive than finding a stool at the end of the bar. It's not until he sits that people gradually turn away. The hum of conversation resumes, and Liam breathes a sigh.

He can do this. Claire is wrong. He's perfectly fine.

"You a weekender?"

Liam startles like a bomb's gone off. The bartender standing in front of him stares with yellowed eyes and an arched brow. What's left of the man's hair is pulled back in a low ponytail, the top of his head shining bald. He polishes a clean glass with a dirty cloth and looks at Liam like he's a spy.

"No," Liam says. "I live here."

"What do you want?"

"A ... beer?"

A blank stare.

"Something local?" Liam adds. "An IPA?"

The bartender doesn't speak when he fills Liam's pint and slides it to him. He shakes his head, sighs heavily, and turns away. As Liam nurses a few welcome sips, he has an urge to people-watch. He isn't confident he can look over his shoulder without drawing ten sets of eyes, so he has little more to occupy himself than watching bubbles pop in his beer foam and confronting the reality that leaving the house was a mistake.

"You just move here?"

Liam startles again, spilling foam down the back of his hand.

"Jesus Christ," he gasps, clutching his heart. A woman his age has taken the seat beside him. She watches him from behind a curtain of dark hair, her cheekbones sharp as her eyes. There's a swizzle stick shaped like a sword tucked behind her ear.

"You're a bit squirrely, huh."

A man a few stools down watches them intently. Liam's throat is tight.

"Where?" she says.

"Excuse me?"

"Where do you live?"

Old defenses kick in. He doesn't give out his address to anyone, not when some yahoo with a fantasy or a grudge could bang down his door.

"Uh …"

"I'm not asking so I can steal your doll collection," she huffs.

"As if you could find it."

The corner of her lip twitches. "I have a bet going with my partner." She indicates their spectator with a thumb. He waves back. "About where you live. Not the dolls."

"Why?"

"What else is there to do in a bar but bet on stupid shit?"

"You could try getting drunk, for a start."

The woman snorts. She clinks their glasses together in a toast. He reaches out with his senses to gauge the edges of her Phren and finds it open and clear. There's nothing overtly intense or sneaky. He takes a chance. "I'm on O'Connor Ave. On the river. Actually, I'm in the O'Connor House."

Her eyebrows climb. "Well, well, well. 'Bout time we got ourselves a fucking O'Connor in Shoalport again. Teddy!" she barks, turning. "Come meet yourself a 100% Angus grassfed O'Connor."

The attention of the entire room swings to him again. Liam shuts his eyes, as if that will hide him. He feels the Nether staring too, incessant as always. Everyone knows his name now. This is how they start to swarm, to ask their questions, cast their blame. He can't believe he gave this woman his address.

He waits … but no one comes over. Miraculously, everyone goes back to their drinks.

The man called Teddy pulls up a stool on Liam's other side. He, at least, has the tact to be bashful about it.

"Sorry if we're bugging you," he says, pushing up his fog-rimmed glasses. He seems to be one of those perpetually sweaty people. "Just never thought we'd have an O'Connor around here again."

Liam shrugs. He feels boxed-in, snared into socializing. He glances at the exit.

"I'm Ingrid. Wanna tell us your first name?" the woman says as she signals to the bartender without looking at him.

"It's … um."

"Did you forget? What are you, a lightweight?"

"Hardly. It's Liam." He closes his eyes, tensing, sure this is the moment he's been dreading. It was inevitable that he was going to be recognized. Now they're going to accost him for autographs, bombard him with more invasive questions until he has a panic attack in public and the internet gets wind of it and—

"Welcome to Shoalport, Liam."

"I … thanks."

"Sorry if we're making it weird," Ingrid says, picking up her fresh beer. "Thanks, Buck," she says to the bartender. "Oh, hey Buck—this dude's a friggin' O'Connor."

"I know," Buck the Bartender says. He eyes Liam with unnerving focus. "Didn't see you at Peter and Deb's funeral, did we."

Liam's starting to wonder if the whole town has a copy of the funeral guestbook. Must have been the event of the season.

"I had work."

Buck snorts. A curd of snot shoots out of his nose and lodges in his stubble. "People these days don't know what real work is. I bet you'd cry to mommy after one day in a real job," he says, not too seriously.

"You guys bet on a lot, don't you?"

"Just on the new guy in town," Ingrid says.

"Ah, but this one's not new." Buck leans on the bar top. "Guy was practically a townie when he was a pissant."

Liam looks at his hands. "Only in the summers. My parents took trips that weren't exactly kid-friendly, so they dumped me at my grandparents' place." He's surprised at himself. He never gives out personal information to strangers. It's gotten back to the press too many times. Maybe he is becoming a lightweight.

"Oh man," Teddy says, shivering, "I think I'd be traumatized if I had to sleep in the O'Connor House as a kid."

Liam doesn't say that he very much *is* traumatized, but it had nothing to do with summering in a creepy old house.

"It was fine."

"Did you ever see the ghost?"

For a moment, Liam thinks Ingrid's teasing him again, but she's staring at him with her mouth set in a line. The others watch him expectantly.

"What ghost?"

"The Man Who Drowned Waiting," Ingrid answers, like it's obvious. When Liam shrugs, her jaw drops. "No one ever told you about The Man Who Drowned Waiting? Shit, all the local kids knew that one when I grew up."

Liam shrugs again. "I'm not a true local."

"You know that house on the island right next to your property? Looks just like yours?" Liam nods. "It's called the Knox House. Back in the mid-1800s this dude from the Knox family killed himself in the river because his girlfriend broke up with him—"

"Wait, that's not quite what happened," Teddy says. Ingrid arches an eyebrow at him. Liam has the sense she'd eviscerate anyone else for interrupting her, but Teddy's sincerity is so obvious it's impossible to be offended by him. "Sorry, I don't mean to mansplain. You know I love this shit. The kids are sick of hearing it every Halloween. I'm a high school English teacher, Liam."

He seems like the type.

"Anyway, this Knox guy fell in love with his neighbor. She was an O'Connor, probably your great, great aunt or something. Her father—who was mayor and a bit of a dick, by all accounts—had some rift with the Knox's, so he forbid the lovers from being together. They made a secret pact to meet and run away together, happily ever after. Only, it didn't work out that way."

"It never does," Ingrid snorts.

"They decided to rendezvous on this little tidal island in the river between their houses. Poetic, right? Problem is, when Knox went to meet her, she wasn't there. And he kept waiting, and waiting, unwilling to give up hope. Now, the thing about some of the islands in that part of the river is that you can walk out to them when the tide is out, but they flood when it comes back in. And sometimes, if it's a king tide or there's a storm, the islands go under all the way. So there he was, waiting on this island, his heart breaking, but still, he refused to leave, hoping against hope that she'd come to him. Unlucky for him, a king tide did come in. By the time he realized, it was too late, and he drowned."

Liam thinks of the small islands dotting the river. It's easy to imagine someone drowning in their heavy Victorian layers and leather shoes. And then there are the rip-currents. He'd been warned about them as a child. Liam shivers. His imagination is too vivid, spiked with Nether echoes. He smells the icy water, hears the distant squawk of a gull on his skin. He tastes old salt.

"It's a sad story," Buck says as though daring Liam to disagree. He puts a fresh beer in front of him.

"And that's not even the saddest part," Teddy says. His passion is revitalizing. "Legend has it that she had been held captive by her father the whole time. She didn't abandon him after all." He looks off wistfully into the distance. "When she realized her lover had died, she went mad. Rosie was her name."

"And the ghost?" Liam says.

"There are accounts of O'Connors seeing strange shit on the island or in the Knox House," Ingrid says. "People say it's the ghost of the poor drowned Knox guy, haunting the place to get his revenge. Some claim they've seen Rosie in the tower windows. Weird that your grandparents never mentioned it."

"They didn't mention much. And, anyway, I'd assume that they were talking about Sophont visions. All those old ghost stories are usually misinterpretations of Fissure side-effects or minor Sophonts picking up telepathic visions they didn't understand, and I'm sure I had other Sophonts in my family, since I'm—"

The words catch in Liam's throat. What the hell is he thinking? He looks up, hoping he didn't just reveal himself. Buck rolls his eyes. Teddy looks contrite, and Ingrid stares, unimpressed.

"Did you think it was a secret?" she says, arching an eyebrow. "Even if you weren't a town celebrity, your face was all over the internet for weeks. We just don't care."

"You aren't the only famous person hiding around here, you know," Buck says. He takes Liam's empty pint glass and tosses it in a nearby sink. It very likely shatters. "We got all sorts of writers and retired TV hosts and actors with their summer mansions. This is New England. Your business is your fuckin' business."

Liam shakes his head, finding himself surprised by people for the first time in a long time.

"Well, not all of you are like this," he says. "My estate manager, for example—"

"Ohhh, yeah, we know about that," Ingrid says, grimacing.

"Know about what?"

"Maggie is a bit of a gossip," Teddy says gently.

"And a drunk," Buck says, less gently. "I've kicked her out of my bar more times than I can count for falling off stools and starting shit. She threw a drink in here once because she was pissed about something or other and almost hit Frank Marietta's dog. I got no respect for that woman." He takes a slug from a glass of clear liquid that cannot possibly be water.

"Wait, sorry," Liam says. "What did Maggie say about me?"

"Maggie is an avid Facebook user," Ingrid says with a cringe. "And she has a blog—a gossip page called *The Mouth of the Port*. I've never read it. Don't want to give her the hits. But her Facebook posts can be kinda entertaining." Ingrid pulls out her phone and starts scrolling.

"She wrote about me?"

"She kinda blasted you, if I'm being honest. Yeah, here it is: 'Never meet your heroes, they say. Well, Calico should be on no one's hero list. He was a stuck-up, mean client with no manners, and I've never been so attacked in my life for simply offering my services as a good Christian. He has a darkness in him. Anyone who walks in the light of Christ can see it. He was threatening, and I wouldn't be surprised if we find out he wasn't so innocent as he wants us to believe. I'm not the first to be suspicious of how his partner *really* died...'" Ingrid shuts her mouth. She shoves her phone back in her purse and dodges eye contact. "This goes on for a few paragraphs and links to her blog, but you get the gist."

Liam pulls at his hat, itching under it. A familiar rush bubbles in his chest, heating his face.

"I have to move," he hears himself say. "Again."

"Ignore that gremlin," Buck spits. "She's not fooling anyone. Every day she has a new target. Christian, my ass. She'll forget about you as soon as someone else gets in her way. Besides, you're an O'Connor. You belong here."

"Who makes Facebook posts that long anyway?" Ingrid says, nudging Liam in the arm. "And Jesus, you should see the grammar."

"She's probably just lonely," Teddy says. Ingrid rolls her eyes, but she takes Teddy's hand beneath the bar top.

They settle into an easy chat. Most of it is mundane, which is just fine with Liam. They gracefully avoid topics related to Fissures, and Liam likes Ingrid's scathing sense of humor. Teddy airs his frustrations about his students' aversion to literature and learning in general, and their inability to read a conventional clock. Buck complains about rising property taxes. Ingrid talks at length about the video game she's playing. Liam relaxes. He smiles, even if he can't manage a laugh yet.

He gets complacent.

"Calico!?"

Liam startles, spilling his drink. As Buck wipes it up, Liam slowly turns. Behind him is a woman his age. Her eyes are dilated with naked admiration, her face lit up with a smile and a blush. She wrings her hands and giggles before finding words.

"Oh my. My gosh. I can't believe it's you," she all but shouts. "Finally. I've waited so long. So, so long. The most famous Wedge in the world. Wow. I almost didn't recognize you with the hat on. Faye Cleary," she says, taking his hand in a jittery shake. Behind her, all eyes are back on Liam. A hiss of whispers starts to rise. "That's my name, I mean. Faye."

Liam doesn't answer. His eyes dart to the door, searching for a means of escape. He sweats between his shoulder blades. Each breath comes shorter, tighter.

"When I heard that you were moving to Shoalport I couldn't believe it," she barrels on. "Gosh, you probably don't remember me. We went to school together, you know. You were a few grades above me but of course everyone knew who you were. You were already a legend when I got there."

Liam blinks. For a moment he thinks she means the University of Chicago, but something catches at the fringes of his Sophont senses. Slowly, he reaches out and grazes the edges of her mind. He feels her Phren nudge back. Faye goes scarlet. She clutches the cross on her neck like it's a string of pearls.

"Oh. I knew you were powerful but to feel it like that. I'm not that strong a Sophont. But of course you know that now," she says, tittering shakily. "I'm just the town Patch."

Liam had purposefully avoided looking up the local Fissure authorities when he moved to Shoalport, determined to stay as uninvolved as possible. He was foolish for thinking they'd be oblivious to him. Every cop and Sophont in the state probably knew they had the country's strongest Wedge within their borders. Still, towns like Shoalport had no need for a Wedge. There were probably one or two Wedges working in the whole state, serving as specialists to be brought in on the rare occasion that a Red or Yellow Fluke needed exterminating. A Patch, or local lesser-Wedge, was a weak Sophont. They did little more than confirm the presence of a Fissure so the big guys could be brought in. Faye had probably graduated from the Academy by a hair. There's no way she's ever faced a Fluke or seen the wasteland of a mangled Host. Compared to being a Wedge in a major city like Chicago, a Patch in Shoalport lived a life of rainbows and cotton candy.

Liam envies her.

"It's nice to meet you," he hears himself say.

"Liam was just heading out," Ingrid says from beside him. Liam's Phren radiates gratitude at her before he can help it. He's tired, rusty at holding his abilities at bay. It's an amateur mistake. Most people run in terror if they feel a Sophont touch their mind. With trepidation, he watches the projection hit her, but she does nothing more than flinch slightly. The swizzle stick falls from her ear.

"Yeah, sorry. I gotta be on my way." He stands, tossing a fifty-dollar bill on the bar top and not bothering to ask for change.

"Maybe we'll see you soon, Liam," Ingrid says. Teddy smiles and waves. Buck nods once.

"Yeah, maybe we can get tea sometime, Liam," Faye says. He winces at the volume of her voice. "And don't worry about what Maggie said. Everyone knows you didn't murder Makoto. Or at least, most people do."

Liam pushes past her without speaking. He feels peoples' Phrens, hears their thoughts.

I thought he'd be taller.

He used to be so hot.

Never thought he'd return after what happened all those years back.

By the time he stumbles out into the alley, he can barely breathe. His vision blurs. He strides out of the alley and back onto the street, into a sea of people. They're dressed in T-shirts, bell-bottoms, petticoats. A barrel of rotten apples falls from a window and crashes. He's the only one who sees it. He tries to run back to his car, but he can't get enough air. Everyone is staring. He thinks he's having a heart attack.

He loses time. When he makes it home, he picks up Kermit and buries his face in soft, black fur.

"I'm never leaving the house again."

CHAPTER THREE
VICE

Liam is asleep when it happens.

He's dreaming of the light—the wisp—again. It follows him to Makoto's funeral, fluttering around his hair. It taps at his neck as the casket is lowered down. That's when Liam realizes he's dreaming; he'd never made it to the funeral in real life. Makoto didn't care about that kind of thing, but Liam has convinced himself that he'd be disappointed. Liam deserves to feel like a disappointment; guilt is justice for what he's done.

Glass shatters.

He wakes with a gasp. Maybe he'd dreamt the sound. Maybe it's the Nether again. Then, a dull thud. There's a non-zero chance a raccoon has come down his chimney.

With a sigh, he kicks the covers to his feet and grimaces at the dampness of his sheets. Everything is damp by the sea, and nightmares make him sweat. Sitting up, he rubs his eyes and reaches over to flick on his bedside lamp.

"Fucking house."

With a stretch, Liam puts on his glasses and heaves to his feet. The sight of his reflection in the nearby window catches his attention. For a moment, he doesn't recognize himself. A Spiderman T-shirt and plaid pajama pants hang on his body. He's never been so thin. His stubble is patchy, his hair overgrown like a neglected garden.

He blinks, eyes adjusting to see the world beyond the glass. A chill rattles through him as the Knox House comes into focus, looming from its island, painted in moonlight. There's something unsettling about how closely it resembles his own home. It looks like a mistake. Or perhaps Liam's house is the aberration. A sense of unease pressures him to look away, as though he's been caught staring at a stranger.

Then he sees something he can't make himself understand: a faint yellow light flickering from one of the windows. It must be a reflection. Or a spot on his glasses. He takes them off and cleans them on his shirt. When he slides them back on, the light is still there. It flashes to an odd beat—short flickers, then long pauses, then short again. It's coming from the room identical to his own. Is there a squater?

Another loud crash from downstairs. A scuffling sound.

Liam freezes. Instinct tells him the sound is human, and close—and a threat. Is it a rabid fan? A past client? How loudly did he tell Ingrid his address? He reaches out with his Sophont senses, fumbling, and grazes a hot slick. Sweet, moldy sickness brushes against him. The crackle of Fissure aura is faint, but distinct.

Of three things he is certain:

1.) There is someone in his house.
2.) He's encountered this Phren before.
3.) They have a Fissure, and a Fluke has crawled through it.

The hall outside his room is dark. He tip-toes down it, breath held tight. Floorboards moan traitorously beneath his bare feet. He twitches at every sound: short bangs and rustles, coming from his living room. A silly vision pops into his head of a giant rat raiding his kitchen for cheese. He wants to giggle. Then a violent retching sound reverberates up the stairs, snuffing out any nervous humor.

Each step down his stairs is an accomplishment. Something about this one is different. His legs fight against him. His heart pounds. Sweat pearls on his back. He realizes too late that he's left his phone on his bedside table. He can't go back now.

Holding his breath, he reaches the bottom step. It's hard to see in his foyer. Someone moans and Liam jumps, slamming his elbow into the wall. He's certain that he's given himself away—then another glass shatters. Seconds inch by.

As slow as he can, he peers around the wall into the living room and the figure comes into view. It sways in the darkness, short and fat. Liquid splashes on the floorboards at its feet. Liam smells ethanol and urine and infection.

And Red Fluke.

Longing, deep and sudden, burns through him. This is the first Fissure he's faced without Makoto's soothing presence, without his Phren linked to

Liam's, keeping him sane. His absence converts fear to terror.

After Makoto died, and when Liam could finally assemble thoughts beyond a deafening roar, he vowed that he would never enter another Phren again. He'd never exterminate another Fluke, never seal another Fissure. And, most importantly, under no circumstances would he set foot in the Nether.

Because without Makoto, the Nether would kill him. Or turn him into something else.

The figure turns. Her face catches a shard of moonlight. Burst blood vessels have inked highway maps in her eyes.

"Maggie?"

Liam flicks on the overhead light. Maggie stumbles back, crashing into Liam's drink cart. She's wearing a pink, fleece nightgown, soaked in vomit. Her bare feet are bloodied by broken glass. She cocks her head to the side.

"You." There's a bottle of Jameson in her hand. She shoves the nozzle to her mouth, cracking it against her teeth. A chunk of tooth breaks off and falls to the floor. She doesn't seem to notice. She chugs, and chugs. More. She pukes yellow foam into the bottle, then gulps it back again. Her nightgown undulates like a slug with every heave. "You think you're better than me. You don't want to be my friend. I just wanted to be your friend. Your sister."

Liam's voice escapes him. Kermit is hiding in his wooden box. Maggie doesn't seem to notice him for now.

"You did this. And look what I've done to my pretty feet."

She stumbles forward, feet slapping wet on the floorboards. Liam steps back. He holds up his hands.

"Maggie, you have a Fluke infestation. I'm going to get my phone and call some people who can help you."

"Oh, because you won't help me? You're the best Wedge in the world, and you won't lift a finger. Of course you won't. My feet. You love seeing me like this. You think I deserve it. She thought I deserved it too. Well, you're a murderer. I always knew it. Look what you did to my feet. You meater. You mumbling cove. You told me we'd be together always. My brother."

Glass crunches under her lumbering steps. Blood spurts out onto his grandmother's frayed oriental rug.

"And my arm. Look at it." She holds it up. Her forearm is crooked, a splinter of bloody bone breaking the skin. "It's your fault that he … he did this to me."

Liam is paralyzed. Reasoning is frozen. His mind is too full of Makoto and the way his eyes looked gray in the Nether, of the scent of his fancy tea tree shampoo and the way he sighed when he found Liam's jokes truly stupid.

He feels the agony of losing Makoto all over again. He hasn't healed at all.

"I can't," he says.

"Of course you can't. You don't care about anyone but yourself. You're just like my mother."

"I'm … sorry."

It's the wrong thing to say. A sharp surge of heat ripples through the room. Maggie's Phren shoves Liam back with the fervor of a Fluke, well fed. He jerks back and hits his head on the doorframe. Maggie sways toward him. Froth drips from her mouth and nostrils.

The Nether breathes to life around him.

"No," he says, as the fabric of his reality frays. Shards of traumatized time come into being. A fire bursts to life in the fireplace. Sheetrock crumbles, revealing fresh, Victorian wallpaper underneath. A wet, fatal cough reverberates from upstairs. Bone snaps. A little girl cries. Liam trembles, fists clenching white, toes curling on the floorboards. A bead of sweat tumbles down his cheek.

Then he raises his eyes to Maggie …

And sees the Fluke. It twines around her—an unfathomable knot of endless pearl-white string. It buds from her mouth and nose and ears, wraps around her throat in a tangle, pulsating. It moves with glee in the whites of her eyes.

The smell of Red Flukes is sweet, almost pleasant, until it binds to the soft palate. Sweet becomes sticky, rotten fruit; mucus and mold. It makes him feel like he's starving. Like he'd take whatever it decides to give him, knowing it will never be enough.

A primal part of his brain calls for him to protect himself, to pierce her Phren and banish the Fluke back into the Nether. He knows the danger Maggie poses like this. She is chaos and misplaced blame. She is desperation. The infection is too complete. Even if Liam did purge the Fluke, her Phren would be ravaged forever. But it's still only a Red, and her mind is weak. He's taken on far worse. This should be easy. Why can't he move? Why does this one feel different?

She ambles closer. The Fluke hums in glee. It's more powerful than it should be, and Liam can do nothing but yield. Her mouth gapes. She coughs, spraying Liam's face with spittle. He shuts his eyes. Something shifts inside him—too much feeling becomes none at all.

And then she barrels past him, crashing through his front door and into the dark. Something in her hand clips Liam on the elbow. He yelps, clutching at it. The room is struck with sudden silence. He doesn't move for a long time.

He blinks.

"She stole my good whiskey."

"So, you had a Fluke Host in your house, and you just let her wander out."

Liam breathes out a shaky sigh. His eyes burn.

"As I said, I called 911 as soon as she left." Only a slight lie. Fending off a panic attack took priority. He'd washed his face in cold water and held Kermit until his breathing slowed.

The officer named Sloane fixes him with a glare. Her skin is tired, her hair flecked with gray. It's obvious she's not a local like her sidekick, and not just because she's a black woman in "white bread, extra side of mayo" New Hampshire. Liam has worked with enough inner-city cops to identify her type. She fought to get where she was in her job, and then she walked away because she could, and she'll never let anyone forget it.

"Hear that, Applebaum? We got the legendary *Calico* here, and he couldn't even handle a Red Fluke."

"I'm not a Wedge anymore."

"There's nothing wrong with quitting. Gotta do what's right for you," Applebaum says, earning an eye roll from Sloane. Liam can't tell if Applebaum is taking her Good Cop™ role too seriously or if she really is this peachy keen. Her curly brown hair plumes behind her, eyes creasing with echoes of endless smiles. She's the mom everyone wanted as their chaperone on school field trips. And yet, for all her unflappable softness, Liam senses that her Phren is very far away, guarded like a fortress.

Sloane, on the other hand, practically shoves her Phren in Liam's face.

"It's wrong if someone's mind goes to mush because Mr. All-Star Wedge was too chicken shit to help. Maggie might be an insufferable fuck but she's ours," Sloane's Boston accent punches the word "fuck" so well Liam can't help but be impressed. "I pulled your file when you rolled into town, *Calico*. You're still licensed whether you're a practicing Wedge or not. Internationally, in fact. You have an obligation to intervene."

"Not legally," Liam says. Sloane's Phren energy surges, and Liam flinches. Applebaum's smile falters.

"No one leaves a big city job like yours without good reason," Sloane says, low. "You had a reason."

"What was yours?"

Her eyes bulge. Fresh sweat rises on Liam's back. He never could keep his damn mouth shut. He clenches his fists to hide their tremor. His throat tightens.

"Excuse me?"

"I just wanted to leave Chicago," he says, quiet.

"And you did. Doesn't explain why you didn't do shit to help Maggie."

"I didn't … it's not my job anymore. You have a Patch anyway. Why don't you—"

"Everyone knows your partner—"

"Sloane, why don't you check the perimeter. There's a chance Maggie is still here," Applebaum says without volume, touching Sloane's elbow. For a moment, Sloane doesn't seem like she'll back down. Then she turns and walks out his back door.

Liam's shoulders relax in increments. Applebaum casually observes the wreck of shattered glass and blood that Maggie left in his living room, her hands folded over her pelvis. She tips back and forth on her heels.

"Sloane can be passionate," she says. The house creaks in a gust of sea wind. "I'm sorry this happened to you. We don't get a lot of these in Shoalport. A Vice Fluke will pop up here and there, what with the opioid epidemic, but never like this." She gestures to the wreck Maggie made of his liquor stock. "It's just unfortunate it went down in your living room."

"Maggie hates me."

Applebaum doesn't look at him. She tips her head to the side. "I *am* on Facebook."

Liam exhales. God, he hates Facebook. "I just wanted to be left alone."

"Maggie isn't very good at that. She's a … *people* person."

"That's a term for it."

"Any idea why she came to your house of all places?"

Liam shrugs. "It's not uncommon for Fluke Hosts to seek vengeance on whoever was the last to wrong them. I was probably the last person to piss her off. And sometimes Hosts seek me out because of the … my thing."

"Because you're a Sophont."

Liam bites the inside of his lip. He doesn't say the word "Trypanon" if he can help it. Applebaum seems to intuit it anyway.

"Sloane isn't the only one who saw your file. The … other thing you can do," she says. "That cannot be easy."

Liam meets her eyes. "Nothing is easy."

"I might disagree with you on that."

"Shoalport isn't Chicago."

"It certainly isn't. But you were from here once, weren't you? I should warn you: everyone connected to you will remember that."

"I've noticed."

"Sloane isn't from around here, though."

"I've noticed that too."

"Our Patch, Faye, mentioned she met you. Several times. In great detail. She'll be here soon."

"She can handle the Fluke."

Applebaum glances at him. Her eyebrow twitches up. "Better than you?" Her words are gentle but the veiled barb finds its mark. He feels like he's disappointed her, his mother, and every grade school teacher he's ever had in one fell swoop.

He's spared from replying when his back door crashes against the wall. Sloane charges in, her Phren radiating hot-cold shards—red and blue. It scrapes over Liam and fills up the room. He jerks away from her.

"Maggie Short is lying dead on your beach. I called it in. Care to tell me how that happened, Calico?"

Liam's in for a long night.

"Can you believe we finally have a Fluke death?"

"They told me she drank her weight in Jame-o before she bit it. Haven't touched that shit since my 20s. Last time I did, I looked a lot like her, let me tell you what."

"Are we allowed to take pictures?"

It's a damn feat that Liam has kept from screaming. Shoalport's finest are a clinic in small town cop bullshit. They hardly bother to conceal their giddiness at finally having something interesting to investigate, and at being in his home. His house was clearly the subject of childhood ghost stories. He's seen more scene contamination tonight than during his entire stint in Chicago. He may have just caught an officer eating one of Kermit's baby carrots out of the fridge.

A gasp. Low tide smell rushes into the room on a breeze. Liam turns to find Faye Cleary standing in his foyer.

"Calico," she breathes, eyes glistening as she scuttles up to him. Her ashy brown hair is strapped into a low, colonial-looking ponytail. "I got here as soon as I could."

"Thanks," Liam says, at a loss.

"I can't believe I get to investigate a Fissure scene in your house, of all places. You're probably going to think I'm such an amateur. Well, I'm here to learn from you, so any bit of advice you have, any critique, please tell me.

Please. Don't be afraid to ride me." A pause. Then her cheeks rise red like a thermometer.

"Cleary!" Sloane barks, stomping over. The tight bun in her hair has started to fray. "You're here to assess the scene, not mingle. *Calico* is not a Wedge anymore, so don't bother filling him in. As far I'm concerned, he's a civilian and he's liable for negligence."

"Won't be admissible in court," Liam hears himself say.

Sloane puffs up like a wood pigeon. Faye cuts in.

"See, that's something I never would have known—the legal stuff. Gosh, I'd love to pick your brain. I don't need my hand held or anything, but, ha, you can if you want to."

Sloane appears to be contemplating the merits of seppuku.

Liam's horrible night spreads into an equally horrible day. When Sloane and her crew finish loitering on his property and finding absolutely nothing useful, they drag him down to the station to fill out columns of paperwork. He barely has the will to speak by the end of it. His hand is curled with a cramp. It seems every officer in the town is eager to ask him about his glamorous life as Calico the Wedge. He can't imagine a more personal form of hell.

He stops at the liquor store on his way home for three bottles of tax-free scotch and tequila (Live Free or Die), and at a gas station for something processed to eat. When he finally returns home, he avoids the carnage in his living room, diverting to his wraparound porch. He plops down on the stairs leading to his backyard. The sun sits low, splattering the sky in oranges and purples. The river is high, choppy, and gray.

She died in that water.

He shivers, riding out a wave of guilt. The soggy ham sandwich he was about to eat is rendered repulsive. Without seriousness, he wonders if Maggie will haunt him. Though, he realizes with a snort, she is hardly the first person to die on this property. Or the first person with reason to haunt him. The more ghosts the merrier.

The Man Who Drowned Waiting falls into his thoughts. Liam seeks out the little island where he might have died, but it's mostly hidden by the high tide. The top branches of its only tree—dead and black—break the surface.

While gas station ham may not be palatable, whisky sure is. He's a third of the way through a bottle by the time the sun tucks beneath the horizon. Some things go numb. Others are cast in stark relief.

He is so very sad.

And he pities himself. And that pity makes him hate himself. And when he hates himself, he pities himself. The cycle revolves—a rolling, buffeting tide. He fights it until he's too fatigued to try anymore. It's better to sink, to accept. He deserves this.

Kermit sits up like a prairie dog when Liam tosses him a few dandelion leaves and a carrot. His eyes sparkle with a delight Liam can only imagine. At least someone has an appetite.

When he shuffles up to his bedroom, he doesn't bother changing. His sheets are a tangle. Sleep takes him fast.

The moment he wakes, Liam knows something is wrong. He sits up, fighting a wave of nausea, and winces. The room is brighter than it should be. It hurts behind his eyes. He listens for Maggie sloshing around in his living room, but it's silent.

He moves to the window, trying to identify the source of the light. The moon is absent, and the world outside his home is pitch black. He's confused. His heart pounds. The Knox House is gone.

And then he sees it in the distance—a Fissure, horrible and luminous. It buzzes like a reactor, torn through the air above the river. *Come*, it commands. Before he's aware of what he's doing, Liam bursts from his bedroom. He moves impossibly fast—almost hovering. He's suddenly outside. The damp grass on his lawn is cold and dewy. His feet are bare. The position of the Fissure strikes him …

It's on the island. *That* island. Certainty washes over him: this is the place where the Knox man drowned. It must be.

The tide is low. A path to the island appears, leading from his little beach, and seems to glow. There's no reason to resist. It's a path made for him. A gift, a beckoning.

The sand is pregnant with seawater. It clutches at his feet with sucking mouths, weighing his steps until he's gasping for breath and covered in sweat. The black water is still around him. He knows he's being watched. The light inside the Fissure pulses, but it's not threatening—it's begging. And Liam must help it. He must help the wisp. If only he could touch it, hold it. Why did he run all these years?

He falls to his knees on the shores of the island, cutting his palms on mussel shells. The constant hum of the Fissure is too much. It itches like nettle. The weight of his own skin is too much to wear.

The light whines.

Liam is running out of time—of energy. It's now or never. He climbs on hands and knees up the rocks, fingers slipping on beads of seaweed. He feels something pulling him back, coming closer, trying to snare him. But he can't leave yet. He's going to end this. He's going to reach inside the Fissure. Behind him, something draws closer, desperate to stop him.

With a shout, he hurls himself up, knees cracking against stone. He reaches and takes hold –

Of an ankle, covered in wet fabric.

Above him, in a halo of Fissure aura, stands a man. He's wearing a black suit and a tailed coat. And an ascot tie. His face is a matted growth of seaweed, speckled with barnacles; they open, clasping/unclasping with feathered digits. Where his mouth should be—a black, depthless hole. Silt dribbles out and down his chin.

But his eyes, sea-gray and human, pierce into Liam. It's agony. The man's fingers unfurl, revealing the light that drew him—a golden wisp. It has followed Liam in his dreams and in the Nether, pursued him like a hunter. And now, he's been caught.

Their eyes lock again, and the man screams, stripping Liam down with the sound—remaking him. The light warps into a thin, sharp line. It pierces Liam's chest and wraps around his ribs, tethering them, tighter. Too tight.

William.

He wakes up and vomits onto his pillow. His hands are bloody.

CHAPTER FOUR
DIRE NEED

IT'S NOT HIS own needs that draw Liam out of the house. He's grown accustomed to a hermit's life, and the longer he's alone, the more it latches onto him. The hunger pains and dizziness don't faze him anymore. Canned soup and stale Triscuits taste better than nothing. Who cares if he skips showers or brushes his teeth without toothpaste? He's not entertaining.

But Kermit has run out of carrots.

"Not everything is about you," Makoto would say. He'd be joking, but it would still hurt.

Liam's hands shake on the steering wheel as he drives to the local Market Basket. He's delicately hopeful that it'll be dead at two o'clock on a Tuesday. The last thing he needs is social interaction. Since Maggie died in his backyard, he's been hounded with calls from Sloane, who seems to think harassment is a suitable method for getting him to take up the Wedge mantle again. And then there's Faye, who went so far as to pay him a visit at eight in the damn morning, though she was too star-struck to utter more than a tremulous "please help me." All that's been achieved by their badgering is Liam committing to never leaving his house again. Or so he thought.

The parking lot is relatively deserted, but he errs on the side of caution, donning a Celtics cap and his sunglasses. He hasn't been to Market Basket since he was a kid, and it's changed in exactly zero ways. The metallic gold garland and paper Patriot's decorations are straight out of the early '90s. It's practically a museum.

Since money is one of the very few things he doesn't have to worry about, he decides to splurge on Kermit. He fills his grocery basket with the finest local greens and carrots with tops. He grabs a few live parsley plants, though the idea of keeping a plant alive is absurd; he's barely managing himself and a rabbit. He buys enough paper litter to last to autumn.

Shopping for himself is rushed since he's less important. He grabs rice, nuts, and canned tuna. Bomb shelter food. He's browsing Campbell's soups when he starts to sense that someone is watching him. Great. Ingrid might have claimed that locals would leave him alone, but this is a tourist town. Anyone could be shopping to stock up their beach rental and recognize him. Keeping his head down, he picks up his pace, skirting past pasta sauce even though he's already grabbed ten boxes of spaghetti. He takes sharp turns, doubles back, and hides behind a display of Doritos, yet his observer only seems to draw closer. He can sense the edges of their Phren following him like a stray dog. Then Liam starts to realize that he doesn't have one stalker; he has many. Every set of eyes is magnetized to him. The whispers rise, shaping the sharp consonants of "Calico." But it's not until he hears the word "Maggie" that he starts to panic.

By the time he's reached the frozen section, which was where he planned to do most of his shopping, his heart is racing. His palms are damp. He's considering ditching his cart and running for the exit.

"Mr. O'Connor?"

Liam slams his elbow into a freezer door and swears. He glances up long enough to identify an overweight, flushed man with blond-white hair.

"Sorry, I'm in a rush," Liam mumbles, pivoting and making a break for the checkout.

He's bouncing on his heels as the cashier takes several centuries to ring him up. He keeps glancing over his shoulder. People around him stare, but no one is brash enough to approach. Maybe those token New England antisocial tendencies are working in his favor.

As he strides across the parking lot, cart rattling, he starts to think he's home free. Then the blond man steps right into his path. Liam gasps, screeching to a halt. The potted parsley falls from the cart, spilling across the pavement.

"Oh, jeez. I'm so sorry," the man says, bending down with a grunt. When Liam shies away from him, he puts his hands up, placating, and backs off. "I didn't mean to spook you. You must think I'm some kind of nut. Gosh, and I'm sure you're a little nervous about people because of ... what happened."

Liam doesn't answer. He thinks of Maggie's veiny cheeks and beady stare, and the way her feet were flayed in his living room, the worms in her eyes. He makes himself breathe.

"I'm Oliver. Oliver Fenton." Sweat pearls on Oliver's crinkled forehead as he holds out a hand. Liam accepts it, barely restraining the urge to wipe his palm off on his pants. There's a film of crusted spittle on the corner of Oliver's lips. His eyes are frenetic and hungry, familiar in a way that makes Liam's gut roll over.

"What do you want?" Liam snaps, then winces as Oliver's red cheeks darken a shade. "Sorry, I'm being a dick. I'm just in a hurry. And ... it's hot out." It is hot. The air is heavy. He glances at his car over Oliver's shoulder, longing for AC and power lock doors.

"I understand. I won't take a minute of your time. Just ... need to catch my breath." He pulls an old receipt from his pocket and wipes at his brow with it. He shuffles back and leans against the hood of Liam's car. Liam droops, realizing he's not going to shake this man unless he runs him over.

"Alright," he sighs. "What's up?"

"Buck told me you were back in town. Do you remember me?"

"Afraid not." Liam throws open his back door and starts loading the grocery bags.

"Really? Well, I guess you were little the last time I saw you. My mother was friends with Deb and Peter, rest them. She's getting up there now, too, as you could pro'lly guess. I'm getting up there myself. Which is a bit of a miracle, really."

"I see." He heaves the paper litter into his trunk with a grunt and busies himself with rescuing the parsley plant.

"I'll bet the reason you don't recognize me is I used to be quite a bit fatter than I am now. Didn't get out much. And if I ever went to a party, I sat in a chair the whole time while my mother fed me hot dogs until I was sweatin' nitrates. But I'm better now. Had to get a bunch of stretched-out skin cut off, though, once the weight was gone. That's the part they don't tell you about. You gotta get surgery unless you wanna look like a deflated old balloon."

If Liam had been interested in a conversation, this was certainly not it.

"Anyway, because I was always sitting at these parties I saw a lot, you know, mostly because people didn't really feel like talkin' to me. I'm not much of a social butterfly, but I do like watching people. And I remember watching you, playing with your friend, that day of the barbeque. You know ... *that* barbeque."

The idea of this man ogling him as a kid isn't exactly sparking joy. Liam knows what barbeque Oliver is referring to. It was the catalyst that first made Liam famous, stealing his privacy and his right to choose the course of his life. He doesn't want to talk about it. He doesn't want to talk about anything. Pulling out his keys, and shaking them a little louder than necessary, he casts suggestive glances at his phone screen. If Oliver gets the message, he doesn't care.

"You know which barbeque I mean, right?" Oliver's Phren flares with growing urgency. Liam twitches and digs his keys into his palm.

"I don't remember much from my summers here," Liam says. "Other than how my grandmother could be a real piece of work when she wanted to be."

Oliver's glossy lips part. He looks around like they're being spied on, lowering his voice.

"You might not want to go around saying that. Peter and Deb were like aristocrats around here, always throwing their elite parties. You weren't anybody if you didn't get an invite, which is why mother always clawed to get one. I just went along to get the food. At the barbeques, they always did a big clam bake and bought up all the lobsters from the pound. Grilled burgers and hot dogs and sausages. There was this spinach artichoke dip—even now I can taste it. But they stopped having these parties after … after the incident."

Liam shoves the last grocery bag into his car a little too hard, grimacing when a few eggs crack.

"What about your friend? Do you remember them?" Oliver says.

Friend.

Liam pauses. He feels a strange pull in his chest, a caged feeling, rattling bars. He doesn't remember a friend.

"Not really."

"What happened that day," Oliver begins, then swallows. He looks around nervously, then whispers, "I saw something. I should have said something then, but I wasn't in a mind to, you know? Sometimes it takes time, decades. And the mind plays tricks. I didn't have the strength back then to trust myself. Everyone said they saw it all happen one way, and they had to be right. I was just some stupid, bloated loser. I had to be wrong. But now I … I know I wasn't. I should've said something."

"Said what?"

"You kids were just swimming, and what I saw, most of me didn't believe it, but I heard about you coming back into town, and Maggie, drowning in that same place, and I knew. She was herself and then she wasn't. There was—"

"Calico!" squeals a familiar voice. Oliver gasps, flinching back and putting his hand over his heart. "I thought I saw you there!" Faye bounds up to them. "It's fate that I keep running into you like this!"

Liam doesn't point out that the last time she "ran into him" was when she came to his house uninvited.

"Oh, Oliver! I didn't see you there. Have you met Calico before?"

Sweat sheens on Oliver's cheeks. His light blue eyes dart around, avoiding Faye. She barrels on, oblivious.

"I did my own full examination of Maggie's corpse, just like you said, Calico. She is definitely a Red Fluke victim. I could see it clear as day in her Phren. Well, what I could see of it. I know I can't see them like *you* can. Oh, Oliver, sorry. This is *Sophont* talk. What I'm saying is she attracted a *Vice* Fluke. Probably because she was such a swizzler." Faye snorts an odd laugh. "We haven't gotten the toxicology report back. Super bummer. Did you know those things take forever? That's not what it's like on TV. Anyway, I'm sure she'll be stuffed like a turkey with drugs and booze and such. Oh shucks! I probably shouldn't tell a *civilian* about this, huh. Oliver—you didn't hear anything, got it? But just between us chickens, it's not a surprise that Maggie got herself that Fluke. Gotta be careful with vice. That's why I never tried drugs in college. Except for ether."

"I need to go," Liam says, hoarse. "I have ... an appointment."

"An appointment? For what? Is it for the investigation? Oh, that would be just wonderful. All Sloane talks about is getting Calico to help us out with the case. He's the best Wedge in the world, you know."

Bile rises. Liam glances at Oliver, who looks equally uncomfortable. Then the last person he wants to see stomps over to them.

"We got a problem here?" Sloane has an innate ability to make Liam feel like he's committing a crime just by existing in her presence. How convenient that they'd both be at a friggin' Market Basket at the same time as him. He'll have to check his car for a tracking monitor later.

"No?" he says, for lack of a better response.

Sloane takes personal offense, as always. "Do we need one?" she growls.

"Why would we need a problem?"

Sloane scowls.

"I'm just gonna leave," Liam says as he yanks open his driver-side door. "Don't want my ... uh ... cat litter to melt."

"Don't you have an appointment with Sloane?" Faye says, showcasing her innate ability to make everything worse. "Liam was just saying he was going to help with the case!"

"Is that so?" Sloane says, arching an eyebrow.

"No, it's not. Sorry, Oliver," Liam says, barreling into his front seat. He can hear his heartbeat in his ears. "We'll talk some other time."

"Wait, Liam, I—"

"Hey!" Sloane barks as Liam slams the door and jams his keys in the ignition. He peels out of the parking lot like an action movie star, and for a moment enjoys a rare swell of freedom. The feeling deteriorates as soon as it forms. He's going to pay for that later.

Back at his house, as he feeds Kermit and puts away his groceries, Oliver's words needle at him. He regrets not passing over his number before he fled. He considers tracking Oliver down on social media but shelves the idea. He knows what reactivating his Facebook would mean: a deluge of fake "just checking in" messages, and all those *In Memoriam* posts about Makoto from people who barely knew him, and Claire's endless "look at my happiness until you feel like shit" albums of her and Ken. No chance in hell.

An itchy sort of exhaustion takes over. It steals the rest of his day from him.

When he jars awake at four o'clock in the morning, his back sore from sleeping on the couch and his mind sticky with dreams, he thinks of Oliver again. He said Liam had a friend. A shadow of memory slinks in. He vaguely recalls playing pretend with someone those summers, and of getting ice cream from the local clam shack, and of riding his bike beside another. He can't remember a face.

He pulls up his browser on his phone and takes a risk. A Google search of "O'Connor BBQ 1990s" yields an instant result from the local paper. He groans when he sees who wrote it:

TRAGEDY AT O'CONNOR AVE—THE BARBEQUE FROM HELL
AUGUST 30th, 2000
By Maggie Short

What began as the perfect summer gathering turned nightmarish this past Saturday. It was a hot, muggy evening. Cicadas were buzzing a melodious symphony on the wind. As the unsuspecting, carefree partygoers sipped cocktails and ate lobsters, their children swam in the Abenaki River, unsupervised. Perhaps the children were trying to escape the heat. Perhaps they were avoiding the zealous revelries of there parents. We can only guess. All we know for certain is that no one was prepared when the cataclysm went off.

What is now speculated to be a rare, massive Fissure Event erupted out of nowhere. A series of Fissures ripped open among select guests, including a child that was swimming. While the child will remain nameless at the behest and legal threats of the family and law enforcement, this reporter regrets to report that it was to late when they finally noticed the little one, fighting for life. CPR was allegedly administered to the drowning victim, but the damage was done.

It is not yet known what suddenly stopped the Fissure Event in its tracks. An investigation into this disaster is at hand, with rumors of a federal institution intercepting the case. A number of party guests were pursued for information by this interviewer, but almost all were suspiciously with-holding and neglected to comment or even pick up the phone despite numerous attempts. One attendee, who has chosen to remain anonymous, offered only this anecdote: "I've been told not to say anything to anybody, but I'll tell you this: we got a real-life hero in our midst. We'd be dead if it wasn't for him. And that's all I'll say about that."

The effect this has on the community will surely not be long forgotten. One thing is for certain: it will be a long time before the O'Connor family hosts one of their exclusive barbeques again. Perhaps if more upstanding local citizens had been invited, this could have been avoided.

Liam rubs at his temples. Aside from suffering Maggie's blaring grammatical errors (Ingrid hadn't exaggerated) and biased reporting, the article doesn't sit right. He remembers the screaming and the mayhem. He remembers running. And he remembers the feeling of power overflowing inside him.

But he doesn't remember a kid drowning.

Makoto's voice pings in his mind:

It's not uncommon for children to repress traumatic memories.

Liam groans and drops his phone off the side of his bed. It hits the floor with a crack that sounds suspiciously like the screen breaking. He stares at the ceiling, just visible in the early morning light. He doesn't want to remember, not right now when he's barely holding on. The last thing he needs is yet another trauma, especially one involving a dead kid. He sucks in a deep breath; exhales slow. He lets the topic go because he must.

Makoto's voice whispers in his head:

Avoidance tactics.

Exhaustion festers and burns over the next few, long days. It wears on Liam—

wilts him. Nightmares are vivid, infesting what little sleep he gets. It's always the same dream: he sees the man on the island, drawing him in with a flickering light like a lantern fish. At times the image stammers and Liam imagines a little boy, indistinct as mist. When he wakes, he smells salt water, and he can't tell if it's real.

He avoids his own reflection. Whenever he catches it on accident, a Tolkien quote pops into his head:

"Like butter scraped over too much bread."

Inspired by this concept, Liam is in the process of eating a slice of bread when someone (it can only be Sloane) starts banging on his back door.

"You're never going to believe this, but this house features a front door with a working doorbell. Have I mentioned that before?" Liam says, pulling the door open. Sloane doesn't respond as she barrels past him, but Liam already knows the answer. Yes. He has. Every single damn time she's come by.

She's especially nasty today. Liam feels it radiating off her Phren, filling the room with a caustic stench. It's humid; he feels like the air is sticking to him. He rubs the phantom feeling off his arms.

"You look like shit, O'Connor." It's an accusation.

"You've caught me on a bad decade."

"You just look a little tired," Applebaum amends, shooting him a sympathetic look as she follows behind Sloane. Her eyes are puffy, her shoulders tense. She masks her feelings well, so something must be really off.

"I think you look great!"

Liam can't hold back a sigh when Faye appears. Makoto would remind him that she's harmless, just a typical fan. Liam can't help but find her annoying. She resembles a walking embodiment of the headache pounding behind his eyes. She bounds into the room, humming with glee. The edges of her Phren radiate simplicity. He doesn't have to delve inside to know her mind is colorless. Exotic as a Kmart. Fun as a twelve-hour layover in Newark.

Faye isn't subtle in anything, including the way she snoops around Liam's living room. Sloane is even less covert, poking at a few of his unpacked boxes and even bending over to look under his couch.

"Jesus fuck, O'Connor, you ever learn how to dust?"

Liam grits his teeth. "What can I help you with today?" he asks with false sincerity.

Sloane shoots him a look. She starts sauntering around the room like a sheriff in a saloon. He can almost hear spurs clicking.

"Trouble follows you wherever you go, huh."

Liam doesn't answer. If he did, he might point out that the only things following him are currently trespassing in his living room without a warrant. Applebaum stands next to him, watching Sloane and Faye and scratching the back of her head. She tilts toward him.

"We're sorry to bother you—"

"No we aren't," Sloane barks. "We've had another Fluke attack. I don't suppose you know who the victim is? You should, since I saw you talking with him five days ago. He seemed pretty upset after you left."

Liam frowns. "Oliver?"

"Yeah, *Oliver.*"

"How do you know it was a Fluke?"

"I could tell right away!" Faye blurts. Sloane ignores her.

"Because as far as we know, the poor bastard locked himself in a closet and ate until his stomach burst. And he wasn't eating normal food, mind you. I've never seen a damn thing like it and let me tell you—I've seen some shit. So, answer me this: why is this the second person to die of a Fluke attack in my town?"

"He's *dead?*"

"Yeah, he's dead. What part of 'stomach burst' didn't you understand? Died right after seeing you, just like Maggie. I've seen Fluke deaths before. Had a guy in Boston once—some druggy. He got infested with a Yellow Fluke and went catatonic. His house went up in an electrical fire and he was too fucked up to get out. I've seen plenty like that. But these two—they aren't normal. And they don't happen in a place like this. So tell me, what's the catalyst here? Huh? Because I think I'm staring right at it."

Liam has to give Sloane this one. A sudden Fluke death in a town like Shoalport is rare. To have two within a month is unheard of. Even when a Fluke *does* manage to claim a Host, it usually takes weeks or even months for it to erode them beyond repair. And even then, the Host is reduced to a shell of themselves, their Phrens vacant as a Blockbuster Video. These poor bastards are usually left to rot in assisted care facilities, where no amount of rehab will make them remember the voice of their mother, their favorite color, their own name. All memory—gone. Husks, they're called. Liam envies them on his hard days and feels like one on his worst. They mark them as 'deceased' on the paperwork. Good as dead.

"That's odd."

"Odd? That's all you have to say?" Sloane's nostrils flare.

"What else do you want me to say?"

"We need your help, Calico," Faye cuts in. "We didn't just come to tell you about Oliver. Sloane, can I tell him?" She looks like it's Christmas and Santa brought her a Tickle Me Elmo.

"Jesus fucking Christ."

"We got preliminary autopsy results back on Maggie," Faye says. She's bouncing on her feet again. "Guess how she died."

"She drowned herself in your whiskey," Sloane says. "Her lungs were full of Jame-o, not water. Care to explain that? And why did Oliver Fenton lock himself in a closet and eat 'til he popped? You said yourself that shit ain't normal."

He did and it isn't. It takes a lot for a Fluke to override someone's survival instinct, even if the Host is suicidal to begin with. It takes time. Flukes aren't interested in killing their Host before they take their meal. Usually, deaths like this are accidental—a Host tripping off a balcony or getting hit by a car. An electrical fire. But filling their own lungs with liquor and walking into a river? Eating through agony until your stomach splits? That takes full possession. Power. Intention.

He's seen it before, and the memory is electric. Liam can't touch it, can't even name it.

"I'm not a Wedge anymore," he hears himself say. The room feels far away.

"Of course you're a Wedge," Faye says. "You're the best Wedge there is."

"I need you to come down to the station. Phoebe Shelton wants to meet you. Do you know who that is?" Sloane says. Her eyes are narrow. He can sense her thoughts grinding like teeth.

"Head of the New Hampshire Fissure Control Department." He hears his own voice from far away.

"Holy shit, give the guy a medal. That's right, Calico. Seems like you know more than you let on. Just come down to the station and have a chat with her. She's an old buddy of mine. She's stationed out in Concord, but she said she'll come out right away. It's for the best if you wanna avoid any additional problems."

"Like what?"

" 'Like what,' he says. *You* work it out. You move into town and we get two Fluke victims in a month, when we haven't had a single Fissure in twenty years. And guess who was here when the last one happened? The one that made national fucking news? You. How do you think that looks? And then you do nothing to help? Seems like a problem to me."

"Are you threatening me?"

"No, Liam, she's not," Applebaum says, stepping between them. "She just wants to fix this, and you're the best person to do it. We're lost on this one. I know you don't want to come in—"

"I don't."

"But if you'd consider just talking to Phoebe, it would mean a lot to us. A lot to me."

A stab of betrayal sinks into Liam's gut. Applebaum was the one he liked. Trusted. Her kind brown eyes, now boring into him like they want something from him, is too much. She's just like everyone else. The need to escape crests inside him, and with it, the Nether steals into his periphery. He hears the crunch of feet on glass, smells whiskey in his ears. The yellow jacket stings him in the neck again.

"I need you to leave."

"Liam—"

"NOW! I know my fucking rights. Stay the hell off my property or come back with a warrant."

They all stagger back. He can't bear to look at them as they file out, knowing that he just made his life a whole lot worse. Sloane fires one last glare at him before she leaves. It's a promise and a threat. It doesn't matter right now.

He can't breathe. He can't think. Air comes in thin gasps. A fluttering pain sizzles up his chest. Spots flutter in his vision. The Nether peeks through— taunts him, beckons him. He can't hold it back when he's like this—when he's cracking and weak. He has no control. He can't fucking breathe.

I'm dying.

The certainty rocks through him. He braces his hands on a window frame, tries to focus on the water in his backyard, and the sunset. His last sunset. This is the moment. This is finally the end. He can't fucking breathe.

He bursts into tears. He's not sure how long he stands there, shivering and weeping. He blinks. Gasps.

And sees the light.

It's almost funny for a moment. Of course the last thing he sees before he dies is that stupid light. It's followed him his whole life. But then the moments drag, and breathing comes easier, and the edges of his vision clear. The Nether fades back. He's not dead, and he's not dreaming either. Yet there, undeniable, is that light.

And it's flickering from *the* island, just like in his dreams. Denial battles with sight. Is the Nether playing a trick on him? It doesn't feel like the Nether. He stumbles onto his back porch, eyes fixed on the light. It's still there, blinking at him from the rocks on the island, just below the dead tree. Is it a candle? No. Maybe it's a piece of a reflector or a broken mirror.

The tide is low. A wet path is illuminated in the fading sun, leading straight from his small beach to the island. He recalls his dream, and The Man Who Drowned Waiting. He can see footprints in the silt, leading from his beach to the island. And another set on the other side, tracing a path from Knox Island. Neither can be real.

Need sparks. He *needs* to be rid of his nightmares and of the light that chased him in the Nether—the light that watched as Makoto was lost forever; the light from the man with the gray eyes. He's suddenly angry. It's an energizing force, whetting his resolve. A spectating part of him is befuddled by his own intensity.

Kicking off his shoes and socks, Liam strides to the path. The sand sucks at his feet as he walks, pricking him with hidden shells and rocks. Hermit crabs dodge his steps. A seagull floats by, watching him.

He's gasping for breath and sweating by the time he reaches the shores of the island. A half-buried piece of a lobster cage snags his foot, sending him hard to his knees. Shattered mussels slice at his palms, just like in his dreams, reopening the cuts. He looks up. The light is hidden at this angle, though he feels its presence. The rocks are slippery with seaweed. He doesn't trust his feet. He thinks of Gollum in the Mines of Moria, crawling on all fours in his relentless pursuit of the Ring.

He slips. A gash opens on his shin, but he hardly notices. He pulls himself up. And finds it. There, wedged between two rocks, is the source of the light. His fingers close around it. Barnacles scrape at him as he yanks it free …

It's a pocket watch.

There's a faded compass rose carved into the salt-worn cover. He pries it open just enough to see the fogged watch face. Climbing down, he plops onto his ass in the sand. Fresh cuts sting as the sweat dries. He shivers and stares down at his great reward—a piece of garbage. Shame rises. He laughs, and the sound breaks.

For a moment, he entertains a fantasy of staying on the island until the tide swallows it up, affording him the same fate as the specter of his nightmares. Perhaps it would be poetic. Or maybe he's been dramatic enough for one day.

As he trudges back through the silt, water up to his ankles now, he wonders what Makoto would think of all this. Would he be disappointed in Liam for not helping Sloane? Would he think Liam's little quest for a stupid piece of sea trash was cathartic or unstable? Would he even care anymore? Being Liam's Splint was, after all, just a job. Maybe Liam glorified their relationship in his grief. Maybe Makoto was relieved to finally be free of him.

Maybe that's why he encouraged Liam to quit.

He tosses the pocket watch on his nightstand on the way to the shower. He might as well wash up for what he's about to do:

Get royally fucking drunk.

CHAPTER FIVE
ROCK BOTTOM

IT COMES EASY that night. The first whiskey goes down fast. Then the second. He switches to beer for a scenic detour—a fun little country road in lieu of a highway. Then it's a swift kick with a big shot of tequila, pulled from the freezer. He doesn't have a lime. He chases it with a bite of one of Kermit's carrots. Could be worse.

Before long, he's buzzed enough to be brave. He sashays onto his back porch and faces the river. The water glistens with aggressive moonlight, churning in the rising tide. His gaze slinks to the island. There's no light now. That's disappointing; he was hoping for solid proof that he really has lost his mind. At least then he'd know; some certainty about anything would be a nice change. He toasts to the island and pours a little out for the Drowned Man. It splashes on his foot.

He ambles around the side of the house to get a look at the Knox place, using the porch railing to steady himself. It stares back at him. There's no light in the window there either.

"Well, fuck you too then."

His phone rings and Liam yanks it out of his pocket. It's a number he doesn't recognize. In the biggest display of poor judgment he's exhibited in weeks, he answers.

"O'Connor residence. May I ask who's calling?"

"I didn't think you'd pick up. Maybe Sloane misspoke about you. This is Phoebe Shelton."

Oh fuck, Liam thinks. He may think it out loud.

"I'm guessing you know who I am, then. And why I'm calling." Her voice is quiet and steady, her diction precise.

"I have a theory."

"Then I'll skip the chitchat. I like that. Who has time to beat around the bush?" She pauses. He fidgets in the silence. "It's my understanding that you're not someone who likes to get pushed around."

Liam takes a swig of his whiskey. His hand shakes. He sits on the swinging porch chair, tensing when the chains creak under his weight. Phoebe is probably silhouetted in an oversized office chair, holding a cigar in one hand and petting a hairless cat with the other.

"Does *anyone* like being pushed around?"

"Ooo, good question. I suppose some people do, right? They don't have to worry about right and wrong when someone makes their decisions for them. It takes the pressure off. But we aren't like that."

"We? We don't know each other."

"I guess that's true. Let's learn about each other, then. I know you don't like having decisions made for you. Do you know what I don't like?"

Another silence. Liam's leg bounces.

"I don't like when people die in my territory. And I really don't like when those deaths could be avoided. I've got a problem here, Liam. Haven't had to worry about Fissures in years and now they're popping up like it's a fad. Makes me look a certain way when things like this happen. But hey, as fortune would have it, I happen to have the best Wedge in the country within my borders."

Liam pushes up his glasses and rubs at his eyes, as if that will sober him up. He's beginning to sense his own disadvantage, yet he can't clear his head. Rational thoughts shy away when he reaches for them. He feels the stare of the Knox House.

"I'm not a Wedge anymore."

"Hmm. Well, maybe not in spirit, but you're fully certified as an international consultant. You can technically take any case you want, anywhere you want it. All I have to do is sign off on it, which I'm more than willing to do."

"Get someone else to do it. You have two decent state Wedges. I've worked with Caraway and Brewster before. Put them on it."

"Caraway is on an extended leave in Bermuda and Brewster is out-of-state on a call-in. And they're not qualified for this. I'd rather have the best."

"It's not … it's not good for me."

"Not good? Oh, sure it is. It's right in your wheelhouse. In fact, I have your file right in front of me now."

Liam goes cold. He can't find words.

"It's impressive, I'll give you that. You graduated valedictorian at the Northeastern Academy for the Paraphrenically Gifted. You nabbed an accelerated PhD from the University of Chicago by twenty-three. That's one hell of a timeline. I get that you're smart, but someone had to know someone to make that happen, right? Then you traveled the world and even took down a Big Bad, but we won't get into him right now. I mean, by all rights you're a real, gen-u-ine hero. But FUSE, they wanted you stationed here, on American soil, serving your country. Chicago won the bid for you, only it seems they had quite a bit of trouble finding a Splint willing to work with you. 'Incompatible,' it says. 'Unstable.' Then came Makoto Mori."

She forms each letter of his name with brutal precision. Liam can't swallow.

"That's … not …"

"Oh, gosh, I'm sorry to bring up something painful for you. But trust me—I understand. I lost my mentor years ago. I'm always thinking of her, and what she'd think of me. And my choices. All we can do is make them proud, right?"

Liam should tell her to fuck off, that it's none of her business, that she'd better keep Makoto's name out of her damn mouth. But she's right, and she's good at this, and he hates himself so damn much he can barely speak.

"Mak—Agent Mori doesn't think anything. He's dead."

"Yes, and what a tragedy that was. FUSE did an impressive job keeping the details out of the papers, but that didn't stop the press from speculating. That's what the press does: they *speculate*. They don't have your file right here like I do. Still, these are just words. You're the only one who saw what really happened that day. So I have to ask: what could have possibly made you decide to enter the Nether that night? Sure, the Nether won't kill you. You're special. Only a few people in the world can do that and survive. But Makoto wasn't like you. For him, there was no coming back. Why did he follow you? Why would he choose certain death?"

"I … he—"

"When you came back without him, you were heard saying some horrible things. Like, how it was your fault, what happened to Makoto. They say you clutched his empty body for hours, long after he stopped breathing. They had to pull you away in cuffs to keep you from grabbing him again. You must have felt so alone.

"But you know, Sloane and I can empathize with you. I've known Sloane a long time. We used to work together in Boston. It took a lot to get us where we are now, and do you know the main thing we learned?"

"No."

"That we'll both do absolutely anything to protect people we care about. Anything. I think Makoto was trying to protect you that day. And you would have done anything to protect Makoto too, right? To keep what happened from happening, especially if it was your fault. Thing is, for Sloane and I, the people we care about most are our citizens and our crew because they're our responsibility, just like Makoto was your responsibility and you were his. Protecting people is the *right* thing to do. We'd take care of you, Liam, just like Makoto did. Nothing bad would happen on our watch. That's what responsibility means to us."

Her tactics aren't new to Liam. Archer pulled the exact same shit on him years ago, coercing him into accepting the job in Chicago when all he wanted to do was quit and never look at a Phren again. She'd backed him into a corner, played on his guilt and hit him from too many angles, just as Phoebe is doing now. Archer probably trained her. He's struck with the suspicion that Phoebe knew he'd be drunk tonight. She knew about his outburst at Sloane and the liquor collection Maggie gorged herself on. Hardly a Sherlockian deduction; Liam's never met another Wedge who didn't have a substance misuse issue. This is a person of consummate deliberation, a master tactician. She probably plays Risk like a monster. Part of him is impressed.

She delivers her finishing blow:

"This file of yours … it really is incredible that your superiors have kept its contents out of the public forum for so long. You must have had a lot of allies. I hope you consider making some friends in Shoalport too. Think of it as a symbiotic partnership. We need you and you need us. Then you can go back to that quiet life you're hoping for. Once this is all resolved, of course."

A deep, hollow feeling yawns open inside him. From a distance he observes himself as an amused spectator.

Ah, there he finally goes. He's hit rock bottom. This is as low as you go, folks.

"Liam. Don't make me beg."

"Fine."

He ends the call.

The alcohol was a mistake. It opens up the floor beneath him—sucks him down. He's gotten low before, especially in the months after Makoto died (oh, was that something to behold), but that was grief. That was normal. This is different than that; it's scary, profound, unstoppable.

This is the first time he truly wants to vanish—to fade away to nothing.

It just seems easier. All of this would go away. Phoebe is right; Makoto would hate him now. He's so fucking pathetic. Anyone can push him around.

He totters to his feet. The journey to his bedroom is a mystery. He doesn't even look at Kermit. Somehow, he ends up in his ensuite. Maybe he was hoping a mirror would help. Boy, was he wrong.

He stares at himself, at his dull green eyes behind his black-rimmed glasses, at the overgrown calico-colored hair and the perpetual rash on his forehead. He's lost weight he couldn't afford. He looks old. There was a time when Liam thought of himself as a handsome man. Now, he searches for anything other than a flaw and comes up empty.

He throws up in the sink.

A profound kind of hopelessness cocoons him when he falls into bed, exhausted beyond reckoning. He doesn't want to get up the next day. Or ever again. He can't face Applebaum, who is just like the rest, or Faye, who's dumb enough to see him as a hero, and especially not Sloane, who he'd almost respected until she'd loosed Phoebe Shelton on him.

The last thing he sees before sleep claims him is the stupid pocket watch on his nightstand.

The Man Who Drowned Waiting is in his bedroom.

Liam smells him first—the prickling gloss of fat and flesh, washed ashore and baked in the sun. Droplets of seawater hit the floorboards in a warped rhythm. There's a wheeze, like air squeezing between shipboards. When Liam comes into awareness, it's a sudden shift.

The room is suffused with blue early morning light. The man is tall; the top of his hair grazes the doorframe. His gray eyes are singular, and they're fixed on Liam, pristine against the horror of his face. The black hole where a mouth should be widens, emitting that low hiss. He regurgitates a tangle of bulbous seaweed down his front. Liam remembers popping the air pockets in that seaweed as a child. He did it with a friend he can't recall.

Liam tries to scream, and his teeth fall out. He feels like wads of gum are clogging his throat. He reaches into his gullet to pull them out and can't.

William.

The man's arm rises slow, his crooked finger extending like driftwood. It points to the nightstand. Liam gasps against a horrible tugging at his ribcage. He throws himself from his bed, landing hard on the floor—

And wakes up.

It's hot and muggy. Liam trembles as he takes a sip from his third cup of coffee. He leans against the kitchen island and counts each rapid beat of his heart. He's overheating in his old university sweatshirt, but he's too vulnerable to wear anything less.

The doorbell rings, and Liam drops the mug, shattering it. With a yelp, he ducks below the kitchen island and peers just over the counter. For a horrible moment, he thinks Sloane is at his door. He's contemplating hiding in a cabinet when he hears wheels screeching. He sneaks to the window in time to watch the mailman peel off down the road.

It takes a while for him to muster the resolve to check what's been delivered. He keeps imagining the Drowned Man in his periphery. He refuses to turn on his phone.

There's a box on his front porch. There are only a few possibilities of who would send him a package, and Liam doesn't like a single one. Phoebe could have sent him the case files, though it seems unlikely Sloane would pass up an opportunity to deliver them personally. Archer is a possibility, but given how they left things, Liam doubts she'll reach out to him any time soon. That leaves Claire. He wouldn't put it past her to craft him a patronizing care package, littered with pity and subtle recriminations and Necco wafers, which he's never liked.

He scuttles out, snatches up the package, and locks the front door behind him. He tosses it on the counter and circles it, assessing. A stamp tells him it was redirected from his old apartment in Chicago. The return address reads:

Kaoru Mori. Kyoto, Japan.

Liam steps back. He rubs at his stubble. He's never met Makoto's mother. Does she blame him for Makoto's death? He rips open the package with a dull knife.

Inside, atop an elegantly folded cushion of tissue paper, is a note scribed on rice paper:

> Dear Liam,
>
> I am sorry my English is so poor. I am writing on behalf of my son. Before his passing, he entrusted this to me for safekeeping, until the appropriate moment arose to forward it to you. It seemed his intention was for me to keep the contents discreet. I am sorry the shipping takes so long.
>
> I am grateful that he had you as a friend all those years.
>
> You were significant to him.
>
> Sincerely,
> Mori Kaoru

Liam pulls off his glasses and drops them on the counter. He's not prepared for this, but the curiosity is there. It nibbles at him as he nibbles his lip. He gives in, folding back the tissue paper and revealing a journal with his name written on the cover. Lifting it with gentle hands, he clutches it to his chest. He backs up until he hits a wall and slides down to the floor. It's as if Makoto just walked into the room.

With legs crossed, Liam examines the journal. It's so very Makoto—clean and sleek. Nothing extraneous. The leather is warm under his fingertips. Smooth. He turns to the first page.

WITHIN IS MAKOTO MORI'S ACCOUNT OF HIS TENURE AS
LIAM O'CONNOR'S SPLINT

Makoto always wrote in all capitals. On impulse, Liam buries his nose in the binding and breathes in the scent. It doesn't quite smell like Makoto, but he senses the phantom of him. It's easy to imagine Makoto, with his perfect posture and calm features, writing in this journal, a cup of green tea steaming close by.

At first, Liam is terrified of what he'll find. In his hands could be the proof that Makoto didn't care about him, that he thought Liam was insane and past saving. He's already teetering on the edge. He can't take the blow of knowing Makoto thought as little of him as he thinks of himself.

But that's not what he finds. Sure, there are recriminations of his poor self-image and coping mechanisms, but nothing Makoto didn't say to his face. And the rest is … fond. In his detailed accounts of their cases, there are nods to Liam's sense of humor and snark, which Makoto seemed to find amusing. He cites private jokes and Liam's little mannerisms. Apparently, Liam rubs at his nape when he's nervous. He takes his hand off his nape when he reads that, and smiles.

He's hesitant to tread over the land mines of past cases, so he skims over most of them, though a few do snag. The McKinley case, for one. A Violence Fluke had infested a former college football player whose Phren was scrambled by a few too many tackles to the head. He'd been let go from his security guard job after several "excessive force" allegations. It became clear at the scene that Joe McKinley had long been overtaken by the Violet Fluke, and that he'd been taking out his rage on his old yellow lab. Her name was Lucy. As Joe snarled from a kitchen chair, the Fluke swelling in him like a boil, the dog shivered in a corner with her tail tucked. Joe was hyper-fixated, his mouth frothing as he panted, bloody eyes locked on her. "Bitch won't ever do what she's told. Chewed on my shoes to spite me. I'll teach her a lesson. Kick her into next week."

The first responders on the scene—a few rookie cops—had handcuffed Joe so Liam could do his work. Unfortunately, they hadn't done a very good job. Joe snapped his own thumbs like wishbones, breaking free. He charged at his dog. She didn't move—just sagged and closed her eyes. Liam threw himself between them and got a broken wrist and a chunk bitten out of his ear (by Joe, not Lucy). Everyone but Makoto teased him about that. *We got Holyfield in the building*, they'd say. At least they weren't calling him Calico. Makoto ends the passage with a line that makes Liam's throat ache:

IN THAT MOMENT, LIAM BELIEVED HIS OWN LIFE TO BE LESS VALUABLE THAN A DOG'S, AND FOR THAT, HE WAS SUPERIOR TO THE REST OF US.

Another case that catches his attention is what Makoto cheekily refers to as "The Trip." It was a simple Vice Fluke, but the Host had dropped acid just before Liam arrived on the scene. Makoto seemed amused by Liam's befuddled stumbling through that Phren. There was a room made of rainbows and giant turnips and a relentless floating banjo that followed him around. It had taken ages to find the location of the Fissure. Eventually, he pinpointed it to a kiddie pool full of glitter. He sealed the Fissure but was completely coated in glitter in the process. For a week Makoto couldn't look at him without smirking. Apparently, the damn stuff littered his Phren.

But that case was an anomaly. They usually left a Fissure scene with Makoto peeling Liam's psyche off a bar floor while Liam made noble attempts to drown memory with whiskey. He hadn't considered how that wore on Makoto. Liam feels Makoto's concern for him on every page, and the toll it took to watch Liam decline. But it didn't just upset Makoto; it also made him angry.

Liam never knew how Makoto truly felt about FUSE. He was always subtle when they discussed it. Diplomatic. But here, he castigates their practices on every page, harsher than anything he expressed out loud. He claimed that their bosses saw Liam as a commodity—a tool—but one with a shelf life. They knew the job would get the most of Liam one day, and that he'd either crumple into a drooling catatonic or break bad. It was in their interest to milk him dry before that day came. They cared about statistics and told Makoto as much when he tried to register his concerns. "Just get him out there," Archer had apparently responded. "That's your job. The greater good is all that matters." Makoto didn't see it like that:

O'CONNOR IS A DEEPLY MORAL, THOUGHTFUL, EMPATHETIC
INDIVIDUAL. DESPITE HIS NUMEROUS TRAUMAS, HE IS
ENDLESSLY COMMITTED TO THE HEALTH AND WELL-BEING
OF STRANGERS. HE IS STRONG, BUT NOT WITHOUT FEELING.
TO SACRIFICE THIS MAN FOR THE SAKE OF POLITICALLY
DRIVEN STATISTICS IS EGREGIOUS MALPRACTICE OF THE
HIGHEST FORM. I INTEND TO SUBMIT A FULL REPORT, AND
IF IT'S NOT SERIOUSLY CONSIDERED, I WILL GO TO THE
PRESS.

Liam's cheeks are hot and wet. He sniffles, trying not to get snot on the pages. The final sections are the hardest. Liam doesn't want to finish. It's as if this is his last conversation with Makoto. He feels close to him—connected. Every day, he's wondered what Makoto would think of him and his choices.

Then he comes upon a passage that stops him short.

WE NEVER DISCUSS IT, BUT AT 12 YEARS OLD, O'CONNOR
WAS SUBJECT TO A SEVERE TRAUMA INVOLVING A FISSURE
EVENT IN HIS FAMILY'S HOMETOWN. HE SUCCESSFULLY
SEALED SEVEN FISSURES, DESPITE HIS YOUNG AGE AND
COMPLETE INEXPERIENCE. I BELIEVE THERE WERE ASPECTS
OF THIS EVENT THAT O'CONNOR HAS REPRESSED. I THINK IT
MAY BE THE CATALYST FOR A LOT OF HIS TRAUMA.

Something shifts as Makoto's words reach into him. He comes to the final page. It's dated to the day before he lost Makoto.

IT IS MY OPINION THAT LIAM O'CONNOR IS NOT DESTINED
FOR A PSYCHOTIC BREAK OR A LIFELONG CAREER SEALING
FISSURES. HE IS RESILIENT, INTELLIGENT, AND FEARLESS. HE
IS ONE OF THE BEST PEOPLE I HAVE KNOWN. IT WOULD
BE A GREAT SHAME TO REDUCE HIM TO ANYTHING LESS. I
DO NOT BELIEVE HE SHOULD BE A WEDGE MUCH LONGER.

I HAVE ALWAYS SEEN HIM AS A HISTORIAN. HE'D MAKE AN
OUTSTANDING PROFESSOR.

Liam was royally shit-faced when he confessed his secret professor fantasy, and Makoto never brought it up. He should have known Makoto remembered everything.

A memory bobs up in his Phren.

"If you weren't a Sophont, what do you believe you would do?" Makodo had said.

"Be a lot less bitchy, for one."

"I mean as a career."

"Oh, I dunno. Doesn't really matter does it," Liam had slurred. But Makoto had only watched him, waiting. Finally, he'd admitted, *"I've always liked history. Took some classes in college when I could sneak them in."*

"Why do you like it?"

"I guess I like the mystery. I like feeling like I'm unearthing something old. Like I'm a pirate with a treasure map. And I suppose I've always felt a special connection to the past. I always wished I could be a professor. But that will never happen."

"You never know."

Liam had laughed. *"I may be drunk and stupid, but I'm not drunk and delusional."*

"I wish you thought more of yourself."

Liam puts the journal down. He stares at it, then paces back and forth in the kitchen. He cycles into the foyer and the dining room, does a circuit past the squirrel's nest in the corner, and the wall of empty built-in china cabinets, then into the living room. He trips on a stack of boxes and swears so loud that Kermit jumps across his pen.

"I need to do something," he says. He looks at Kermit. "I don't know what I'm supposed to do." Kermit's nose twitches. Liam looks around, hands on his hips. The unpacked mess feels more obvious without his usual fog. It's oppressive. Maybe he hadn't noticed how much it wore on him. "I need to fucking clean."

But he's on the precipice of something. He's choking in the collar of his own talent. It made it famous and infamous, wealthy and consistent. Yet, he never had a choice. Agency was a luxury for normal people. And here he is, desperate for Makoto's guidance—for someone to tell him what to do. Maybe Phoebe was right: it is easier to be told what to do. He thought he was finally taking control, but fear has been a constant. And not fear of the Nether or of any Fluke, but fear of who he'll become if he doesn't step away. Makoto was his barometer. He was always honest, even when it meant pissing Liam or his superiors off. He would know if Liam should take this case or walk away. He would take the pressure off.

And then he thinks of the journal, and of their last conversation in the bar the night Makoto died. Makoto said he could quit if he wanted to. Makoto thought his fantasy of being a professor wasn't just some pipe dream. He peels away all the layers of self-doubt. What would Makoto really want?

"If you did not want to do this anymore, I would advocate for you."

But Makoto didn't know a Host would drop dead in his backyard. In *Shoalport*, no less. If everyone around him is begging for his help, shouldn't he give it? Makoto said he's a good person. Many times. Isn't taking this case what a good person would do?

"Perhaps your sense of responsibility for the lives of strangers is crippling you."

He paces. And he thinks. And he keeps bumping into fucking boxes. With a growl, he kicks one over, sending a herd of Blu-ray cases skidding across the floor. He can't clear his head in the house. The air is stagnant, sour with old wood and old memories he can't recall.

He throws off his sweatshirt and barrels out of the back door onto the porch. A wave of hot air comes, carrying the clean scent of high tide. He glares out across the river. It's peppered with kayakers and paddleboarders, gliding around anchored lobster boats. As he strides down the path to his beach, flat inlayed stones warm under his bare feet, he peels off more clothes. Impulse pulls him. He's too damn hot and sweaty. He definitely smells. Why hadn't he noticed before? God, he needs to mow the lawn.

He breaks into a run. He doesn't hesitate when his feet hit sand, then water.

He dives in.

And it's fucking freezing.

Liam gasps, shaking his hair. The cold is shocking. At first, he wants to run right back out. But he breathes through it, surrendering to the chill and the swaying waves. And then his skin begins to adapt. There's something oddly pleasant about the cold. It's purifying. He's clean and awake. The haze recedes and the sky is bright, and his mind isn't stuck in memories or on his future. He is exactly where he is.

Eyes closed, he floats on his back for a while, only getting out when his ankles ache. He shivers as he walks back into the house and up to his room for a hot shower. When he's done, warm and pink, he doesn't have a headache. He's had a headache for so long, he'd stopped noticing. Its absence is stranger than its presence.

The rare clarity is a high and he wants to ride it. He wants to *do* something with it.

Before he can think of all the good reasons not to, he calls Phoebe Shelton. She answers on the last possible ring.

"Liam. I was just in the process of finishing your case forms. Anything you need?"

"Yeah, about that. I gave it some thought. I've decided I'm not going to take over the case."

"Excuse me?"

"What I mean is … I cannot take on the full responsibility of it. I'm retired. But I can take a look at the files and offer some suggestions. You know—meet you in the middle. But yeah, sorry, I don't work as a Wedge anymore."

There's a long, barbed pause. Each second winds tighter.

"May I ask what changed your mind?"

"I didn't change my mind. I've never wanted to take this case." He catches himself before he says "but you made me take it," like a child.

"Well, I'm afraid what we want isn't always an option."

"I'm sorry?"

"'Meeting in the middle' is not an offer I'm willing to accept." Her voice has gone cold, crisp—a rapid drop.

"I don't understand."

"Trypanons are rare."

That word clicks like a trigger. In speaking it, Phoebe burns away any false confidence or clarity he'd mustered. He can't respond. All he can do is accept the slow certainty that he is tremendously outgunned. Again.

"You move back to Shoalport and suddenly we have two Fissure incidents when we haven't had one since … you were last here, two decades ago. At your family's barbeque."

"I don't know what that has to do with—"

"You were only twelve then, yet you sealed all those Fissures that opened that day. Seven total, wasn't it? Did you know that day is classified as the most catastrophic Fissure Event New England has ever seen?"

"Of course I do."

"FUSE saw how powerful you are. They've been keeping you on a tight leash ever since. Dragged you to the Academy before you could pack a bag."

Liam's heart pounds in his ears. His chest burns. "They always bring children to the Academy when their Sophont abilities present," he says, and despises how meek he sounds.

"Don't be modest. Most Sophonts can barely dream hop. Few are as powerful as me, and I have nothing on you. When I presented, I kept manipulating my parents' thoughts. I got whatever I wanted for Christmas, you can be sure of that. I was advanced for a ten-year-old, sure, but not extraordinary. I couldn't seal seven Fissures in one go. I don't know any *adult* Wedges who could pull that off."

Phoebe's most disarming tactic is that she selects truths; nothing she's said is a lie. Though Liam knew that Phoebe had to be a Sophont to get her position, the implications hadn't struck him until now. Usually, weaker Sophonts were the ones to take on an administrative role like Phoebe's since they weren't able to work in the field. But there were exceptions. Makoto once commented that he wasn't the only one to use his abilities to manipulate the emotions of others, he just did it on a small scale and only when it was essential (usually to protect Liam). Liam read between the lines: there were some people in power who used any means necessary to meet their goals. Manipulating minds at age ten wasn't some common little trick. It took years of training for Sophonts to learn this ability, and it wasn't something they taught at the Academy. Since it was, you know, *illegal.*

Even if her powers don't work on a Trypanon, he never wants to be in a room with Phoebe Shelton.

She slithers on, each word formed with precision. Again, despite his disgust and discomfort, Liam is impressed.

"People have always known how special you are. One of only seven known Tryps in the world, in fact. I read up about them. I like to do research. Seems five out of the seven of these Tryps are in high security prisons after they ripped open a bunch of Fissures in their victims. Most weren't even aware they were doing it."

"What's your point?" Liam rasps, as if he doesn't already know.

"I'm so glad you asked. I probably shouldn't tell you this, but Wendalyn Archer got in touch with me when you moved here. She asked me to keep a close eye on you. Apparently, that request came from high up. I say 'request,' but we both know that it's as good as an order with FUSE. Trust isn't something afforded to people like us. I can't say I trust our kind either. We can do a lot of damage without realizing it, even as kids. FUSE knows this better than anyone. I don't want to report back to them that you aren't being cooperative, especially when two people have died after getting in confrontations with you."

"Oliver wasn't—"

"It's all about how things are spun, right? You get that. Surely, you've worked closely with the press before. As of right now, most people still see you as a hero. Broken and tragic, but still a hero. Shoalport, though … heck, you've been a town legend ever since that barbeque. I can see why you'd want to retire here. As long as your reputation stays intact, that is."

"I have to say, this is starting to sound like a threat, Phoebe."

"Perhaps. But it's more than that, isn't it? What if you *are* linked to their deaths in some way and you don't even know it? It's happened before. It's happened a lot, with Trypanons."

It strikes fast—a scalding, instant fury.

"If you're calling me a suspect just because I won't do what you want, that's pretty fucked up, Phoebe."

"No one is calling you a suspect."

"Yeah, 'not yet'—is that what you mean? If I don't bend over and take what you want to give me?"

"That's a little crass."

"Oh, fuck that. Just say it. Stop dancing around your point."

"Alright, Calico: if you don't take this case, there will be consequences. I don't think that's a mystery. I do not necessarily believe you are our killer. But someone is and I have my suspicions, and you are the only one who can go into the Nether and prove me right. Something strange is going on here, something I've never seen before. I'm blind to something, and I'm never blind to anything. I need help. I need someone stronger than me. And the more you refuse to take this case, the more suspicious you look. And not just to me. What if we have an unidentified, unregulated Trypanon running wild? What if they followed you here? I know you're aware of how dangerous that is. You have no choice but to take this case."

"I'm not taking it."

"You're making a big mistake."

"I usually am."

Liam feels a shift. Phoebe doesn't take 'no' for an answer often. She's angry. Angrier than he is. He hears her breath hiss on the line before she speaks, cold and low.

"Makoto Mori would be ashamed of you."

And that's officially his limit.

"You know what, Phoebe—fuck off. I'm not doing shit on your fucking case. And if you want to come after me, I fucking dare you. You said it yourself: I'm much more powerful than you, and you're nothing but a bully."

He hangs up the call and turns off his phone.

And then a slow, crawling realization rises.

Well shit.

Barnacles popping. The stink of tidal mud exposed to the sun. A painful tug, deep in Liam's chest. The Drowned Man is in his room again, framed by the doorway. He coughs, fog misting out of his mouth. He reaches out with a white hand, the skin gnawed down to the bones and tendons by little fish. Extending a long finger, he points.

He returns the next night. And the next.

CHAPTER SIX
INDEPENDENCE DAY

𝔇AYS PASS IN intervals of extremes. At times, each second stings by. Others, he seems to blink from morning light to a setting sun. The mess gets worse. He'd rummaged through a few boxes looking for a spatula one afternoon. Now, their innards are strewn like guts after a battle. He never did find the spatula.

Phoebe doesn't contact him. There are no more threats, no cops banging down his door, no articles about him in the paper. It's worse than an immediate confrontation, and he thinks she knows that. She's biding her time and he's on constant edge, waiting for her to take her revenge. He can't believe he told her to fuck off.

Well. Maybe he can.

July 4 is hot and hazy. The sun blares into his bedroom, bullying him into waking far too early. He'd forgotten how hot old houses can get in the summer. He's still refusing to buy an air conditioner until it becomes unbearable like a true New Englander. But he's sick from lack of sleep and washing his sweat-soaked sheets is becoming a constant necessity. Caving, he pulls up Amazon. He buys two window ACs: one for him, one for Kermit, who's been laying out like a Roman emperor to stay cool. Liam's phone buzzes with an email receipt. Without thinking, he opens his inbox.

Oh no.

He's managed to avoid his emails since the great "Fuck Off" incident. Cringing, he covers his mouth. If he sees something from Phoebe or Claire or Archer he won't be able to resist opening it. But there's nothing from any of them. Or anyone back in Chicago. He glances at his full trash folder and feels a moment of gratitude for how thorough he'd been about blocking contacts before his move.

There is one unopened email that catches his attention, dated a few weeks prior. He holds his breath. And clicks:

From: IngridNess@gmail.com
CC: burnerteddy@hotmail.com
Subject: July 4th BBQ invite

Liam!

This is Ingrid from The Salt Cellar. We didn't have time to catch your number before you Irish-goodbyed, but we managed to track down your email address ... not in a creepy way. Teddy and I are having a BBQ on the 4th around 3:00PM and wanted to shoot you an invite. Gonna be a small gathering of non-obnoxious people, drinking beer and eating processed tubes of meat. You should fit right in. If you have plans or don't feel like coming—cool. If you wanna show up late—cool. If you don't celebrate the birth of our nation—cool. You do you.

Regardless, we should hang out soon. Hope all is great.

Ingrid

Re: July 4th BBQ invite

Really hope you can make it, Liam! This is Teddy, btw. I'm that guy who wouldn't shut up about local folklore, because I forget when I'm not in a classroom *facepalm*

Speaking of which: Here's an article about *The Man Who Drowned Waiting*, in case you're curious (I hope you're curious). I had the privilege of contributing to it through the Historical Society, as my students never get tired of hearing (they get very tired of hearing anything).

LINK

Hope to see you Wednesday! (what a bogus day for a party, but we'll make it work) (historically we actually declared independence on July 2nd but no one seems to care when I tell them that … especially my students) (they don't care about anything) (are you sensing a theme?)

Teddy

Re: Re: July 4th BBQ invite

I already took the fifth off. Anticipating an epic hangover in honor of our great nation.

Oh, and please ignore how my boyfriend has a fucking Hotmail account. I try to.

Ingrid

Re: Re: Re: July 4th BBQ invite

But what if I like my mail hot?

Re: Re: Re: July 4th BBQ invite

Is it possible to delete someone's entire history of terrible jokes from your memory, Liam? Asking for a friend.

Though there's no way in hell he'll go to a party, Liam is curious about the article. Perhaps if he gets more information on the Drowned Man, the nightmares will stop, like purging a song that's been stuck in your head by listening to it. He'll do anything for a decent night's sleep.

He clicks.

THE LEGEND OF "THE MAN WHO DROWNED WAITING": FACT AND FICTION

Though the seacoast is rife with local legends, none are more well-known than "The Man Who Drowned Waiting." While many residents purport a version of the tale, and each swear by their iteration's legitimacy, there are only a few details we know for certain. Over the years, fact and fiction have coalesced. Reliable documentation is sparse, partly due to the Fire of 1922, which destroyed many important records. Furthermore, the Knox and O'Connor families have stringently guarded their family secrets. Trespassers, including historians, are still barred from the Knox property. Regardless, a great deal of effort has been dedicated to uncovering the mystery of "The Man Who Drowned Waiting."

Sebastian Knox (born 1837 in Cambridge, England) was an English architect of some repute. Following the birth of his son, Jasper Knox (born 1862), and subsequent death of his wife, he relocated to Shoalport, NH. His talents were widely sought after; several notable New England structures are accredited to his design.

The most famous of which are his own residence—the Knox House—and its identical twin—the O'Connor House— standing across the perilous, tidal Abenaki River. The design boasts a wraparound porch, intricate dentils, and a tower. It is classically Victorian yet unique to Knox's signature style. The only characteristic distinguishing the two homes is the paint; the Knox House is dark gray while the O'Connor House is white. The color has been maintained to this day. The structures are also mirror opposites, as if one house casts a reflection of the other from across the water.

Despite the beauty of the homes, it is speculated that a rift formed between Sebastian Knox and Declan O'Connor, who commissioned Knox to build to the O'Connor House. This is not confirmed. O'Connor was a decorated Civil War veteran, celebrated political figure, lawyer, and prominent abolitionist, known for his favorable term as mayor of Shoalport from 1884-1888. His grave lies on the O'Connor property, along with the rest of his family.

Here is where legend begins to blur with fact. Town myth has it that Sebastian Knox's son, Jasper, fell in love with Rosie O'Connor, the neighboring Declan O'Connor's daughter. Their parents disapproved of their union. A bitter rift began to form. In the wake of their parents' objection, the star-crossed lovers made plans to run away together. They would meet on an island in the Abenaki River, only accessible from their properties at low tide. When the young man, Jasper, went to the island to meet her, she never arrived. As misfortune would have it, a rare king tide occurred, and he drowned. It is said that when Rosie discovered that her lover had died, she went mad. To this day, there is no evidence to indicate the romantic relationship or the cause of Jasper Knox's death. Some even speculate that Jasper

Knox was murdered, though this is pure conjecture. Jasper's grave has never been located.

A single salvaged document confirms that Jasper did die on August 28, 1888, which was also his birthday. He was twenty-six years old and had been living at home with his father after graduating from Harvard with a degree in Natural Sciences. Following Jasper's death, Sebastian Knox lived the rest of his life in solitude in an apartment in downtown Shoalport. He died in 1905. The Knox House has not been occupied since, due to a prohibition Sebastian established before his passing. It is said he wanted the house sealed as a tomb for his late son.

The only record of Rosie O'Connor indicates that she also died in 1888 at the Danvers Lunatic Hospital. The cited cause of death was "hysteria." Her body rests in the family plot on the O'Connor property.

There's a slideshow of old photos below the article. The first few show Liam's house and the Knox House from different angles. They've changed little over the years, though the Knox House has taken a beating since. He clicks through—to a portrait of a painfully serious young woman, with an over-large cross on her neck. Her thin hair is greased into a tight, low bun. He can't tell if she was miserable or just looks like it, as most people do in old photos. There's a young man standing behind her with his hand firmly gripping her shoulder. "Declan O'Connor Jr. with Rosie O'Connor" the caption reads. He clicks again.

And stops.

The grainy image of Jasper Knox stares back at him. The man sits rigid in a chair, his father looming behind him. Liam's first thought is that Jasper is handsome, and so is Sebastian. They're lithe and tall, with high cheekbones and dark, lightly curled hair. He zooms in on Jasper's face. Though the eyes are hard to make out, he senses familiarity in them. Liam cleans his glasses on his T-shirt, blinks, and stares at the image again. The eyes. They were in his bedroom the night before, staring at him. They've been in his bedroom every night for weeks.

Several explanations fly through his head and he doesn't like any of them. The Nether snickers in his ear.

Liam slams his laptop shut and shoots to his feet. He bounces on the floor—paces. He's on the precipice of something. He needs to act. But what can he do? He can't think when he's surrounded by a mess.

So he decides to clean his house. For real this time.

Liam wipes the sweat from his forehead with his T-shirt and surveys his handiwork. Though there are still a few boxes left to unpack, he's sequestered them into corners where he's less likely to trip over them. He put away most of his kitchenware (even found the damn spatula), not that there was a lot of it, dusted, and did a good sweep. The bubble wrap is gone. The furniture covers are stuffed in a closet. There's more to do, but he allows himself a hum of accomplishment. Unpacking had been insurmountable. It's not anymore.

"I think this is cause to celebrate, huh little man?"

Kermit ignores him. He gets a handful of romaine and a strawberry anyway.

Liam is feeling good. After a shower he feels even better. He wanders around, eager to do something that isn't wallowing in self-pity or hiding from Phoebe. He checks the time—five o'clock in the evening. Ingrid did say he could come to the barbeque late. Maybe it wouldn't be so bad. Ingrid and Teddy were good company. It makes sense that their friends would be bearable too. Ingrid didn't seem like the type to bullshit him or put up with people who annoy her. His stomach grumbles. He could go for a hot dog and a beer.

He's rummaging through his booze collection for something to bring to the party when there's a cracking, erratic knock at his back door. He reaches out with his senses, back muscles tensing as he catches the fraught scent of a Phren. He considers pretending he's not home, but the knocking persists. He hears the glass wail, not likely to prevail under the onslaught. He peeks around the door-frame of his kitchen and sees a familiar figure on his back porch. Of course. Sloane always uses his back door. At least it's not Phoebe.

He sighs, knowing she won't leave until he talks to her.

"Open the fucking door, O'Connor."

There's a clumsy edge to her voice that calls Liam to a sharper awareness. He opens the door halfway so she won't come inside. She barrels in anyway. Her shoulder catches his and he stumbles back. The odor of alcohol follows her. She's in casual clothes, which is odd. Sweat stains spread across the back of her T-shirt and the pits. Her hair is frizzed. There's something unsettling about seeing Sloane distressed. Though she's always emotional, she's never this disheveled.

"What happened?" he says.

"You know what fucking happened," she spits. Liam rolls his eyes.

"No, I don't. Unless you're here because I'm not taking the case. I told Phoebe I'd take a look at the files but she—"

Sloane slams her fist onto his mantel. A cloud of dust billows into the light. Apparently, Liam forgot to clean that spot.

"She's dead."

"Who's dead?"

"Phoebe Shelton, you bastard. And Jake Shelton, not that you give a damn about him. Or any of them."

Liam blinks. "I don't understand."

"Oh yes, you fucking do. Big ole Calico comes into town and now we got a fucking Fissure plague on our hands. You know, I was excited to meet you," she laughs humorlessly, shaking her head. "Now I wish you'd never set foot in this town. Now my best friend is dead."

Liam rubs at his temples and takes a deep breath. "Hold on, back up. How do you know there was a Fissure? And what happened?"

Sloane sags a little. She rubs the back of her hand across her mouth and shuffles to his couch, collapsing down onto it. Her head hangs.

"Car accident yesterday morning. Phoebe was at the wheel. Her husband, Jake, was in the passenger seat. I got a couple runners who said they saw her driving erratically. They claim she was yelling at Jake, that she looked *possessed*. Then Jake," her voice catches. "Then Jake just … just opened the door and tumbled out of the moving car. Got his head caught under the wheel. And Phoebe kept going. Didn't even pause, like it didn't mean nothing. She was on West River Bridge. It's narrow, like all the bridges around here, and she collided headlong with an oncoming vehicle. Betsy Cross was driving it. She was just this little old lady everyone knew because she had an ice cream truck. Her granddaughter was in the back seat. They were on their way to the beach. Little girl is fine, thank Christ. Well … fine as an eight-year-old can be after watching her granny get brutalized right in front of her, spurting blood all over her little yellow sun-dress. She had part of a denture stuck in her hair. There's not enough therapy in the world. The old lady survived, but she'll be bedridden for the rest of her life, however long that is."

Liam stares at her.

"Don't you dare look at me like that. I know my friend and she wouldn't have behaved like that unless something was in her. 'Possessed,' the runner said. It was a Fluke; I know it."

"Sophonts don't get Flukes. And one getting a Fissure is very, very unusual," he tries, gentle.

"Everything happening in this town since you showed up is 'unusual,' don't give me that. You know what—fine. Let's say it's unusual. Let's say I can't tell a Host from a junkie and Phoebe had a secret life and Faye is a small-town Patch who got the job because no one else wanted it and Phoebe felt bad for her. You know who that leaves who can make some sense of this? You. All you have to do is come take a look. Faye doesn't have the stuff."

Liam agreed to peruse some files, not tour dead Phrens. "There are other Wedges in New Hampshire."

"You know who those Wedges are. They're not much better than Faye. I know the guy who works Nashua and Manchester and he's a glorified box-checker with a beach house in Bermuda. You're the best Wedge in the world, O'Connor. Why won't you just help us? It's suspicious as hell, and you know it. I know that you were at the other end of a call from Phoebe and that you fought with her. That's motive enough. We've got you linked to all three Hosts. I'm not looking to prove you did it but you're not giving me much of a choice."

Liam leans against the wall. The embers of that old headache catch fire. A heaviness blankets over his back like a cape.

"Is it so hard to understand why I wouldn't want to do this anymore?" The words are quiet. He doesn't think she hears him at first.

"No." Sloane digs her fingers into her eyelids, then cocks her head to look at him. She rubs at her temple, and in the edges of her Phren Liam sees the same headache burning. "I wanted to quit too. Why do you think I'm not in Boston anymore?"

He looks at her—at her Phren—and sees himself. He's always seen it. His resolve sloughs away like snow from a roof. "Same reason I'm not in Chicago."

He sinks against the wall, shoulders hunching. It's suddenly impossible to keep his eyes open.

"Phoebe can be persuasive." Sloane's tone has shifted. It's conspiratorial. Wry. Almost like they're friends. "She got me here by guaranteeing that it wouldn't be like Boston. 'Shoalport is a small, quiet town,' she said. I wouldn't see the shit I saw in a big city. These aren't my first Fissure scenes."

"I know."

"One time I responded to a domestic abuse call in Southie. Routine. Me and my partner had more of those than I care to remember. Just small-dick bastards beating up their wives. Sometimes these fuckers would even say a Fluke made them do it, but we had a decent Wedge in Boston who always squashed that bullshit."

"Yeah, Valerie. She was a couple classes above me at the Academy. She's a good Wedge."

"Makes a wicked old fashioned, too. Anyway, nothing I'd seen prepared me for this scene. Didn't know it was a Fissure incident until we got there. We didn't get a lot of Violet Flukes. It was in a young woman. Pretty. You could tell her face had been sweet before and that something was *in* her now. She was a caregiver for her father—a nasty old bastard with half his face drooping like melted putty from a stroke. I don't know what happened to rip open her Fissure, but that Violence Fluke had a field day with her. And by the time we got there she had done … things, to her father. I can't say them. I can't even think them." Her hands start to tremble. "But what she did to him was nothing compared to what she'd done to herself. We tried to get her to stop with all those kind, de-escalating words they train you to say. She didn't hear them. I should have restrained her. I wanted to but my partner said … she said to hang back. So I did. I didn't react fast enough when it happened. I didn't think someone so small could be so strong. My partner had her throat eaten out. Hit an artery. She died in my arms while the Host flayed herself with a hedge pruner."

Liam can do nothing but nod. The story could be his own.

"I turned in my badge the next day. I'd failed my partner. And I failed the girl too. I should have called FUSE and gotten help the second we walked into that house. I should have gotten help. If I'd been like you, if I had your abilities, things would have been different."

"It's not your fault."

"Does that help when people say it to you?"

Liam bites the inside of his mouth.

"Please," Sloane says. "Make this stop." He hears the notes of sorrow and regret, her genuine desperation. Worse, the swamp of grief spreads from Sloane's Phren, sinking into his own. It pulls his own grief to the surface, coalescing into something new. "Then I swear—I'll leave you in peace to drink yourself stupid in this old house or take up paddleboard yoga or whatever the fuck else you feel like doing. Just … help me put this one to bed. Something feels off here. Ever since it started, I haven't felt right. All the control I thought I had is gone. I don't feel like myself. It's gotta stop. I don't want to do this anymore either."

Liam feels a collar tightening around his throat. He takes a long pause, hoping Sloane feels each second; hoping she feels guilty.

"What's your rabbit's name?" Sloane says.

Liam blinks. "Kermit."

Sloane stands and brushes her hands off on her jeans. She smooths back her frizzed hair.

"It's a rabbit, not a frog," she says. "I'll pick you up tomorrow morning at ten, take you to the morgue. Phoebe got all the paperwork set; all you have to do is sign and you're our consulting Wedge."

She turns to leave.

"You know," Liam says as she opens his back door. "I'll never forgive you for this." His voice doesn't sound like his own.

"I know. I never forgave Phoebe either."

Despite his best efforts, Liam can't get drunk enough to numb his thoughts that night. Each pull of whisky only drags him lower, until he forfeits the battle and crawls into bed. He isn't aware of falling asleep. One moment he's alone, and the next Jasper Knox is standing in his bedroom.

Liam stares at him from his bed. Gray, penetrating eyes stare back. There's no seaweed, no gaping black mouth or click of barnacles. The scent of tide is still present, but it's softer. His expression matches the melancholic severity of the photograph Liam had seen online. His tall figure is framed ominously by the doorway. His skin is as gray as an old photo.

"Alright, get it over with," Liam says on a sigh.

"Pardon?" It's startling to hear him speak beyond the haunting growl of *"William."* The word is sleek with an English accent. Liam grabs his glasses off the nightstand—not that he needs them in his own Phren—and props up on his pillows. He conjures a hat, pulls it on, and crosses his arms on his chest.

"Tell me what you want," he says.

"I—"

"You might as well cut to the chase. I'm already at rock bottom so it's not like I can go any lower."

He waits for a reaction—annoyance or perhaps a flutter of embarrassment. But there's nothing. Jasper merely stares at him.

"Come on, don't be shy," Liam prods. "You've already seen me in bed."

Jasper's expression gives away nothing, though his eyes dart to the side as if he'd only just noticed he's in Liam's bedroom. Liam is used to reading great swathes of emotion and memory from people without trying. Phrens blare at him constantly, shouting secrets. Jasper is blank. His eyes are shallow pools.

It strikes him: Jasper has no Phren.

Yet, there is something there. He's not an illusion or a nightmare, as Liam hoped. When he feels around the edges of Jasper's being, the unmistakable presence of life nudges back. It's faint, like Wick energy.

"Why are you here?" Liam tries.

Jasper opens his mouth, frowns, then shuts it again.

"No clue? Okay, how about where did you come from?"

Nothing. Just a gray stare.

"Alright, why don't I share my ideas, then." He cracks his knuckles and smooths out the fringe of his duvet. "Up until now my prevailing theory has been that you're a Wick. The line between me and the Nether blurs every day. If I see pieces of the Nether while I'm awake, it stands to reason that I'm even more connected to it while I'm asleep and can't fortify my boundaries. Shit, maybe I even go inside. And let me just say, that is some bad news, buddy. Like, epically bad. I've been hoping you were just a nightmare, conjured by my endless list of traumas and odd fascination with that *Man Who Drowned Waiting* legend, but that would mean I'm a normal person, and given my track record, I'm not counting on it."

Jasper looks as though he's about to interrupt, but Liam barrels on.

"And I suspect you've been following me around the Nether for a while, long before I came to Shoalport. Can't mistake that low tide perfume of yours. Which brings me back to my Wick theory. A Wick made sense when you were all dressed up with seaweed and Nether shit. You looked like a Fluke-eaten soul if I ever saw one. But look at you now—fully realized."

"I don't know what—you—"

"And semi-articulate. So that leaves one conclusion, outside of the distinct possibility that I've lost my whole fucking mind."

Jasper's chin tilts up, his eyes narrow. He achieves a quick aristocratic superiority. "Well?"

"You're a Hitch. *My* Hitch. And that, my ascot-wearing specter, is some bad news fucking bears. And also tremendously bizarre because unless I'm 150 years old and didn't notice, I've never met you before, and Hitches only happen with two souls that are exceptionally linked. So?"

Jasper maintains that damn stare. Liam rolls his eyes and lets his arms flop down at his sides.

"Forget how to talk, with that posh little accent of yours? What are you? A Wick, a Hitch, or the harbinger of my inevitable descent into madness?"

"I haven't the faintest what a 'Hitch' or 'Wick' is."

"Of course you don't."

"Might you … please, cloth yourself in proper attire? It's quite indecent to discuss such matters when you're in a state of undress."

Liam punches out a laugh. "Like I said, you're the one who came into *my* bedroom. I don't have to do what you say." He crosses his arms over his chest defiantly.

Jasper fidgets—only a little—and sets his gaze on the wall above Liam's headboard. He seems to deliberate. Liam waits.

"My name is Jasper Knox."

"Oh, we're doing introductions? Lovely. I already knew your name, Jasper. And I know you already knew mine since you like to creepily whisper it to me every night while I'm sleeping. I go by Liam, though. Only my grandparents called me William."

"I … don't …"

"What?"

"I'm not sure how I know your name."

"That makes two of us. Not sure how you weaseled your way into my Phren either, and not just because I'm, frankly, buzzed right now. I've always attracted Wicks, but if you broke into my friggin' mind that makes you a special little snowflake. And also almost definitely my Hitch. So let me reiterate: this is all really fucking bad." Liam slaps his palm into his forehead. "Of course! How didn't I see it before? The light on the island; that must be my Hitch marker. Usually it's some kind of tie like a string or a chain. That's why it didn't occur to me."

Jasper huffs, crossing his arms as well. "These terms you keep using—I don't know what they mean."

Liam sits with that for a minute. If Jasper really is some poor bastard who drowned in the 1880s, likely from a Fluke attack, Liam now realizes, he'd have no idea what the modern jargon meant. Most of the terms were invented in the 20s and 30s, after the Trypanon mess of WWI. He asks the logical question: "What do you call yourself?"

"I don't understand."

"Seems like a theme with you."

Jasper's eyes dart down to him, narrowed by a frown. "I'm a scientist, an English immigrant, the only son of a reputed architect, a New Englander, a Harvard graduate, a—"

"I didn't ask for your dating profile."

"And I believe that I am dead."

"Bingo."

"And that I've been trapped in some sort of purgatory."

"You're not wrong."

"And that I've witnessed a murderer coming in and out of that purgatory at will."

Um. That was not what Liam was expecting. His thoughts screech to a halt. He feels them bunch up onto each other like a car pile-up. His mouth opens, closes, opens again. "I don't understand," he says.

"Seems to be a theme with you."

Liam sits up. The covers fall around his waist and Jasper swiftly looks away again, as if the sight of Liam in a T-shirt and shorts is the pinnacle of scandal.

"What do you mean you've seen a murderer coming in and out of the Nether?"

"Exactly what I said."

"Alright, smartass, but how do you know that?"

"I've seen them. I believe I clarified that already. Perhaps you are too inebriated to recall."

"Well, what do they look like?" Liam says, throwing up his hands.

"Like a person."

"Jesus fucking—"

"I have never seen their face."

"Oh, great. Very helpful."

"But I am certain that I know them personally, somehow. I just cannot remember."

Liam rakes his hands through his hair. He takes a slow breath. "Jasper. What you're describing is a Trypanon. Do you know that word?

"Yes. It's a mind-surgeon. Derived from the Greek word meaning 'to bore,' as in to dig a hole, not as in to irritate someone by being obtuse, as you are doing now."

Liam pauses. "Wow."

"I have, on three separate occasions, witnessed this person exit my purgatory through what appear to be tears or doors. I can only assume these doors lead to an individual's mind, for shortly after their departure, the murderer returns with a soul in tow. The soul seems dead, or at least mutilated beyond repair, and the door seals behind them and disappears. I've searched for this individual's point of entry but have yet to discover it. It's difficult to follow them when I must avoid being seen."

Liam covers his mouth with his palm and frowns so hard it hurts.

"Does this behavior fit your definition of a Trypanon?" Jasper says.

Liam stares at his duvet. "Yeah, but it's not possible."

"Why?"

"Because Trypanons are, like, ridiculously fucking rare. There's only one in the United States." Liam casts his eyes down.

"Which is you."

Liam stumbles a bit at that. "How do you know that, but you don't know what 'Hitch' or 'Wick' means?"

"You said you have the ability to enter the … *Nether*, just as our murderer does. It stands to reason that you are also a Trypanon. The way you speak of yourself indicates you have a long history with my purgatory and with the souls that inhabit it. Additionally, the more I speak with you, the more I seem to glean your mind, your thoughts. It's puzzling."

Liam rubs hard at his scalp, squeezing his eyes tight. "Yeah, probably because you're trespassing in my fucking mind. Listen—there can't be a Trypanon murderer in friggin' Shoalport, New Hampshire, okay? That would be so unlucky that it's almost funny."

"I see nothing comical in the situation."

"I've already had my big Trypanon battle, dammit. I did this shit. I put my archnemesis behind bars."

"That settles it then."

Liam looks up. "What settles what?"

"If you've already apprehended a similar perpetrator before, then you are an ideal candidate for the endeavor."

Liam samples several responses to that, all of which die on impact. He laughs. Stops. Laughs again.

When Sloane finds out a Trypanon is behind the Fluke deaths—if one actually is—it's going to validate every tactic she employed to get him to take the case. He's ashamed to admit he's glad Phoebe isn't around to gloat. None of the Patches or Wedges working in New Hampshire could handle a case like this. No other Sophont in the country could. There's a reason he was shipped off to Russia when Iris happened.

The only person who can stop a Trypanon on a murder spree is another Trypanon.

"Did Sloane hire you to do this?"

"I do not understa—no."

Liam shakes his head. A sense of surrender pulls at him, casting the room in shadow. He can't fight from so many different angles. "I didn't sign up for any of this," he whispers.

"I can assure you: neither did I."

Liam shakes his head. "You have no idea what we're talking about here. A Trypanon using their power to rip peoples' souls out of their bodies is a once-in-a-generation thing. It'll be damn near impossible to identify them, especially since this one isn't registered, which is absurd. They'll be able to hide their tracks, even from me. Shit, they might not even know they're doing it. It could be anyone."

It could be me.

"I already mentioned that I know them somehow," Jasper says, tilting up his chin.

"Yeah, and you don't know how."

"It's true that I recall little from my life. In fact, these new details have only come to me today. The degree from Harvard, my father being an architect, my immigration from England—"

"In other words, you only know what I read about you today in that article. And you only look like yourself now because I saw that picture of you. Gray scale and all."

"Correct."

"So you're just gleaning stuff off my Phren. How does that do anything? Beyond creep me the hell out."

"It presents a simple solution. Surely you must see it."

"*Surely*, I don't."

A short huff of air from his nose is the only indication of Jasper's annoyance. He's either extremely self-controlled or mostly vacant. Or both.

"The more you learn about my life, the more of my memory is unearthed," Jasper says slowly, as though Liam is a moron. "In order to uncover the identity of our Trypanon, you need only to uncover me."

"And how am I supposed to do that? I don't know if you know this but people in this town have been trying to 'uncover' you ever since you died, and they didn't find much."

"I am aware. But they didn't have what you have."

"What's that?"

"Me. I may not remember anything in detail, but I have impressions. Inclinations. You can start by investigating my home."

Liam throws his hands up. "Hey, now I haven't agreed to do shit for you. Everyone is always pushing me around. I don't need a dead Victorian with frankly fantastic hair doing it too."

The smallest hint of pink blooms on Jasper's cheeks.

Got him.

"You would prefer people died while you sat idle?"

Liam winces. Familiar weight settles on his back and neck. "I have to go to the morgue first."

"Morgue?"

"I'm examining the bodies of the murder victims."

Jasper looks at him. One refined eyebrow arches. "Convenient."

"Isn't it just." Liam sighs. "Alright, if Phoebe Shelton had a Fluke, then fine: I believe you, because only a Tryp could put a Fluke in a Sophont. But if not, you gotta leave me alone."

"As you wish."

"Confident, are you?"

"Yes."

Liam grabs a pillow and holds it against his face. Maybe if he tries hard enough, he can suffocate himself. "You can leave now," he mumbles against the fabric. He waits through a long silence before peeking to see if Jasper is still there.

He's gone, though the scent of sunbaked seaweed and wet sand remains. It's not until the light shifts that Liam realizes he's already woken up. He breathes deep, chasing the last of the smell, and shivers on the exhale.

He lays marinating in his own sweat, staring at his cracked ceiling and stewing on the absurdity of what he's learned: he has a Hitch from the 1800s named Jasper Knox. And there's a Trypanon murdering people. And to discover this killer, he must first discover who Jasper used to be.

But first, he needs to go to a morgue. To look at dead bodies.

It's going to be a long day.

CHAPTER SEVEN

CONSULTING WEDGE

"Are you sure you're alright?"

It's the third time Applebaum has asked him since they picked him up that morning.

"He's fine, Jackie. Back off."

If Liam thought Sloane would warm after their conversation the day before, she has liberated him from the delusion. With her hair tied tight and her uniform sharp, she is a fortress again, and not a friendly one. He feels the first stings of resentment.

The truth is that Liam is not fine. He's exhausted. He's reeling from his little interaction with Jasper the friendly Hitch. He's despondent at the idea of another Trypanon murderer. And he's hungover.

"Wake the fuck up, O'Connor," Sloane says, apparently holding the door open for him. He blinks. Oh good, he's already dissociating. Hooray. "You look like shit, by the way."

"Not all of us can hold our liquor like you can," Liam mutters. Applebaum's head jerks toward Sloane. Oops.

The familiar sterilized perfume of formaldehyde, chlorine, and embalmed flesh inundates him when he steps over the threshold. Faye's face lights up when she sees him. She's wearing a turtleneck sweater and paying for it, given her sweaty hair and flushed cheeks.

"Calico! Oh my gosh, this is so exciting. I didn't get any sleep last night after Sloane told me you'd taken the case." She flashes him a lipstick-stained smile. "I've never seen anyone teletravel inside a dead Phren before. I was so worried I was going to have to do it. This is the best thing to ever happen."

A woman with asymmetrical black hair and red-rimmed glasses stands at Faye's side, looking smug. "The best thing to ever happen to you is people dying?" she says. Faye looks embarrassed, though not enough to counter the point. "I'm Dr. Felix," the woman goes on. "Medical examiner. Your reputation precedes you, Calico."

"You don't say."

"Really looking forward to seeing you work today. Normally I just get domestic dispute deaths or accidents. Lots of red necks in New Hampshire shooting their own femoral arteries. Boring. Don't need to do more than swab up some DNA and determine cause of death, though of course it's obvious. My buddies here," she gestures to Sloane and Applebaum, "normally don't even need to see the bodies after I autopsy them. Pictures do fine. But you … you need to go *inside* them like I do. In a way, you're performing a mind autopsy."

Liam winces. "I guess you could say that." Though he'd rather she didn't.

Everyone seems to be waiting for him to say something else, but he has nothing polite or useful to add. The less time he spends talking the better.

It's a small morgue compared to the ones in Chicago. Small enough that he can see through the glass door behind Felix to a body laid out on a mortuary table, covered by a white shroud. The Nether hums, poking at him. It's stronger in here. Liam clenches his teeth and blocks it out.

"He signed all the paperwork in the parking lot so, according to the federal government, he's ours until this bullshit is over," Sloane says. He hears a note of conquest in her voice. And scratchiness, the only indicator of her hangover, aside from the sour burn coming off her Phren.

"Yes, we all appreciate Liam stepping in like this," Applebaum says.

"We really, really do." Faye's eyes sparkle. She may be drooling a little.

"I've got Maggie Short out and ready for you." Felix gestures behind her with a thumb. "The rest are in the cold lockers. I didn't know if you needed all of them on tables or if the sliders will do."

Liam takes a deep breath. No going back now. "Sliders are fine. Let's not waste time." He goes to a supply counter and sanitizes his hands. Reluctantly, he hangs his baseball cap on a nearby hook, then puts on the PPE. He can tell from their hesitation that Applebaum and Faye are not used to latex gloves or medical masks. Sloane, however, is as practiced as he is.

Without waiting for them to finish, he pushes open the glass door and heads inside.

The smell hits. He stumbles a little. The shape of Maggie's stout, bloated form seems to taunt him from beneath the white sheet. Her stench is similar to the one that follows Jasper: low tide and baked shellfish, silt and death. He hears the phantom snort of laughter again.

Dr. Felix enters first.

"Jesus, she's a fragrant one. We got her in the fridge as fast as we could, but the body went fast. Never seen anything like it. Phoebe Shelton was adamant about keeping them exactly as they are for you, but I had to do some work. Cut her open to determine the cause of death, as you know. Didn't think it would take so long for Phoebe to convince you to sign on, knowing her. She was *persuasive*, huh?"

An understatement if Liam's ever heard one. His teeth clench as he looks at the cold lockers. He can sense which one holds Phoebe. She's probably pleased as punch with her victory over him, even in death.

"Please remove the sheet," he says. Felix hesitates, frowning at him as her Phren radiates puzzlement, like she can't figure him out. Still, she collects herself and does as she's told.

Liam is no stranger to the sight of a dead body—of the tinted skin and blisters and open, cloudy eyes. The swift shut down, the way he recedes into himself, is automatic. Makoto used to say the way his face went blank was unnerving. Sloane, Applebaum, and Faye come up behind him. He feels their scrutiny and knows they feel the same as Makoto once did. It wasn't always easy for Liam to shut down and block out the horror. Yet, the more he saw, the less it touched him, which was more upsetting than the alternative.

"I'm going to examine each of the bodies and their dead Phrens," Liam says. "If I look strange while I'm doing this, it's because my Phren is untethered from my body. Under no circumstances should you touch me while I do this." He and Sloane shoot Faye a look. She crosses her arms. "I'm looking for indicators in each Host to identify the location of their Fissures and determine what type of Fluke, if any, attacked them. I'll need the medical files so please get them ready. Now, can you all take a few steps back and give me some space?"

For a long moment, everyone stares until Liam starts to fidget. Sloane looks pissed even behind her surgical mask, probably because of his "if any" comment. As far as he's concerned, Phoebe and her husband died from a domestic dispute until proven otherwise. He already knows Maggie had a Red Fluke, but she's a clinic on Vice Fluke bait. It doesn't mean the others are Fluke deaths. It doesn't mean a Trypanon is killing people. It doesn't mean Jasper Knox is right.

"Okay?" Liam snaps, jarring them into action. Dr. Felix goes to a nearby filing cabinet and pulls out a few folders. Applebaum and Sloane back away; Faye rushes across the room and into the corner. Liam shuts his eyes, takes a shaky breath, and looks at the remains of Maggie Short.

Any imagined horrors Liam had conjured to prepare him for the state of Maggie's corpse swiftly prove inadequate. She no longer looks human. Her body is bloated like a pruned, pink bladder. Her eyes bug out of her skull, bleached white and green. There are gouges taken out of her skin where gulls and crabs got to her before the cops did. The Y-shaped incision on her chest strains against the stiches. Her orange hair is abrasive to the eyes, synthetic like a doll's.

Swallowing hard, he braces himself, goes neutral, and makes his vision shift.

The unseen—the angle only a Sophont can perceive—comes into view. A map of dark striations appears on Maggie's skin—the former highways of her parasite. He visualizes her standing in his living room with her feet bloody and arm broken, the white worms gyrating inside her. They're gone now, having gorged themselves and returned to the Nether. He glances down at the split skin on her feet.

"Give me her file." He reaches out without looking and Felix puts it in his hand. He rifles through. The photographs of her back are adequate; he won't need her corpse flipped over. The external indicators of a Fluke don't mean much without a Phren examination anyway, and Liam will avoid manhandling a dead body if he can. Her X-ray is innocuous beyond the broken arm and mild scoliosis. The toxicology report, however, boasts an impressive array of prescription pills and a staggering blood alcohol level. Even with Fluke energy, it's remarkable that Maggie was able to walk. But there was something different about that Fluke. It had power—strange power.

He looks over the file again. And again. Sweat starts to bead on his brow. He's stalling.

This will be the first time Liam has entered another Phren since Makoto died. His hand grasps for the warm grip of Makoto's fingers. He wants to stop, to be alone. A tightness winds in his chest. His gaze darts for the exit. Then, oddly, he hears Jasper's words in his head:

You would prefer people died while you sat idle?

It's annoyance more than anything that halts the panic rising in his chest. He needs to do this, if for no other reason than to prove Jasper wrong. There can't be a Trypanon murderer in a town like Shoalport. The odds are astronomical. Even he's not that unlucky. This string of deaths is a coincidence, pure and simple.

He reminds himself that this is just a dead Phren. He won't have to interact with any needy souls or Flukes. He won't have to go in the Nether. All he needs to do is look.

He shakes out his hands and begins.

It's always chilling to leave his own Phren, no matter how well he tethers the link to his body. A fan once asked him what teletravel felt like back when he still took questions from fans. He remembers saying "like your mind is a kite and you just tossed it off a cliff into a hurricane." "Why would you ever choose to do that?" they'd asked. Stupid question. There was never any choice. At least it was easier when Makoto was with him, as with everything else.

If he wasn't already certain that Maggie had a Red Fluke, he would be now. Her Phren is pungent with the same smell she'd brought into his home the night she died: bad tequila and vomit and sickly sweet. He knows it well. Red Flukes are by far the most common and vice has the most obvious traits.

He almost cracks a joke about one of his more memorable cases—a Red Fluke Host that was addicted to having sex with balloons. Then he realizes Makoto isn't there to hear it.

He banishes the thought before it drags him down, focusing on the Phren instead. White walls, crumbling and moist, surround him. Yellow liquid oozes down to the industrial carpet. In the first couple rooms, he doesn't see much—broken glass and empty bottles, an empty reception desk, a terrible mural of a donkey—so it takes him a moment to realize Maggie's Phren is a 70s era evangelical church. A rotted cross gives it away, hanging upside down above a stripped bed, standing in place of a pulpit in the chapel. Figures Maggie's Phren would be a church. Self-righteous little troll.

A chill hisses from a door in the far corner. Slow, he approaches. A flash. Liam stumbles back as blackness bursts around him. He blinks. Light returns. Moonlight spreads across still water. There's a small island. Its bare tree reaches for the sky like skeletal fingers. He watches Maggie wade into the water, a bottle in hand.

"Never cared," she mutters. "Sinner. He took him from me."

She shoves the nozzle deep down the back of her throat, tilts her head up, and inhales. The bottle acts like a cork in her gullet—a vacuum seal that keeps her from coughing up the liquor as it fills her lungs. Liam watches, frozen, as she slowly drowns in whiskey, her body convulsing before slipping beneath the glassy black.

The vision fades, dissolving into the barren back room. There's a perfect incision through the floor and wall, soaked in Nether echoes. This was

Maggie's Fissure, and it's not normal. It's too pristine, too man-made. Liam has seen Fissures like this before.

Iris.

Liam stumbles back. His hand squelches through the drywall behind him and comes out filthy with river silt. The world shudders. He chokes on imagined air.

Look at my pretty feet.

The Nether pushes against the dead Fissure. Tendrils slither between the seam.

You're just like my mother.

He vaults his mind from Maggie's Phren, recoiling fast, and falls back into his body. He blinks and gapes into the Waking World to find everyone staring at him, wide-eyed. He clears his throat.

"Confirmed Red Fluke," he says, hoarse. "And I can verify Dr. Felix's assessment of the cause of death. An echo of her last memory was imprinted on her Phren. I saw her inhale a bottle of Jameson. Like, literally." Shame, too. That was sipping whiskey.

"She had a memory in there? A full one? Isn't that not supposed to happen?" Sloane says, for once genuinely curious rather than incessantly antagonistic.

"It's rare. I've only seen it in specific infestations."

"And?"

"And what?"

"And what does that mean?"

Liam frowns. "It means I haven't finished my assessment yet. Dr. Felix—please take out Oliver Fenton."

Sloane takes an aggressive step towards him and is quelled by Applebaum's hand on her elbow.

Liam breathes a little easier once Maggie's corpse is covered by the sheet again, though he wishes her feet were hidden. Then Oliver is yanked from the cold locker.

Any hope Liam had that Oliver isn't a Fluke victim abandons him: his skin, blistered and stretch-marked, is mustard yellow. He's gained an impossible amount of weight since their Market Basket meetup. Liam doesn't need to be a Sophont to see that. He looks like an overfed tick, close to bursting. Then Liam switches on his Sophont sight. Like Samantha, there's a constellation of white-rimmed holes covering Oliver's body.

Liam shouldn't have blown him off at the grocery store.

He closes his eyes, and sees the alleyway where Samantha sat, mouth gaping. Makoto knew he hated Yellows, knew they made him want to throw up.

Samantha Munn. Why had her Fissure reopened?

"He looks pretty gross," Faye says, startling him. "All those little holes … I don't like it."

Liam is surprised. He almost forgot Faye is a Sophont. "No one likes them," he says.

"Holes?" Felix says. "There are holes?"

"Paraphrenically," Liam amends. "A Fluke attack manifests physically on the Host if you have the Sophont perception to see it. I'll still need to examine Oliver's dead Phren to be sure, but this is obviously a Neglect Fluke Host. They're always covered in little holes."

"They showed us a cadaver at the Academy once," Faye says, too cheerful for someone talking about cadavers. "One of my classmates threw up. I didn't though." She looks at Liam like he'll be impressed.

"Christ, Faye, let him do his damn job," Sloane barks. "You'll only get in the way."

Faye blushes and slinks back into her corner.

"You're fine, Faye. I just need some space," Liam says.

Faye smiles like he just proposed.

"His weight gain," Applebaum says. "Is that from the Fluke?"

"It can happen," Liam says.

"He looks like a different person. Or … well, like he used to look a few years ago. I guess I assumed neglect would make a person *lose* weight."

"Oliver was most neglected when he was most obese."

"Oh. Right, that makes sense."

Liam glances at Applebaum. The soft sadness in her eyes makes him uncomfortable. If he stares too long, he won't be able to see Oliver as a case, but as someone who liked people-watching and hot dogs, which wouldn't help anyone.

"What was the official cause of death?" Liam asks Felix.

"Torn esophagus. He ate too much for his lap band to handle, so it just packed into his esophagus until it ripped open. Which is very odd because usually people vomit before that can happen."

Odd, yes, but Liam has seen it before.

"There's a list of his stomach contents in his file. Most of it was raw animal meat, including bones. Chicken wings and drumsticks. But there were other things, too: photos, toothpaste, his own baby clothes. All that probably contributed to the tear." For the first time, Felix shows some sign of unease.

She picks at one of her nails as she speaks. "And there was some of his own … flesh, in there too. You can see the wounds on his arm where he bit himself. And he ate his own tongue."

"Yikes," Faye whispers. "At least he didn't eat someone else's."

Sloane rolls her eyes. Liam opens Oliver's file.

It's much thicker than Maggie's; Oliver seemed to be collecting diagnoses like Pokémon. The list goes on for pages. While most of his ailments are tied to his morbid obesity and subsequent laparoscopic surgery (Liam could have done without another reminder that Oliver had excess skin sliced off), some strain credulity: fibromyalgia, asthma (though his oxygen levels were always normal and no wheezing was detected), restless leg syndrome, non-celiac gluten sensitivity, chronic Lyme disease, psychosomatic limp, adrenal fatigue, leaky gut. He's hardly surprised when the word "Munchausen" makes the cut.

Then he looks at the X-ray. Oliver broke his arm right before he died. The same arm as Maggie, in the same place. Liam frowns. It's probably a coincidence. Still, a feeling rises. Something is wrong.

This time, when he ties the link and leaves his body, he doesn't reach for Makoto's hand. It's small; another surrendering to the fact of Makoto's death. It takes something from Liam. He's more tired when he sets foot in the wreckage of Oliver's Phren.

The smell is miasmic, permeating the air in a stagnant, snot-like cloud. It's invasive, suffocating. Liam scrambles to dissipate it. When he finally does, he finds himself in a home cluttered with shadows. There are no visible objects left—the Fluke has taken them—though Liam still senses their echo. This Phren was once congested—a hoarder den. Though the hoard is gone, the smothering, cluttered energy remains.

There's an open door at the end of a hall. Liam senses Nether remnants beyond, pulsing to an agitating rhythm. He twitches at each discordant note. Slowly, he approaches, bracing for a vision to hit him, just as Maggie's last memory did. He steps into the room. A cross hangs above a large bed with a deep, stained crater in the mattress. A precise Nether scar splits it down the middle. The similarities to Samantha's case strike him again.

Why didn't her Fissure stay sealed?

Liam stumbles back with a shout as a door to his left flies open, banging into the wall and revealing a closet. A dark, silhouetted shape sways inside it. Coat hangers rattle against its shoulders. The guts of the closet—old shoes, photo albums, molded stuffed animals—are suddenly strewn across the floor. Liam realizes he's witnessing Oliver's last memory.

Cautious, he inches closer. Oliver's face shifts into the light. Blood and chunks of meat dribble down his chin. His eyes are bugged out, his skin jaundiced and cracked like the heel of a foot. Liam can hear the sluggish thumping of Oliver's heart. His distended stomach strains against his shirt buttons. His arm hangs crooked. There's a mess of empty raw hamburger and whole chicken packages on the floor of the closet. Shredded photo albums and baby clothes. Liam is reminded of a nest.

"No more, Mother," Oliver slurs, slowly crumpling to the floor. His head tilts at a crooked angle, his eyes bleach white. There's something violating about watching someone simply lay down to die. The forfeit is unnatural, intimate. "I'll be holy. I'll punish him. Please, no more."

Just as Oliver's last breath creaks from his lips, a flash—

Then screaming. Sand. People in summer clothes scramble around a small beach. Liam's mother is standing on the shore. She isn't moving or screaming, just staring.

What about your friend? Do you remember them?

The vision dies. Liam stands frozen. There's a caress against his shoulder. He jerks and turns. The dead Fissure seems to smile at him. The scent of tide whispers by.

The Fissure is too perfect. It's inorganic. Man-made. Again. Liam can't breathe.

He comes back into his body with a gasp. Someone's gloved hand is in front of him, holding his glasses.

"You alright, Liam?" It's Applebaum. She's looking at him like a mother. Not his own mother, but like one he's seen on TV. "These fell on the floor."

He takes his glasses from her and slides them back on. "I witnessed Oliver's last memory," he says. And another memory, but he doesn't mention that one.

"Again? Is it normal to have two Fluke victims back-to-back with memories like that?" Sloane says. Some of her hair wisps out of her tight bun.

"No," Liam says. He feels numb.

This can't be happening.

"What's going on?" Sloane snaps. Her eyes keep finding the cold lockers.

"I'm not positive yet. Dr. Felix—can you please take out Jake Shelton now?" Liam catches the slight release in Sloane's shoulders. Of course. She doesn't want to see the corpse of her best friend. But this is a case, and if she wants to stay on it, this is inevitable. He can at least give her time to prepare.

"Alright, but as you know, he did get his head run over by a car," Felix says as she approaches a locker. "There's not a whole lotta brain matter left in his skull. I've been wondering about that: do you need a brain to see a Phren? Oh, and also: does a Phren decompose over time like a body? Is that why Phoebe wanted them fridged for you?"

Liam sighs. He's not interested in explaining the intricacies of the brain/Phren relationship, not that much is understood about it, even by him. Sophonts and Paraphrenology were approached spiritually, not scientifically, until teletravel was weaponized in World War I. And Fluke Hosts were treated the same as schizophrenics and manic depressives until about the mid-'50s. Which is to say, not very fucking well.

"I'll be able to get what I need." It's all she needs to know. She looks disappointed. That's fine. He's encountered quite a few people like Dr. Felix in his field: the unusual type that look at a corpse like an object to be studied. Liam can fake that alright, but he hates himself for it. People like Felix are always fascinated by what Liam can do. It's off-putting.

When Felix slides Jake out of the cold locker, Sloane turns away. Felix was not exaggerating; Jake is barely a step above decapitated. Seeing a body without a head is so bizarre that it's almost less horrifying. It dehumanizes the corpse, makes it harder to remember that it was once a person with feelings and opinions and a favorite flavor of ice cream. It's almost funny to look at, but not quite.

Damn, maybe he's more like Felix than he thought.

Sloane still won't look at the body. When Applebaum leans in and reaches out to touch her, she waves her off.

"I guess the cause of death here is pretty obvious," Dr. Felix says. "Not much to look at in his file. Toxicology report came back clean. Great blood pressure, exercise habit, no chronic illnesses to speak of. Far as I know there was no documented history of mental illness. Hard to believe he'd wanna just jump out of a moving car like that."

"He wouldn't," Sloane bites. She levels Liam with a glare that he chooses to ignore.

"What can you tell me about him?" Liam says to the room, knowing Sloane will answer. "What did he do for work? What was he like? Did he have many friends? What did people like or dislike about him?"

"Jake was a damn good man," Sloane says. "He was a wicked good father and husband."

It's not helpful and she should know better.

"And? I need details. Real ones."

Sloane at least has the self-awareness to wince. People always want to paint a perfect picture of the deceased. It's a normal compulsion but it never solves cases. Everyone has flaws and secret grievances. She crosses her arms tight over her chest and stares at the floor. Her voice is even when she speaks—more like a cop.

"He was like a stay-at-home dad type. Phoebe's life was her career. Their son, Bert … he's a Sophont like Phoebe. Jake isn't, so I guess that was probably hard for him, living with two Sophonts. And Bert fucking worships Phoebe even though she wasn't around much. Phoebe's his damn hero."

Her voice catches. It occurs to Liam that she must be the one who told Bert Shelton that both of his parents were dead.

"I don't think Bert respected Jake, but it was hard to blame him. Jake was …" Her throat bobs as she swallows. "Jesus, feels like taking a cheap shot at a dead guy but … Jake was kinda wimpy. He didn't talk much but he didn't have much to say, and Phoebe and Bert were a little more … dominant. He did love them though, I know that. Did whatever they asked. Especially Phoebe. She could snap her fingers and he'd know she wanted a martini or a grilled cheese or a phone charger without her even opening her mouth."

He thinks again of Makoto's words: he wasn't the only Sophont who could use his abilities to manipulate others.

"How did they meet?"

"They were both studying in Boston. Phoebe was getting her masters at Harvard, and Jake was pre-law at BU or Suffolk or something. But that didn't pan out for him. If he had ambition, he never showed it. He followed Phoebe to Shoalport when she got the job in Paraphenic Social Services. Worked temp jobs doing data entry and office admin stuff once. He didn't have a lot of friends that weren't Phoebe's friends first. No way Jake had enemies because no one thought enough about Jake to hate him. He was just … there."

"Thank you," Liam says. "That's helpful."

Sloane glares at him. "But he wouldn't just jump out of a car and off himself. Jake was a doormat, but he adored Phoebe and Bert. He had a good life, better than most. He wouldn't end it all out of nowhere."

Liam doesn't have a response for her. Sloane knows as well as he does that people have secret lives. Seemingly happy people live in bad domestic situations or have suicidal ideation or a hidden addiction all the time, and sometimes it has nothing to do with how good or bad your life is. No one really knows anybody.

He opens Jake's file. "Why does it say his name is Jake Mausser?"

"He took Phoebe's last name when they got married," Sloane mumbles.

"Was that his choice?"

Liam feels the mood in the room shifting. He's not trying to assassinate anyone's character, but Phoebe and Jake's relationship seems far from a fairy tale. It's easy to imagine Phoebe dominating or manipulating a man like Jake, having been at the receiving end of her persuasion skills himself. There's nothing wrong with a man taking a woman's last name, but he's starting to gather that a lot of Jake's choices weren't his own. But hey, maybe he liked it that way. Liam hears his own teeth grinding together. "I manipulated my parents' thoughts," Phoebe had said.

"What do you fucking think?" Sloane bites. A bead of sweat drips down her temple and gets absorbed into her mask. "Phoebe called the shots. Jake was along for the ride."

"I'd want to take my husband's name," Faye announces. Everyone looks at her, says nothing, and turns back to Liam.

A look at Jake's file confirms Felix's summary of his health history. Jake wasn't on any medications, he didn't have a therapist, and he'd never had surgery beyond wisdom tooth removal.

Then he finds the X-ray results. He closes his eyes before reading and takes a breath.

Broken arm.

But he'd fallen out of a car. Of course his arm broke. It doesn't mean anything. Liam shuts the file.

"You know something we don't, O'Connor?" Sloane says.

"Probably."

Sloane growls, throwing up her hands. "You gonna share with the fucking class or do you have something to hide?"

Liam feels his nerves start to tingle, his muscles bunching. He's flooded with the urge to run from the room. He glares at Sloane. "Unless you have something valuable to contribute, I request no more interruptions until I've finished my assessment. I'm not interested in spouting theories prematurely. You insisted on hiring me. This is how I work, so accept that, or tear up my contract."

Sloane seems about ready to stab him.

"You're right, Liam. We'll let you do your job," Applebaum says. She tactfully inserts herself between Liam and Sloane, using some sort of secret power to edge Sloane to the back of the room.

It takes a long moment for Liam to calm down. If he can avoid it, he won't do anything paraphrenic when he's stressed. That's how accidents happen, like a Sophont's Phren permanently severing from their body. Again, he recalls the incident at the Academy that taught him why he should tie a tether. Seventeen-year-old Franky Mason was hysterical over his girlfriend leaving him and tried to break into her Phren to convince her to take him back. He didn't bother to tie himself. She expelled him immediately, and he couldn't make it back to his body. It was the first time Liam saw a Husk in person. He'll never forget the dead eyes and the drool, the chilling hollowness of a body without a mind.

After cycling through a few of the breathing exercises Makoto taught him, Liam switches his vision and examines Jake's body. At first, he sees almost nothing paraphrenic. Jake's skin is extremely pale, but that's common. He was pale to begin with, and blond, judging by the shard of skull still attached to his neck by a few heroic tendons. Bruises and lesions from the accident make it difficult to catch subtle Fluke signs. The photographs from his file offer nothing.

He's starting to feel a hint of relief, of validation. There was no Fluke here, no Trypanon on a murder spree. This was a normal domestic abuse incident that tragically escalated.

Then he rounds the head and looks into Jake's severed neck. There, inside the trachea, is a white, fungal film, encasing a vacant shell. Liam jerks back, covering his mouth. He can almost feel the carapace lodge in his own throat.

"What? What is it?" Felix says. "Is there something in the throat?"

"Not something you can see."

He closes his eyes against a blooming headache. There's no avoiding it. He tethers his mind to his body, and slips into Jake's Phren.

It's the most difficult yet: a fragmented wasteland, a shredded reality that scalds at being touched. Any semblance of structure is absent. The sky yawns with desolate gray. The ground is cracked pavement, pockmarked by large potholes full of utter nothing. It's one of the worst destructions of a Phren that Liam has ever seen, and not just because Jake's skull was popped like an over-easy egg yolk. A Fluke has devoured this Phren.

White Flukes are sneaky. They can feed on a Phren for years without being detected. They prefer their host alive and incubating in subjugation, at least until they decide it's time to finish their meal. An average Sophont could meet a White Fluke Host and carry out a full conversation without ever suspecting they're infested. And their tastes swing two ways, too; they like the flavor of a Host being subjugated just as much as one doing the subjugating. It can make victims tough to identify. Though they're the least common Fluke, aside from Blues, Liam was assigned to quite a few in Chicago. Only a highly proficient Wedge can flush out a Subjugation Fluke, let alone exterminate one.

More exploration of the Phren yields nothing, not even the source of the Fissure. He's about to give up and return to his body when something shiny at the edge of a massive pothole the size of a small swimming pool catches his eye. As he approaches, a slow hum rises. He feels the scar of the former

Fissure before he sees it.

The twisted skeleton of an old car lies inside the pothole. He peers through a half rolled-down window. Cigarette butts fill the cup holders, and a few rotten keepsakes pepper the car's floor and back seat, but there's not much. Then he looks at the dashboard. It's split, the leather cut like a scalpel to skin in a perfect line. The old Fissure. It smiles at him.

It's fitting that Jake's Phren was a car. He's seen it before, usually in teenagers. Was Jake's Phren always this compressed, or did it change once Phoebe entered his life? The car must have been his single personal space—an outlet of freedom and of keeping secrets. He wonders if Phoebe knew Jake smoked.

Then he spies something shiny on the little shelf below the speedometer. He gets on his knees at the edge of the hole and leans over, reaching through the driver's side window. His fingertips touch the steering wheel—

And suddenly he's in the car. The world is suffused in early morning summer sun. He's in the backseat. In front, Phoebe sits at the wheel and Jake is hunched in the passenger seat. Liam flinches at the sound of her voice. The penetrating, sharp tone rakes through him.

"Why can't you just be a man?" she says. "You think I like walking all over you like this? You think I like feeling guilty every time I open my mouth? I mean, you just crumble. You fold even when I have no cards to play. It makes me feel like a monster."

Jake just shrugs, staring down at his hands, clenched in a ball on his lap. One of his arms hangs crooked. The fingers are blue.

"That's it? Nothing? You can't even say anything?"

He doesn't respond.

"It's like talking to a corpse. If you weren't here, I don't even think I would notice. God, you're just such … a *pussy*, alright? You're a goddamn pussy. What is the point? Why do you even stay? You might as well just open that door and throw yourself from the car if you can't even fight back."

And then Jake does exactly that. He unclicks his seat belt, opens the door, and tumbles out. The car bounces like it's hit a speedbump, and the vision dies. Liam finds himself sitting in the driver's seat, his hands on the wheel as if he had been driving.

He yanks his hands away and scrambles, but he can't get out. The seatbelt is stuck around his body. When had he put it on? He reaches to unclip it, but his arm won't work. It's broken.

Makoto Mori would be ashamed of you.

The scar across the dashboard starts to stink, filling the car with low tide stench. The seatbelt fuses to his chest, tightening. He writhes, clambering to break free. He can't breathe. He can't get out.

A voice breaks through. It's faint, nothing more than a whisper. It forms a single word:

William.

With a shout, Liam pulls hard on the tether to his body. He throws himself out of the car and the wasteland—out of Jake's ruined Phren.

He falls back into his physical form hard, back into the morgue. He can still see gray shadows and broken pavement in his periphery.

"Water," he says. "I need water."

Faye launches into a mad scramble around the room; it's obvious she has no idea where a cup is. Felix calmly exits and returns with a plastic bottle of water, handing it to him. His fingers shake as he rips off his latex gloves and twists off the cap. Tilting up his mask, he drinks. The water is cold. It puts him in the present. He wishes he could put his hat back on.

"It's a White Fluke," he says after a moment, sounding calmer than he feels. "His Phren was devoured."

"I fucking told you it was," Sloane snaps.

"I said that Jake was a Fluke Host, not Phoebe," Liam bites back. His nerves are frayed, his head pounds. He hasn't teletraveled in a long time and he isn't used to entering so many Phrens in a row. And he's still hungover. "It's highly unlikely that both of them were Hosts. And she was a Sophont. I already told you: it's impossible for a Sophont to get a Fluke." Unless …

"You don't know for sure."

Liam did not expect Applebaum to give him pushback. He glances at her and can't quite read her expression.

"It's just that a lot about this case seems unusual or rare. As you said: best to wait until you're done with your assessment before drawing conclusions."

"Yeah, and you'd better—"

Applebaum holds up her hand, effectively cutting Sloane off. "So, we should let him finish. This must be exhausting work."

For the first time, Liam realizes Applebaum's status in the room. She's easy to overlook, with her unobtrusive, accessible prettiness and unshakable calm, but there's still a quality to her that says, *don't fuck with me.*

"Alright," Liam says. He turns to Sloane. Though most of her face is covered by the PPE, her Phren is loud enough that he knows her expression beneath the face mask. "Now is the moment to leave if this will be too difficult for you."

She glares back but the acid isn't quite there when she speaks. She knows protocols and respects them, even if they piss her off. "I can handle it."

"Are you sure?"

"If I can't, I'll leave."

Liam nods. He turns to Felix and gestures for her to open the last cold locker. He puts on new gloves as she draws Phoebe out.

Sloane doesn't react physically as metal screeches in a long whine. Her Phren, however, seems to erupt. Her grief hits Liam like a wet slap on the side of his neck. But he doesn't say anything. She said she'd tap out if she needed to.

Liam never saw Phoebe alive. There's a government headshot in her file, probably from her ID. She doesn't resemble it anymore. Her face is swollen beyond recognition. A broken cheekbone protrudes from beneath her eye, which has been sliced in half by a shard of glass. Lacerations mark her neck and torso. In a gash on her chest, white fat glistens like teeth in a smile.

He doesn't look at Sloane.

Phoebe's file is a bit more interesting than Jake's, though she was also healthy, especially for a fifty-one-year-old. He does note that she once had a stint in a rehab facility fifteen years prior. The reason is not specified.

She also has a broken arm.

"Is there anything else I should know about Phoebe?" Liam keeps his eyes on the file as he speaks. He waits through a long pause.

"She saved my life," Faye says. Everyone turns to look at her. "She's the one who identified my Sophont skills. I didn't have much. My grandmother didn't see, but Phoebe did. She got me into the Academy. Got me this job too. She was a bit imperious, but I don't know where I'd be without her. Gives me the morbs. It's a real drag she had to go out like this."

Though no one would be flattered to hear their untimely death referred to as a "drag," he appreciates Faye's sentiment. Sloane, however, radiates agitation. He senses there's something personal going on between them and decides to move on before it becomes his problem.

"Then I'll begin. To reiterate, I'd like silence until I'm done."

Liam sets the file aside on a metal rolling tray. He rolls his neck and adjusts his face mask. He makes his vision shift.

A rotten, transparent tangle covers Phoebe's mouth, eyes, and ears. It's a wet, hollow bloom, resembling coral or lichen, yet also being nothing like those things. Among the fronds are carapace shells, identical to what was lodged in Jake's throat. Liam's mind struggles to process it, as is the case with all Flukes. They're organic yet unalive. Recognizable yet utterly foreign.

He shuts his eyes and sighs. A small, stupid part of him had hoped that today would be the end of this, that he'd waltz in and declare this all a coincidence, that he'd be allowed to go back to his life of solitude and binge drinking and having exactly one friend (who he's starting to suspect only likes him for the carrots). That Jasper was just a bad dream.

He ties the tether and enters Phoebe's Phren.

At first, nothing about it feels dead or devoured. He finds himself standing in a large penthouse office. There are no framed pictures on the wall or books on the shelves or stacks of files. A Fluke could have eaten some of them, but swanky big city offices are always aggressively minimalistic, and dead Phrens are always somewhat barren. The room is bordered by large windows, with a cityscape and blue skies beyond. The city is nondescript, and there are no people or cars mingling below. An imposing desk stands at the center of the room with an office chair behind it. He has a pressing desire to sit in it and spin like a Bond villain.

He rounds the desk. The smooth leather of the chair is warm and inviting. It draws him in. He sits.

And is back in the car. It's like the scene from Jake's Phren, and Liam watches again from the back seat. But there are differences this time.

"Why can't you just be the man I need?" Phoebe says. "I hate walking all over you like this. You think I like feeling guilty every time I open my mouth because you just crumble? Please stop acting like you don't care."

Jake just shrugs, staring down at his hands, clenched in a ball on his lap.

"That's it? You won't say anything?"

He doesn't respond.

"It's like talking to a corpse. It's like you don't even *like* me. You look like you'd rather throw yourself from the car than be here with me."

Jake opens the door and tumbles out. Liam stares at Phoebe. Her eyes don't stray from the road. Her face is empty, as if she left when Jake did. She has no reaction as she drifts onto the narrow bridge. Though part of him knows this is just a vision, the sight of another car approaching sends Liam into a panic. He reaches to take the wheel from Phoebe, to turn the car before they collide. The oncoming driver must not see them. But the wheel won't budge, and neither will Phoebe, and there's nothing Liam can do but take the hit. Glass and plastic burst.

He falls from the office chair onto a cold marble floor. The chair turns slowly.

The Fissure scar is carved up its back. It has the same signature precision as the others. When he sees it, the Phren shifts, revealing remnants of a White Fluke attack. There's a bleached, stripped quality to each piece of furniture, each adornment. The city buildings beyond the windows look like bland cardboard cutouts. He may not have known Phoebe well, but he knew her passion. There is none of that here—it's been sucked dry.

A wisp of cold air sneaks from the old Fissure, caressing him feather-light. He shrinks away from it. Phoebe's sharp voice pricks like a stinger.

Something strange is going on here.

She'd said it. She'd been right. His thoughts dart to Samantha Munn. Why hadn't her Fissure stayed sealed? He hears the whisper again—*William.* Louder. He feels it like a poke at his side.

Liam has seen enough. None of it is what he wanted. None of it is right. He travels back into in his body and stands motionless for some unknown length of time. He's barely aware of asking Felix to put Phoebe's corpse away, of leaving the room, and removing his PPE and putting his hat back on. He doesn't notice that the others have followed him until he's leaning against the wall in Felix's office. They all look at him with an eager fascination. Even Sloane seems captivated.

Liam takes off his glasses and pinches the bridge of his nose.

"I think," he begins, then stops. The words don't want to come. Once he says them, they're true. He swallows and forces them out. "I think you might have a murderer. And it's a Trypanon."

No one says anything. They seem to be waiting for Liam to say more. He can't yet.

"Fuck," Sloane says, appropriately.

"But how is that possible?" Applebaum says.

Liam shakes his head. "I have no idea. It shouldn't be possible. Every living Trypanon is monitored carefully, or they're in prison. The idea that one could be in Shoalport and no one knows about them is … very troubling."

"But how do *you* know?" Applebaum says. "How can you be certain?"

"I'm not certain. But the signs are there. When—" Liam stops again. He hasn't talked about Iris since it happened, not even really with Makoto. He combs through his words before speaking, trying to divulge as little as he can. He has no desire to relive it, and the case is top secret. If Archer finds out he's sharing stories willy-nilly, there'll be hell to pay. "When Iris happened, when he ripped open Fissures in his victims, they were precise. There was something about them that looked man-made. I've never seen it since … until today. And the Flukes that came through Iris's Fissures were superpowered, just like these. Maggie shouldn't have been able to walk, Oliver shouldn't have had the fortitude to eat himself to death, and with Jake… well, usually White Flukes keep their Hosts alive. But all of that could have been coincidence, until I looked at Phoebe's Phren. I told you: Sophonts don't get Flukes. Unless … unless a Trypanon gives them one."

There's a coiling energy in the room now, a blend of fear and excitement. Liam does not understand the latter. He feels like he's being swallowed by the air.

"And there's something else," he goes on. "There's something called a Tryp Mark. It's a scar or an injury or genetic trait that the Trypanon possesses that gets passed on to their victim. Now, broken arms are common in corpses when there's been significant physical trauma. I don't know the rate, but I've seen it a lot."

"Yes, they are common," Felix says, gleeful to chime in. "I see them all the time. People tend to protect themselves with their arms and hands."

"I've never broken my arm. Never broken any bones," Faye announces, sticking her chest out.

"Fuck, Cleary, no one cares," Sloane barks. Liam decides to ignore them.

"It could be nothing," he continues, "but all four Hosts had broken arms. A Trypanon is impossible to rule out."

Another silence.

"This is kind of a big deal, huh?" Faye's Phren radiates giddiness.

"Yeah, I'd say it's a pretty big fucking deal," Sloane says, voice rising. She takes a step toward Liam. "Imagine if you'd taken this case when we first fucking asked you to. This shit could have been prevented."

"I highly doubt it."

"What?"

Liam pushes off the wall, rising to his full height. He stands eye-level with Sloane. "Do you have any concept of how difficult it is to catch a Trypanon? Dumb luck is the only reason I was able to take Iris down. We have no idea who this Trypanon is. It could be anyone. They might not even know they're doing it."

Sloane takes another step. Applebaum comes up behind her but doesn't make a move to stop her.

"It could be you," Sloane says, low.

Liam shrugs. "Or you."

"Gee willikers," Faye whispers.

"Then how do we stop them?" Applebaum says.

Sloane frowns at the floor, chewing on the inside of her cheek.

"The same way you catch a normal killer," Liam says. "I'll need to interview people close to the victims and try to find a motive. If this Trypanon has managed to keep their exceptional powers hidden, then they must be very good at blocking out other Sophonts. They might even be able to manipulate them. Phoebe said she felt like she was being *made blind* to something. She may well have been sensing our killer. I'll need everything you have on the victims and a list of Sophonts in the area. I doubt the Academy would have failed to identify a Trypanon student if they attended the school. They watched us like hawks, so maybe our killer never went to the school. Paraphrenic abilities are genetic, though recessive. Even if our Trypanon is hidden, their parents might be registered. It's possible this person presented late, never went to the Academy, and is related to a known Sophont."

"And what about us?" Sloane says.

"What about you?"

"What are we supposed to do while you play detective? Can't we pursue leads too?"

"You could, but you'll likely be manipulated in the wrong direction as soon as you get remotely close to our killer. This is an unregulated, violent Trypanon with no compunction about violating boundaries or human agency. Do you know what a Pelt is?"

"Yes, I know what a fucking Pelt is."

"I don't," Felix cuts in.

"A Pelt is a person under the control of a powerful Sophont. Like a puppet," Faye declares, proud.

"Exactly. And we know this person is powerful enough to attack a Sophont, maybe even make a Pelt out of them. I wouldn't even have Faye go near them. It's too dangerous. You need another Trypanon or no one at all. A Tryp can put a Fluke in anyone, even Sophonts. The only one they can't touch is another Trypanon."

"So you're saying you'll take the case?" Faye says, beaming.

"I'm saying I have no choice."

"And what if you're wrong? What if this isn't all because of a Trypanon murderer? What if this is all just a coincidence?" Felix says.

"Then the deaths stop here and none of you ever have to talk to me again."

"I'll always talk to you!" Faye squeals.

Sloane won't look at him. Something has changed in her. It's a transition he recognizes. She knows as well as he does that these things rarely end in a best-case scenario. They were both running from something. Shoalport was meant to be their haven.

Now, the haven has gone dark.

CHAPTER EIGHT
THE KNOX HOUSE

"**I** ALREADY KNOW what transpired today."

Liam blinks at Jasper. He's posted in the bedroom doorway as usual, his arms at his sides. His shoes are muddy, leaving a trail behind him in the hall. He's still colorless.

"How do you—oh. Right. The Vulcan mind-meld thing."

Liam takes his glasses off the nightstand and slips them on. The truth is he doesn't really need the glasses. He started using them to hide his face and the habit is hard to break. He leaves the hat off for now. There isn't much point in hiding his hair from Jasper when the man is already inside his head.

"Did you come here to gloat? Well, congrats. We're all fucked."

"I came to give you instructions."

Liam snorts, shaking his head. "Oh great." He throws back the covers. Jasper looks away as he rises to his feet and stretches. "Might as well have a real introduction, if you're gonna start bossing me around." Liam holds out his hand. Jasper doesn't take it. "You can invade my mind but shaking my hand is out of the question?"

Jasper clears his throat but says nothing.

Liam rolls his eyes. "Is it my 'state of undress' again? Fine. You know, these aren't real clothes anyway; they're just a figment of my imagination, or I guess *our* imagination, but if it untwists your knickers …" Liam conjures plaid pajama pants and, appropriately, a *Star Trek* sweatshirt onto his body. He plops down in an old armchair in the corner. A cloud of dust bursts from the cushion. Even in his Phren, his house is filthy. "Now that I'm not offending your delicate sensibilities—let's talk."

"You need to investigate my former residence—the Knox House."

Liam blinks. "Rifling through your shit isn't exactly my top priority. Or getting arrested for trespassing."

"Did you not confirm earlier that a Trypanon is likely committing these murders? You vowed to explore possible leads and I am the best lead you have."

"And how do you expect me to get to your house, anyway? It's on a friggin' island. And I'm not just gonna walk out at low tide and get myself marooned. You of all people get why." Liam winces. Bringing up how a guy died is probably not very polite.

Jasper looks at him and arches one dark, refined eyebrow. "Do boats still exist?"

Liam decides he doesn't like Jasper very much. "I think you know damn well that they do."

"Then I suggest you procure one."

Liam takes a moment to process the staggering unreality of his situation. He'd come to Shoalport to be alone, to rot in grief and burn away at his savings. Being ordered around by a specter to solve a Trypanon murder case was not on his vision board, had he made one. Ever.

"How will I know what to look for?" he sighs.

"You won't, but I will do my best to nudge you in the right direction. When you were at the morgue today, I was able to watch your actions, at least partially. It was like looking through a haar."

"Haar?"

"A sea fog. I attempted to contact you at several points."

Liam thinks back to the whispers of "William" and that smell of low tide. "Yeah, I thought you might have. And I told you: my name is Liam."

"You will need to be thorough. Leave no crevice unexamined."

"Because I have all the time in the world."

"I doubt you have anything more pressing than this. Other than cleaning your decrepit living quarters and practicing a modicum of personal hygiene."

Liam's teeth clench so hard his jaw creaks. He had no idea Victorians were such assholes. "You know, there's another theory that I didn't mention today."

Jasper tilts his chin up. "What theory is that?"

"This person you've seen in the Nether—they must be from your time. You said you knew them, right? Maybe they're a Tryp from the 1800s who got stuck in the Nether. It would explain why they're not registered."

"A feasible theory."

"You say you have no memories. How do you know what you've been up to all this time? You're not exactly a reliable narrator."

"What are you implying?"

"Maybe you were a Trypanon, and you don't remember. Maybe you're the one we're looking for."

Jasper's eyes, gray as a storm, fix on him. Impossibly, he stands even taller. "You stated our culprit can possess a living Host. Clearly, you are susceptible to a Wick invading your mind, as my presence proves. And your own memory is muddled by liquor and years spent galivanting in the Nether. Are you so certain you can trust yourself?"

Liam leans back in the chair, crossing his arms over his chest. He hates Jasper's stupid ascot and his sharp nose. He hates his relentless gaze and perfect posture. He hates that he isn't saying anything Liam hasn't considered himself.

"Alright, smart-ass, let's say I am possessed. That doesn't disprove my point. You are literally possessing me right now. What if you're making me kill people?"

"What if, indeed." Jasper stares at him. "If only there was a way to know for certain."

Liam glares at the ceiling. A counterpoint refuses to come. In the game of logic chess, he tips over his king. "Where the fuck am I gonna get a boat?"

"It's a coastal town. I'm sure you'll find something. It will be best to wake early. I know you are a late riser, assuming you elect to rise at all."

"Well, maybe if *someone* wasn't fucking up my sleep schedule by being gross and creepy and annoying in my dreams, my rising wouldn't be so late."

"Maybe."

Jasper turns and leaves like he won something.

When Liam wakes up, he's more pissed off than he's been in a long time. And not just because it's seven o'clock in the morning and he's inadvertently done exactly what Jasper ordered him to do.

With a grumble, he grabs his phone off his nightstand and Googles "kayak store near me."

Carl's Kayak Shack is exactly what Liam expects: a small shop by a tidal marsh full of way too much crap that no one needs. As he shuffles through the thin, congested aisles, he's bombarded with the phrase "Live free or die," adorning everything from mugs and bumper stickers to toilet seat covers. There's an array of taxidermy, all decorated with kitschy hats or flannel. A junky-looking

raccoon dons a T-shirt with a dog on it that says, "Come to the bark side."
Woof.

He's staring into the void of a dead beaver's fake eyes when someone comes up behind him. "Can I help you with anything, dude?"

Liam turns. He's face-to-face with a heavily-tanned, blond twenty-something with a broccoli cut. There's a string of puka shells around his neck.

"Yo, sorry, bro. Didn't mean to scare you. Name's Kyle. Anything I can assist you with on this fine morning?"

"Uh, yeah. I'm looking to buy a kayak."

"Then you came to the right place, bro. Did you have any, like, specifications?"

"I don't need anything special. Just something I can use in the river that won't flip."

"Right this way."

Kyle flashes an unnaturally white smile and leads Liam outside to an array of neon kayaks. Kyle is both knowledgeable and too laid back (or too stoned) to bother upselling. Liam picks out a basic river kayak in an un-assaulting shade of forest green. He splurges on decent oars that won't annihilate his tremendously out-of-shape arms.

Kyle has just finished helping Liam tie the kayak to the top of his Honda Civic when someone calls his name from across the crushed-shell parking lot.

"Never thought you were the outdoorsy type," Ingrid says as she approaches. He's surprised to see her in hiking boots and a North Face tank top.

"Didn't think you were either."

"I contain multitudes." She pulls her short hair into a dinky ponytail. "Teddy and I like to paddleboard, especially when there are no people around. People are annoying. Anyway, how you been? We missed you at the party."

"Yeah, I … had work."

"Work? Like, Sophont shit?"

"Unfortunately, yes."

"So they guilted you back on, huh? I'm guessing that had to do with those deaths in the news."

"You guess right."

"Well, in case I didn't make it clear in my email, we got a nice, chill group of friends and I think you'd fit in great. We're doing another hang tomorrow night. Super casual. You should come."

Liam scratches the back of his head. Today, he wants to say yes, but there's no telling what he'll feel like tomorrow. He stares at his feet and kicks a chunk of oyster shell.

"How about this," Ingrid says. "I'll give you my number and if you decide you wanna come, shoot me a text. Last minute is fine. We always make way too much food anyway."

Liam looks at her. There's no fawning adoration or goading, no intense energy coming off her Phren. He can't imagine Ingrid hiding anything. She is refreshingly authentic, even for her bluntness. Or especially for it.

He puts her number in his phone and thanks her for the invite. She asks what he's doing for the rest of the day, and he doesn't offer details beyond "trying out the new kayak." No need to mention that he'll be trespassing on private property because the dead Victorian in his dreams told him to.

It's a miracle Liam doesn't flip his kayak.

The high tide current is strong; it tugs him side to side like he's a new favorite toy. The water is clear, and he almost tips over a few times trying to see a fish or hermit crab below.

The sea air is purifying and crisp, offering a respite from the July heat. On the water, he has new perspective for the shoals and small islands, for the trees shifting in the wind. If he didn't know better, he'd think this was a pond rather than a river, but he learned as a child that the current is sneaky; it hides beneath the surface.

Every summer, a lobsterman diving for their cages would never resurface, or a tourist looking to cool down would get swept out to sea, their swollen corpses beaching in Massachusetts or Rhode Island. When he was ten, his grandparents' neighbor had a body wash up on their yard. At the time, he wanted to pull a *Stand By Me* and check it out. Now, he never wants to see a corpse again.

His arms burn when he finally reaches the shore of Knox Island. He casts a note of gratitude to Kyle for suggesting the "wicked baller oars from New Zealand."

Despite his best efforts to maintain grace and dignity, he slips on some seaweed trying to climb out of the kayak and falls to his knees in the shallows. He barely manages to keep his backpack dry.

Once he's yanked his kayak beyond the tide's reach, he makes his way from the thin beach to a grassy meadow. The island is small and verdant, with a hill rising at its center. A gnarled old tree stands at the highest point like a grave marker, silhouetted by the sun. There's a patch of forest in the opposite direction of the house and a large deadfall of driftwood. He has the sense that he's been here before.

He turns towards the Knox House.

It stares at him, looming tall. As he approaches, the effects of coastal weather become evident. The dark gray paint is salt-worn and dull. Many of the protective plywood boards have fallen off, exposing broken windows. As he rounds the wraparound porch, the ruins of a greenhouse come into view. The brick base is coated with lichen. Most of the glass has shattered. He climbs over an old stone fence and looks inside, but there's not much beyond weeds and cracked terra-cotta pots. A warm wind sighs by, rustling dandelions. Liam feels a twinge—a sudden sadness. Again, he feels like he's been here before. Maybe Jasper's memories are leaking into his.

Shaking it off, he turns back and is struck again by the impression that the house itself is watching him. His brain stutters on how closely it resembles his own home. It's as though he's fallen into a mirror universe where everything is the same yet exactly the opposite. He must still have *Star Trek* on the brain.

Through a walk around the perimeter, he finds that the front door is heavily boarded up, while the back door is not. As he stares at it, standing at the base of the porch stairs, he's reminded that he is, in fact, trespassing. He looks around for any indications of human life—a sign or a security camera— and can't find anything beyond a rusted shovel. It seems odd that a house like this would be held off the market, even if it's tied up in some sort of legalese, and odder still that there isn't a caretaker. No one has been here in a long time.

He decides that if he gets busted for breaking and entering, Sloane can deal with the paperwork. She owes him one. Or forty.

He frowns at the porch boards. Several have rotted through, exposing rusted nails. He scratches his scalp under his hat, hesitating. He'd stupidly left his phone back at his house, for fear of dropping it in the water. If he falls through the porch and breaks a leg, no one is going to find him for a long time. Maybe that wouldn't be so bad; then everyone would stop bothering him.

Tiptoeing up the stairs and onto the porch, he twitches at each ominous creak. His fists clench white. His palms sweat. The nail-in-foot scene from *Home Alone* plays in his head.

When he finally makes it to the door, he wipes his damp forehead with the front of his T-shirt. Cool air slips out from under the door. It slinks through the humid heat, curling up his wet leg like an eel. Liam wriggles and makes a "blech" sound. He feels the Nether skittering against his barriers.

"Alright, Jasper, I don't know if you can hear me, but if this door is locked, there's no way I'm climbing through a broken window to get in there. I don't need tetanus on top of—"

With a long, slow creak the door eases open. Liam staggers back. Chilly air flows from the doorway, washing over him and carrying the scent of cigarette smoke and something herbal. He hears the echo of a child coughing.

With a deep breath, he shakes out his hands and allows himself a little laugh. He's acting like this house is haunted, when he knows better than anyone that ghost stories are all myths rooted in misunderstood paraphrenic incidents. The Nether is just sneaking through and fucking with him again. Right? Right.

He steps inside.

And has the befuddling impression that he's just walked into his own foyer, yet everything is inverted, more dilapidated, and totally unmodernized. The stairs, covered in a sheen of dust, lead up to darkness. In the room to the right, which is the dining room—not the living room as it is in his house—there's only a warped wooden table. Piles of dead leaves fill the corners, and there's a mound of detritus where part of the ceiling fell through. The wallpaper is speckled with mold.

He peers into the living room to the left. Stained shrouds still cover a few furniture pieces, but most have slipped off, pooling on the floor. There's a chaise lounge pocked with mouse holes, and a dusty grandfather clock. The fireplace has regurgitated an old squirrel's nest onto the floor.

Then, something catches his attention. A shroud has partially slid off the sharp edge of a large object, revealing a striking, intricate carving of a star pattern on dark wood. Liam pinches the corner of the sheet and drags it off.

A pulse beats in his mind at the sight of the desk. Though faint, he somehow knows Jasper is trying to communicate.

Liam takes hold of the handles on the roll top and tugs. It screeches like a dying rabbit, metal connectors rusted and grinding together. By the time he manages to shove it up, his ears are ringing.

"Was this your desk? Is that why you want me to look at it?" He doesn't get a reply—he wasn't expecting to—yet somehow, he feels the "no" anyway.

An array of books and papers fill the numerous slots. Liam has always had an affinity for old, Victorian writing desks. They remind him of puzzle boxes, with their hidden compartments and secret treasures. As he looks through the books on landscaping and architecture, he recalls from the online article that Jasper's father was an architect. Delicately, he extracts several rolls of manila paper, and hopes he's not damaging historical documents. In his college history classes he learned all too well that idiots like him were the worst enemy to preserving artifacts.

But dammit, he's curious. A couple documents won't matter much. There are dozens of others, and he has the sense that Jasper is encouraging him. Gently, he splays one out, and reveals a stunning hand-drawn blueprint. He doesn't recognize the building, though it resembles some of the older structures in Shoalport's downtown. Sebastian Knox's signature is scrawled in the bottom right corner.

He rolls the paper up and puts it back where he found it. Fiddling through a few more documents, he finds mostly boring professional letters and contracts. Then, he opens a small drawer tucked near the back of the desk. A flush of excitement flutters through him; it's a collection of letters, and the first is signed by Jasper Knox. He tucks them into a plastic folder in his backpack. He'll read them with some gloves on. He's not without some respect.

Once Liam forces the roll top closed, he makes his way to the kitchen. He finds a rusted cast iron skillet and a mouse's impressive acorn collection in a drawer, but little else. The door to the basement is locked, which he's frankly relieved to discover, and while the bathroom provides insight into late 1800s plumbing, he finds nothing relevant to Jasper.

Back in the foyer, Liam's not sure how long he stands at the base of the stairs, staring up into the darkness. A niggling dread has tied his feet to the floor. The Nether hums down to him.

He's contemplating turning around and going home when a little sting jabs in the back of his mind. He senses a huff of English recrimination.

"Yeah, yeah, message received," he mutters.

As he works his way up the stairs, mice scuttle under the boards, setting his teeth on edge. One board teeters under his weight. He grabs the railing.

"I can't believe I'm fucking doing this. What if I fall through the fucking floor? Not that you give a shit. Asshole."

The instant he reaches the second floor, he's hit with a thick cloud of Nether aura. It rushes over him and scrapes in his ears. He struggles to block it out. It takes a few slow breaths for him to get his bearings again.

The benefit of the Knox House being a mirror image of his own is that he knows his way around. He checks out the first bedroom. It's barren except for a wooden bed frame and a dresser with no drawers. Then he starts to approach the other bedroom—the one that matches his own. With each step he feels the strength of the Nether grow. His breath catches; his heart races in his ears. He suddenly recalls seeing the light in this room's window when he'd first moved to Shoalport.

He'd seen it on the night Maggie died.

He turns the knob. The door whines open. Like the other room, there's a bed frame and a dresser with no drawers. But there's something else. Excitement that doesn't belong to Liam blossoms in the back of his mind.

A writing desk.

It's massive—a wide tabletop below two thick cabinet doors. When Liam pulls them open, he's met with an array of compartments and small shelves, all full of vials or jars. He rubs the dust off a few, revealing the seeds or dried leaves inside.

"Oh, right," he whispers. "You said you were a botanist. Or a natural scientist, or whatever."

He continues to explore the desk. There are books on the flora of New England, bound wax paper albums with pressed leaves and flowers inside, and ink drawings of plants. He grimaces at some of the preserved animal specimens he finds: a pink baby mouse suspended in liquid, a jar of fish eyeballs, a taxidermized bluebird. With a twitch, his eyes dart to a black bound book, tucked beside a brass kaleidoscope. The cover is engraved with intricate gold vines. He turns to the first page and reads, *"Jasper Sebastian Knox's Journal of Natural Science."*

An overwhelming, bright warmth flutters in him. It's insistent, tugging on him like an excited child.

"Alright, alright, I'm taking it. Relax."

Carefully, he wraps the journal in a bandanna from his backpack and tucks it inside. He feels Jasper's relief like it's his own.

"I think we have enough intel for today. This Nether stink is starting to get to me," he says, trying not to feel nuts for talking to no one.

Carefully, he closes the desk cabinets. He turns to leave … and stops. A small table catches his eye. It stands directly below the window that faces his own bedroom. On it, a candle, burned down to a stump, juts up from a pewter taper. He'd been too focused on the desk to see it. Is this the source of the light he saw in the window that night? Maybe the house isn't abandoned. Maybe someone has been watching him. He hasn't felt another Phren nearby, but he's been focused on keeping the Nether out. It's possible another Trypanon could block Liam from sensing them …

Like a nervous cat, he approaches the table with his shoulders bunched. He leans down and examines the candle.

And sighs. There's a film of dust coating the wick and wax; it hasn't been lit in a long time. Which means Liam saw something that wasn't really there. Again.

An unsettling thought dawns on him. Jasper. He's been linked to him from the start, and their Hitch marker is a light. Was Jasper communicating with him the night Maggie died? Was he reaching to him from the Nether, even then?

The table has a single drawer and Liam pulls it open, revealing a book on Morse code and a small tin box. The box is rusted shut, and it takes him a few tries to wrench it open. Inside, he finds several hand-rolled cigarettes. He sniffs them and detects a strange herbal note distinct from tobacco. He's smelled it before—at the porch door. There's also a medicine bottle in the box with the words "Syrup Ipecac" on the label. Did this belong to Jasper? Was he sick?

He can ask him later. He closes the drawer and turns to leave.

Under the bed.

Liam jumps, hands flying up to cover his ears. It was Jasper, clear as if he'd been in the room. And yet Liam felt it *inside* himself. It's exactly how Makoto's voice sounded when they were linked.

The bed frame. There's something under it, half-covered by a faded sheet. He approaches, and bends down, reaching. With a tug, the sheet falls away. It's a painting, face-down. Carefully, he picks it up. There's a note elegantly scrawled on the back:

For you, Father, so you may recall what I look like.

Liam turns it over.

And his breath stops. Two familiar eyes stare back at him. It's arresting how accurate the portrayal is, capturing the pale curve of Jasper's strong cheekbones and the slight curl in his hair where it covers the tips of his ears. But the most astounding feature is the defiance in his gray eyes. There's more substance here than Liam has ever seen in the man that's been haunting his dreams. The longer he looks, the more he sees the hidden flecks of sadness, the complexity and caged passion. Liam sees color in his cheeks and lips for the first time. He doesn't want to damage the painting by putting it in his backpack, so he covers it back up with the sheet and places it on the nightstand.

"Alright, I really mean it this time. I'm going back." He strides to the door.

The instant he steps into the hall, a grating, horrible rattling fills the air. His heart jumps to his throat. He covers his ears and scrambles to find the source. It's everywhere and nowhere all at once, both real and unreal.

Then, he turns—the door to the tower. Part of him wants to run. To flee. He hears his grandmother's voice in his head, commanding him to never enter the tower, and castigating him when he disobeyed, even as his neck swelled from the yellow jacket sting.

The door shakes against its brass hinges. Wind hisses on the other side. Liam wipes his sweaty hands on his shorts. Something pulls him toward the door, moving his feet without his command. He stares down at his own hand as if watching found footage of someone else. The fingers take hold of the door handle, turning it. *Wait*, he thinks. He doesn't wait. The door flies open, shoved by a gust of wind, and crashes into the wall. His hat nearly flies off as steps inside, and ascends a narrow, spiraling staircase. It leads him to a ladder, and he climbs, hands slick on the splintered bars. Bright light burns his eyes. They're still adjusting when he peers over the ledge at the top, looking into a round, windowed room with a pointed ceiling.

There's something on the floor. Liam pulls himself up to his feet. The wind whips through the broken windows, spiraling dust around him like a twister. He bends down and picks up a square, wooden box. On it, a golden inlay of a compass rose. He flicks the latch and opens the lid.

A dented velvet cushion outlines the absence of a round object, once kept inside. It's a perfect fit …

For a pocket watch.

He needs to get out of the house.

Clambering back down the ladder, then the stairs, he skips steps. He crashes into the wall as he rushes down the spiral and into the hall. The Nether growls around him. He smells herbal cigarette smoke, hears someone panting, then the scratching of a fountain pen on paper. A dull crack resonates—a bone breaking. He almost falls running down the main stairs to the foyer, and just manages to catch himself before he steps on a rusted nail on the porch. It's not until he's back in the meadow near his kayak that he bends over, hands on his knees, and fights for breath. He dry heaves. A garter snake slinks off a rock close by and into the grass.

The house seems to poke at his back, demanding attention, which he refuses to give. He doesn't look at it until he's safely across the river and back in his own yard. He shakes his head and sits on his porch steps until his breathing slows. And, gradually, he starts to feel like a fool. If the Nether was more powerful in the Knox House, it's only because he allowed it to be.

His heart doesn't stop pounding until he's had a long shower and stiff drink. As he sits on his couch, watching Kermit saw through a romaine leaf, his eyes keep being drawn to his backpack. His foot bounces on the floor.

"Fuck it."

Heaving to his feet, he grabs a pair of new cleaning gloves from the kitchen and empties the backpack on his dining room table.

He starts with the letters first.

"Well, well, well. Look who it is." Liam pushes up on his pillows and puts on his glasses. "Mr. *I Keep Dead Shit in Jars.* And Mr. Artist, apparently."

"I have many interests."

"And a taste for cigarettes and ipecac, apparently."

Jasper takes a few steps into the room and the blue light hits his face. His cheeks are flushed, his lips pink. It's the first time he's crossed the threshold.

"You look different," Liam says, a little struck.

"I feel different," he says. He looks around the room like he's seeing it for the first time. "It's strange how this room resembles my bedroom."

"Yeah, that weirded me out today too."

"But we aren't in your bedroom right now." Jasper says it like he's taste-testing the words. "This is your Phren. I think I understand the term better now."

"Some people have apartments that were important to them or theatres or gardens."

Jasper's brow dents in thought. "I imagine mine was a garden. Or a greenhouse. Seems logical given what we learned today."

Liam sits up more. "That was an impressive journal you had there. I read through it when I got home."

"I have an affinity for things that grow. I liked being outside … when I was allowed to be."

Liam arches an eyebrow. "Allowed?"

"Some memories returned when you discovered the cigarettes and ipecac. I was sickly—asthmatic. My physicians claimed it resulted from my difficult birth. My mother didn't survive. We knew that already."

"They gave you cigarettes for asthma?"

"Laced with nightshade."

"Fuckin' A," Liam laughs. Jasper winces. "Let me tell you, buddy, from a modern medicine perspective, that is pretty fucking off-base."

"I had my suspicions."

Liam throws off the covers and stands. Jasper turns away as Liam conjures pajama pants and the *Star Trek* sweatshirt onto his body.

"What do you say we head downstairs and chat about today. I don't think either of us want to hang out in my bedroom."

As Liam leads Jasper to the hall and down the stairs, he's careful to keep any errant memories from sneaking out around them. In most Phrens that resemble homes, there are photographs on the walls that hold living memories. Samantha's Phren had many. Liam trained himself long ago to keep his memories locked away in the basement and closets. Makoto called it "repressing." Liam pointed out that Makoto was one of the most repressed people he knew, and the subject was dropped.

"Don't mind the rabbit," Liam says as they enter the living room. "I keep a re-creation of him in my Phren. Guess I like having the little guy around." He nudges the manifestation, and it comes to life, hopping around the pen in a circle.

He looks back at Jasper.

There's more expression on his face than Liam has seen yet. His eyes sparkle. His hand moves to his chest and rests on top of the ascot.

"You alright?"

"What's his name?" Jasper says, quiet.

"Kermit." Liam sighs, waiting for the inevitable "that's a frog's name" response. He's the one who suggested the name when Makoto got the rabbit. He wasn't expecting everyone to having a fucking opinion on a pet's name.

"It suits him."

Liam starts. Their eyes meet. A flush rises on Jasper's pale cheeks. Then, swift as a curtain falling, his expression shutters again.

"We should discuss the evidence you collected today." His accent takes on an abrupt smugness. "I have no interest in idle chatter."

"Whatever you say."

Liam takes a seat on the sofa and gestures for Jasper to take the armchair. When Jasper sits, his back is rigid, his hands placed flat on his thighs. He looks like a statue, except for the way his eyes keep darting to Kermit's pen.

"I read the letters between you and your father," Liam says.

Jasper's gaze locks on him. "Titillating, I'm sure."

"Seems like the relationship was strained."

"If you're implying that my father is the Trypanon we're seeking, you are not as skilled as people claim you to be."

Liam huffs, leaning back on the couch. He puts his foot up on the coffee table. "Then we are shit out of luck, because I didn't find evidence of anyone else you might have known."

Jasper folds his hands together on his lap. "You hardly made much of an effort. You were too craven to perform a thorough search."

Liam bristles, leaning forward. "As if you've done shit. Why couldn't it be your father? Seemed to me like you hardly knew each other. Guy was barely around."

Jasper's lips thin to a line. "My father was a distant, implacable man who lacked an ability to invest in my life, skills, or passions. I believe he was ill-equipped to raise me following my mother's untimely death. But he was not a violent man, nor was he ... a ... *Sophont*, I believe is your term. He was a pacifist, a master architect, and a gentle, if stoic, individual. He would not wish suffering on anyone, including me. Perhaps especially me. I believe he loved my mother dearly and my presence was ... a reminder of her absence."

"You think he blamed you for her death?"

"In a way—yes. But that doesn't render him a murderer. Furthermore, I would know instantly if the Trypanon was my father. I know I cannot prove why, but you will simply need to trust me. I would know if I had seen him in the Nether. Especially now."

Liam sinks back in the couch cushions. "Fair enough. Shit, I'm not close to my parents either. Haven't spoken to them in years. I'm not even sure where they are."

"Why is this house not in their possession? Shouldn't they be first in line to inherit it?"

"It belonged to my grandparents, and they had a falling out with my parents, so they left the house to me. Why does that matter? Anyway, I'm not clear where we take this little investigation from here. Think we've hit a dead end, buddy."

"Surely, you are not this inexperienced with a modicum of hard work and reasoning. Return to the Knox House, visit the local magistrate, speak with a historian. You must be familiar with the fundamentals of research. Do libraries still exist in your time or have people forsaken the written word? Your colorful vernacular is hardly a substitute."

Liam scowls, irritated. He crosses his arms over his chest. "You know, I could just say 'fuck you' and go to a dinner party tomorrow instead and get drunk and have a good time for once in my damn life."

"Consuming an excess of alcohol has hardly afforded you the 'good times' to which you refer. But I do believe you should attend a social gathering. You can interview the locals in attendance and report back after. That man Teddy seems to possess historical acumen. I will attempt further communication with you during this time. I think I comprehend the mechanism now. Clearly, my guidance is essential if anything is to be accomplished."

Liam throws his hands up in the air. "Un-fucking-believable."

"As I said: colorful."

Liam storms back upstairs, leaving Jasper alone in the living room. He realizes on his way out that he's doing Jasper a favor by leaving; he's already staring at Kermit like he's the most interesting thing in the world.

As Liam sits cross-legged on his bed, stewing like a child in time out and waiting to wake up, he takes stock of what he's learned about Jasper so far. The man can be a selfish, poncy dick when he wants to be. He's also annoyingly talented and smart, if socially awkward, not that Liam understands the social norms of the nineteenth century. He must have been isolated, living alone on an island with a distant father. Their suspect list can't be long. How many people did he even know, besides some classmates at Harvard?

He thinks of Declan O'Connor, and the legend of The Man Who Drowned Waiting, but that's the problem—without finding a journal or letters, there's no way to confirm what aspects of the legend are true. And if no one has managed to find any proof yet, why should his search yield anything different?

Still, if the Trypanon was from Jasper's time, it stands to reason that it could have been a member of Liam's lineage. Sophontism is genetic, after all. Maybe the Trypanon is one of his ancestors. Maybe Declan's soul is taking his revenge for a lost daughter.

There's only one way Liam can get a direct look into the past: going back into the Nether.

At the thought, he's shoved back into consciousness. He wakes covered in sweat, staring at the morning light streaking across his bedroom ceiling. His phone buzzes with a text on his nightstand. It's from Ingrid.

Hope to see you tonight!

Liam stares at the phone, a headache growing behind his eyes. He can't believe what he's about to do. He texts back:

I'll be there.

CHAPTER NINE

EXPOSURE THERAPY

IT DOESN'T OCCUR to Liam that he's made a mistake until he's standing on Ingrid and Teddy's front porch, finger extended toward their doorbell. It's absurd that he agreed to attend a dinner party with strangers. He didn't even enjoy parties with longtime friends in Chicago. Granted, they were Claire's friends. People who didn't worship Liam found him off-putting. He never seemed to say the right thing, always made off-color jokes, got too morbid, or didn't speak enough. And it didn't help that everyone was terrified he'd read their minds. Claire could never understand.

"What is with you tonight?" she would say on their way home. *"It was like you didn't even care what my friends thought of you."*

He did care at first, then he didn't, and she came to know it and it signified the beginning of the end. He didn't want to talk about work or politics or current events, didn't want to one-up anyone with his achievements. He was always raw from Fissure cases, running on empty. The only type of socializing he desired was playing games in his apartment with Makoto, sharing thoughts without speaking so he didn't have to talk.

The door opens and Liam retracts his arm like he's been caught doing Ding-Dong Ditch.

"Jesus, Liam, you scared the shit out of me," Ingrid says, almost dropping the bouquet of empty beer bottles she's cradling against her chest. "How long have you been standing out here?"

"Uh … not long? I … here." He holds out the bottle he'd brought from his collection. "BenRiach 12-year-old single malt. It's a good scotch."

Ingrid blinks. "Thanks. Let me just dump these bottles and I'll grab it from you."

"Right. Of course."

Liam wants to slap himself. He waits awkwardly as she tosses the bottles in a blue bin at the end of her driveway and returns.

"I think maybe I should go home," Liam says, staring at his feet as she comes up to him.

"Why? You anti-recycling or something?"

"Yeah, and I hate sea turtles. No, I just think maybe this wasn't a good idea."

Ingrid takes the scotch from him. He looks up.

"You can do whatever you want, but I'm taking the scotch. Would be a shame to miss out on your own scotch."

Liam sighs, adjusting his baseball cap and pushing up his glasses. "I guess so."

"Listen, Liam, I'm not a big dinner party person either. This is just a couple of nerds playing table games and drinking beer—probably too much of it, as you can see from the recycling. Give it a try and if you decide to ghost, I promise no one will give you shit for it. You probably won't even be the first."

Ingrid has a talent for identifying exactly what Liam doesn't want to hear, and then saying the opposite. It's frankly tactical of her. He wonders what she does for a living, and decides that whatever it is, she must be good at it.

Liam reminds himself to breathe as he steps inside the house and follows Ingrid to the living room. The house is old, like most of the homes around downtown Shoalport. It's a little crooked, with high ceilings and scuffed wood floors. The walls are covered in framed fanart from *Star Wars*, Studio Ghibli films, *Lord of the Rings*, Nintendo, and just about every other niche nerd interest.

"We go to a lot of cons," she says when Liam pauses to look at a digital art print of Princess Leia straddling a giant D20. "You ever been to one?"

"Only once." Makoto had dragged him into it. The crowd had gotten to him. They'd left after an hour.

When they enter the living room, no one looks up from the game spread out on the coffee table.

"Good to see you, Liam!" Teddy says, standing and coming over to them. A fat orange cat follows and rubs up against Liam's leg. "Glad you could make it. You like table games? We're playing Carcassonne."

"Yeah, and you just stole my city, you dick," says a woman on the couch.

She's wearing sweatpants and a flannel top, her hair pulled into a messy bun.

"That's Jill," says Ingrid.

"Hi." Jill waves without looking up.

"And that's Benny," says Ingrid, gesturing to a husky, relaxed-looking redhead beside Jill. He bears an uncanny resemblance to the cat.

"I'm the one losing horribly. Don't know why you're complaining," he says. Then he looks to Liam. "Glad you could make it. We missed you on the fourth."

"Yeah," Liam mumbles.

"And that's pretty much everyone," Ingrid says. "We have one more coming after you. Her name's Cedra. You'll like her."

"Is that whisky?" Teddy says, eyes sparkling. Ingrid hands it to him. "Oh, hell yeah. I like a man who brings good scotch into my house. You want a glass? Can I get you a beer? Jill brought over some good local stuff."

"Better than the piss water my students drink," Jill says.

"Do you teach with Teddy?" Liam asks, taking a seat in an armchair and folding his hands on his lap. His leg bounces and he forces it to stop. Claire hated when he did that.

"Naw, I went for higher education because teenagers are terrifying. I'm an assistant professor. Anthropology. I wanted to be like Indiana Jones. Instead, I teach overcrowded lecture halls of dead-eyed students about the lurid history of corn and try not to feel like an imperialist."

"I used to want to be a professor," Liam says.

"That makes two of us."

Teddy hands Liam a beer and a whisky shot just as Jill indignantly declares the end of the game. When Teddy takes a seat next to Liam, there's a nudge in the back of Liam's mind. Jasper. Liam had almost forgotten that he's only here on business. He's still gonna drink on the job.

"Teddy, could I ask you a few questions? That whole *Man Who Drowned Waiting* legend ... I read the article you sent me. Seems like the records are kinda sparce."

"Unfortunately, yeah. The O'Connors and Knoxes were notorious for guarding their secrets."

"So, there's nothing else to know about, say, Declan O'Connor or his kids?"

Teddy shrugs. "Declan had a lot of control over the records, since he was both mayor and a lawyer. There's never much on the women, which should come as a shock to no one. We know that his wife, Emily, died of consumption. Pretty common back then. We know Rosie died in an asylum, which took a lot of digging to find out, let me tell you what."

"And you never found any evidence that she was Jasper's lover?"

"No, none at all. I wish we had, but sometimes the simpler answer is the best. Between you and me, I think the guy probably went for a stroll to a tidal island, took a nap, and woke up just in time to drown."

Liam can sense Jasper absorbing these words. If it's hard for him to hear about his own death, Liam can't tell.

"Did Declan have any other kids?"

"Only one. His son, Declan Jr., took over the family law firm eventually. He married and the lineage went on, etc, etc, and here you are today. There's a rumor that Declan Sr. had another son, but we've never been able to prove that. If he existed, a lot of dirty work was done to get him erased from the record, and he's not in the family plot."

"And what about Jasper Knox? Anything else I should know about him?"

"Man, this story really caught you, huh? I get it. It's what got me involved with the Historical Society. I'm sorry, though. You know about as much as I do. There were some rumors that Jasper Knox was a sexual deviant, but I think that's just some puritanical gossip. Other than that—nothing. The poor guy didn't even get a grave, as far as we know. I guess there might be something hidden on the Knox property, but like I say in the article, we can't go near it. I'm sure some delinquents have tried to get on the island, but fear of the whole haunting thing keeps them away."

"You're not talking about that dumb folktale again, are you?" Jill cuts in.

"Jill hates legends," Teddy says to Liam. "And fun."

"I like my history to be factual, based in evidence, excavated and catalogued, fuck you very much."

Teddy shrugs.

The doorbell rings. No one goes to answer it, and the visitor comes in anyway.

"Who wants poutine?" The woman who must be Cedra waltzes in, holding up a large takeout box. She's blonde and flushed, her eyes squinted by a broad smile. There's an obvious easy quality to her. Her Phren glows, soft.

"You're late," Jill says. "But the fries make up for it."

"I knew they would." Cedra hands the box to Teddy and takes a seat in the armchair beside Liam. Liam says nothing as Benny and Jill put away the game and Teddy and Ingrid go into the kitchen. He isn't sure what to do, especially without Ingrid in the room. He knows it would be polite to introduce himself to Cedra, but he's never been a fan of introductions.

"I'd say 'nice to meet you,' but we've actually already met," Cedra says.

Liam looks at her. "Have we?"

"I don't blame you for not remembering. We were kids and it was kind of a big day for everyone."

Liam has no idea what she's talking about. Any comfort he'd felt in her presence sloughs away. It's common for people to claim to know him, either to feign intimacy or because of some small interaction he doesn't remember. His eyes dart to the exit.

"You could leave now, but you'd regret it later," she says.

He looks at her. Her eyes are easy, her expression peacefully neutral. He's suddenly reminded of Makoto. "You're a therapist, aren't you." Liam doesn't mean to say it out loud.

Cedra laughs. "I guess we have a look, don't we. Yeah, I'm a counselor. But don't worry—I make it a point not to psychoanalyze at dinner parties."

"Isn't that the best time to do it?"

"Not if you want friends."

"If you pulled that shit on me, I'd kick your ass," Jill cuts in.

"See." Cedra smiles. Ingrid comes back into the room, hands Cedra a beer called "Donkey-Hoté," and pulls up a chair.

"What did I miss?" she says.

"Jill was threatening physical violence against Cedra," Benny replies. Jill glares at him.

"Classic."

Once Teddy comes in and sets out the poutine, a veggie platter, and some dinosaur shaped chicken nuggets (Liam was not aware they still made these), the conversation ebbs into a comfortable lull. This seems to be a group of people that don't need to talk to enjoy each other's company. He can see why Ingrid thought he'd fit in.

As they work their way through the spread, Liam learns a few details. Ingrid works in marketing and met Cedra by helping promote her non-profit—an at-risk youth after-school program. Cedra seems to be the only one in the room who loves what she does for a living. Benny's an engineer, though he's far more passionate about video games and his pet conure bird, Dorito. Jill and Teddy pass a few stories about the tribulations of teaching disaffected students. Neither of them like their jobs or have plans to give them up any time soon.

After the snacks are sufficiently vanquished, they play a round of Catan. Liam decides to watch, though there are great efforts to get him to play. He hasn't touched Catan since Makoto, and he's not ready. Besides, he'd rather watch the group dynamics play out over the game. Even if he couldn't read

Phren energy, it's obvious that Benny has a crush on Jill and will never do anything about it. Liam doesn't blame him; Jill's temper is something to behold. He can imagine students liking her as a professor, though. As for Ingrid and Teddy, his positive impression of their relationship holds up. It's obvious they're best friends, if different people. Ingrid is logical where Teddy is emotional, cool where he's warm. He enjoys their presence, though it draws a sharp contrast to his relationship with Claire. He's having trouble remembering why he thought they would work.

And then there's Cedra, who makes it her personal mission to make everyone in the room as comfortable as possible. Her jokes are horrible, which is somehow funny, her laugh so buoyant that Liam can't help but feel lighter. There is no pretention, no prying.

When they finish the game, he finds that he doesn't want to leave, even as Jill and Benny pack up and head home. Ingrid brings the scotch into the living room and pours him another shot. Cedra takes one too.

"I think Radagast and I are gonna call it a night," Teddy says. It takes Liam a moment to realize Radagast is the cat. Teddy scoops him up, getting a face full of fluffy orange tail, and heads upstairs.

"Last ones standing, as always," Ingrid says, toasting at Cedra. "Bunch of lightweights."

Liam is starting to feel warmth in his cheeks and a pleasant buzz in his chest. Cedra's flush is spreading to her neck and ears. Ingrid looks the same.

"So, Liam," Ingrid says, leaning back on the couch cushions. "Your verdict? You glad you stayed?"

"Yeah, I am. You guys are an easy group of people to be around."

"Minus Jill's meltdown over Benny stealing her sheep in Catan—yeah, I'd agree with you. There's no bullshit here. We're all pretty lame." Ingrid takes a long pull from the scotch. "Shit, this is good. Where'd you find this stuff?"

"I spent time in Scotland."

"Oh right, you've been all over, haven't you? All that travel must've been cool."

"Yes and no. I could do without being recognized everywhere I go."

"It must be especially hard for you around here, then," Cedra says, looking at Liam. "I'm sure you get a lot of unwanted attention. If I were you, I wouldn't leave my house."

At the acknowledgment of Liam's fame, he isn't as uncomfortable as he expects. He's almost relieved. "Yeah, I didn't know it would be like this when I moved here. I thought I'd get some privacy."

"Really? I'm surprised at that, after what you did at the barbeque."

Liam throws his hands up. "Everyone keeps bringing that up. I barely even remember it."

Cedra leans forward, elbows on her knees. "Repressed childhood trauma," she whispers.

"Hey, no psychoanalyzing, remember?" Ingrid sends, pointing at Cedra. Her finger sways, missing its mark.

"Oops. It's the booze, I swear. Good thing I Uber'd here."

"What kind of counselor are you anyway?" Liam says, taking a strong sip of the scotch. It doesn't burn, which is a sign that he's getting drunk.

"Well, I work with at-risk youth, as I said—running groups and facilitating events and classes and what-not. If I had to pick, I'd say my best skill is helping them overcome fears and phobias. Hey!" She bounces a little excitedly. A few drops of scotch spill onto the floor. "What's your biggest fear?" she says, eyes darting between them.

"I'm worried Teddy will want kids." Ingrid's response is immediate. Her eyes glaze into the distance, unfocused. Liam gets the sense her and Cedra have discussed this before. "I don't want them. Never have, never will. He says he's okay with that, but I'm worried he'll change his mind."

Liam and Cedra nod in unison. Claire had wanted kids too. Liam said he didn't think it was right for him, but she always insisted he'd change his mind.

"I'm afraid of my uncle," Cedra says. There's something in the tone of her voice that shifts the mood. Liam is struck by the honesty that comes so easy to them both. He envies it.

"He's in prison, Ced," Ingrid says.

"But he won't be forever."

"If that motherfucker comes near you, I'll fuck him the fuck up."

"Thanks," Cedra says with a genuine laugh. It's miraculous how fast she sheds the dark thought. He's envious. His own tend to stick to him like burrs. "What about you, Liam?"

Liam blinks. Their honesty is contagious, and he wants to match it, but he has so many fears; it's hard to pick just one. He might have said "losing Claire" or "losing Makoto" in the past. An answer presents and leaves his mouth before he has time to examine it:

"Losing myself."

Cedra and Ingrid offer him a long silence.

"What does that look like for you?" Cedra finally says when he doesn't seem inclined to elaborate. It's something Makoto would say.

He huffs a laugh and shakes his head. "It looks like hell." He takes off his hat and rubs a hand through his hair. He realizes belatedly what he's done.

When they don't react to his hair, he keeps it off. "I can't go in the Nether again." The words keep coming. Whether from the booze or the company, he can't seem to hold them back. "Every time I do, I'm different. I'm … less-than. I care less. I'm more … apathetic. It's like it takes something from me. I don't want to be like that."

"So, don't go back in," Ingrid says, like it's simple.

"You guys must know about the Fluke deaths." They nod. "Well, they finally got me signed on to work the case. I just wanted to be done with this shit. Now I don't have a choice."

"But why would they need you? Can't they just use Faye or one of the state Wedges?" Cedra is more familiar with the system than Liam expects. "I guess Faye isn't much help, huh."

"There's a Trypanon murderer." Liam winces. "Fuck, you can't tell anyone about that."

"We won't," they say in unison.

"But that is some heavy shit," Ingrid adds. "Man, here you are, just trying to retire after you took one of those Trypanon fuckers down, and now you gotta do it again. That sucks."

"Yeah. I hate my life."

"Well, if anyone can do it, you can," Cedra says. She raises a toast. They all finish their shots. Ingrid refills their glasses. "Is there anything we can do to help?"

A sharp ping radiates through Liam's mind. The scent of low tide wisps past his nose. He'd completely forgotten about Jasper or the investigation. He feels Jasper's irritation spike, and he slaps it back.

"Actually, yeah. Do you guys know any of the victims?" he says.

"Oh yeah," Ingrid replies, slurring a little. "It's a small city, if you can even call it a city, and we both work with a lot of different people. I already told you about Maggie. RIP or whatever, but I was not a big fan."

"I don't think many people were," Cedra says.

"You'd never know that from the Facebook posts. Suddenly everyone was her best friend. 'I'll never forget her,' 'I'll miss her every day,' 'she was the greatest ratchet bitch of all time.' Fucking annoying."

"People want to feel important," Cedra says, shrugging. "And they lie."

"Damn right they do," Ingrid slurs. "But yeah, if you're looking for motive there, it might be hard to pinpoint. She had dirt on everyone and liked to use it. She was big in the local Baptist church. It's this enormous, offensive '70s-style fortress. Crazy money there. Shit, maybe I should go into the God business and stop paying taxes too."

"Oliver was sort of a friend of mine," Cedra adds. "We didn't hang out, but I knew him because of my father. He was a good man. Really struggled with weight loss, which was absolutely a result of childhood trauma from his mother. I've always theorized some Munchausen by proxy going on there. But of course I can't diagnose someone who isn't my patient. Or so I have to say."

"Yeah, I clocked that from his file," Liam says.

"Her name is Angelica. His mom, I mean. I'd pay her a visit, if for no other reason than to paint a better picture of Oliver's life. He could never totally escape her, I don't think. She was always finding ways to suck him back into her vortex. He was bedridden for years, and I swear, she liked him that way. Once he got that surgery, though, it was like he was a new person. He moved out and got a lot healthier. I was surprised when he moved back in with her. Guess she had her ways with him. Friggin' narcissist. Oops. I mean, I can't diagnose."

"What about Phoebe and Jake?"

Ingrid shakes her head and shrugs. Cedra answers: "I didn't know them well. Maybe met Phoebe a few times at a non-profit function or town parade. Jake was never with her. But Bert, their son … he's a real piece of work. He lives in New York City now. I don't think he has a job."

"If he did, I'd know the name," Liam says. "The Sophont circle is small and Chicago and NYC are in bed together."

"Bert's got a reputation," Ingrid says. "He went to a bougie elementary school in Shoalport. When he came back to town after college, he drove around in a loud lime green sports car. Used to rent a huge condo downtown. Since he's a Sophont, pretty much everyone knows about him. And knows not to mess with him because mommy always bails him out."

"There's a rumor that he got into a fight in a bar a few years ago and Phoebe covered it up," Cedra adds, voice low like someone is listening in. "She had some connections in the police department. Actually, I think it was Maggie who spread that rumor. I try not to read her blog or her Facebook, but we all get bored sometimes."

"Okay, good to know," Liam says. He wonders if Sloane was Phoebe's police connection. "I'll take a look at Maggie's blog, even though I'd rather light myself on fire."

"Same." Ingrid scrunches up her face.

"Anything else?" Liam says.

There's a long pause. Cedra seems to be ruminating on something, chewing her lip and frowning. Ingrid's still riding a wave of disgust over Maggie's blog.

"Trypanons are rare, right?" Cedra says, tentative. "Like, really rare."

Liam tenses. "Yeah …"

"Are you worried people will suspect you?" She's so direct about it, so open, that Liam doesn't feel the usual rush of panic.

"I'm worried I'll suspect myself." The admission is barely a whisper. He wonders if they even heard it. Then Ingrid shakes her head and Cedra covers her mouth.

"That's heavy shit, Liam," Ingrid says. "I'm sorry."

He nods.

"You really don't remember me?" Cedra says.

Liam looks at her. "I'm sorry, no. When did we meet?"

"On August 28, 2000."

At first, Liam is perplexed by that date. It's familiar. He's heard it recently, but he can't remember why.

Then he feels a nudge in the back of his mind, hears the slightest whisper:

The 28ᵗʰ of August is my birthday.

"It's the date of the barbeque … the Fissure Event. When you sealed seven Fissures and you were only twelve years old."

It's as though two gears just shifted and locked together. The Nether whispers against the back of his ear. He shudders. The warped sound of rapid thuds mocks him. It's as though a body is falling down the stairs, ending with a final crack at the bottom. He clenches his teeth through it and shoves the Nether back. It puts up a fight.

You see the Nether this frequently? Jasper's voice is clearer than
before.

Shut up.

"You alright, Liam?" Cedra says.

He blinks back into the room. "Yeah, I … sorry. It's just, the Fissure Event—I know it mattered a lot to people, but I only remember fragments. I know I was swimming with a friend, and I know something bad happened. And I remember the after-effects: the fight between my parents and my grandparents, getting sent to the Academy. I remember being told what I am and not understanding. That's it."

"There's probably a reason for that," Cedra says. "It was a very traumatic day. It certainly was for me." She offers a small, conciliatory smile. "My dad was one of the Fissure victims."

Liam swallows and it hurts. Did Ingrid set this up? She must have known. His heart pounds.

Cedra goes on: "I don't remember much either. Just what his face looked like. And I remember what you looked like when you saved him."

"I'm sorry," Liam rasps. He doesn't know what else to say. He wants to leave.

"Don't be sorry. If it wasn't for you, I would have lost him. We did lose a lot of him, but not all. He's at a long-term care facility. That's how I know Oliver. He was an orderly there. He was always good with my dad."

"Jesus." Liam takes off his glasses and covers his eyes. He needs darkness for a moment. He's too vulnerable. He let his guard down and he wasn't ready.

"I'm sorry if that makes you uncomfortable," Cedra says. She doesn't sound drunk anymore. "It felt dishonest not to tell you. We didn't plan to corner you with this, if that's what you're wondering."

"I was just using you for free scotch," Ingrid says.

Liam breathes a laugh. "It's alright."

"Maybe not at this moment, but I think it will be," Cedra says.

"Damn, shit got heavy fast, huh? We need another shot."

Hardly, Jasper mumbles, faint.

Mind your business.

The Fissure Event doesn't come up again, and Liam is happy to let the conversation swing back to more benign subjects like who serves the best pizza in town and which Miyazaki movie is their favorite. It's nearly two o'clock in the morning by the time they call it a night. The room veers to the left when he stands up, so he decides to retrieve his car in the morning and share an Uber with Cedra.

"Thank you for peer pressuring me into coming tonight," he says to Ingrid on his way out. She pats him on the shoulder. He's glad she doesn't try to hug him.

After pouring themselves into the back of the Uber, Cedra and Liam enter a fuzzy, comfortable silence. It's starting to mist outside, and Liam closes his eyes, enjoying the slow ride and the hum of the engine. Her stop is first. When the driver pulls over, Cedra looks at Liam.

"You know, the saying is true; there's only one way to get rid of a fear," she says. Liam blinks. The edges of his vision are blurred, and Cedra's face is hidden in shadow. "Apathetic people don't care if they're apathetic, Liam. You're better than you think you are."

She throws open the car door and stumbles out into her driveway. "Mic drop," she says, and slams the door shut.

Liam is barely aware of the rest of the drive or of the walk into his house. He kicks his shoes off in the foyer and shuffles into the living room. The couch beckons. He collapses onto it, lounges back, and closes his eyes.

"Sleeping in the sitting room tonight, I see?"

Liam groans as a blurry, cracked ceiling whirls into focus. The room contracts; the scent of low tide and floral scotch swirls around him. He has the sensation of little bubbles popping on his skin.

"Because whisky, that's why."

"You're inebriated."

"I'm gonna start calling you Sherlock with deduction skills that sharp." Liam's head tips to the side. Jasper looms over him, looking down his nose with his brow furrowed.

"Who is Sherlock?" he says.

"Jesus, are there any references you *do* get?"

"Your objective this evening was to gather information relevant to our case, not drink to excess. I feel as if I've been consuming alcohol just by being in your mind."

Liam sighs, folding his hands behind his head. "Good. Maybe bogarting my buzz will unclench your derrière a little. And I *did* get information. Which I think you know since I could hear you bitching in my head. You're getting better at that."

"I am beginning to understand the mechanism for communication. It will take further practice, however."

"So you can invade my thoughts at all hours of the day? Great. That's just what I need."

Jasper turns away, gracefully taking a seat in the armchair facing Liam. As always, he's wearing the black suit with the tail, shiny buttons, and white cuffs. The fit is flawlessly tailored. His shoes are still caked with silt.

"I am someone who values privacy," Jasper says.

"Just not mine."

"If there was an alternative, I would choose it. But this is temporary. Once you discern my history and we apprehend the murderer, you will never see me again."

Liam sits up against the armrest. "We have a Hitch link, buddy. Shit doesn't just go away."

Jasper blinks once. "I see."

"Oh, come on, am I that bad?" The residual impulse to be honest is still strong, bolstered by the booze. "We have some stuff in common. I like your sense of humor. And the nature thing is cool. The art stuff too. I can't draw for shit."

Jasper stares, expressionless. He opens his mouth and closes it again. This repeats several more times before words manage to form. "I merely wish to apprehend the killer. I have no use for flattery."

"Come on, *everyone* likes a little flattery. What made you get into that stuff, huh? Like, what draws you to natural science?" When Jasper's gray eyes narrow, Liam shifts tactics. "Maybe if you talk about your past, you'll remember more of it—unlock something we don't know yet. You know, for the sake of the case."

Jasper licks his lips once. Liam has the odd thought that it's the first time he's seen Jasper's tongue. He prefers it to the black, gaping hole he used to have for a mouth.

"Very well." Jasper straightens his posture more, which Liam hadn't thought possible. "You want to know why I studied natural science?"

"Sure. What is it about plants that gets you going?"

Jasper takes such a long pause that Liam doesn't think he'll answer. Then, slow, he says: "I like the variety. Each variant has unique traits and needs, behaviors and weaknesses. When you study them and slow down to match their pace, you behold their personalities. You start to see them move, however gradual. I also liked to collect them. There was always more to learn, more to see. And I suppose they brought me peace. For a long time, I was not allowed off my property, for fear of my waning health. As a compromise, my father procured a collection of seeds and bulbs for me to foster in the greenhouse. I could not travel to their habitats, as I'd wanted, so they came to me." With each word his eyes grow sharper, more alive.

"I guess I never thought about them that way."

A slight bloom of color rises on Jasper's cheeks. He picks an imaginary piece of lint off his trousers. "I've divulged to excess."

"Not at all. I liked it. In fact, you can talk to me about plants any time you want."

Jasper doesn't find his way to a response. He fidgets, which is out of character, eyes darting around at everything in the room but Liam. Finally, his gaze settles on Kermit. "What made you decide to get a rabbit?" he punches out.

"I wouldn't say I decided." Liam sits up, putting his feet on the floor and leaning forward on his elbows. "He belonged to my best friend. He died, so the rabbit went to me. I'm surprised you didn't get that knowledge out of my Phren."

"I did not."

"You would have liked him—my friend, I mean. He had a lot of house plants. Bonsai trees, actually. Do you know what those are?"

"Of course I do."

Liam huffs a laugh. "Of course you do. They seemed like more work than they're worth to me. Makoto was always fussing over them in the summer."

"He must have been a patient person."

"Oh yeah. He put up with me, didn't he?"

Jasper blinks. Liam looks at Kermit, or rather the Phren version of him. He's staring back over his shoulder at Liam with a sly gaze. Liam loves when he does that. "He might not have been my pet to start, but I do love that little puffball. He's a lot funnier than I thought he'd be."

"Rabbits are extraordinary creatures. Had I been allowed, I would have owned many pets and explored numerous ecosystems to observe the flora and fauna. But my doctors feared my asthma would flare in a foreign environment."

"At least you don't have to worry about that now."

"Yes, but it's not as though I can travel now, can I?"

"I guess not."

"I spent most of my life on an island. My father did not want me to attend Harvard for fear of my health, but I defied him. When four years in Boston only improved my fitness, I came to suspect the prognostics of my impending doom were overly cautious."

"Better that than the alternative, I guess."

"Perhaps." Jasper adjusts his sleeves. He licks his lips again. "I'm not accustomed to talking about myself."

"I'm not either."

"I don't see the point of discussing plants. It doesn't help us identify our murder suspect."

"Not everything has to be all business, all the time. Don't you want to know more about me too?"

"Not particularly."

Liam glares. "Why, have you already seen it all from snooping around my Phren?"

"As I mentioned, I value privacy. I have tried not to glean anything from your Phren that you would not show me willingly. Hence why I did not know Kermit's origins. It's not relevant to the case."

"I didn't exactly invite you in here, though, did I?"

"That's not—" Jasper's mouth snaps shut. He looks away. "Allow me to posit that the weights of our scale have evened," he says after a long moment. "I invade your mind, and you exhume the private history of my life."

"Only because you're forcing me to."

"The murderer is forcing you, not I. Do you have any idea how frustrating it is to not remember oneself?" he says, running a hand through his hair. "I don't even know why I was on that blasted island in the first place."

"Do you have any theories?"

"No, not especially. I know I was waiting for someone. I'm not confident it was your ancestor Rosie. I have no memories of that person, and I am positive she was not my lover."

"How?"

"What?"

"How are you positive if you don't remember?"

Jasper's expression shutters. "I simply am. That is all you need to know."

"What, you never had a girlfriend? No slight Victorian maiden clutching your handkerchief to her swelling bosom?"

Jasper stares at him.

"Guess not," Liam says. "I had a girlfriend, you know. She sucks, though. I mean … she doesn't suck. I sucked. Never fully invested … couldn't be myself around her. I've never told anyone, but I was kind of relieved when she left me. Devastated, yes. Heartbroken, sure. But really, she did me a favor. I never would have pulled the trigger and ended it. Would've just stayed in that thing, plugging along, forever. Always thought she wasn't the one, but no one else could deal with my lifestyle, so I'd have been an idiot to leave. It was her or no one."

"The only woman in my life was my governess."

"Yeah, you mentioned her in the letters. You weren't a big fan, huh."

"Decidedly not. She was adamant I stay indoors for my health, though I came to understand it was more for her benefit than mine. She returned to Europe when I was twelve."

"There's really no one else? Come on, you're a handsome guy. There had to be someone pining after you. Or someone you pined for."

"No."

Liam throws up his hands. "Great. So, in conclusion: we are shit out of luck."

"Hardly. You will investigate Angelica Fenton and Bert Shelton. Both exhibited suspicious behavior, according to your new friends. Additionally, I think Cedra's advice was sound; it would be foolish not to overcome your fear and search the Nether for clues. I was going to suggest we do it tonight, but since you've soaked yourself into a stupor—"

"Hey, hold on for one fucking minute," Liam says, sitting up. The room veers to the side, then rights itself. He points at Jasper. "I'm trying to be nice here; I don't need you giving me fucking orders like I'm your little pet. I'm not going anywhere near the fucking Nether again. I don't care what you or some stupid therapist says."

"You didn't think she was stupid earlier."

"I—"

"When I agree to a responsibility, I dedicate myself to it. I do what needs to be done to ensure that it is completed properly, with dedication and personal sacrifice. In this case, I have nothing to gain other than the satisfaction of doing the right thing, of saving others from my fate. Yet you, for all your privilege—the privilege to live and explore and form relationships—you would rather sit in your home, drinking yourself to death. I was beginning to think you a noble man. Now, all I see is a coward."

The room groans into darkness, the wallpaper fraying, the ceiling crumbling. Kermit disappears.

"You don't know anything about me."

Jasper arches an eyebrow. He looks around suggestively. The message is clear: he knows everything about Liam. He's in his mind. Any illusion of Jasper's respect for his privacy dissipates. Liam's perception narrows to a blurred tunnel. Flame erupts in the fireplace as if a bottle of 150 proof has been smashed on an old ember. Behind Jasper, Liam sees the faded image of Makoto slipping into darkness.

"Get the hell out of my mind." The words reverberate. He doesn't open his mouth to speak them.

"With pleasure."

And then Jasper is gone. Slowly, the darkness recedes as the room bleeds back into its familiar state. Kermit returns, but he's facing away from Liam and not looking back this time. An oil of shame slicks over Liam. He wishes he wasn't still drunk.

CHAPTER TEN

OLIVE BRANCH

Liam is shocked when he first wakes up. He doesn't have a headache. He isn't nauseous or dizzy. He's … almost relaxed. He thought days like this ended in his mid-twenties, but by some miracle, he's avoided a hangover. He gets out of bed with a skip in his step.

That's his first mistake.

It's not until he's put on a pot of coffee and eaten half a piece of toast that he realizes the horrifying truth: he didn't avoid a hangover. When he woke up, he was still drunk. Now, with the bread churning in his stomach and sweat breaking out on his back, he feels every sip of whisky with painful acuity. The room wobbles, saliva fills his mouth. He turns off the coffee, grabs a Polar Seltzer out of the fridge, and heads right back to bed.

And that's where he stays for the next six excruciating hours. He manages to text Ingrid that he won't be getting his car until later. She seems to be in a similar state, responding with a succinct:

Who cares life is meaningless I'm never drinking scotch again

While the hangover is miserable, it's not as bad as having to stew in his thoughts all day with nothing to distract him except Maggie's horrible blog. When he's done sifting through as many posts as he can stand, learning little beyond what he already knew, his focus turns inward. He agonizes over his behavior at the dinner party, combing through everything he said to find flaws. Before long, he's convinced everyone hates him. Worse, he can't stop replaying his conversation with Jasper. It had been going so well until it wasn't.

Jasper's words were eviscerating, stabbing at the sensitive underbelly of Liam's fears about himself. And Liam can't even blame Jasper. In fact, he agrees with him.

He *is* a coward. He's known it for years. Maybe he's been using Makoto's death as an excuse to avoid the Nether. He doesn't want to be that person. He doesn't want Jasper to think he's that person, and he doesn't want more people to die.

He doesn't know why he's been so stubborn about helping Jasper regain his memories. It's not like he's doing anything else with his time, and he should love an opportunity to do some research. This is a chance to redeem himself. Perhaps there's some karmic absolution in helping Jasper reclaim himself from the same place that claimed Makoto. Maybe, if he does this, Jasper will be able to move on to another plane. Though the concept of the Other is just that—a concept. Liam has seen enough to believe that souls go *somewhere* when their bodies die, somewhere better than a Fluke-infested collage of trauma. If the Nether exists, why can't the Other?

By midday, Liam gathers enough resolve to launch an effort to communicate with Jasper. Though he'd told Jasper to get out of his Phren the night before, he can still sense him, hiding deep inside. He's annoyed by that until he realizes he can't blame anyone for evading the Nether.

He puts on some classical music and meditates, sitting cross-legged on the floor in front of his fireplace. He inverts his focus, looking inside himself. The real O'Connor House fades as the one formed by his mind takes shape.

Liam can see the effect of his hangover on his Phren; the walls are soggy, glistening in burning, bright morning light. There's a musty smell and the floor is sticky. He rides out a wave of shame before beginning his search.

He takes his time checking each room and closet, letting Jasper's aura draw him like a dowsing rod to water. He finds him in the last place he thinks to look: the tower. As Liam climbs the spiral stairs, Jasper's soul radiates distaste. When he reaches for the latch to open the trapdoor in the low ceiling, the presence shoves back, keeping it shut. Liam pushes at it, over and over until a pompous English voice reverberates:

    Desist! I wish to be left alone.

    I just want to apologize.

    Leave.

Liam recoils, defeated. He blinks away the world of his Phren, coming back into his body and the present. The air conditioner in the window is battling nobly with midday summer sun. Dust floats in the light. Warm air wafts out of the fireplace.

He recedes into his bedroom and pities himself into a nap. He doesn't dream. When he wakes, he's able to shower and eat a bowl of instant ramen. The hangover has begun receding, but the shame remains. A slight nudge at Jasper's presence yields another rebuff.

He pulls on jeans and a T-shirt, calls an Uber, and retrieves his car from Ingrid's, grateful that he doesn't feel obligated to socialize with her, before returning home. The house is more solitary than before. It's confining. He attempts to unpack more boxes but quits when a few waves of nausea roll over him and he's sweaty enough to merit a second shower.

Now that he's pinpointed Jasper's presence in his mind, he notices how little it moves. He wonders if Jasper's been camping out in there, avoiding the Nether. The invasion doesn't bother him as much as it should. Jasper doesn't poke around or change anything. He just … hides.

Liam indulges in a delivery order from Domino's that night, slaying the last of his hangover via processed cheese and too many (never enough) sides of ranch. Despite doing nothing all day, he's exhausted when he crawls into bed. Still, it takes him a while to fall asleep. He's nervous to talk to Jasper, and for what he's planning to do.

"Please let me in," Liam says, staring up at the trapdoor to the tower. He braces a foot on the ladder.

"No, thank you." Jasper's voice is muffled, though no less cutting.

Liam sighs. "You can't keep me locked out of part of my own mind."

"Apparently, it seems I can."

"Jasper, come on."

There's a long pause. Jasper must know that Liam could force his way in if he wanted to. He won't, though, as a gesture.

The latch turns and the door swings open, clattering onto the floor. Liam climbs up the ladder and into the round tower room. Jasper is facing away from him, staring out a window into darkness. A yellow jacket flies down from the ceiling and buzzes past Liam's head. He ducks, and quickly banishes it.

"You know, I wasn't allowed up here as a kid. I snuck in once and got stung by a yellow jacket."

"Perhaps you shouldn't have disobeyed."

Liam rubs a hand through his hair. "Will you look at me?"

Jasper doesn't budge.

"Christ, you're stubborn. I'm trying to apologize, here." Liam plops down on the floor, a cloud of dust billowing around him. He crosses his legs.

"I prefer action over words. Unless you've come here to dedicate yourself to bringing this murderer to justice, then I have nothing more to say to you."

"Funny you should mention that," Liam says. "Because I came here to make you one hell of an offer."

Jasper cants his head, looking over his shoulder at Liam with narrowed eyes. It's a remarkable impression of Kermit, right down to the black hair. "Elaborate."

"I can't believe I'm about to say this but," Liam takes a deep breath, shaking his head, "let's go into the Nether tonight."

Jasper doesn't react for a moment. The yellow jacket reappears, diving for Liam's neck. He banishes it again, swearing under his breath. Jasper turns to fully face him. "You're serious."

"As a funeral. My own, probably. You were right—we need clues and the Nether is the best place to find them. Though let me be clear: this is a one-time offer. And we take my lead. I'm not gonna to do anything I'm not comfortable with. For whatever reason, I'm putting a ridiculous amount of trust in you. Blame it on the Hitch link."

"You have no reason to suspect my motivations," Jasper says.

Liam brushes the dust off his hands and heaves to his feet. He meets Jasper's eyes, then looks away. "You know why I don't want to go back there."

Jasper heard his entire conversation with Cedra and Ingrid; he knows Liam's fears. And if he's been holing up in Liam's mind, then he knows some of his history. He implied as much the night before.

"I think I may understand better than anyone in your acquaintance," Jasper says. Liam chances a glance up at him. "Surely, you know my reasons for hiding here in your Phren instead of returning to the Nether as you demanded."

"I haven't asked you to leave, have I?"

Jasper frowns. "No, you have not. What I mean to say is: yes, I do understand, and I sympathize. But the horror of the Nether and what it does to human souls is precisely why we must work together to stop this individual. No one should be forced into the Nether. I wouldn't wish it on anyone."

"Not even me?" Liam raises his eyebrows.

Jasper's expression is shielded. "I would never force you into entering the Nether, though I reserve my right to disapprove of your choices. Whether or not you value my approval is at your discretion."

"That's fair."

"Then we are in agreement."

Liam nods. He takes a couple steps closer to Jasper and is surprised when he doesn't recede. "Does this mean you forgive me? Or maybe see me as less of a coward? Just a little bit?"

Gray eyes narrow. "I am undecided."

Liam rolls his eyes. "Stubborn as hell."

Liam turns and climbs down the ladder. Jasper follows. As they make their way through the hall and back downstairs, Liam has the dawning realization that he isn't exactly sure where he's going. He's moving with purpose. He knows he's drawing closer to his own personal door to the Nether, but he'd never truly contemplated the nature of it before. It was always intuitive more than physical.

For common Sophonts, the Nether is only accessible through a Host's Fissure. They don't encounter the Nether until their first Fluke case. And they never go inside. What makes Liam different—what makes him a Trypanon—is that he has a permanent door to the Nether inside his own mind. Technically, this door is a Fissure, but it's one that is completely under Liam's control. He can use it, seal it, and reopen it as he pleases. Nothing comes in without his permission.

Well, nothing except Jasper. He hasn't allowed himself to fully comprehend the implications of a Trypanon having a Hitch. He's never heard of it happening before.

He keeps moving, with Jasper just a step behind him. They're down the stairs and out the back door—then walking across the lawn. The grass is cool on his feet. It's turquoise in the moonlight. He's ankle deep in salt water before he realizes where he's going.

The island. The light.

He stops. Jasper almost crashes into his back.

"My Nether door is on the island," Liam whispers.

"Obviously."

"I never really thought about it. I just … felt my way there. This is the first time I've made this path so … material, I guess?"

"I see."

"I wonder if there's something here. This is the island you died on, and the light I imagined came from your pocket watch. Could this have something to do with you being my Hitch?"

Liam turns to look at him. Jasper shrugs. "I know only what you know. I have no theories on why we are connected. It's one of the mysteries I'm hoping to illuminate through our investigation."

"Right."

"I suppose it's possible that you're producing this visual in response to my presence. It only presented after you learned of my history. And after you stole my watch."

"I didn't steal it. I *found* it."

"Convenient semantics."

Liam frowns. He continues on the path to the island, but he's unsettled. He feels as though he's missing something crucial. He doesn't admit to Jasper that he'd been seeing the light and smelling the low tide long before he came to Shoalport. Liam had been hoping that his connection to Jasper was only formed recently. But even now, with Jasper in his mind, he senses the attachment has always been there.

It's a conversation for later.

They reach the island's shores. A thin, clear incision cuts up the fabric of his Phren, right through the center of the island. It's as if the world is a canvas, torn by a frustrated artist. He feels the Nether push against the seam, eager. Liam shivers, fighting the craving to turn away and never approach this door again. He glances at Jasper and finds him staring back with narrowed eyes, as if he's waiting for Liam to disappoint him.

Liam rallies. He cannot tie a tether here, as much as he wants to. He could never figure out how. When he was growing up at the Academy, Liam taught himself everything he knows involving the Nether, with Archer fumbling to coach him. There was only one other Trypanon on the continent when Liam was young, and she was locked in a high security Canadian prison. Liam couldn't exactly ask her for guidance.

Since he had no mentor, it took years for Liam to understand his relationship to the Nether. When Liam first started opening his door, he didn't realize he was doing it. At the Academy, his dreams grew dark and complex. He'd wake up covered in sweat, with a patch of newly colored hair on his head and memories that weren't his own. He was absorbing stains from the Nether, but to him, they were merely nightmares. Archer had suspicions, but it wasn't until he developed a fear of the Academy's North Tower that they were confirmed.

There had been a hushed suicide a decade before, when a student tied an extension cord around her neck and jumped out of the tower's highest window. Liam knew details about it that no one could possibly know except a few staff members and a retired janitor. That was when his private lessons began. Archer trained Liam to control his back door to the Nether, to keep it sealed even while he was sleeping. He was constantly fighting with an intrinsic, ineffable desire to open it, as if something was calling him from the other side.

He wonders now if that call was Jasper.

He shakes off the thought and centers himself, clearing his thoughts of anything extraneous or troubling. The Nether will feed on the baggage he takes with him.

Then, drawing on power deep within, he pulls, and the seam of the Nether door splits, revealing the grim world beyond.

"I despise going back," Jasper says. When Liam looks at him, he finds his gaze turned inward, lost in memories. "I could forget what you've helped me remember."

"As long as I remember, I think you'll hold onto it."

Jasper nods.

Liam is about to move when a thought makes him pause. "When you come into my Phren," he says, "do you open this door yourself? Or do I, like, subconsciously open it for you?"

"I'm not certain. Since you stole my watch, I always simply enter."

"I didn't steal—well anyway, we'll have to talk about that later. Ready, then?"

"I suppose."

"Hey, this was your idea."

"Thank you for reminding me."

With one last breath, in unison, they step through the tear.

At first, the Nether looks no different than Liam's Phren. They're standing on the same island. The water and distant trees are silver with moonlight, the tide low and calm. But Liam feels the perversion. His senses switch, as they do when a Fissure is nearby. He hears the scent of salt and decay, tastes the sound of lapping water. There's a sinister energy soaking the shadows. Everything here is dead.

Including the man standing next to him. Jasper's eyes are wide and dilated, darting back and forth. His fists are clenched, his shoulders bunched nearly up to his ears.

"You alright?" Liam says.

"I do not like this island."

"Why—oh."

Liam catches sight of something in the shallows beyond Jasper: a crooked shape half-buried in soggy sand. There's a white tuft of fabric standing out in the moonlight. It takes Liam a moment to realize it's an ascot.

"It's just a memory," he says. "Like … an echo. It's not real."

"Don't be a fool. Your pity is useless when you couple it with inanity. The Nether is more real to me now than you are."

Though he doesn't appreciate the choice of words, Liam can't argue with him; the Nether is as dangerous as the Waking World. By its very nature it convinces a trespasser of its veracity. It's powerful and unpredictable, full of pitfalls and mazes. There are no rules. Space and time warp and change. It knows what it wants. It manipulates to get it.

A shape undulates in the water about twenty feet away. Across the water, a distant tree splits with a resounding crack. Then it reforms, sways, and cracks again. A ragged boat drifts by with a white arm hanging off the side, fingertips grazing the surface of the water.

"We should check out the Knox House."

At Liam's words, the world around them jerks with a woosh. One moment they're standing on the island, and then, with a single step, they're across the river. The Knox House looms above them, lit by orange twilight. It's raining, though the sun is out and there isn't a cloud in sight.

"Jesus, I'll never get used to that," Liam says riding out a surge of nausea.

"Likewise."

It occurs to him that this is the first time he's explored the Nether with another person. He's never been able to talk about the Nether with someone who understood, let alone experience it with them. It makes it all a bit less desolate.

Liam looks around for anything that stands out from the Waking World. It strikes him first that all the plants he can see are dead. There's not one green blade of grass. Everything is tan and crisp with dry decay. Liam looks at Jasper. There's resignation in his eyes.

"I'm sorry," Liam says. "This kinda feels like a personal 'fuck you' from the Nether, killing all the plants like this."

"I haven't seen living plants in a long time."

"Could you see them through me? Like, when you're in my mind and I'm walking around?"

Jasper looks at him. A small smile curls the corner of his lips. "Not until yesterday."

"Have you been in there?" Liam points at the Knox House. "Since you came to the Nether?"

Jasper tilts his head to the side, brow furrowing in thought. "Up until recently I had no thoughts, no concept of my actions. I simply existed. But I remember now." He points a long finger up at the window to his bedroom. "I vaguely recall entering my old room, and of lighting a candle in the window. I'm not sure what led me to do it. It wasn't long ago, though it's hard to be certain when that occurred. Time is fluid here."

"The night Maggie died," Liam whispers. Jasper nods once.

And the world around them contorts again. A rush of wind circles them, breaking off blades of dead grass in a tan whirlwind. They're staring up at the Knox House, then they're inside a building.

Around them, yellowed walls rise and click into place. An inverted cross hangs above a bed. Liam doesn't realize what he's seeing at first. It's the smell that reveals it to him: tequila and sickly sweet. "What the hell," Liam whispers. "This is—"

"Maggie Short's Phren. But how could it be in the Nether? It was my understanding that a Phren is left behind in the body and only the soul crosses over. Is that not why you could enter it in the morgue?"

"Yeah, this can't be her Phren. Something is wrong."

The sheetrock rattles and cracks. An inchoate hissing rises, cresting into a deafening screech. Large books drop from the ceiling. Liam and Jasper barely dodge out of the way, with Liam just missing taking one to the head. He catches sight of the cover: a tattered modern copy of the Bible with a childish drawing of baby Jesus on the front.

A crackling static joins the cacophony, emanating from large speakers in the high corners of the chapel. The bed begins to whine, as if someone is jumping on the old springs, though it doesn't move.

"Let's get out of here," Liam yells. He reaches for Jasper.

Look what you did to my pretty feet

The wall splits. Sheetrock and chunks of brick spill across the floor. The bed flips, careening across the room. Liam stumbles back, reaching to grab Jasper's shirt sleeve, but Jasper pulls his arm away.

A deranged, stout shape emerges from the fresh crack in the wall. Maggie is hardly recognizable. She's naked, her skin sagging where the white worms of the Fluke carved their tunnels. Her feet are bloated with sepsis, pustules splattering white paste with each lumbering step. Her joints are contorted like a broken toy doll.

"Fuck, that's one of the worst Wicks I've ever seen," Liam shouts to Jasper, face scrunching up. The scent of her fetid feet fills the room. "Jesus Chr—"

Jasper begins to respond when a shrill voice cuts him off.

Never take the Lord's name in vain, sinner. Fall to your knees.

The Wick of Maggie Short crumples to the ground, curling prostrate in the sheetrock dust. The voice echoes. The words change with each reverberation, though the theme remains the same: harsh religious castigation. The voice becomes two, then three. Soon there's a jury of gossipers, all directing their judgment upon Maggie, multiplying into infinity. Figures move in the shadows.

Did you see the way she behaved? What would the pastor say?

Never married. Was that God's plan for her? Or do you think she's hiding something sinful?

I always thought she was a dyke.

What would her mother say?

Always in everyone else's business, passing judgement. But what of God's judgement?

She acts like no one knows she's high. Everyone knows. You can't hide from us. You can't hide from God.

She was drunk at yesterday's sermon. What an embarrassment.

You almost wish a Fluke would teach her a lesson. All that vice …

Liam has witnessed this only once before. Most of the Wicks he's seen in his time as a Wedge were empty husks, totally devoid of memory or personality, wandering aimlessly through the tapestry of the Nether. Samantha Munn's husband was a rare exception, but he was powered by a Hitch link.

Maggie is different. She's locked in a prison of memory and torment, not of her own making or the Nether's. Liam senses a power much like his own. This is a controlled, created space, as complex and intricate as his own Phren.

A Trypanon built this.

Crouching down, he takes a few cautious steps toward Maggie.

"Maggie," he yells above the panoply of hissing whispers. "This isn't real. You need to leave this place. It can't hold you."

Maggie's head twitches on her neck like a bobblehead. One of her swollen eyes swivels in the socket and locks on him.

"The voices aren't real," Liam says. "I can prove it to you."

Liam hasn't done this since Iris. He never told anyone he could alter the Nether to his will, just as he alters his own Phren. He can't imagine what Archer or Makoto's reactions would have been if they knew.

It was a power he's witnessed in only one other:

Iris.

But Maggie's torment is unacceptable to Liam, no matter how little he liked her. To imprison her in never-ending agony, to wrap a Wick in corrupted memory, is unspeakable. It would be better if she felt nothing. There's intent here. Retribution. When Iris did this, he was enacting his own warped perception of justice upon those he deemed evil. There's a similar self-righteousness here, but also a flavor of bitterness and maliciousness that Iris didn't have. This is personal. Maggie knew this Trypanon. But how?

Liam harnesses his power. He holds it like a grenade, taking one last look at Jasper before he detonates. He feels stronger than before. Perhaps because he's not alone. Or maybe it's that he feels Jasper's energy, charging him the same way Samantha did to her husband. Jasper's eyes are wide, his lips parted.

He'll look at Liam differently after this.

In one single flourish, Liam wipes their surroundings clean. He imagines a sterile, caustic world, and makes it happen. The walls, the cross, the dirty carpet all strip down and cleanse, becoming new again. The smell of rotten flesh and sickly sweet is cauterized by bleach and synthetic lemon. He fills the room with light, giving it a holy essence. Maggie will respond to that. He wants what's left of her to see this as a purification, a baptism. He wants it to make her feel free.

Liam tumbles to the ground, hands splaying on the clean carpeted floor. He feels wrung out like never before. He doesn't want to see Jasper's expression. He looks at Maggie's Wick instead.

And is stunned. Around her, an alabaster glow, stark even against the light Liam concocted. It reminds him of a spotlight. Or a halo. Her flesh melts away, pooling on the floor in a pink puddle. Then evaporates. In the space where she had been, more light. It diffuses into the floor. And then, with a pop, disappears.

With Iris, Liam couldn't free the Wicks. He could destroy the prison, but the Wicks would continue to wander the Nether in their torment. Maggie has simply dissolved. No—*crossed over.*

Did she pass into the Other?

With a grunt, Liam pushes to his feet. He brushes the sheetrock dust off his clothes and turns to face Jasper. "Well, I guess you know my little secret now," he says. His shoulders feel heavy.

"Which secret is that?"

Liam meets Jasper's eyes, expecting to find derision, even fear. Jasper stares back with a cool neutrality.

"The whole bending the Nether to my will thing," Liam says, frowning. "It's pretty dark stuff."

"I assumed you had powers that I was not aware of. It's logical that this would be one of them."

Liam shakes his head. "If you understood what this means about me, you'd never talk to me again, no matter how much you want to save people," he says.

"Save people as you have just done, you mean?"

Liam opens his mouth to reply. He shuts it again. Jasper leans down and picks up a shred of paper off the floor.

"A bit of Corinthians," he says. "I never much enjoyed the Bible." He flicks the paper away. "If this power of yours is seen as frightening, then it's because it has not been wielded by a moral man. You have just used it to free a Wick. It's the opposite of what our killer is doing. I have no reason to sever communications. You're doing what I requested of you. Finally."

Liam blinks. He still can't find words.

"Now, what should we explore next? Perhaps we should return to my house," Jasper says.

Liam clears his throat, unsticking his thoughts. It takes him a moment to shift his focus back to the case. "I have to call it a night. I want to unpack what just happened, and frankly, I'm fucking drained after this shit."

Jasper's brow furrows. Liam feels his irritation spike.

"But we have not gathered nearly as many clues as I'd hoped."

"I get that, but I'm done here, and I told you that I call the shots. That was the deal."

Jasper puffs up like a bird, a prickly aura misting around him.

Liam rolls his eyes and throws his hands up. "Fine, we can come back here again if the leads we got don't pan out, okay?"

Liam watches as Jasper absorbs his words, slowly softening into acceptance. He offers a short nod.

Liam uses what remains of his energy to imagine the island, with its damp, sandy shores and dead tree, and the door back to Liam's Phren. The world stutters, trembling, before it shifts, bringing them to the island once again. It's dark. Liam catches how Jasper's back tenses. With the very last of his energy, Liam banishes the corpse on the thin beach. Jasper glances at him. He doesn't say "thank you."

Liam reopens the door, and they step through. Once they make their way back to the living room of Liam's Phren, Jasper takes a seat in his usual armchair close to Kermit. Liam collapses onto the couch, and covers his eyes with his forearm. He feels a headache building.

"You are exhausted," Jasper says. Liam moves his arm aside enough to look at him with one eye. Jasper's looking around the room. "I can feel it."

"I'm not as lazy as you think I am, you know. It's not every day that I save a Wick from a Nether prison. And I didn't even like Maggie."

"You did it because it was the right thing to do."

"I guess."

"You said 'prison.' Am I to understand our Trypanon engineered a kind of cell for their victim?"

"Yeah, like a handcrafted fun house of torture and bad memories. Takes a lot of power to do that."

"Power that you also possess."

Liam rubs at his eyes, pushing out a breath through his nose. "This is why I never told anyone I could do that."

"Again, you used your power to do the right thing. Power in itself is not immoral, only the manner in which it is wielded. I see no need to discuss the subject further."

"I … okay."

"More relevantly, I am curious about Maggie's relationship to the local church."

Liam sighs, pushing up on his elbows. He conjures a pillow behind his back and nestles against it. "Yeah, I think there might be something there. Whoever made that prison had to know Maggie. They knew she was a religious nut with some major insecurities. That all felt pretty damn personal. And this isn't the first time we've heard a victim use religious jargon."

"Perhaps it was a fellow parishioner. Or the pastor she mentioned."

"I'll scope out the church tomorrow."

Jasper nods. Liam gets the sense he's contemplating whether to say something. He waits.

"What is the nature of our connection?" Jasper says at last. He takes a breath. "You found my pocket watch. When did I start visiting your dreams?"

Liam stares at him. "The night after I found the pocket watch."

"Maybe finding it opened that door in your mind to me."

"I guess it's possible. I have no reference for this shit. Hitches are rare as hell, and on top of that I'm a Trypanon. There are no guidebooks about this. I know about as much as you do."

"But logically …"

Liam rakes a hand through his hair. "Yeah, I guess logically you and I had some sort of dormant connection, and when I found that pocket watch it, I dunno, *activated* it. You said it yourself: the more I learn about you, the more of yourself you get back. Maybe that's part of my Tryp powers. Maybe I'm building you like I build my own Phren."

"Or it's analogous to your ability to create your own reality in the Nether."

Liam frowns. When he speaks, it's barely a whisper: "You're saying it's possible that I'm manifesting you."

Jasper suddenly directs his attention to his sleeves, peeling off imaginary bits of lint and straightening the already-straight cuffs. "I'm not ruling out the possibility, but I certainly don't think we have enough evidence to draw that conclusion yet. And if I may, I do not *feel* like a creation of your subconscious."

Liam hopes he's right. If Liam is pulling Wicks out of the Nether and pumping them full of life and personality, then they have much more to worry about than a murderer.

"I may have seen you before the pocket watch," he confesses. Jasper looks at him. "I think I've sensed you in the Nether before. And, when you lit a candle in your old room, I saw it; it was the night Maggie died. It's not the only time. But you already knew that, didn't you."

"To an extent," Jasper says. Liam waits for him to go on. Jasper changes the subject instead. "When you visit the church tomorrow, I am going to attempt to hone my skills at communicating with you."

Liam sighs.

"Is that," Jasper swallows, "agreeable to you?"

Liam looks at him. His eyes are blank, but there's a tint of pink on his cheeks. Liam smiles. "It's agreeable. I'm gonna take the rest of the night to rest, but I'll see you tomorrow?"

Jasper nods, then blinks out of existence. Still, Liam feels him in the tower again.

Liam takes the rest of the night to mediate, drifting with his eyes closed in his own Phren. He welcomes the darkness. His insides feel gutted, but he's not as cold as he normally is after he visits the Nether. Instead, he feels connected. To Cedra and Ingrid.

And to Jasper.

CHAPTER ELEVEN

HOUSE OF GOD

LIAM DOES NOT like churches.

As he waits in the massive lobby of the duly massive church, he feels like a fussy kid in a pew again. He feels the ghost of his grandmother's scornful gaze on the side of his face, can smell her miasma of floral perfume. He twitches and sniffs, rubbing his nose.

The bad mural of the donkey on the wall is familiar; he'd seen it in Maggie's Phren. He frowns at it from where he sits on a crunchy blue chair. He shifts on his ass, wincing at the crinkling plastic. It's as if churches aim to make everyone uncomfortable. Maybe it makes people more likely to crave salvation. Or sacramental wine.

He turns his gaze from the deformed donkey to a large portrait painting of a man with stern eyes and crevices of wrinkles. "Our Devoted Shepard, Pastor Douglas Gartlett. Born 1933—Died 2015. May angels carry him home!" is scribed on a gold plaque below the frame. Liam tries not to fidget.

"She should be with you shortly," says the woman with a butter-yellow smile, startling him. She sits beneath the portrait at an overlarge reception desk made of tan, fake wood.

"Thanks."

When he called that morning, she treated him like a solicitor and claimed he had no chance of meeting the illustrious Pastor when he wasn't even a member of the church. She didn't budge until he dropped the law enforcement card. After some needling, he learned Pastor Gartlett—aka "creepy portrait guy"—had apparently retired years before and died of a stroke shortly after.

Pastor Riverton would be the one meeting with him.

He's contemplating the creative liberties taken with the donkey's unnatural anatomy when Jasper's voice cuts through his thoughts.

>*Perhaps this Riverton is the pastor spoken of in Maggie's Phren. If not, surely Riverton will know something of Gartlett. It's a lead worth pursuing.*

>*Jesus—you scared the crap out of me.*

>*I told you I'd be attempting to communicate with you verbally today.*

>*Yeah, I just didn't think you'd be this good at it already.*

>*It's a more intuitive mechanism than I had anticipated. And it feels easier today.*

"You must be Liam."

Liam jumps. A young woman with thick, black-rimmed glasses, a sharp gray blazer, and orange Converse All Stars stands in front of him. Liam blinks up at her.

"Didn't mean to scare you. You looked like you were a mile away," she says. "Pastor Riverton." She reaches out and Liam takes her hand.

"I'm Liam O'Connor."

"Didn't think we'd have a celebrity in our midst."

"Wait, you're *that* Liam O'Connor?" blurts the woman at the desk. Her eyes take on a familiar, hungry sparkle. "Meaning like ... *Calico?*"

>*Disturbing.*

Liam twitches.

"Yeah," he mutters.

"Oh my gosh, why didn't you say so? I read *all* about you." Her tone is sharp at the edges, heavy with implication. He wonders if she's a *Mouth of the Port* fan too. "Can I get a selfie with you?"

"I'm sure Liam is flattered, Barbara, but he's on the clock right now. Let's not waste any of his time. Liam—care to follow me to my office?"

>*Figures her name is Barbara.* He doesn't mean to say it to Jasper.

The response is immediate. *In Greek it means "strange."*

Liam snorts and Riverton raises an eyebrow. She turns, leading him out of the lobby and down a familiar hall. He sweats as they approach the door to the chapel.

>*Why are you so disquieted?*

>*I don't like churches. My parents weren't into this God shit but it was like crack for my grandparents. They always made me go to Mass in the summers. Was just never for me. I hated it.*

>*As did I.*

Riverton pushes open the heavy double doors and gestures for Liam to go inside. He swallows hard as he steps over the threshold.

The chapel is similar to Maggie's Phren, though much cleaner and less like a horror movie. There's no inverted cross hanging from the wall, rotten sheetrock, or ominous old bed, though the room possesses the same 1970s style. The chairs are metal with thin gray cushions. The walls have a few framed prints of religious art. The pulpit is modern and drab; the carpet, industrial. A large wall vent pumps frigid air into the room.

"Not exactly the Sistine Chapel," Riverton says, startling him. When he turns to look at her, the Nether shoves at him; a Bible falls from the ceiling with a thud.

It's concerning how often you see the Nether when you are awake.

Liam pretends not to hear him.

"You don't like houses of worship, do you, Liam?"

There's no point in lying. "Not really my thing."

Riverton shrugs. "I can't say they're my favorite either. I'd much rather conduct services outside. Who wants this air-conditioned, sterile crap when God made us a beach? Anyway, my office is back there."

Liam shivers when he realizes where she's leading him. He feels Jasper examining his thoughts.

Despite the bits of the Nether sneaking by, Riverton's office is far less nightmarish than Maggie's Fluke-warped version of it. There are houseplants and trinkets from various cultures. The walls are covered with pictures from all over the world, usually featuring Riverton giving a thumbs-up with an epic foreign landscape in the background.

She owns a healthy Monstera deliciosa, Jasper says. Her areca palm needs more consistent misting, however. And ... oh, my. Is that an orchid? In a north-facing window? It'll be dead within a fortnight.

Liam clenches his teeth. *You're not helping.*

I'm merely being observant.

You're being annoying.

"I like to travel," Riverton says, pulling his focus back into the room. She gestures to the photos on the wall. "Not on missionary work, just for fun," she adds when he raises an eyebrow. Liam witnessed some shady church business abroad. He has the tact not to mention it.

"Take a seat." Riverton gestures to a green velvet couch under the windowsill as she sinks into an armchair. Her couch is vastly preferrable to the plastic-stuffed chairs in the lobby. "So, I'm guessing you're here to talk about Maggie Short."

Liam blinks. He folds his hands on his lap. "She was a parishioner of yours," he says.

"She was. Or rather one I inherited."

"From Pastor Gartlett."

"That's right. I'm sorry to hear about Maggie. She's been a dedicated member of the church her whole life. I know she shared a close relationship with Pastor Gartlett. Her and I never had time to … acclimatize to each other."

Liam senses a veiled opinion buzzing below the surface. "Did you know the late pastor?"

"Only a little. Him and I had a … difference of approach. I prefer the tenets of open-mindedness and acceptance. Diversity. Evolution is key to the survival of all things, religion included. Gartlett was more traditionalist."

"So, he was a Bible thumper."

Riverton shrugs a shoulder. "You could say that. I know he had an extensive resumé of missionary work."

Liam nods, receiving the message. "And do you know anything about his relationship to Maggie?"

Riverton wipes invisible dust off the table beside her. She seems to be selecting her words like fruit at a marketplace. "Maggie had some objections to my style of worship. I gleaned a bit of her relationship to Gartlett through her issues with me. I think …" She adjusts in her seat. "I think Gartlett valued a certain kind of social currency. Maggie could provide it."

"Gossip, you mean."

"She certainly knew everyone's dirty laundry. I think it made her feel powerful, and from what I gather, Gartlett did nothing to dissuade her from that notion. I have no tolerance for gossip. If people care to share something with me or seek guidance, I'm happy to help. I have no interest in gathering private details without someone's consent."

"So she was no fan of yours," Liam says.

Riverton could be a suspect, Jasper says.

I doubt it. Maggie wasn't a problem for her. If anything, Maggie would be the one with the motive.

Perhaps. Maggie was hardly making her life easy.

I don't think Maggie made anyone's life easy.

Except Gartlett's, it would seem.

"From what I gather, she was no fan of you either." She offers Liam a wry grin.

"Guess you've read her blog, then," Liam says.

"And the Facebook posts. Maggie didn't like being snubbed. I think people like her try to collect secrets and use them as a shield. Or perhaps a smoke screen. She was protecting herself from her own shame."

"You sound like a therapist."

"I've worn many hats."

Ask her about Maggie's family. I believe she mentioned a mother.

"Do you know anything about Maggie's family?"

"She has a younger brother and an older sister that live in Tucson. Her father hasn't been in the picture for a long time and her mother is in a nursing home out near Maggie's siblings. I asked her once if she planned on visiting and she said she was 'too busy' working on her blog. Said her followers were counting on her. I gather there's been estrangement there for a while. I only know about her siblings because they're well-liked around here. People bring them up a lot. Her brother was valedictorian at the high school and her sister was an all-star swimmer. Maggie never wanted to discuss them. Perhaps she felt overshadowed."

"Classic middle child."

"You could say that."

I was content with being my parents' only child.

Yeah, same.

"I should mention, though I'm guessing you already know," Riverton says. "Maggie had a substance misuse issue. It wasn't exactly a secret, though she liked to believe it was. I had to take her aside after a sermon or a group to address her behavior a few times. She always carried a pink water bottle around."

"Maybe she was just committed to being hydrated." Liam smirks.

Your jokes are strange.

Gee, thanks.

"While I don't like the rumor mill, it can be impossible to avoid," Riverton says, shrugging. "I heard she had a Vice Fluke attack her."

"You heard right."

Riverton licks her lips, as if taste-testing her next words before serving them. "May I ask why one of the best Wedges in the world would need to be consulted on a Red Fluke case? Is it because they rarely kill their Hosts?"

Liam leans back on the couch. "You seem to know more about Flukes than a layman."

"As I said, many hats."

She's definitely got a psych background, he says to Jasper. *Probably worked with some Hosts on aftercare.*

If only she afforded that level of attention to her orchid.

Liam barely suppresses an eye roll. "What about Oliver Fenton?" Liam says. "Did you know him at all?"

"I know his mother. She's a member of the church." She pauses. "I was sorry to hear about Oliver. Apparently, he used to accompany Angelica to service, but he stopped before I came along. Angelica is very … how do I say this? She's intense."

"Intense?"

"I want my parishioners to be passionate, don't get me wrong. If I weren't also passionate about this, I wouldn't be a pastor. But Angelica approaches it like she's looking to get something. Or at least she did; I haven't seen her since Oliver passed away."

"What do you think she was trying to get?"

"I think she wanted Oliver back. She was upset he moved out. I think she saw it as an abandonment. Her husband—Oliver's father—left her a long time ago too."

Could Angelica be a suspect? Jasper says.

Mhmm. Maybe she was pissed at Oliver for leaving her and she wanted to punish him. Don't see a connection to Maggie or Jake and Phoebe yet, though.

"Did Angelica and Maggie have a relationship at all?" Liam says.

Riverton crosses her arms over her chest. "You know, years back, in my first gig as a pastor out in California, one of my parishioners was murdered."

"Oh?"

"The police came and asked me questions about who the victim might have known in the church, looking for suspects. They talked to me just as you're talking to me now."

Liam chooses not to respond. She seems to take that as a response in itself.

"If you're asking me if there was motive for Angelica to, let's say *inspire* Maggie or Oliver to be attacked by a Fluke, then it's not something I witnessed. Like I said, I avoid gossip. But you'd be hard-pressed to find someone who didn't have an issue with Maggie. She collected dirt on everyone, friend or foe, and used it when she could. As for Angelica, I don't know the details of her relationship with her son. But I do know that all she wanted was for him to come home, and eventually he did, and she was happy again. I think she was much more interested in keeping Oliver close than losing him to a Fluke. But I suggest you ask her yourself. Here, I'll give you her contact information."

She goes to a laptop on her desk and copies an address and phone number onto a Post-it note. "Is there anything else?" she asks as she passes him the paper.

    Ask about Phoebe and —

    I was about to.

"Did you know Phoebe and Jake Shelton at all?"

"Not personally."

"I see. What about impersonally?"

"I only know of them because of the recent accident."

    Sounds suspicious.

Liam reaches out, tentative, feeling for the edges of her Phren …

And finds a wall—a fortress. He's not gleaning anything from her unless he does a full breach, and that wouldn't be ethical. Still, she may simply have boundaries and a strong mind. He gets the sense she has seen a lot, just as he has.

    I believe she could be a suspect, Jasper says, cutting through Liam's thoughts.

    Why?

    You said everyone could be. She is more knowledgeable than a layman regarding Flukes and the like, and she is religious. You said yourself there was a religious element to these cases. Also, she is charismatic.

    That doesn't make her a murderer.

"You haven't asked me about Betsy," Riverton says. Liam isn't sure who she's talking about.

    Jasper cuts in: Betsy Cross is the elderly woman who was injured in the vehicular accident involving Phoebe and Jake Shelton.

    Oh shit, you're right. And just say "car accident." "Vehicular accident" sounds weird.

    Did you not understand what I meant?

    I did, but——

    Then my phrasing was sufficient.

    Stubborn as hell.

"She's my mother," Riverton says. For the first time, the barrier in her eyes slips away. A fragile sadness mists to the surface. "Joley, the little girl, is my niece. That's how I found out about Phoebe and Jake."

"Oh. Shit, I'm sorry, I didn't know. I haven't looked at their files much." Guilt swells. He hadn't thought about the old lady or little girl much since they weren't Fluke victims. Or maybe he was sparing himself from the responsibility.

    Your thoughts are not productive. Don't take accountability for a murderer's misdeeds.

I'll try.

"You know, sometimes you seem to be having a conversation with someone else in your head."

Liam startles like he's been caught passing a note in class. "No, I—ha, yeah, sorry. Was just thinking about the case and … how tragic it is. I'm … you have my condolences. For your mother. I hope she heals up fast. Shit, sorry, that's probably not helpful. And sorry for swearing. I'm in a goddamn church and I'm swearing. Aw fuck. I mean!"

Your eloquence is astounding.

Riverton laughs. "Relax, Liam. I talk to God in my head; I'm hardly going to judge you."

"I am sorry, though. I heard she ran an ice cream truck."

"She did. She's just about the best person I've ever met. She has good people taking care of her though. I have to believe God will take care of her too."

"Yeah, I get that."

"But you don't believe in it."

Liam sighs. "No. Not with what I've seen."

What about the Other? Did we not witness it last night?

Please shut up.

"Fair. You have seen more than most. Maybe more than anyone."

Liam doesn't know what to say.

Ask about the child.

"Is … the girl okay?"

"Not yet, but she will be. It was nice meeting with you, Liam. If you don't have any other questions, I'll have to be on my way. I have a group in about ten minutes, and I need to prepare."

"Thanks for taking the time for me."

Riverton escorts him back to the lobby, courteously barring Barbara from talking to him with a sharp "he needs to be on his way." When Liam's back in his car and on his way home, he reaches out to Jasper:

Still think she's a suspect?

It seems highly unlikely given her mother and niece's involvement. I doubt she'd want to harm them. Her grief seemed genuine.

Yeah, I think the same.

Though it is suspicious that her Phren was closed off to you.

Some people are just like that. Doesn't make them a Trypanon. You're not exactly an open book yourself.

I believe it's wise to err on the side of suspicion.

Fine, but it's okay to rule out suspects. I think we should pay Angelica Fenton a little visit tomorrow.

And explore the Nether again tonight?

Liam can sense Jasper's tentative eagerness.

Fine. But we take my lead again.

As you wish.

A waft of approval fills Liam's Phren.

His phone vibrates. Sloane is calling. Again. He doesn't answer.

CHAPTER TWELVE
MOMMY DEAREST

"**R**EADY?"

Jasper looks up from where he's sitting, hands folded on his lap. He'd been staring at Kermit.

"Of course." Jasper rises from the armchair with elegance and adjusts his waist-coat. Liam finds himself staring. Jasper's starting to look like he belongs in Liam's Phren. It's not an idea he wants to examine. He turns away.

As they take the path to the island in silence. Jasper's posture is rigid, his hands clenched to fists. Liam isn't used to being the one with more composure, but the job feels easier with a partner. He's reminded of when Makoto was first assigned as his Splint.

The door to the Nether hums, eager like a child, as they approach. "You sure you're good?" Liam says. Jasper flinches, then glares at him.

"My disdain for the Nether is precisely why we must proceed, or have you forgotten?"

Liam rolls his eyes. "I was just asking, asshole. Fine, let's go."

With a tug, the door splits open, and, in unison, they pass through it. Liam shivers and tenses as the Nether takes shape around them. The atmosphere has the cloying, heavy weight of the worst day of someone's life. He takes a deep, imaginary breath, and gathers himself.

Their surroundings are both the same and different. The boat with the white hand is beached on a distant shore. The breaking tree is moving at an unnatural, slow speed. The light is cool, like an early winter morning. It's as corrupted as before, yet in a lull now, like a sleeping rabid animal. Anything feels possible. The worst feels inevitable.

"Last time, I wasn't clear what mechanism transported us to Maggie and her prison," Jasper says.

"I think it was me. You know how I can manipulate the Nether? I think I manifested it. I said Maggie's name, so the Nether took us to her."

"We should assume the Trypanon has made prisons for the other victims as well."

"Yeah. Fuck."

Jasper frowns. "I do not understand why they are doing this. Such needless cruelty."

"They must think they're giving these people what they deserve. Like some divine retribution."

"Cruelty is never justice," Jasper says, shaking his head. "We should seek out the other prisons. Perhaps we will catch the Trypanon inside one of them, surveying their work."

"Right, like returning to the scene of the crime to get off. Maybe if I think hard about Oliver, I can reveal something, like—"

With a gust of wet wind, they're thrust off the island and into the air. The river and the forest soar by. They're past roads and a string of houses— spinning, disoriented. Then everything stops with a snap.

"—like that."

Liam shivers, shaking his hands. Jasper adjusts his ascot. Then Jasper gags, his hand flying up to cover his mouth.

"The smell," he grits, muffled. He draws a handkerchief out of his pocket and covers his nose.

As if on cue, the stench hits Liam. He tugs his shirt collar up over his nose, but it does little to shield him. Urine and rotten food and sweat converge. His eyes burn. His senses jumble, each one assaulted by rot.

Their surroundings creep into focus: a house, packed with mountains of junk. Piles upon piles of boxes rise around them. Children's toys lay strewn amongst rusted pans and stained clothes. There are countless old Powerade bottles, half-filled with cloudy yellow liquid.

It's not the first time he's been inside a house like this. Neglect Flukes have a taste for hoarders. They offer the perfect cocktail of paralytic trauma, isolation, and hopelessness—potent Fluke bait. While Liam now understands on a personal level how a mess can get out of control, given the state of his own house, he can't fathom living with maggot-covered food and a broken toilet.

"This is abhorrent," Jasper says, his voice nasally from pinching his nose.

Liam tries not to find it cute.

"No kidding. Uggh, I can't take it. Let's get out of here—"

A cooing sound trickles out from a door at the end of a short hall, slightly ajar. Jasper and Liam freeze.

"Is this another prison?" Jasper whispers.

"I—"

Liam's eyes lock on a tilted framed picture on the wall. In it, Oliver Fenton leans on a cane beside a woman. She looks miniature by comparison. The picture itself sweats, liquid dribbling down the sheetrock below. The woman smiles with large, gray teeth. Her grip on Oliver's arm is too tight.

Jasper comes up beside Liam. "Oliver's Phren was empty when you investigated it, but you felt the echo of objects, didn't you?"

"Yeah. Hey, how'd you know that?"

"Uncertain. Perhaps I sensed it as well."

Liam's foot squelches on something round and moldy. He can only guess it was once a cantaloupe. "Ick, gross. Looks like this is where the mess ended up."

"And that's the room Oliver died in." Jasper points to the door.

Liam clenches his fists. The cooing starts again, followed by the click of a "tsk-tsk."

"I don't wanna go in there," Liam confesses.

"Irrelevant. If Oliver's Wick is trapped in there, you must free him."

"Don't tell me what I have to do," Liam snaps, louder than he means to.

Jasper is silent. Liam cringes. "Sorry," he mumbles. "I sound like a teenager."

"No. I should not dictate orders to you. You stipulated that you would 'call the shots,' and I should have respected that. If you believe the best course of action is to leave, then I won't argue with you."

Liam blinks. "Thanks."

Jasper nods.

Then Liam shakes his head. "But you're right; I have to stop it."

"What's that you say?"

"Huh? I said I have to stop it."

"The first part."

Liam pauses. Then rolls his eyes. "I liked you better when your mouth didn't work."

Box towers teeter as they shuffle between them, making their way to the door across the room. The floor is slippery with mystery liquid, dotted with dead bugs and fluffy patches of mold. The sheer array of detritus piled around them seems to have a pull. Disgust and fascination tap at him like a needy child's fingers. One look wouldn't hurt. Doesn't he want to see? Isn't it gross? Isn't it strange?

"Hey!" he barks at Jasper, who's staring at the petrified corpse of a white cat. There's a nest of rigid kittens beneath her. "Don't dwell on any of it. It's a trap. The Nether wants you to look, so don't."

Jasper nods. He sidles up close behind Liam, though not enough to touch.

They reach the door. Slow, Liam pushes it open. It catches on a few crumpled-up newspapers. He pushes until it flies open, crashing into something against the wall. The room beyond is dark except for a single yellow lamp. They take a few tentative steps over the threshold. The light grows.

On the large, dipping bed is Oliver. He's wearing nothing but white underwear, and it strains against his crusted, bulbous mounds of fat. An absurd collection of medical supplies encircles the bed.

The light from the lamp blacks out, then returns. A figure has crossed in front of it.

Silly little monkey. Have you wet yourself again?

Oliver shudders and moans. He shrinks away from the shadowed figure whenever she draws near. She flutters around him like a moth, periodically swooping in to wipe him with a washcloth.

"Please, no, Mother," Oliver rasps. He tries to get up and can't. "I'm fine. I can take care of myself."

Nonsense. You're still my little boy. My little angel. And look at you. You're filthy. You're Unclean. One of the sinners. But, as a woman of God, it's my mission to save you. Mommy's here. Mommy is going to feed you, cleanse you, baptize you.

Her voice is disembodied. Something about it is off. Liam is reminded of a play he saw once, where an actor performed a dialogue with a recording that played from the speakers. The actor tried to sell it, but it was so obvious to Liam that the recorded voice wasn't live, wasn't reactive. The same disconnect is present here.

"Is that specter meant to be Angelica Fenton? The mother?" Jasper whispers, pointing at the shadow.

"I think so. I knew she was overbearing when Oliver was bedridden, but I didn't know it was this bad. I guess the Nether could be exaggerating it, but still."

"It's torture. To be trapped inside and fawned over, the lack of privacy … of autonomy …"

There's a ghost of memory in Jasper's eyes. Liam thinks of the governess Jasper mentioned, of how he was barely let outside as a child. Liam draws his power to him. He feels a spark—an outlet—from Jasper, from their connection. He pulls on it, absorbs it, lets it charge him like a battery. Around them, the mess begins to collapse out of existence. The windows fly open, sucking out the funk of dust and stench, dousing the room in light. The shade of Angelica Fenton screeches like a rodent. It scurries into the closet where Oliver ate himself to death. Liam dissipates the closet door. Angelica holds up her clawed fingers, dark and immaterial as soot, caught out like a burglar.

Liam takes a step toward her. A clawing surge of anger rises inside him. He hates Angelica, hates the hoard, hates how the mess reminds him of his own house, his own failures. More than anything, though, he hates the Nether. And he wants to make it bend and break. It's all his to purge. He has the power to destroy what deserves to be destroyed. Jasper was right. There's nothing wrong with power. He can use it how he pleases.

The room dyes red. Angelica shudders, whimpering as her form is ripped like a leaf in the wind.

With her gone, Liam turns his attention to Oliver. The form of him is frozen, blinking up at the ceiling. Liam now sees the Fluke-induced holes covering his body. They dilate with each labored breath. His eyes are clouded, his hair like withered straw. He has the bewildered look of someone who thought they'd escaped this life, only to be yanked back into it for no reason other than horrible luck. A Wick should never be this cognizant.

It's cruel beyond measure. He can understand why Maggie would have made enemies, but Oliver never hurt anyone. All he wanted was to escape. It's all Liam has wanted too.

Liam's fingers spread. He feels the power tingling beneath his nails. With one final push, he cleanses the last of the sickness from Oliver's prison.

Exhaustion roils through him, cutting his strings. He collapses to the floor. Jasper's muddy shoes come into his eyeline.

"It's happening again," Jasper says. "The crossing over."

Liam blinks the fuzz from his vision and looks at Oliver. He's coated in that same bright light that had taken Maggie. It fills the holes covering his body, turns him to liquid gold. He melts into the dented mattress. It's impossible to look at, impossible to turn away from. The last of him disappears with a pop.

"It's as though he's been pulled into another realm," Jasper whispers. His eyes are bright, his lips parted.

"I doubt it." Liam shifts onto his rear and holds his head between his knees. His insides itch. He feels as hot and exposed as a sunburn.

"Why?"

"The two *realms* we have are more than enough for me to deal with."

"Whether or not you want to 'deal with' something has no bearing on its existence."

"I'm fucking aware." Liam glares at Jasper and finds him frowning down at him.

"We need to leave," Jasper says. "You look ill."

Liam sighs, sagging. "Yeah, I feel like shit."

Liam uses the last of his energy to transport them back to the island, swaying on his feet when he reopens the door to his Phren. He trips as he climbs through.

"Shit!" he squeaks, reaching out for Jasper as he teeters forward. Jasper dodges out of his grasp and Liam tumbles through the door, landing hard on the other side. He gets a few thin cuts on his palms and knees from broken mussel shells. Again.

"Son a bitch," he growls. "You couldn't have given me a hand?"

"It's not as if you will be hurt in your Waking World."

"Uh, think again, jerk. I wasn't focused so these stupid cuts will be on my body when I wake up. I hope I don't need stitches. My hands just fucking healed."

"You should exercise better focus in the future, then."

Liam grumbles and pushes back to his feet. He doesn't speak to Jasper again until they're in the kitchen of his Phren and he's washing the blood off his hands in the sink. Jasper watches him with a raised eyebrow, like he knows Liam is wasting time. He is, but he's not about to admit it.

When he's done, he shuffles into the living room and collapses on the couch. Jasper claims his perch in the armchair by Kermit.

"That was gross," Liam sighs after a moment. He takes off his glasses and rubs at his eyes.

"You were angry."

"Could you blame me? That was fucking sadistic. And to someone who never did anything to anyone."

"As far as you know."

Liam huffs. A headache cramps behind his eyes. "I don't think there's anything Oliver could have done to deserve that."

"I concur, but I believe it's important to search for motive behind this Trypanon's actions. How else will we ascertain their identity?"

Liam wants to argue. He doesn't have the energy. "Can't say I'm looking forward to meeting Angelica after that one," he says instead. "Or going in her house."

"As you mentioned, it's possible the Trypanon's rendering of her was an exaggeration."

They glance at each other. Jasper doesn't look any more optimistic than Liam feels.

"So, we have one dead religious alcoholic and one morbidly obese hoarder who got tortured by Mama Munchausen. If there's a connection between them other than the religious thing, or a link to your past, I'm not seeing it."

"I have also noted the Christian element in their Nether prisons and Phrens, and the fear of sinning, but everyone in my acquaintance shared this trait. It could be anyone I knew, except me and my father. I'm afraid we were anomalous in our atheism."

"Yeah, I'll bet. Not being religious is way more common these days. But I can't tell if our Trypanon hates religion or is a devout Christian. Could go either way at this point. Phoebe and Jake had no connection to the church, so the religious shit could be a coincidence. Uggh, my fucking head."

The walls around them pulse and shudder, emitting a pink aura. Liam shifts on the couch cushions and shuts his eyes tight.

"Is it safe?"

"Is what safe?" Liam asks through clenched teeth.

"What you're doing in the Nether to dissolve these prisons. I feel the toll it takes on you. Are you certain you're not doing irrevocable damage to yourself?"

"Oh, now you care? You were the one who wanted me to do this shit in the first place."

Silence.

With a thought, Liam dims the lights in the room. He opens his eyes, wincing against the headache, and looks at Jasper. Two dimples pucker the space between his eyebrows. Liam waits for Jasper to say something, to argue, but nothing comes. He doesn't feel like assuaging Jasper's guilt tonight. Liam can't deny the sprig of resentment he feels.

If Jasper cared about his health and well-being, he'd never have pressured him to go into the Nether. It's a fact, and one Liam reminds himself not to forget. Their relationship is a means to an end. They may form something like a friendship in the process, but the ultimate goal is catching the Trypanon, at whatever cost to Liam. Jasper said so himself.

"I think I need to rest before tomorrow," Liam says. "I need—"

"Understood."

Jasper vanishes. Liam blinks at the indent in the chair where he'd been sitting.

"Angelica Fenton? My name is Liam—"

"Officer Sloane told me Calico might come knocking on my door."

"May we come in?"

"We?"

Shit.

"I mean me. Just me."

She bites her lip, glancing behind her and scratching her long thumbnail on the doorframe. "It's been a long time since I've had company."

Liam shudders at memories of piss-filled bottles and dead cats. "If it helps, I just moved in, so my place is a mess."

She stares at him.

She's hiding something, Jasper says in his mind.

"Alright, but I can't talk long. Errands to run. And of course, I'm in mourning."

"I understand. I'll be quick."

She exhales long, like he's putting her out. "Fine."

Liam takes a deep breath, knowing it will probably be the last clean air he gets for a little while, and enters.

There is clutter—a lot of it—but it's nothing compared to the Nether prison. Stacks of boxes fill the corners of the living room, and every surface is covered in knickknacks—dolls and painted bird houses and ceramic ducks. It smells like cigarettes and that indefinable "old person" scent. The floor is covered in a stained maroon carpet. The peeling wallpaper is a pale-yellow flower print. As Angelica leads him to the sitting area, he sneaks a glance into the kitchen. It's packed with pots, appliances, and cooking accoutrement, but he doesn't see rotting food or stacks of dirty dishes. The hall beyond it leads to a shut door; Oliver's room.

The barriers of reality are thin here. Liam can hear the Nether scampering like mice inside the walls. Something behind the door to Oliver's room coos at him.

"So, you're here to talk about my poor baby Oliver," Angelica says as they sit. The couch—covered in plastic—crumples under Liam's ass. "Do you want something to drink? Some water? Or I have Powerade?"

Liam shivers. "No, thank you. I'm fine."

This home is very odd, Jasper says in his mind.

No shit.

Though not as derelict as we were expecting.

Not from what we can see. I doubt she'll let us in Oliver's bedroom.

The energy emanating from it is difficult to ignore.

"It's so shocking that a Fluke attacked him," Angelica says, holding her palm against her chest. She sniffles and her nose whistles like a recorder in a fourth-grade music class. "He was the last person anyone would have expected to get one—especially a Neglect Fluke! No one has ever been less neglected, at least by their mother. Must have been his darn father's doing."

"I'm sorry for your loss," Liam says. "I'm investigating the recent Fluke deaths to make sure nothing is going on."

"What could be going on? I thought Fluke attacks were mostly random. Is there foul play?"

> *Subtlety is not your strong suit. Surely you don't plan to tell her of the*
> *Trypanon. Do try for a modicum of subtlety.*

Liam's eye twitches.

"Oh, it's probably nothing. Unfortunately, coincidences like this do happen sometimes. We just want to make sure we're being thorough and checking every angle. To, you know, understand why this happened. If it's alright, could I ask you a few questions?"

Angelica folds her hands on her lap. Liam scans over her appearance, clocking the bleached hair and gray roots, the sun damage wrinkling her face like a date, and the outfit that is too pink and frilly for an adult. She's missing a canine, not that her smile would carry much charm if she weren't. And she's thin like a greyhound.

"I'm happy to talk about my little boy any time," she says at last. "Especially with a celebrity. You're the talk of the town, you know. Lots being said about you at church."

Liam holds back a cringe.

"You mind if I smoke, dear?" She draws a cigarette from inside a ceramic clamshell on the coffee table and lights up without waiting for a response.

> *You said smoking was unhealthy.*
> *It is.*

He tries to keep the conversation on track. "Did Oliver have any enemies that you know of? Any difficulty with people, say, at his job or at church?"

"If Oliver had problems at work, he didn't tell me about them. As for church, Oliver was the perfect little lamb. When he was a kid, he always sat right up front with me in his Sunday best. Oh, he just had the sweetest blue bow tie. Looked like one of my dolls! But, well, as you know, at a certain point Oliver was too ill to attend church for many years. Poor angel was cursed with every ailment you could imagine. I took care of him as best I could, but something new always came up. Went through every doctor in the area getting second opinions. Doctors think they know everything, but mother knows best."

Yikes.

*I'm not entirely sure what that word means, but I concur with your
    sentiment.*

"Did Oliver have any interactions with Maggie Short that you know of?"

"Hardly. Maggie was not the type of person we associate with. She was
a gossip. Slander is a sin, you know. She was always secretly drinking and
popping pills at services, as if we didn't notice. And you know what? I think
she was a ..." her voice dips into a whisper, "... a *lesbian*. Lord knows what
she got up to on the world wide web. I pray for her, but shudder to think
where her soul has ended up."

Hates gossip, my ass.

Your "ass?"

It's a figure of speech.

"What about Phoebe and Jake Shelton? Did Oliver know them?" Liam
says.

She scoffs. "Of course he knew *of* Phoebe Shelton. Who doesn't? But he
hardly ran in that crowd. Oliver didn't have many friends."

*Doesn't sound like she knew too much about what was going on with
    Oliver,* Liam says to Jasper. *We may be hitting a dead end here.*

Inquire as to her theories on why he might have attracted a Fluke.

"I know you said it was a surprise that Oliver attracted a Fluke, but he got
it for a reason. Are there any instances of neglect in his life that you can think
of? You mentioned a father."

A scowl deepens the puckered wrinkles above her lip. "When Oliver was
very little, he didn't get to live with me, where he belonged. His daddy had
him. I thought it would be best for him to be with a male figure. A man needs
to act like a man. But I was wrong. Bob was too busy with floozies and bars
to take care of my little boy. Luckily, the courts gave him back to me. I made
it my mission to undo what his daddy had done."

Think she might have gone a little overboard, Liam says to Jasper.

Your ass.

That's not ... never mind.

"You're sure nothing happened recently?" Liam asks.

Angelica's pale blue eyes narrow. The corner of her lip twitches. "I doted
on Oliver every second. I fed him, cleaned him, loved him more than any other
woman could. He didn't have to make any decisions. I took care of everything.
I made life easy for him. But there was that phase he went through."

"Phase?"

"Oh, just one of those rebellious phases every teenage boy goes through. He was in his 30s at the time, but mind you, Oliver was a little stunted. He was a preemie and without a good daddy, it was hard for him to become a man, just as I'd feared. He was soft. It's why I didn't want him playing with kids his age. They'd just bully him. One day he woke up and out of the blue, he decided to leave me." Her eyes well up with tears. She wipes them on her lacy sleeve, smearing mascara. "It was such a dark period. I should have known his father had passed his wicked ways onto Oliver. My baby abandoned me just like his daddy. I was so worried about Oliver, out there, living on his own with no one to take care of him. I'd call all the time, show up at his apartment to surprise him. You should have seen him. He was emaciated, spending all hours at his stupid job when he should have been home resting with me. And his apartment … there was barely anything in it—antiseptic and empty. It was like a prison cell."

A sour taste coats Liam's mouth, filling his cheeks with saliva. It takes every ounce of his control to keep from grimacing.

I do not believe her perception is accurate, Jasper says.

No shit.

I am curious as to why Oliver chose to return to her.

"So you believe this … neglect, occurred while he was living on his own?"

"It's the only possible explanation."

"Right. But he was living here with you while he was attacked, and he died in your house. In a closet, in fact. Is that right?"

Her lips catch on her teeth when she tries to respond. Splotchy red blooms on her cheeks. "He wasn't the same when he came home. Being without me *changed* him. He was always such a good little boy. When he came home, he was disobedient. He talked back, went out at all hours doing whatever he wanted. Wouldn't let me cook for him or even come in his room without his permission. He even put a lock on the door."

"What was his reason for moving back home?"

"Well, I'd become very ill."

"You seem healthy now."

Angelica's lip twitches, her eyes flashing.

You've made her angry.

"I had a bad bout," she says, low. "You know, Oliver became a bit obsessed with you in the days before he died. He'd talk of nothing else. He'd mumble your name under his breath. Kept saying there was something he needed to tell you."

A creeping unease rises. "He did say that he had something to tell me when I met him. I never got to hear what it was."

"Oh yes, he told me all about that. How you blew him off. He came into the house in a state. Broke a few of my china dolls."

He should have broken more. Jasper mutters.

"Did he ever tell you what he was going to tell me?"

Her face flushes almost purple. "I didn't ask."

I think he chose not to tell her, Liam says. *Sounds like Oliver didn't want to be here any more than we do. I just can't imagine why he moved back home with this nutjob. We may never know.*

It is a bit strange that he attracted a Neglect Fluke with such an overbearing caregiver. You could argue he was the opposite of neglected. Smothered, rather.

Neglect is a weird word. Because of the way she raised him and isolated him, he neglected himself. His socialization and growth and health were neglected. She saw it as love but overfeeding him until he was confined to a bed is absolutely a kind of neglect. Think of it more like, "failing to care for properly."

I see.

"What is the matter with you?" Angelica says, pulling Liam back into the room. "Your eyes, you … you keep looking off like you're talking to someone in another world."

Liam laughs weakly. "I … no, I was just wondering what could have caused Oliver to attract a Fluke."

"I told you, it was all that gosh darn time alone, without me. Why don't you ask the monsters at the God forsaken care center he worked at? They're the ones who did this to him!"

You did it to him and you know it.

A pause. Angelica's jaw drops in enraged horror. Liam reaches up to cover his mouth but it's too late. He said the words out loud.

She shoots to her feet and points a spindly finger in his face. "You're just like them," she spits, voice cracking. "Bert Shelton warned us about you. I should have listened."

Liam is in the middle of rising to his feet when that stops him short. "What did Bert say?"

"He told us a Trypanon killed our loved ones. He told us it was *you* who did it; that's why you're investigating. To, you know, cover your tracks. He said you got in a fight with Maggie, and Bert's parents, and even my dear sweet Oliver right before they died."

A spit bubble inflates and pops in the corner of her lips as she speaks.

The Nether rustles through a stack of boxes to his side.

"That's not …"

"Why else would you be investigating? If it was just a regular Fluke attack, why would you be here? Bert says Trypanons are rare. Bert says it has to be you. Wait, that means …"

Her face drains of color. She stumbles back, hitting the edge of a glass table. Her eyes are wide as she backs away toward her kitchen.

"You can control minds. You could be controlling mine right now. You could be trying to kill me. Get out! Leave!"

With pleasure, Jasper snarks.

"Okay," Liam says simply.

As he turns and strides toward the front door, something flashes in his periphery. He glances into the kitchen and down the hall to Oliver's bedroom door.

It's open now. A shadowed figure crosses beyond it. Liam blinks, and the door is closed again.

"Get out!"

Liam trips, hurrying toward the door before Angelica throws a wooden duck at his head.

Did you see that? He says to Jasper once he's back in his car
and peeling out of the driveway.

Yes. It was the Trypanon.

Liam's tires screech as he slams on the brakes. "What?" he says out loud.

It was the Trypanon. Trust me. I told you: I know them.

Fuck.

Indeed.

But how? Were they in my mind?

Liam is having trouble catching his breath. The air is too hot, too thick.

*Calm yourself, Liam. You know that the barrier between you and
the Nether is fraying. It is most plausible that you were simply
perceiving the Nether and they passed by.*

Or that they were spying on us.

Liam cranks up the air conditioner. It blasts hot air into his face, but it's better than nothing. He absorbs Jasper's logic, lets it stabilize him. He wipes the sweat off his forehead with the front of his T-shirt.

Well, at least now we have a solid suspect, Liam says. He steps on
the gas again, easing onto the main road. *Other than me, I
mean.*

Bert Shelton is a Sophont. It stands to reason that he could secretly be a Trypanon, and that he'd try to deflect blame onto you.

It's not hard to do. I'm pretty fucking suspicious apparently.

You do seem to keep getting into arguments. You're hardly endearing yourself to the townsfolk.

Gee, thanks.

You are welcome.

Liam rolls his eyes.

I don't like that we were being spied on, Liam says. *If the Trypanon can peek in on me during the day, they could be spying on us at night, while we're in the Nether. Or maybe even in my Phren.*

If they were in your Phren, one of us would be aware of it.

Who knows? They're sneaky. We need to go on the offensive; catch them out before they infiltrate us, or whatever.

Are you sure it's wise to go into the Nether again when you are still fatigued from last night?

Liam pulls onto O'Connor Ave. His house comes into view, with Jasper's house standing, identical, across the river behind it.

No, it's probably not fucking wise. But we gotta act fast. We don't know how much they know about us. They might even know you're helping me.

For my sake, I hope not.

Liam is on the couch, just starting to doze, when Jasper speaks again:

I have a question.

Liam sighs, rubbing his eyes.

Hit me with it.

Why do some people get Fissures while others do not? I've been contemplating it. Scores of people abuse drugs, experience violence and neglect and subjugation. Why do Fissures and Flukes only affect a few?

Liam weaves his fingers together on his chest.

You're asking an age-old question, Friendly Ghost. If I had an answer, I'd give it to you. The only sense I could make of it is … life is just harder for some people.

But why?

Fuck if I know. Why do some people have asthma or pancreatic cancer or migraines? Genetics? Environmental factors? Bad fucking luck? We just haven't learned enough to know.

Jasper is quiet for so long that Liam starts to doze again.

Why did it happen to me?

Liam bites his lip. He's searching for an answer when Jasper speaks again.

Blue Flukes, he says, making Liam go rigid. *I've gleaned the specific baits for the other four from your conversations and thoughts. Red is Vice, Yellow is Neglect, White is Subjugation, Violet is Violence. But what is a Blue?*

Liam closes his eyes. He thinks of Claire and Makoto. His parents. Iris. He thinks of the mess he's made. He thinks of the Nether. He thinks of the gasping black.

Despair.

CHAPTER THIRTEEN
BETRAYAL

Liam isn't in a good mood when they enter the Nether that night.

That afternoon, Sloane, Applebaum, and Faye showed up at his door not long after he'd gotten home. Apparently, a colorful call from Angelica Fenton provided Sloane with the justification she needed to interrogate Liam over his progress with the case. Without elucidating his sojourns into the Nether, Liam sounded like he'd been slacking at best, harassing an old lady at worst, and Sloane let him know it. Not that any of them had made much progress either. They had no leads from investigating the long-term care facility where Oliver worked, or the victims' emails and phones. Interviewing close friends and family yielded little. As predicted, they were useless, and it clearly bothered Sloane, though she hardly claimed any responsibility. She informed him not-so-gently that certain individuals were not too happy with Liam. Code: the FUSE goons were putting the pressure on, and Bert Shelton was dragging his name through the mud. And clearly, Sloane was not taking Liam's side. Bert could do no wrong in her eyes; he was family.

Liam should have considered this before he declared Bert a suspect. Sloane just about pulled her gun on him. "He's been in New York this whole time and I'll verify that alibi any fucking day in court, if you want to go there. Bert wouldn't kill his own parents. Not everyone has mommy issues. Go project your bullshit trauma somewhere else." Liam didn't bother responding.

And Sloane wasn't the only one fraying his nerves. Faye fawned on Liam in her usual bubbly, unhinged manner, and Applebaum stayed carefully neutral, which helped no one. Not even Jasper's little remarks in his head helped.

The hard truth is that they have no ironclad leads. Sure, Bert is an option, but on what evidence? That the guy got in a bar fight once? Hardly a steppingstone to serial killing. With no other suspects, all signs point in Liam's direction, even to Liam. He's not confident in his own mental state. He wasn't well before his Victorian crime-fighting buddy came along, assuming Jasper isn't a hallucination.

The case is too big, too convoluted, too uncertain. Liam is too suspicious. And he's tired. He hasn't had a break, not even in sleep.

He knows Jasper can see the burn of Liam's exhaustion and annoyance on the walls of his Phren. As they enter the Nether, Jasper orders Liam to focus and relax. It only irritates him more.

"Where should we begin?" Jasper says, looking out over the dark water at the re-breaking tree. Liam can hear the caution in his voice, as if Liam is a spooked rescue animal in fight or flight.

Liam kicks a wad of Nether seaweed. "If the Trypanon is spying on us, they know who I am, and they probably know we've been taking nightly trips into the Nether. Let's check out the O'Connor House. We might catch them in there, snooping around."

Jasper goes still. "Are you certain you wish to do that?"

"What do you mean?"

"I confess, I am hesitant to enter my own house here. The Nether is composed of horrible fragments in time. 'Trauma' is the word you use, I believe."

"Yeah, and?"

"It stands to reason that there may be memories imprinted on that home that you would not like to relive."

"It wasn't even my home. I was only there in the summers as a kid."

"It is more of a home to you than anywhere else. You modeled your Phren after it."

Liam isn't sure what's more annoying: that Jasper is speculating wildly about Liam's own experience, that he gleaned this knowledge from poking around inside Liam's Phren, or that he's right.

"I'll be fine."

"If you insist."

"What else do you expect me to do? Go looking for Jake or Phoebe's Nether prisons? Because I don't have the energy to dispel them tonight. I'm running on fumes."

"Then perhaps we should not have entered the Nether."

"Too fucking late now." Liam's aware that he's being snappy, and that

Jasper doesn't deserve it. He'll apologize later. "You knew my ancestors who lived in this house, correct? There might be memories inside that can help you figure out who our killer is. Maybe there's a memory in there about Rosie, or that Declan character. Everyone says he was a dick. Maybe he's a suspect."

Jasper says nothing.

The O'Connor House seems to draw them to it. It's effortless to fly across the dark water of the river, their feet barely touching the sandy shore or the dead grass in his yard. It's as if a fishing hook has ensnared Liam's ribs, a fisherman reeling in his cast with purpose, if not haste.

"I do not think this is wise." Jasper's eyes are wide, his jaw clenched.

"Why? You don't think I can handle it?"

"No." Jasper doesn't elaborate. Liam can't decide if he's saying, "No, I don't think you can handle it," or "No, there's another reason." He can't help the stir of resentment. Jasper said he wouldn't wish the Nether on anyone. Apparently, that didn't include Liam.

Jasper side-eyes him with the corners of his lips turned down, as if he can hear Liam's thoughts. Maybe he can.

The door to the Nether iteration of Liam's home creaks open. It's warped. Aberrant. As soon as they step inside, it's obvious how different this house is from his Phren. Though there are elements he finds familiar, like a whiff of dusty wood or the signature creak of a particular floorboard, it's corrupted and patchy. There's wallpaper he doesn't recognize in the living room. Antique, yet new and pristine, except for a mottled dark smear on the wall from a leak. There's a hint of smoke coming from the fireplace, where the coals still glow amber. Muffled, wet coughing reverberates from the second floor. There's a dead cat curled up in the corner, its eyes dried out like sunbaked fruit. It reminds him of Oliver's hoard. And the dead dog in the alleyway.

"It's not so bad," Liam says, turning to face Jasper. His eyes are darting around the room. "Relax, will you?"

"I sense something."

"What—"

A cabinet door slams in the kitchen. Liam whirls around. The kitchen is shrouded in darkness. Slow, he approaches. Another slam. The sound of glass shattering carves down his spine. Then, crunching, as if the sole of a shoe is grinding into the shards.

Look at the mess you made.

The voice is low and faint, but Liam recognizes it immediately. His grandmother always had grit in her throat, sharpened by crackling mucus from a daily pack of Salems.

Too bad for you that your grandpa's not here. He's too soft.

The memory comes to him quick and bright. The kitchen light flicks on, as if revealing the stage. His grandmother looms over a little boy with brown hair, who's half-climbed up on the counter.

It was an accident. I was trying to get something from the top—

You were trying to get sweets. You know the rules. And now look what you've done. You've broken your great grandmother's china. It was a wedding present. Your grandfather will be heartbroken. But you don't care, do you? Everything is a joke to you. Nothing matters as long as you get your fun. You're lucky my father isn't with us anymore. He'd take the belt to you. Kids don't know discipline anymore.

The little boy tries to climb off the counter and slips with a gasp. He lands hard on the broken china. Blood spurts across the tile from his hands and knees. His grandmother doesn't react. Her jaw is tilted up, her yellowed green eyes staring down her nose with righteous satisfaction.

This is what happens when you disobey, she says. They call that divine restitution, you know. First the wasp, now this. Maybe you'll finally learn.

The figures flicker out, then reset. The whole scene begins again. Liam turns away. He looks at his palms. The thin white scars are still there between the mussel cuts, and they throb. Jasper is inches behind him. Liam looks over his shoulder and their eyes meet.

Jasper doesn't say "I warned you." Liam hears it anyway.

"You go check the dining room. I'll try upstairs," Liam grits.

"Are you certain you want to go alone?"

Liam glares. He stomps by him, having every intention of roughly bumping their shoulders together to make a point, but Jasper dodges him with ease. Liam's halfway up the stairs when he hears the muffled hum of a resonant voice. He slows, creeping up to the top, and follows the sound to his grandparents' bedroom. He hardly ever goes in here in either his Phren or the Waking World. Echoes of his grandparents' chastisement bounce off the walls.

Don't even think about going in there, young man!

He pushes open the door.

At the far end of the room, a large man looms over two children. Their faces are blurry, their bodies shifting in and out of focus like a computer glitch. Liam blinks, woozy with the effort of trying to perceive them. One of the children is a little girl with a heavy dress. The hem is soaked in mud, and there's a large tear up the side, revealing the petticoat beneath. She's trying to cover it with her hand.

If neither of you will be honest, both of you must be punished.

She was speaking in tongues, the boy says. *She was seeing things. Dark, evil things. Devil speak. I had to make her stop.*

Is that true? the man says to the girl.

She stares at the floor, frozen. *He lies,* she whispers. *He always lies.*

She's the liar! The boy shoves her shoulder. *She's a witch, Father! I always catch her doing dark spells. She was making potions down by the water. Even made a shrine. She put a dead seagull on it, Father. And a poppet. You can check for yourself!*

Is that true? The father is eerily calm. It's worse than if he were shouting. The girl starts to tremble. *If I look, is that what I'll find?*

The girl looks around, panicked. Two wide green eyes come into detail among the blur of her face.

I was trying to save it … to bring it back to life—

The father steps forward and locks his large hand around her forearm. She yelps as he turns and drags her toward the door, toward Liam. His pace is slow and deliberate. Liam stumbles back out into the hall and out of his way. As he passes by, Liam catches the expression of the boy. The sparkling giddiness and the spread of a toothy smile comes into stark focus. The Nether titters with joy.

You'll stay up there with your Bible until you learn to accept the Lord into your soul, the father says as he drags her up the spiral stairs.

Liam can't see from his angle, but he hears him throw open the trapdoor and hoist her up. She whimpers and keens, sobbing now through desperate pleas.

No. Please. Anywhere but here.

Man doesn't meddle with life or death. Only God can or those chosen by God may do that.

Father, please. I don't want to be stung. You know there's a nest of—

The vision disappears when the trap door slams shut. The boy evaporates. The father never comes back down the spiral stairs. Liam's shoulders start to relax, his breath easing.

Then two shadowed figures materialize in front of the door to the tower. They aren't out of focus, and they aren't wearing antique clothes. Liam knows them both.

Did you know what he was? You did, didn't you. You were hiding it from me.

He hasn't heard his mother speak in months. She didn't call when Makoto died, and neither did he. She's distant—always has been—but there's a raw vulnerability now that he hasn't heard in her voice since he was a child.

Will you keep your voice down? I don't know where he's hiding.

Answer the fucking question, Pete.

His grandfather, who was always composed, never a hair out of place, looks wound tight. His shoulders are halfway up to his ears, arms crossed over his chest. He looks guilty.

They're so rare. How could I assume—

He's dangerous, his mother spits. *You knew, and you didn't say a word. I'm his mother.*

And why didn't you notice, then? You said it yourself: you're his mother. Maybe if you spent some time with him—

Oh, don't pull that shit on me. As if you weren't dying to take him every summer, trying to bend him to your ways. You know I have business.

Liam remembers this conversation. He'd been hiding in the tower. Why was he hiding? The truth keeps slipping out of his grasp. Then his mother says:

Seven people, Pete. They say some of them will never recover. And the child—

Seven people he saved.

That's not the way these FUSE people are playing it. They seem to think he's a threat.

He's not. He's a good boy. His grandfather says it quiet, like it's a weak defense, like it's irrelevant.

They're taking him away from me, Pete.

When his grandfather doesn't respond, his mother takes his arm hard and shakes.

Do you understand that? They're sending him to that boarding school for Sophonts. This Archer woman says that until they get him trained and under control, he shouldn't come home. It wouldn't be safe.

They can't do that.

They can and they have to.

His mother sighs. She turns away, and Liam ducks, expecting to be caught out, as if he's still a little boy spying on a conversation he was never meant to hear. This is only a memory, though. A trauma. And he feels the Nether savoring it, swirling it against its soft palate, relishing the taste of one of the worst moments of Liam's life.

Why didn't you tell me? his mother says again.

Because I didn't want it to be true. Deb, she ... she's the one who figured it out first.

His mother shakes her head. *This is all your fault.*

How? Even if we'd known—

He didn't get this ... this defect from me. You all knew that this defect ran in your family. And no one ever told me. I carried him inside me and no one ever told me what he could inherit. I never would have—

What—never would have had him?

Yes! Liam's mother whirls around. *You know why I'm always gone? Why I never felt close to him, even when he was a baby? He's different. He's … creepy. I thought I was crazy, but I swore I could feel him in my mind sometimes. He'd know my thoughts, my secrets. It scared me. And here you were, always treating me like half a mother, like I was never enough. And now I find out that you knew why the whole time and you never told me. How could you do that to me? I hated myself, and you let me. I should have known my child could be a Sophont before I even married Finn.*

Finn didn't tell you either.

He says he didn't know.

His grandfather's lips stay sealed. He looks at Liam's mother with tired, old eyes.

I'll never forgive you for this, his mother says. *Any of you.*

It hadn't happened for generations. We assumed it wouldn't be a problem.

Not a problem? You know what this means. Liam isn't just some fucking paper-pushing Sophont. He's … he's a …

I know what he is. But he's still my grandson. He's still your child.

He's a mistake.

The words hit. Then they repeat. Once, twice, ten times, as if the record of the Nether is skipping. But this is intentional. The Nether feels his pain. It's drinking it from him now, forcing him to take that statement from his own mother over and over and over again. *Mistake. Mistake. Mistake.*

He's flooded with a desire to find the childhood version of himself, hiding in the tower. If he could just reach him, maybe he could make the memory go away. Maybe he could change things. It's not rational; some part of him knows this, but he's losing himself. Jasper was right: he never should have come in here.

He barrels past the shadows of his mother and grandfather. They don't acknowledge him. He throws open the door to the tower, clawing up the narrow spiraling stairs with his hands on the steps like a child. He reaches the ladder, and climbs it, toward the growing insect buzz. He shoves open the trapdoor.

There is someone in the tower, but it's not Liam as a little boy.

The circular room is dark and hazy. He sees the shadow of an adult, cloaked in heavy fabric. The power emanating from them is familiar; it matches his own.

"What—"

The figure jerks and turns, sending a cloud of dust billowing behind them. They crash through a window and plunge into the night beyond. In their wake, the room floods with a swarm of yellow jackets, spiraling like a twister.

Liam must act fast. He claws deep inside himself, pulling on his tired power. In an instant, he's in the dining room downstairs, away from the buzz, with Jasper standing stunned before him.

"They're here! They jumped out the window when they saw me. We have to hurry."

Liam turns and runs before Jasper can respond. He lets his power draw him toward the Tryp. They're easy to sense now that he's come so close. He reaches behind him to take hold of Jasper's hand and clasps at nothing.

"Take my fucking hand!"

When Jasper still refuses, Liam growls in frustration. If Jasper gets left behind, that's on him. He pulls harder on his power, gasping as he tumbles with wrenching speed across the water, past the white hand and the tree that keeps breaking. Jasper stays close behind him; for the first time, Liam notices how aware he is of his presence without needing to look at him. He feels the tie between them, pulling Jasper along, keeping them close.

The silhouette of the Tryp is relentlessly fast, flying above the black water like a vulture. Liam shouts. His stomach aches. And, somehow, he begins to close the gap between them. The Tryp reaches the shore and scurries up a hill toward the road, ripping gray grass up into the air in their wake.

Then, suddenly, they stop. It's so strange that Liam falters. With a stumble, he reaches the shore. Jasper is so close Liam can almost feel his breath on his neck. Clawing up the grass, Liam reaches the road. Yet just as his feet touch the black pavement, the Trypanon does something that stops him dead.

The hint of a parked car appears like a watermark beside the Tryp. A person leans against it. Liam can barely see them. There's a stark difference between this car and this person and the rest of the Nether. This is not a traumatic memory stuck on repeat. This isn't a part of this world.

This is real. This is the Waking World being pulled into the Nether by the Trypanon.

With a single, appalling motion, the Trypanon slices a clean gash down the center of the veiled figure. The figure jerks, shuddering. Without looking back, the Trypanon steps through the slit and disappears.

A profound horror freezes Liam where he stands. The sheer violation of it—of a Tryp tearing open a mind and invading. It makes him feel exposed and guilty, as if he'd done it himself.

Then Jasper steps in front him, advancing. Liam stares in shock at his back.

"What the hell are you doing?"

"We need to apprehend them before they escape." Jasper approaches the tear.

"They've already escaped. We can't follow them. Get away from there!"

"No."

"Jasper! Are you insane? You can't go into someone's mind."

"We need to catch the Trypanon." His voice is blank, devoid of emotion—of conscience. Liam watches as tendrils of seaweed sprout from the dark hair on the back of his head. Seawater drips from his sleeves. The low tide smell billows out.

"We will! But this isn't the way." Liam reaches out to grab Jasper's hand, to hold him back, but Jasper dodges him without looking. Jasper raises his arm, reaching into the tear—into a mind. Into a victim.

"You can't! Jasper, stop—"

"I must. I must be free of this place. I cannot stay here. I'll do anything."

"No!"

Reaching deep inside himself, Liam gathers every bit of power he has. He takes Jasper by the shoulders and spins him around. With a final surge, he pours the last of his reserves into sealing the tear.

He meets Jasper's eyes. They're wide as saucers, almost glowing. His lips are parted. The seaweed falls away, his clothes suddenly dry. His face contorts with fear.

Liam is suddenly aware of why Jasper always barred them from touching. At their contact, Jasper's emotions pour into him—his guilt, his fervent need to escape the Nether, his shock. There's a sprig of something pleasant too, but it's overwhelmed by need—a primal desperation to get out of the Nether by any means necessary.

With brutal clarity, Liam sees the truth:.Jasper doesn't care about the victims; he only cares about himself.

Liam collapses to the ground, his kneecaps clacking against the pavement. They'll be bruised when he wakes. A cold, gutting certainty sluices over him. He can't look at Jasper. The grief rises inside him like a king tide. The Nether slinks in, thrilled by his profound sense of betrayal, his surrender.

"Liam. I … I apologize. Please—"

"I have to go back to my Phren," Liam rasps. He can barely open his eyes. The Nether is needles on his skin.

"Right. Of course, I'll—"

"Just stay out of my way."

Liam has nothing left. Jasper doesn't offer his hand to help him up.

Liam isn't sure how he manages to claw his way back to the island, or amble through the door to his Phren. He moves in a fog. He's pushed himself past the brink. He's been flayed. Searing pain radiates. The walls of his Phren burn red and white like an infected sore. Furniture and decorations flutter in and out of existence, as if the integrity of his mind is compromised. He doesn't have the energy to hold it in place. Stacks of boxes appear around the room, full of agitated memories. Some tumble out across the floor; the afternoon he got lost in Florence, his first day of college, the failed date he tried to plan for Claire to patch things up, the last time they had sex.

He ambles to his couch, collapsing onto it. He turns the room to blackness. Time spreads and bends. He isn't sure how long he lays in the mire.

When he finally comes back to himself, illuminating the room again, he turns his head on the couch cushion. Jasper comes into focus. He's sitting in his usual chair, as if he deserves to be there. His face is neutral, his back straight and hands placed with inhuman deliberation on his thighs.

Liam doesn't have the energy for much, but he still manages to be angry.

"Do you have any idea what you tried to do?"

Jasper looks away. His eyes fix on Kermit. With a flick of his wrist, Liam dispels the illusion of the rabbit. It startles Jasper, sets him off-kilter, which is less than he deserves. The privilege to enjoy Liam's Phren is no longer his.

"I was attempting to apprehend a murderer."

"Bullshit. You were trying to escape." Jasper doesn't respond. "Was that your plan the whole time? To use me so you could get closer to the Trypanon? All this investigating bullshit. It was just so you could catch a ride out of the Nether and into some poor soul's Phren."

"No, I had no such plan. I merely saw an opportunity."

"To steal someone's mind and body? Do you have any idea how fucking evil that is?"

"'Evil' is a religious concept. I am only human. You don't understand what it's like to be trapped in the Nether. The desperation is hard to suppress. It corrupts your thinking. It … primal-izes you, devolves you down to your most feral form."

"If you're looking for sympathy from me, you can shut up right fucking now. You think I don't get what temptation looks like? You think I've never been desperate, that I've never considered using my abilities to get what I want?"

"You frequently enter peoples' minds without their explicit consent. It's the nature of your career."

"To save them, not to possess them. And I only do it without consent when they aren't able to consent. It's part of my job. It's surgery to save a life. It's regulated. I abide by clearly defined rules. This is totally different."

Jasper's hands curl on his lap. His chin tilts down.

"All that righteous shit you pitched at me about saving people from the Nether," Liam goes on, voice low. "You were just baiting me to get what you wanted. You don't care about me, and you sure as shit don't care about the victims if you don't see a problem with invading someone's mind."

"I wasn't—"

The sentence dies. Jasper's shoulders, always set in perfect posture, droop.

"You've been violating me, reading my thoughts and memories. I thought you wouldn't let me touch you because of some Victorian propriety shit. But you were hiding this from me."

Jasper shakes his head. Liam speaks in a voice not his own:

"You're no better than the man we're hunting."

Jasper's lips part in a small gasp. "I do not believe that can be true. I don't want to hurt anyone."

"My whole life people have feared me, hated me, even envied me for what I was capable of doing—for what other Trypanons had done, like the one we saw tonight. But I never did it. I've never ripped open a Fissure in someone's mind and walked through, and do you know why?"

Jasper looks up at him. The usual distant steadiness in his eyes is strained.

"Because it's wrong," Liam says.

Jasper nods. His lip twitches only once. "Would you have me leave?"

"Yes. I would. Funny, isn't it? I've been letting you camp out in my Phren all this time so you didn't have to go back into the Nether. And now, because of what you've done, you're not welcome here anymore."

"Liam."

"I mean it. I never should have let a Wick into my mind in the first place. Then again, I didn't exactly invite you in, did I? You came in like you owned the place, just like you were going to do to that poor bastard on the road."

"It wasn't as simple as that. You're my Hitch."

"No. I'm not."

"Liam—"

"Don't pretend like I mean a damn thing to you. You're just like everyone else. You're not my friend. You're just using me."

"William, please—"

"Get out!"

The walls shudder. The floorboards clack together, toppling the mountains of boxes. They spill across the floor, filling the room with a barrage of memories. Jasper gasps and flinches.

Then he's gone.

And Liam is alone.

THE DAYS SHIFT in and out of focus. Liam ignores Sloane. Any cleaning he'd done is rendered meaningless as the dust accumulates and more boxes spill their guts onto the floors. He loses muscle. He barely showers or shaves. Texts from Cedra, Ingrid, and Teddy get deleted before they're opened. His mailbox is overstuffed. He can't bring himself to care.

He's been low before. It was bad when he first entered the Academy. And worse when the fifth Splint assigned to him resigned citing "irreconcilable differences." He felt it when Claire left, and when Makoto died. But it's never been quite this bad.

Jasper keeps trying to reach him.

Please, let me explain myself, Liam.

I realize you are cross with me, but I believe there has been a misunderstanding.

I deeply regret my mistake.

I'm not who you believe me to be.

Liam doesn't respond. Jasper's tone doesn't affect him, no matter how much pitiful affectation he puts on. Liam is numb.

He wonders what Makoto would say if he saw him now. It doesn't matter. Makoto is dead.

After two weeks of floating around his house, his phone dead and back sore, there's a knock on his door. He's sitting on his kitchen floor eating peanut butter with a spoon, and he waits, frozen, for a long minute, hoping whoever it is will go away. His shoulders are relaxing and he's stuffing another spoonful into his mouth when a shout nearly makes him choke on it.

"We know you're in there, jackass! Your car is in the driveway. Open the damn door."

Slowly, sets the peanut butter aside, and pushes to his feet. His back creaks in protest.

"Please? We just want to make sure you're okay."

With a sigh, Liam ambles to his front door and pulls it open. Ingrid has her arms crossed over her chest. Cedra's frowning.

"Jesus, you look like a walking hangover," Ingrid says.

"I'm not hungover." It's probably the worst lie he's ever told. They all wince.

"May we come in?"

Liam is about to say no. He doesn't want to talk to anyone, and his house is a mess. He's also been wearing the same clothes for … he isn't sure how long.

"Fine," he says, turning. "Let me just get changed. You can hang out on the back porch."

He shuts the door and goes upstairs to put on his last remaining clean clothes: a T-shirt and a pair of shorts. He brushes his teeth, tames his hair with a wet comb, and pulls on a hat. He doesn't bother with the glasses.

"I wouldn't trust that swing if I were you," he says when he makes his way to the back porch. Ingrid and Cedra shoot to their feet.

"Told you so," Ingrid hisses at Cedra. "Could've broken my whole ass."

"You're the one who said 'I've always wanted a porch swing. They look so fun. So literary. Let's sit on this one.'"

"I didn't—"

"Why are you here?" Liam says. He doesn't find their banter amusing like he had at the dinner party. He grabs the only lawn chair he owns and drags it down to the yard. He faces it towards the porch steps and collapses down into it. After shuffling awkwardly, Ingrid and Cedra sit on the steps.

"You stopped answering our texts. Then we called and it just went to voicemail. We wanted to see if you were okay," Cedra says, slowly.

"Well, here I am," Liam says, holding out his arms. "Better than ever."

Ingrid snorts. Cedra elbows her in the side. "We don't mean to invade your space or anything, Liam," she says.

"Good."

"But you shouldn't stay cooped up in this haunted old house. You're gonna turn into a vampire or a Victorian attic wife or some shit," Ingrid says.

"I'll be careful to avoid that."

Ingrid frowns. "Something happened. Something bad."

"What happened, Liam?" Cedra says.

Their stares are piercing. They hit his armor at the seams.

"I just don't think there's any point anymore," Liam says. The words spill out. "Does anyone really care about bad shit happening to other people? Is it all just some bullshit farce? Jesus Christ, just … everyone fucking lies. They act like there's some great morality behind what they do, but really, all anyone cares about is themselves. Why do I have to be any different? Why is it my fucking responsibility to fix this? No one gives a shit about me or what I want. At this point, neither do I."

Ingrid and Cedra don't respond at first. Cedra opens her mouth to speak first, but Ingrid beats her to it.

"It's not your responsibility. You don't have to do anything you don't want to do. It sucks being a good person."

"How the hell do you know if I'm a good person? Maybe I'm not. Maybe I've only ever helped people against my will because I'm a goddamn puppet who does whatever he's told."

"You're a good person, Liam," Cedra states, like it's a fact.

"You don't know me."

"I know enough."

Liam itches under his hat.

"Who's making you think like this?" Ingrid says, voice rising. "Was it Bert? Because, sure, he's grieving, but he's also kind of an asshole. Or—wait, don't tell me it was Maggie or any of those religious nut jobs, with all their crazy ass Facebook posts. They're all just looking for someone to crucify. Is Sloane giving you a hard time? People aren't happy with the way she's has been acting, just so you know. Apparently, she hassled the hell out of some folks at the long-term care facility. A buddy of mine at the station says she's behaving like a totally different person."

"I don't care what anyone says."

Cedra leans forward, elbows on her knees. "Why do you think you're a bad person, Liam?"

Liam shrugs. "Why does it matter? People are always going to do shitty things to get what they want, no matter what I do. None of my work has made one goddamn bit of difference."

"That's not true."

"Like hell. I'm just a fucking fool, out here putting Band-Aids on tumors. None of it has been worth anything."

"I would like to take you somewhere," Cedra says, shooting to her feet and brushing off her linen shorts. She turns and walks around his house to the front.

Ingrid looks at him and shrugs. "Might as well follow her when she gets like this."

"I can't. I'm busy."

"Oh, please. You're bored and you know it. Get your ass up and come on."

Liam isn't sure why he decides to follow Ingrid to his driveway, or why he climbs into the back seat of Cedra's Subaru. He wants nothing more than to lock himself back inside his house, to stare at the ceiling in silence. Maybe he is bored.

He zones out for most of the drive, staring out the window and letting the hot sun brand floating silver shapes against his eyelids. He doesn't immediately recognize the building when they pull up to it. At first, he thinks it's a mental institution, and that Cedra is about to have him committed. Then he remembers: he came across photos of it during a Google search for the case.

The long-term care facility is smaller than he's expecting. Its grounds are strictly landscaped, boasting manicured shrubs, stone fences, and a pergola. Automatic sliding doors part as they enter. The smell of fresh carpet, chlorine, and something subtly sweet wafts over Liam.

The woman at the front desk gives them a nod. Cedra waves. Their pace doesn't slow. His thoughts are sticky, and he keeps slipping in and out of the moment. The Nether lingers in the shadows. He doesn't realize they're visiting Cedra's father until they're standing outside a room with the words "Patient: Harold Parsons" on a label beside the door.

His feet adhere to the linoleum floor. The last thing he needs is to see a ravaged Fissure Host that he didn't manage to save in time. He looks to Ingrid for help. Her expression is sympathetic, but she gestures to Cedra as if to say, "she's driving the car; I'm just here for the ride."

"Liam," Cedra says. "If I thought this would make you feel worse, I wouldn't be doing it."

He's skeptical, but the edges of her Phren are clear and calm. She's not setting a trap.

He follows her inside.

Harold Parsons sits in a cushioned chair by the window. A tree outside shifts in the wind, casting his face in spots of shade. His expression is serene, if vacant. When Cedra says, "Dad," he turns toward her. A light breaks through the clouds in his eyes.

"Sparky," he says, voice crackling like kindling.

"Hi Dad," Cedra says, walking over to give him a hug and a kiss on the cheek. "I brought someone very special to see you." She drags over a couple chairs.

"I'm gonna go check out the vending machines," Ingrid says, making a strategic exit. Liam glares at her back.

"This is Liam O'Connor, Dad. Do you remember him?"

Harold's blue eyes, identical to Cedra's, softly land on Liam. There's only a hint of recognition, and it wavers in and out. Liam feels the edges of his Phren. It's fragmented, like a fossilized skeleton with bones missing.

"Nice to meet you," Liam says, stumbling over the words. "Or, I guess, to see you again."

He doesn't usually talk to Hosts this long after an attack. Or at all, if he can avoid it.

"I know you," Harold says. He seems to surprise himself with his own words. Liam feels the strained effort of his Phren, struggling to conjure memory.

"That's right, Dad. This was the little boy who saved you."

"I don't—"

Harold cuts Liam off. "Thank you," he says. He reaches out with spindly fingers. The back of his hand is speckled with liver spots. His grip curls in Liam's T-shirt sleeve. "Tear in my mind."

Liam doesn't know what to say. He doesn't remember helping this man. He doesn't remember sealing the Fissures. Only the smallest bits of the barbeque come to him: cold water and charcoal burning and his mother's horrible grimace. *Mistake.*

"Your friend," Harold says, a shudder rattling through him. His eyes go wide, his lower lip quivering. "I saw them. I saw what happened. Their face."

Then, with no warning, Harold heaves into a scream. Liam and Cedra skid back in their chairs. Spit sprays across Liam's face. Harold screams again. Stops. Screams again.

"Okay, okay, here we are," a nurse says as she bustles inside. "We having a little moment?"

She takes Harold by the upper arms and squeezes. Cedra stands and tries to take Harold's hands. He jerks away from her. The nurse takes a syringe out of her pocket.

"No, wait. Please, he'll calm down. He hates being sedated. Please, just give him a minute," Cedra says.

The nurse shakes her head. "I have no choice. He could hurt himself."

"Wait," Liam says. He can't take it, can't handle another scream. He hates the idea of being sedated against his will, of doing *anything* against his will. "Cedra, may I have your permission to enter your father's Phren? I can help."

"Do it."

The nurse double-takes. Her face illuminates with recognition as she gapes at him. "Holy shit. It's Liam O'Connor."

Harold screams again. Liam doesn't spare time to acknowledge her.

Entering Harold's Phren is easy. There is no barrier to push through, no resistance. Once Liam is inside, however, he's disoriented. The structure of Harold's Phren is utterly illogical. Liam stumbles between the deck of a beach house, a '60s-era childhood bedroom, and slivers of absolute nothingness. Everything is coated in an air of fear and confusion. He needs something to harness, to expand; a good memory to draw to light.

He's scrambling through a hot attic, sifting through heirlooms. There's a trunk of old clothes, laced with memories of a mother long gone, and a stack of comic books, projecting images of a little boy hiding under a blanket at night to read. It's not enough.

Then he finds what he's looking for: a weathered basketball. He touches it, and is weightless, then moving, then dropped onto a driveway. Harold appears in front of him. He's younger, his eyes clear and bright. He's holding the basketball now. In front of him, a little girl in purple shorts points back.

"That's 'H. O. .' Dad. You better not be letting me win."

"If I did that, it would never mean anything when you finally do beat me."

"You mean like I'm gonna beat you today?"

"Still got two more letters to go, Sparky."

The sky is glowing purple and orange. The air is warm and breathless, the cicadas buzzing loud. Liam holds onto the memory, even as Harold's broken, frantic mind tries to tear it away. Liam's still weak from the Nether, even now, but he uses what little he possesses to expand the memory, letting it fill Harold's Phren to the brim and demand his attention.

As the scene plays on, Liam feels Harold relax in increments, until the last of his panic has faded. When the scene ends, Liam replays it again. And again, until Harold's mind takes hold on its own.

"I beat you! I can't believe I beat you!" little Cedra shouts, bouncing around her dad in a circle.

Harold smiles wide. His eyes are warm as he watches her. No one ever looked at Liam with such pure, depthless pride.

"Two out of three?"

Liam wants this to stay for Harold, to take up residence—a haven that

Harold can enjoy for the rest of his life.

Slow and gentle, Liam recedes. When he eases back into his body, he blinks into the sight of the nurse and Cedra gazing at him. Their faces are wet.

"Oh, Liam," Cedra says. "That was remarkable."

Liam's cheeks heat. "I didn't … it was nothing."

"It wasn't nothing!" Cedra says, looking offended for the first time in their acquaintance. "You gave him back a memory, didn't you? We saw it happen, the moment it struck him. Did you know he was talking? I remember that night, playing basketball. It was like I got to watch him live it all over again. I got to play basketball with my dad again." She sniffs. "Shit, I haven't seen him that happy in a long time. You did that, Liam."

Liam wants to deny what Cedra is saying, to push back. He can't find the words.

Then the nurse says, "I guess you probably don't remember me, right?"

Liam blinks up at her. "Uh, sorry, I—"

"It's alright. Nora Ashwood," she says holding out her hand. Liam shakes it tentatively. "I guess there's no sense beating around the bush. You sorta saved my life."

Liam still doesn't recognize her.

She swallows and goes on. "I was at the barbeque that day too. Just like Harold. I was one of the seven."

Liam's mouth drops open. He looks to Cedra. She offers a soft nod, her eyes still wet.

"But you're not …"

"A Husk? Or half of one like Harold? No, I'm not, thanks to you. There are others like me, you know. You saved a lot of people that day."

"I'm sorry, I don't remember it. I don't remember much from that day."

"I don't either. But I do remember feeling you in my mind. I remember the pain and the moment you made it go away. I barely knew you. I was fourteen and it just … set the course for the rest of my life. It's why I wanted to work here. I had to give something back. You're probably sick of people saying you're a hero. Can I just shake your hand instead?"

Her hand trembles in his, and she holds it a little too long. She excuses herself, wiping her nose with a tissue as she exits.

In the silence she leaves behind, Liam lets the weight of her words drape over him. He'd always thought he was too late that day, that most of the Fissure victims turned to Husks. He was, after all, only twelve, and utterly untrained. He assumed he did more damage than good in trying to seal Fissures.

Still, not everyone was as lucky as Nora.

He looks at Cedra. She's watching her father as he rocks gently, staring out the window.

"I'm sorry I couldn't save your father like I saved her," Liam says.

Cedra's head snaps to him. Her brow furrows in disbelief. "But you did save him. If it wasn't for you, there wouldn't be a memory of playing basketball. He wouldn't know my nickname was Sparky. He wouldn't be able to feel anything at all. You saved parts of my dad for me."

"But I made a mistake. I didn't do enough. You have to understand. I mean, in your job, haven't you had kids like that? Kids you've tried to save, but you didn't do enough and now they're lost?"

"Of course. But I have to forgive myself for that. We aren't perfect. We can't control everything. No matter how hard we try, we will always make mistakes. We will always be flawed and selfish. We'll always fall short. But we gotta see the good in what we do, forgive, and keep trying to be better. You're a good person, Liam." Cedra stands and Liam follows. Slowly, giving him ample opportunity to move away, she steps forward and puts her arms around his shoulders. Liam can't remember the last time someone hugged him. He isn't sure what to do. His hands lay limp at his sides. She pulls away.

"Aw, did I miss a sappy moment?" Ingrid says. Liam jerks back like he's been caught with a girl in his dorm.

"You can have a hug too, if you want one," Cedra says, holding out her arms and shuffling toward her.

"Not until you buy me a drink." Ingrid holds her back with a finger to her forehead.

"Speaking of which, let's get out of here. My dad needs some rest." Cedra gives her dad a kiss on the tip of his nose, and they file into the hall.

They're almost to the end of the patient ward when a familiar voice gives him pause. He edges toward an open door and looks inside.

"Faye?" he says.

She startles, jerking around to face him and scrambling to her feet. "Calico! I mean Liam! What are you doing here?"

"I was about to ask you the same thing."

"We'll meet you at the car, Liam!" Ingrid says, throwing her arm around Cedra's shoulder and heading for the doors.

Liam turns back to Faye and realizes she's not alone. Behind her, sitting upright in a bed with sheets around her waist is an older woman. She's hooked up to an array of machines. Her cheeks sag, a pool of spittle collecting on her chest. One of her eyeballs bulges like a frog's, the iris murky white. She doesn't acknowledge Liam, or anything.

"I'm visiting my mom," Faye says. "Did Sloane not tell you she was a patient here?"

"Sloane didn't tell me much about you, actually."

Faye frowns. "Phoebe didn't either?"

Liam isn't about to tell Faye what Phoebe said about her.

"Not really."

"Huh. I guess I always assume people are gossiping. Never been interested in idle chatter myself."

"Me either."

Faye smiles at him. He imagines little hearts popping above her head. He looks down to her shoes to avoid eye-contact. She's wearing the kind of white sneakers Liam thought were reserved for nurses over sixty.

"Well, I'll leave you to it." Liam turns to leave.

"She did this to herself, you know."

Liam stops. He looks back over his shoulder. Faye is staring at her mother, frowning. "She's not like a Husk or one of those stroked out people. This was her choice. She tried to hang herself when I was a kid."

People have always tended to confess personal things to Liam. He asked Makoto about it once, and Makoto said the same thing had always happened to him too. They speculated that it had to do with the high empathy levels inherent in Sophonts or some sort of mirroring. Perhaps it was a subconscious compulsion. Then again, Faye was also a Sophont, so maybe she was just open. Or an oversharer.

"I'm sorry to hear that."

"Hard not to be angry with her."

"It's okay to be angry," Liam says, shrugging.

"I suppose. It's not like she can fight back, though. We didn't get along well even before this happened."

"I don't get along with my mother either."

Faye looks at him like this shared trait has somehow proven her theory that they're soulmates and destined to be together for all eternity.

"You know, I really admire you," she says, turning to sit backward on the chair. She rests her elbow on the back, holding her head in her hand and looking at Liam like he's her Disney prince. "You save people who are troubled. You probably could have saved my mother. I've always wanted to be like you. But I know I'm not very good. I know what people say about me. I know Phoebe pitied me after my father died and when my mother did this to herself. I was a daddy's girl. For some reason I think my mother resented that. At least she never found out I'm a Sophont. If she hadn't already hung herself, that would have done the trick." She laughs, too loud. "Still, I always just wanted to save people because of her. If only I could have been a Wedge."

"I'm … glad you're working the case," Liam says. He's unsure of how to proceed. He keeps eyeing the door and can't think of anything appropriate to say. "I really should be going. My friends are probably waiting for me."

"Oh, that's nice that you made some friends here! Maybe I could hang out with you guys sometime. I've been here most of my life and I can't seem to find like-minded people. I think I'm a little too friendly."

"Uh …"

A shard of the Nether pokes through the edge of his vision. A rotten cross falls off the wall, crashing to the floor and evaporating into dust. He hears gargling in the next room over. Then the sound of a flatlining heart monitor. He only knows it's not real when there is no reaction from the nurses outside the room.

"I really need to get going." He pulls out his phone. "Oh yeah, they just texted me." (They haven't.) "See you later."

"Okay, Calico. I mean Liam! I'll get that right someday. Thank you for coming by to see me!" she says, as if he's there just for her.

"I'm sure I'll see you soon. For the case, I mean," he corrects when she beams.

"Call me anytime!" she calls at his back. "Hey wait!"

Liam halts, his sneakers squeaking on the linoleum. He sighs and turns.

"I just wanted to say real quick," Faye says, turning red. "I'm team Calico."

"Huh?"

"In the whole feud between you and Bert Shelton. On Facebook they say you're either Team Shelton or Team Calico. So, I'm just saying: I'm on your side. Bert doesn't know you like I do."

Liam cringes, muttering a quick "thanks" before turning to hustle down the hall, past the reception desk and out the front automatic doors. The Nether claws at his heels. He gasps when he barrels outside into the summer air. He bends over, hands on his knees. Ingrid calls out to him.

"If you're this out of breath from jogging, we really gotta get you to a gym, Liam."

"I'd rather go to a bar."

Cedra and Ingrid look at each other from across the hood of the Subaru.

"Salt Cellar?" Cedra says to Liam.

"Works for me."

As they climb into the car and buckle in, Jasper tries to speak to him again. Liam doesn't answer.

VIOLET

INGRID CALLS JILL and Teddy on the way to the bar and invites them to join. They show up a few minutes after Ingrid snags a table by the fireplace. "Best spot for people-watching," she says as they pull out the heavy oak chairs and take their seats. Liam mumbles that he's usually the one *being* people-watched.

Though only weeks have passed, the underground pub is different than Liam remembers it. At first, he's not sure why. Buck is still perched behind the bar, his bald head glistening in the low light. The nautical décor is the same, though some of it is older and more interesting than he'd first thought, such as an axe in a display case. He squints at the label from his chair, picking out words like "Isle of Shoals" and "double murder."

The smell of fried potatoes is still strong, though Ingrid warned him never to order the fries. Not because of the quality, but because Buck only offered them to comply with state liquor licensing laws demanding that food be sold alongside alcohol. Apparently, all the locals knew Buck would never fill your pint to the brim again if you ordered them and gave him the hassle.

The difference, Liam realizes, is him. When he'd first come to The Salt Cellar, he was barely present. He wasn't engaged with people or his surroundings. He was afraid. Sure, he thought it was a neat pub, but his eyes were half-shut to it. He'd had a good first encounter with Ingrid and Teddy, but he hadn't thought he'd see them again, much less go to their home. Maybe he's doing better than he thought.

"First round is on me," Cedra says as she walks backward toward the bar, pointing at them with finger guns. "But that means you're all getting an IPA and there's nothing you can do about it."

"But I want a sour," Jill whines. "Not all beer has to include 400% of your daily caloric intake."

It seems no one cares about Jill's preferences enough to intervene. Not even Jill, who is the first to finish her pint after Cedra returns and offers a toast. They don't toast to anything specific. It's a silent salute to the joy of day drinking in a pub on a Saturday afternoon.

Conversation is easy and amusing. Liam participates when he feels like it and people-watches when he doesn't, which is why he's the first to notice Faye stumbling through the door. She scans the room, her eyes igniting with joy when she finds Liam. She's smeared on lipstick and tied up her hair. As she approaches, he hears the clopping of her high heels on the stone.

"Crap," he says under his breath.

"What?" Ingrid looks where he's looking. "Oh."

"Liam! I didn't know you would be here! What a wonderful surprise. Guess you can't get enough of me today." Faye grabs an empty chair from an occupied table without asking for permission. It screeches on the stone floor. She sits before saying, "Can I join you guys?" as if she's giving them an option. "So weird—Liam and I were just talking about me meeting his friends. I'm Faye. Liam and I work together. Well, we don't *just* work together."

It's unlikely that anyone at the table doesn't know who Faye is.

Sure enough, Jill says, "aren't you our Patch?" She eyes Faye narrowly over her fresh pint of sour beer. "I just saw you on the news."

Liam watches Faye's cheeks dye scarlet. She tucks a tuft of hair behind her ear and titters something falsely modest.

Liam has a strict policy against accepting interviews from the press while he's working a case, which he's made clear to Sloane and anyone who called. It hadn't occurred to him that the department would rely on Faye to give them instead. He can't imagine she achieved the cool, deliberate vagueness, precise articulation, and strong boundaries necessary for the role during her interview. Or in any scenario he can fathom.

For a dragging moment, no one seems to know what to say. An uncomfortable aura radiates from their Phrens.

Then Teddy rises to his feet. "What are you drinking, Faye?"

"Oh, I don't drink. Can't stand to be around the stuff."

"And yet, you came to a bar?" Jill raises an eyebrow and takes a pointed sip of her beer.

"Ah, yes, well. I happened to notice the car model Liam left in so when I saw it parked outside, I thought, hey—why not stop in and see if he's there? I ran into him here once before so I—"

"Yeah, we were here too," Ingrid says, gesturing to herself and Teddy. "Remember?"

"Oops, sorry, I don't. Well, I can give you a ride home, Liam. My car is much nicer. It's a Dodge Dart." Faye looks at Liam with sparkling eyes.

"Yikes," Jill says under her breath. Teddy shares a glance with Ingrid before he retreats to the bar, muttering something about a seltzer. As Faye sputters on, clearly growing more aware of her missteps, Cedra stares at her.

"I've seen you at the center before," Cedra cuts in during a break in Faye's monologue.

"Oh, right! I thought I recognized you from somewhere. You and I probably have a lot in common."

Liam can't imagine what they could have in common besides a parent that's an invalid, but he lets Cedra handle it. She's polite and validating, but he can tell from her glances at Liam that she sees what he sees: Faye is a lot. Harmless, but not the type of person he'd trust with anything personal. Her desperation for closeness has rendered her a tad invasive. She's not the first Sophont Liam has met with poor social skills. For some, paraphrenic senses gave them insight into other people, made them charming and easy to talk to. For others, they came in too hot or got easily overwhelmed by other peoples' feelings. Liam isn't without sympathy.

Still, he's grateful when Jill shifts the focus away from Faye and onto niche nerd subjects around comics and video games. Faye quiets down and listens, though Liam is aware she's staring at him when he's not looking.

"Liam," Cedra says to him quietly while Teddy is ranting about Magneto and queer culture. Cedra nudges him on the arm. "I'm glad you're here."

"Me too."

"I don't know how I can ever thank you enough for today."

"I could probably say the same thing. You guys were right; I needed to get out of the house."

"Ingrid and I have both been stuck before. We get how hard it is."

Liam nods. He doesn't think it's the moment to ask what she's referring to, but he'd like to know more. It occurs to him that he'd like to know more about Ingrid, Teddy, and Jill too.

"I'm glad I met you guys," he says, then his cheeks burn.

He's about to blame the 8.2% ABV for his sappiness when Cedra says, "We're glad too."

Liam smiles down at the beer foam capping his pint. He smells the bitter hops with his ears.

And freezes.

He smelled something with his ears. He hears a woman's grating laugh with his eyes. He shivers as the bitter aftertaste from the beer ripples through the hair on his arms.

But there can't be a Fissure in the room. He would have known it. That's when he realizes the Fissure is not in the room. It's outside on the street. And it's drawing closer. It drags open the heavy door, stumbles into the stairwell. Liam freezes, bracing himself just before the door slams open, crashing against the wall and shattering glass. Chairs screech on the stone floor as people jerk back. All eyes are on the man swaying with his fists clenched white and blood dripping from between his fingers.

"Liam O'Connor," he gargles.

People recoil, backing away like a school of fish retreating from a shark. Liam knows what they see. They see Bert with his cheeks flaming violet, his joints bunched at odd angles. They see his bloated stomach, pulling at the buttons of his shirt.

And his bare feet, purpled and sliced like Maggie's had been.

That's not what Liam sees, what his senses perceive. No, the hidden layer beneath is far worse. Bert's face is covered by a writhing black mask. It undulates and glistens, reminiscent of a dead pig Liam saw in Haiti once. The corpse was so overwhelmed with flies that Liam didn't know he was looking at a pig until someone told him. He'll never forget the poor creature's eyes and nostrils and anus, overflowing with maggots.

Violence Flukes weren't common in Fissure victims, despite the commonality of violence. It took more than just a moment of rage or a bar fight to attract one. Brutality had to be pervasive and constant, both inflicted and received. It was why Liam was sent to war-torn countries and places like Chicago. This wasn't something a Patch or common Wedge could handle. And often, the damage was done long before a Wedge could intercede. Violence Flukes rarely left their Hosts alive for long.

But it's not a face full of flies or the reality of a rare Fluke that strikes him:

Trypanons don't get Flukes. Bert can't be the killer.

Liam is drawn from his thoughts when Bert's focus locks on him. Someone grabs Liam's arm, pinching his muscle tight. He can't look away.

Liam, you must get out of there! Jasper's voice is a faint brush in the back of his mind.

"You." Pink froth spritzes from Bert's lips. "You think you're the Trypanon in power here." He lurches forward. A strange twitch travels up his side and down his arm. Liam follows its path until it settles in Bert's fingertips. Blood dribbles from where his nails have been torn out.

"Alright, calm down. Cool it, buddy," Buck barks out from behind the bar. He has a phone pressed to his ear. "I'm already calling the police so just turn around, go for a walk, and rethink whatever it is you're about to start."

Bert doesn't acknowledge him, can't even hear him. All his focus is married to Liam. With a swift buzz, the flies recede away from his eyes, revealing what's left of them. They're globular and soggy like sponges, stained with purple blood. The Nether laughs into existence behind him, taunting. Chunks of traumatic memory fall into the room: splintering wood from an old bar fight, a terrier yacking itself to death from a swallowed piece of broken glass, an endless cycle of regurgitation and the glug-glug-glug of chugging beer.

"Liam, we need to get you out of here," Cedra hisses, yanking him back and stepping in front of him. "Whatever pain you're suffering, Bert, it's not worth this. Can we pause for a moment and approach this reasonably," she calls out, her tone professional and even.

"Cedra, you can't reason with him. There's not much of him left." Cedra's blonde hair flutters from Liam's breath.

"I am the Trypanon killer," Bert shouts. Small lumps of flesh spew from his lips, as if he's been gnawing on his tongue. The room gasps in shock. "I have merely deflected blame in an effort to escape incarceration."

"Fuck," Ingrid says, grabbing Teddy by the arm. "He's lost it. What do we do?"

Any chance of forming a plan is taken from them. With sudden, unnatural speed, Bert lunges toward them. He runs with damaging abandon, his ankles twisting and arms flinging hard; Liam can hear the joints crack. A growl bubbles from his gullet like a wet bark. The flies buzz into a frenzy, growing louder the closer he draws.

Then Faye jumps in front of him

"Faye, no!" Liam shouts.

"Desist! You are not to harm—"

Faye cuts off with a chirp. Bert moves through her as if he doesn't know she's there, and she's thrown to the side. Her temple cracks against the edge of a table, and Liam feels her Phren black out. But Liam doesn't have a thought to spare for Faye. Bert isn't stopping.

He reaches out with fingers curled like claws. A red mist forms a halo around his body, speckled with dots of buzzing black. Liam shuts his eyes tight, and braces for impact.

But it doesn't come. He opens his eyes.

Bert's hands are wrapped around Cedra's neck. It happens too fast. The sight is so shocking, for a moment Liam can't move, can't think. And then, in one horrible swipe, a Fissure rips through the core of Cedra's mind. Liam feels the severing as if it's being done to him. It's the kind of pain that is so tremendous, so unfathomable, it feels like nothing.

Before he can breathe, before he can stop it, he witnesses something he prayed he'd never see again: a transfer. The Violence Fluke leaves Bert's Phren, now chewed to a pulp, and slides inside Cedra. The flies jump from one body to the other in perfect synchronism.

Liam swallows, forcing himself to move. Frantic, Liam tries to tie a tether between his soul and his body. If he acts fast, he can expel the Fluke before it feeds. But he's disoriented. His mind is slippery with fear. He's just finishing the link when Bert recoils from Cedra, stumbling away. His bloody eyes are bulging wide. His breath comes in lurching heaves.

"What have I done?" he slurs. "I am the sinner. I am damned."

Then Bert turns, and charges with terrible intention at the wall. Chairs squeal on the floor. There's shouting. Someone laughs in terror. And Bert's forehead collides with brick in a wet, hollow crack. He falls limp to the ground. His mutilated Phren snaps to nothing.

Liam can't focus. Everyone is suspended, unmoving. He'll agonize over this moment for the rest of his life, willing this version of himself to *move*, to do something, to look at Cedra and realize what's happening. But he doesn't.

Death has always held a strange inconsistency to Liam. A body can survive unbelievable trauma and wild, impossible odds. It can withstand savage blows and high falls. A car accident, a gunshot. Yet, if something happens just right (or just wrong), it can come easy as a smile.

Liam feels the moment Cedra's soul is torn from her Phren. The Fluke covets it like a lover, holding it tight, and drags it into the Fissure—into the Nether. One moment Cedra is present and alive, and the next, her mind is as hollow as a ship's hull. She tips to the side, her body going limp. She slips between Liam's hands when he tries to grab her. Down she goes. London Bridge. Liam's heart beats one painful drum in his chest, and he watches, useless, as her jaw catches on the edge of the mantel, over the fireplace that they sat by for the people-watching. With a crisp click, her neck snaps.

Liam's first thought is, "What a funny sound."

Then he thinks, "someone left a tea kettle on." But the high-pitched whistling is not from a kettle. He reaches up and touches his own lips. He's not making the sound either. Then he turns and sees Ingrid. She's screaming.

"God dammit, O'Connor, are you even listening to me?"

Liam hears Sloane's voice from far away. It occurs to him that he's outside, tucked in an alleyway. He doesn't know how he got there. The distant muddle of excited chatter makes him feel like he's underwater.

"Liam, we know Cedra was a friend of yours, but please understand; if we don't get more information, it's not going to look good that another person in your circle has died from a Fluke attack." Applebaum's hair is especially frizzy today. Liam's forehead tickles. He reaches up to touch it and his hand comes away wet. It must be a hot evening. His hat is soaked. Strange. Liam thought it was January.

"Liam?"

"Cut the good cop shit, Jackie. This bastard's been dodging our calls for weeks, avoiding us at every damn opportunity. I've had it. I'm about to fuck my career and cuff him. FUSE can eat my ass—"

Her fingers clasp Liam's bicep. He glances down. She's hurting him. He'll have bruises. How strange.

Sloane shakes him.

"Jesus, O'Connor, what the fuck is wrong with you? That was your fucking friend in there, wasn't it? Do you even care that these people are dying?"

Her question pierces the barrier of unfeeling Liam's built around himself. Does he care? Cedra seemed to believe he did and look where it got her. He didn't do anything to save her. He just let her die. He could have tied the tether faster. He could have gone into Bert's Phren the moment he came down the stairs and stopped him. Typical. Classic.

If he had saved Makoto, then Cedra never would have met him, and she'd still be alive.

"Maybe I don't." He says it ponderously. It's a benign concept. Maybe he doesn't care. Maybe that's why this keeps happening.

"Alright, that's it, you rat fuck. I'm taking you in for obstruction—"

"You guys!" Faye calls out, bounding into the alley. She's pressing gauze to her head. Blood is crusted in her hair. "I finally snuck away from the paramedic. I hope you're not talking about the case without me. Big break today!"

Sloane rolls her eyes so hard she winces. She lets go of Liam's arm and swings toward Faye. "We can't talk about the case because your boyfriend here won't open his fucking mouth."

At the word "boyfriend" Faye blushes scarlet. She sputters and giggles.

Liam sees her through a veil. He feels as though reality is playing around him like a movie in a foreign language. He can't find the subtitles.

"You should go to the hospital," Jackie says to Faye. She sounds tired. Or perhaps just tired of Faye.

"Not in a moment like this! Not when we finally know who the Trypanon is."

Sloane and Applebaum turn to face her fully.

"You can confirm that O'Connor is the Trypanon?" Sloane says.

"What—of course not! Liam's not the Trypanon. I mean, he's *a* Trypanon but not *the* Trypanon. Did he not tell you? Bert confessed. He called himself the 'Trypanon killer.' Then he threw me against a table and I passed out, so I missed the rest of it. But it's pretty obvious Bert ripped open a Fissure in Cedra, right in front of everyone. Then he went and killed himself. Guess he got rid of the problem for us. Too bad about Cedra, though. She seemed nice. Blonde's really don't have more fun after all."

Liam stares at his feet. There's a spot of blood on his Converse, right on the white tip. He wonders if it came from Bert's mouth or Cedra's head.

"Is that true, O'Connor?" When he doesn't answer, Sloane pokes him hard in the shoulder. "Answer or I take you in."

"It's true, right Liam?" Faye says. Liam glances up. Faye's eyes hold a gentle plea.

He nods.

"Fuck," Sloane says, throwing her hands up. "It doesn't make any fucking sense. He wouldn't fucking—God, I don't fucking know."

"So this is … over?" Applebaum says, frowning.

"Yes! All over," Faye says. "Well, not our friendships with you, Liam. You're stuck with us for life." She punches him on the arm.

"Go to the hospital and get your damn concussion checked out, Cleary. Jackie, let's get some witness testimony." She starts to leave the alley, then stops. She turns and sticks a finger in Liam's face. "I'm not done with you. I'm going to assume you had some sort of crush on Cedra and that's why you're shut up like an oyster right now, but that only buys you so much time. And if there is one more Fissure in this town for as long as you live here, I am coming right to your door. Fuck. This doesn't feel right," she mutters, shaking her head like there's a bug on it. "Nothing fucking does these days."

Liam doesn't respond. He doesn't acknowledge Applebaum when she puts a gentle hand on his shoulder and says something about calling her if he needs to talk. He doesn't respond to Faye when she titters an unsubtle confession of love and gratitude for his continued existence.

He's not sure how long he stands in the alleyway, letting the world dip out of focus. Ingrid cries in the distance at one point. Jill berates someone, her voice shrill until it cracks and cuts off.

It's dark when he finally moves. He escapes by squeezing through a narrow pathway behind a dumpster. He walks all the way home, takes some wrong turns. Serpentines. He doesn't know how much time has passed by the time he makes it home. He walks up the stairs of his porch and through the back door. He stands in his foyer, looks up the stairs, then glances into the dining room on his left, and the living room on his right.

He shuts his eyes and recedes into himself. It's like turning inside out. He blinks back into sight. The walls of his Phren rise about him.

Jasper.

He lets the word blare through his Phren, past the tidal pond in his mind, and between the hinges of his own personal door to the Nether.

Liam. The response is immediate. Jasper appears at the top of
the stairs. *"I'm sor—"*

"I'm going into the Nether." Even in his own mind, his voice is cold and remote. It leaves no room for questioning. "Bert's not the Trypanon. I need to find who is."

"Very well."

CHAPTER SIXTEEN
ABSOLUTION

"LIAM."

It's not the first time Jasper has said his name, or the first time Liam has ignored it.

He said it when Liam turned to the back door and stepped onto this porch. He said it again when Liam wouldn't stop, wouldn't respond. He tries again on Liam's path to the island—to the Nether—but Liam won't hear him. He has one purpose. He doesn't care what Jasper has to say anymore. The water hemming in his path is thick like tar. It bubbles over, spitting at his feet and threatening to suck him in.

Liam reaches the door. He's beginning to pour his power into it, to tear it open, when Jasper steps in front of him. "Liam, I don't believe it is wise to enter the Nether in your current state."

"What state is that?"

Jasper looks around, suggestively. When Liam doesn't speak, Jasper fidgets.

"I know what transpired today."

"Of course you fucking do."

Jasper looks to the side. "I … I didn't steal the memory from you. Not intentionally. Even when I don't enter your Phren, I see what you're doing. I don't see everything—I cannot control it. I've tried. I suspect it's the 'Hitch link,' as you call it. I've tried to sever the link, but I cannot."

His words are irrelevant. It seemed important before that he trust Jasper, that he be close to him. Now he doesn't see the point. When he speaks, his voice is a low echo.

"I need to know who killed her—"

Black water ripples.

"You don't believe it could be Bert Shelton?" Jasper takes a micro step closer to him. "He confessed. He transferred his Fluke to Ce—"

Liam refuses to hear her name. The sky flashes with red as if there's a solar flare.

"He couldn't have had a Fluke. Trypanons don't get Flukes."

"But how do you know?" Jasper's voice is faint. His shoulders climb toward his ears. "How can you be certain? You claimed that there is a lot we don't know about Trypanons. And you said Sophonts don't get Fissures or Flukes, but then Phoebe Shelton happened. And now Bert. What if there are more exceptions?"

Liam doesn't plan on answering, but his mind is erratic, his Phren unstable. Jasper's questions provoke something that's been buried beneath the surface.

Suddenly, his Phren transforms. They're no longer on the island in the dark, but inside a bright, sterile classroom. Wendalyn Archer stands at the head. Behind her, a whiteboard has the words "trauma-induced mind tear" written on it. The smell: dry erase markers, chlorine on linoleum, the kid named Ian that refused to shower. It's a home Liam never wanted.

"Fuck," he hisses.

"What is this place?"

"It's nothing; don't look at it."

Liam tries to dissipate the memory, but part of him doesn't want to banish it. He knows who he'll see, and the effort of not looking is too much.

Jasper says, "that's you, isn't it."

Liam gives in. His focus slinks to the boy in the desk near the back. It's always strange to see himself as a child. He's barely thirteen in this memory, sitting with his back rigid and eyes wide. He was constantly on alert then, waiting for the next attack. His hair is simply brown. He's squinting at the whiteboard, his face bare of glasses. One of the boys had stolen them. He never did find that pair.

"Is that Makoto?"

Liam fights to keep his eyes on himself, but he's weak. He hasn't allowed memories of Makoto to appear in his Phren until now. He looks—dark hair, straight posture, the way Makoto folded his hands on his desk. He was more of an adult then than Liam is now.

"Yeah. Yeah, that's him."

"Why is this memory presenting right now?"

The memory speeds up. It sprints through Archer's explanation of how trauma causes the seams of a mind to fray. Not all minds, just some. A kid raises his hand and asks why some people get Fissures and others don't. She says, *"we don't know. We are trying to find out, but for now, all we know is that being alive is just harder for some people."* The memory moves faster. It won't stop even as Makoto starts to squirm in his seat, the hair at the nape of his neck darkening with sweat. Liam wants to stop it, to tell Archer to shut up and leave it alone.

Then it happens. The students squeal and scurry away. Makoto is convulsing. He falls to the ground, clutching his head and writhing.

Everyone get back! Archer shouts. She's too late to stop Liam. They all stare, mouths agape, as young Liam takes Makoto's shoulders in his hands. They weren't friends yet. Liam had acted intuitively, with all the dangerous recklessness of a child. He didn't understand the risk then. All he knew was instinct.

The memory shifts, and the walls of Makoto's Phren form around them. Everything is in a frenzy around the Fissure. The walls are shaking. Picture frames and books and little figurines being thrown to the floor. A strange voice roars. Liam didn't learn until later that he was witnessing Makoto's worst memory: an earthquake. Makoto was only eight at the time. Liam was too busy with the Fissure to watch. It manifested as a crack in the wall beside a small bed, expanding with every jolt of the house and tear of tatami rugs.

Liam was dangerously curious then. Foolish. As he watches on with Jasper, the image of Makoto's Fissure layers over his own door to the Nether. It whines and calls for him. In it, a light—beckoning.

The light had always been there.

But the memory demands attention. He watches himself approach the Fissure and remembers how he'd believed he was so much older than he was. He thought he could handle anything. It's so obvious now how wrong he was. His expression is slack, his eyes entranced as he's drawn to the Fissure like a minnow to an angler fish's lure. Archer had beaten into his head that no one should ever go inside a Fissure, but somehow that didn't matter—all that mattered was getting to the light. He watches the small version of himself enter the Nether for the first time, and the scene changes.

It's appalling at first to see the Nether inside his own Phren, though he feels the difference between this recreated memory and the real thing. There's a flatness to this version. It doesn't evoke the same profound, consuming dread. Doesn't smell like rot.

Back then, he hadn't stayed long. The first thing he'd seen was a ravenous Yellow Fluke, drooling at the feet of the Fissure. It paused for only a moment at Liam's entrance, before charging at him. Little Liam dodges, tumbling to the side and crying out, but the Fluke wasn't aiming for him. It was trying to get into the Fissure—into Makoto. But no matter how much it gnaws and beats against the Fissure, it can't enter.

An aura blocks its way.

Eventually the Fluke turns its sights on Liam. The boy whimpers as the Fluke pounces at him, but the creature is erratic. Liam lunges away, jumping over viscous tentacles and leaping back through the Fissure. The instant he hits the floor of Makoto's Phren, the Fissure seals behind him. Somehow, he'd closed it himself. He wanted it to stop, so it did.Archer hadn't liked that explanation. She wanted to know how he did it, and why. When he answered honestly, she told him to knock it off.

As if summoned, Archer appears in Makoto's Phren. Liam can easily recall the way his heart churned when he'd pulled his hands away from his eyes and saw her. He thought he'd be expelled, that he'd have to go into foster care. As it turned out, violating another student's mind was the least of his troubles.

The vision shifts back into the too-bright classroom. Liam's small face is flushed and wet. A patch of black hair has appeared above his ear. Archer is looming over him, her features contorted with an expression Liam had never seen on an adult before. At the time, he didn't know what it meant. Now, he reads it clearly: she was terrified of him.

The rest of the memory floats by in a blur. He vaguely hears Archer say "Trypanon"—a word he'd never heard before at the time. He aches as he watches Makoto's jaw set. This is the moment Makoto decided that he owed Liam his life. This is why he put up with him for so long. In his code of ethics, he owed Liam a debt. It hurts to see it; cheapens their connection. And yet, Liam doesn't know what he would have done without Makoto at the Academy. The other students became fans or enemies. Makoto was always simply a friend.

When the memory has faded into nothing, and they're surrounded once again by night-stained seawater, with their feet covered in sand, Liam turns to Jasper.

"Sophonts can get Fissures," Liam says. "But they can't get Flukes. You saw it yourself. The aura. If Bert got a Fluke, it's because a Trypanon gave it to him. It's the only way."

"What if he inadvertently drew a Fluke into himself?"

"If he had that ability, then he'd be able to get rid of it too. It wouldn't have shredded him to a pulp like that. Bert can't be the killer."

"I see."

For some reason, Jasper's response annoys the hell out of him.

"I am finding the Trypanon tonight," Liam says. He doesn't recognize his own voice. From Jasper's expression, he isn't alone.

"How? Do you have any theories?"

Liam wonders if Jasper is provoking him on purpose.

"I have one." He stares at Jasper like his eyes could pierce him. Like he wants to hurt.

Jasper blinks. He lips part. With utter disbelief, he says, "you sincerely believe I'm the murderer."

Liam shrugs.

"Liam," Jasper says, then closes his mouth. He frowns and looks to the side. "We saw the Trypanon together. We chased it through the Nether, watched it inhabit a human Phren. How could it be me?"

"The Nether lies. It can be manipulated. I don't trust anything I've seen. I don't trust you."

Jasper doesn't respond for a long moment. Quiet, he finally says, "do you think so little of me?"

Liam doesn't answer.

"Liam, if I could escape the Nether, don't you think I would have done it?"

"But you have. You aren't in the Nether right now, are you?"

Jasper stutters. Liam's never seen him do that before. Jasper gathers himself and tries again.

"If … if your theory is correct, and I am the Trypanon, or if the culprit is currently in the Nether, it is not advisable for you to walk through that door right now."

"I don't care what happens to me."

"And what if you aren't the only one in danger? You said you don't trust what you've seen. You've said this Trypanon can manipulate the Nether. As can you. Are you certain *you* are not the Trypanon?"

"No!" He doesn't mean to shout. Jasper steps back. The word reverberates through Liam's Phren, kicking up waves around them. The smell of a storm fills the air.

"Liam." Jasper runs a hand through his hair, disheveling it. His fingers shake. "I'm sorry, I do not believe you could be the killer."

"It doesn't matter what you believe. At this point, this is all I have to go on. It's either you or it's me."

Liam moves to shove Jasper out of the way and is unsurprised when Jasper dodges him. Fine. Liam doesn't want to touch him either. He rips open the door and strides into the Nether. Jasper follows on his heels. Liam doesn't care. All that matters is ending this.

And, he hopes, finding Cedra's soul before the Trypanon gets to it.

The potency of the Nether is shocking. It greets him eagerly, drawing him in and swallowing.

"Liam, I think we should leave. Something is not right."

What a stupid thing to say. Of course something is not right. Nothing is right here, or in the Waking World, or in Liam's own Phren. It's all wrong.

"We're going to the Knox House." Liam's voice is cold. Emotionless. The Nether rumbles. Jasper doesn't argue, though Liam feels his hesitation as they glide across the water and onto Knox Island. The Nether is annoyed with Jasper. He's spoiling the fun. It tries to weigh him down and alter his path. Jasper fights to stay close.

"Liam," Jasper calls from somewhere behind him. He's ignored. All Liam cares about is gutting the Knox House until he finds what he's looking for. He's going to tear it all open. He's going to figure out why Jasper is his Hitch. Maybe Jasper's been using his body as a vessel to kill people. Maybe they're in on it together. Or maybe Jasper is simply a liar. He's lied to Liam before.

Or perhaps Liam will find nothing and prove that Jasper is innocent. Then he'll have his answer. If it's not Jasper, it's him, and he'll punish himself accordingly. Maybe he'll punish them both. It doesn't matter. Liam needs to stop this. Part of him believes that it will bring Cedra back if he does. Her body isn't rotten yet. He could put her soul back in her Phren. Why not? Why the hell not?

He throws open the porch door to the Knox House, shattering the windows.

"Liam, wait," Jasper says, breathless as he runs up to him.

"Why? Something you don't want me to see?"

As Liam strides into the foyer, the house shudders around him, squealing and warping at the intrusion. In the living room, furniture blinks in and out of existence, the walls quivering as if his very presence is a poison. Or a shot of adrenaline.

"Please, Liam. The Nether is feeding off you. It—"

Liam doesn't hear him anymore. As he strides to the fireplace, the walls billow out, shifting in and out of focus. They grow huge, then small. It's daylight, then early morning. There are voices.

Liam vaguely recognizes one. Jasper's accent is strange and specific, a mix of high-class English and old American. But here, it's the voice of a child.

Liam reaches for a box on the mantel.

"Wait, don't—" Jasper says, voice cracking.

The shadow of the boy speaks.

> *Please, Miss. I am well enough to be outside.*
>
> *Your father decreed that you are not capable of making that decision.
> Only I can make it for you, and I know that little boys like to get
> into trouble out in the mud, left to their own compulsions. No, you
> are to stay here with me.*
>
> *But I do not intend to get into trouble. I just want to see the plants.
> And there are rabbits in the garden. I saw from my window. I
> simply—*
>
> *You want to die gasping for breath over a few rabbits? What if you fall
> and break your brittle bones? Your father would never forgive me.
> As far as you are to be concerned, I am your mother now, and you
> will listen to me.*

The room fills with a peppery scent.

> *You cannot keep me here. I am not a prisoner.*

The patter of little feet on boards, moving toward the door, then abruptly stopping. The boy cries out.

> *See, you are inclined to sin. This is why God gave you such a broken
> body. It is my duty to clean it of corruption. To educate, yes. But
> also to cleanse. Praise Him I got to you when I did.*

Liam watches as the silhouettes of a woman in a heavy dress and the frame of a small, thin boy stumble to the stairs. He hears the boy's shoes clunk on the boards as he's dragged. Liam follows them to the foyer to watch. As the boy is pulled, his shoe catches between the railings, but the woman doesn't stop. She yanks. The boy's arm breaks with a dull snap.

> *You see,* the woman coos over the boy's screams, *this is what
> God does when you are wicked.*

Liam turns. Jasper stares after the boy with wide gray eyes, his skin pallid. He's holding his arm. It's easy to see how the boy grew into the man. He's sharper now, suspended in his late twenties, with his cheekbones defined and eyes less large on his face. Handsome. Then Liam realizes …

"The Tryp's victims always speak in religious terms. Archaic ones."

Jasper's eyes snap to him. "I know."

"They also had broken arms. It was a Tryp mark."

"Yes."

A darkness rises in Liam. The Nether bounces like an excited child. Liam ignores it. Striding to the fireplace again, he grabs the box off the mantel and opens it. A memory spills out: a mother, wailing in pain, the chain of a locket around her neck breaking as she writhes. The smell of blood and shit fills the room. Liam tosses the box aside. This memory is useless for his purpose.

Liam goes to Sebastian Knox's desk and throws open the roll top, letting papers fly out and flutter around the room. More memories. Too many, all mixing.

I have found you a suitable wife. It's time for you to become a man.

No.

Do you really need to leave again, Father? You just returned.

Your governess tells me your interests are not natural.

I am never to be wed.

Call me Mother or take the Birch.

Your father and I will be married.

Confirmed bachelor.

Do you hate me, Father?

I've never known what to feel for you.

None of this is useful. With a growl, Liam banishes the memories, wiping the room clean. He whirls around. Jasper stumbles back, his eyes wide. He's scared. Liam knows he's hiding something.

"Where is it?" The walls shake. Liam's voice echoes.

"What?"

"You're lying to me. You're hiding something. What is it?"

"I'm not—"

"Liar!" Liam shouts. A chunk of the ceiling falls to the floor. Damp rats pour from it. Jasper steps back. He looks appalled by the rats. Coward. Liam lunges toward him, and Jasper retreats until his back hits the wall. His eyes are close—dilated. "Tell me." It's a command. Liam feels the power behind it, lets it rise inside him. The Nether helps, rising with him.

Maybe the Nether isn't the enemy. Maybe the Nether is the only thing on his side.

He feels Jasper's breath on his face. His gray gaze tips down to Liam's mouth, then back to his eyes.

"Tell me," Liam says again. Low, this time—soft.

Then Jasper looks to the stairwell. Liam shoves off him. Moves. He floats up to the top of the stairs in an instant, and then his chest clenches. He blinks, turns, and takes a few steps—stops.

Down the hall, in Jasper's room—the light. It quivers in the dark. It's coming from the small table in front of the window. Jasper is shouting for him from far away. He's trying to come up the stairs, but the Nether won't let him. Good. He'll only stop Liam from finding the truth.

Liam stares into the light. It pulls him, guiding his feet. A righteous conquering pullulates inside him. This is the moment; he once ran from the light—now, he's going to catch it. Snuff it out. He crosses into the bedroom, and the door slams behind him, shuttering the room in heavy darkness. Fear rolls through him, but only for a moment before the light draws his focus again. He drifts closer, reaching out. His hand trembles. Then his fingertips touch the warm edges of the light. It flares at his touch, banishing the darkness. He squints against it. Then, slowly, his vision adjusts.

Cedra stands in front of him. In her hand—the pocket watch. Jasper's pocket watch. An ache digs a hole in his chest and plants in his belly. Cedra's hair is caked with blood. One of her eyes swivels at an angle, split like a cooked grape.

Why didn't you save me? Her voice whistles in her throat. He can hear the broken bone blocking her trachea. *You just stood there. You didn't do anything to save me. Everything I thought about you is wrong.*

"I'm—I'm not—"

The walls around him disappear with a rush of sea air. Suddenly, he's back on the shore behind his house. The sun is out. The air is hot and wet. People are shouting and running. Someone is splashing in the water, their cries gurgling. It's a child. No. More than one.

The world changes again. He's inside a Phren … Harold Parsons's Phren. And he sees himself, only a child, trying to seal a Fissure.

You couldn't save his mind. Not all the way. Not in the ways that matter. Did you know he didn't recognize me most days? His own daughter.

"I tried. I … I was just a boy."

You were always more than a boy. You were a mistake.

Mistake. He sees the form of the word on his mother's lips, though he cannot hear it. She turns and looks at him like he's a monster. She never looked at him like a son again.

Someone is banging on a distant door. Then, brick walls rise around him, closing him in a kind of canyon. The sky above is black and empty. A smell washes over him. He turns … and sees himself with Makoto standing beside him. They're holding hands, looming over the form of Samantha Munn, her mouth gaping and head tilted to the starless sky.

"No."

You failed him too. You didn't act. You just stood there.

The Nether contracts, and laughs, and changes into a hospital room.

"No, not this."

Makoto stands before him. He's not like the boy Liam saved in a classroom, or the man he came to know in dive bars and alleyways. He is devoured—a mauled shadow. He gawks at Liam with vacant eyes, set in rotten skin. Liam can see his heart—the final, convulsing beats. His body couldn't take being a Husk.

Liam reaches for him, fingers spread, and is shoved away. He tries again, fighting to touch him, but Makoto repels him like a rip current. Over and over the scene replays.

You did nothing to save him.

"I'm trying." His own voice startles him. The banging gets louder.

And it wasn't good enough. You couldn't save my father. You couldn't save Makoto. You couldn't save me. Everything you touch dies.

"Don't say that." An icy, suffocating weight crawls up his body. He feels it consuming him—no, changing him. He reaches for Makoto one last time. When Makoto rejects him with a wicked smile, Liam gives up. He sinks and exhales. He doesn't care anymore. The tears sting on his face.

And he's back in The Salt Cellar. A swarm of flies forms the shape of Bert Shelton. It sways and buzzes, fixing Liam with dead, white eyes. Cedra's shadow clings to Liam's back. Her lips graze his ear.

You could have stopped him now, but you didn't. You never do anything. All that power, all that talent and training … a waste. You're a coward. Cedra's words wriggle in his ear like worms. Bert growls, slinking closer. *You are the Trypanon killer.*

It's true. He is the reason so many have died. He deserves this. He belongs in the Nether with the rest of the creatures and the shades.

The banging crescendos. The world shudders, flashing back into Jasper's bedroom, then the shore, then the hospital room.

Two more figures appear.

You did this to us. Our blood is on your hands.

Phoebe and Jake are thin shells of themselves, chopped up by metal and shattered glass. Phoebe sits in her imposing office chair with her legs crossed. At her feet, Jake kneels with collar about his neck. A leash leads from it to Phoebe's spindly hand. She yanks, and Jake moans, and Phoebe moans. Then it's not Jake at all, but Liam on the floor. He stares at his own face, at the euphoria heavy on his eyelids.

You are nothing but a servant, Phoebe says. *And you love it. You crave it. You want to be told what to do, how to feel. I could tell you when to piss and shit and your little heart would bloom.*

She rises to her feet and takes a step toward him, then another. She jerks the leash and Jake—no, Liam—follows.

Close, closer. Bert, Phoebe, Jake, and Cedra—all around him.

Then a resounding crack fills the air.

"It is time for you to leave. Get out of my home."

Jasper's voice is like a melody. Liam is having trouble remembering who Jasper is. He's having trouble remembering anything. There's a scuffle happening around him, but he can't focus his eyes to watch it unfold. He's lost.

"Be free of this place."

Liam's vision clears. He looks at Jasper and sees the light—the same light that's followed him all his life—burning in Jasper's chest. It's so different than the one Cedra used to draw him close. How could he have confused the two? The light grows and expands. It spreads to the broken soul of Cedra, to Phoebe and Jake. It dissipates the illusion of Bert. That's right—Bert died; he wasn't consumed by the Nether. He can't be here. But the rest … oh, he sees the truth now:

They're Wicks.

Even Cedra.

As the light blankets her, he is overwhelmed by her relief, her liberation, even as she crosses out of the Nether, into somewhere new and better. Phoebe and Jake follow, sighing out. Becoming free. Jasper is glowing. For a delirious moment, Liam thinks he's an angel. Then he shakes away the thought, scoffing at himself. He'd never say something like that. Why did he? Who made him? His awareness is coming back. The Nether's hold is shaking loose. It whines and sizzles in the burn of the light.

Harnessing all he has left, Liam shoves the Nether back, out of the house and off of Knox Island. For the moment, the house belongs to them. As Jasper collapses to the floor, the room reverts to his bedroom. Liam senses a distant surge of fury.

"Jasper," Liam says, hoarse, crawling to him on his hands and knees. Jasper is curled up, the tail of his coat fanning out behind him. "What happened?"

"Nether prison." His voice is fragile. "I told you it was not advisable to enter the Nether now."

"You can collect your 'I told you so' trophy later. Let's go home."

"For the first time tonight, I agree with you."

Liam reaches out to grab him and stops with his fingers hovering. "I'm going to need to touch you, though. Is that alright?"

"It will have to be."

Liam is expecting Jasper's thoughts to punch into his mind like they did before. Instead, at their contact, Jasper sighs in relief. Liam feels it too; like sliding into bed after a long trip. He can taste the edges of Jasper's thoughts, but they're fuzzy with exhaustion. They aren't overwhelming, and Liam finds himself sinking into the connection.

He pulls Jasper to his feet, cinching an arm around his waist. Liam's power is different when they're touching. It's calmer, less volatile, flowing between them in a loop.

It's easy to carry them from Jasper's bedroom to the Nether door. Once they're safe inside Liam's Phren, with the Nether shut away, he tidies up the mess he left behind and takes Jasper back to the house. He guides Jasper into his usual armchair and summons the image of Kermit. When Jasper's eyes slide to the little black rabbit, the edge of his mouth ticks up.

"So I was, uh, kind of a dick in there, huh," Liam says, crossing his arms.

"I have never met a Richard to compare you to."

Liam sighs. "I mean I was an asshole."

"I know."

He looks at Liam through the corner of his eyes.

"You made a joke," Liam says with awe.

"You seem surprised."

"I just didn't think you'd want to joke at a time like this."

"I can't imagine a better time to acquire a sense of humor."

Liam shakes his head. "Sometimes I wonder if I know you at all."

Jasper stares at him. There's something in his eyes that Liam can't place. It makes him fidget.

"So, the Trypanon put me in a Nether prison," Liam says, looking at the ground.

"Yes. I could tell when I saw the light at the top of the stairs."

"How?"

"Because I am the source of the light; it could not be me. It was a trap."

Liam collapses onto the couch. Now that he and Jasper aren't touching, his mind burns. He's desperate to rest, but this can't wait.

"I'm sorry," he says.

"I know."

Liam swallows. "I know I barely knew her, but I really liked Cedra."

"I believe your affections were reciprocated."

Liam sighs. "This can't keep happening. I have to stop this person. I can't ... I can't just stand there, not doing anything. Not again."

He tosses off his glasses and rubs at his eyes. The case has become too messy, the possibilities too varied. It wasn't always so difficult to work a case. His mind itches with it.

"I can't think straight. I know there's something I'm missing. Jesus, maybe I'm not as smart as I used to be."

"Then let us talk through it. Who makes our list of suspects now?" Jasper says. He weaves his fingers together on his lap.

"Present company excluded?" Jasper rolls his eyes. "Hey, I can have a sense of humor too."

"Can you?"

"*Anyway*, Bert was my best guess and that's out the window. The only other Sophont in the area is Faye, and I can't imagine her pulling this off; she's too weak. And she was unconscious when Bert attacked Cedra. I also highly doubt she'd try to kill me."

"Because she is enamored with you."

Liam cringes. "Yeah."

Jasper gives him a strange look. Liam isn't sure what to make of it. He goes on.

"I guess there's Angelica Fenton. She's religious," Liam says. "She could have attacked Oliver as punishment for abandoning her. Just seems odd that she'd do it *after* he moved back in, or that she'd let him move out in the first place if she had Tryp powers. And I didn't sense any paraphrenic abilities in her. Though, I'm wondering how much I can trust my senses."

"If we proceed under the assumption that a soul from my time escaped the Nether and is inhabiting a living vessel, there would be a distinct change in personality upon possession. Other people would surely notice it. By all accounts, Angelica's behavior seems rather consistent."

"True, but who knows when the initial possession happened. Time is strange in the Nether. If only we knew more about who this Trypanon was, we could…"

Jasper's gaze narrows. Liam rubs the back of his head.

"I guess you've been pushing me to investigate your past this whole time. And I haven't exactly been nice about it."

Jasper stares at him.

"Sorry," Liam mumbles.

"Unnecessary."

"So, let's talk about you, then. You really don't think your governess could have been a Trypanon?" he tries. "She checks the ultra-religious box and she's someone you knew. Maybe she waltzed through a Fissure and got stuck in the Nether. Then … I dunno, a hundred and fifty years later, the moment presented itself and she escaped, possessing some poor bastard's Phren and using their body like a puppet to enact her holy vengeance."

"We have no evidence that she was a Trypanon, or even a Sophont. Only Trypanons can leave the Nether once they've entered it."

"You escape all the time."

The words herald a silence. It's a moment before Jasper speaks. "Is it possible that a Hitch link enables a soul to escape the Nether?"

Liam's eyes throb. He feels the ache in the walls around them. "I believe one or both parties must be a Sophont. It's the only thing that makes sense. Maybe living in the Nether for years gives a Sophont Wick the ability to travel in and out, if they can draw on a Hitch link."

"Or we are both Trypanons."

"Shit, I dunno. Maybe. At the very least, you're a Sophont. After what we just saw you do today, I don't think we can deny it. Takes a lot of paraphrenic energy to fuck up a Nether prison like that."

Jasper stares off. Liam can almost feel his thoughts churning. "Why is this happening now?" Jasper says, quiet.

Liam throws up his hands. "Shit, I don't know. My brain hurts. I don't know why you're my Hitch; I don't know how anyone but a Trypanon could escape the Nether; I don't know how a Trypanon could avoid detection by FUSE, I don't know how your hair always looks perfect, I don't know why this is happening now, and I don't know why a Trypanon would kill all these people if they're relig—"

The word cuts off. Behind Jasper, the memory of Archer's classroom reappears. Liam stares at it. Something sparks. *Trypanons*, Archer says. But what did she say?

He takes hold of the memory and pulls it out, cleaning off the dust and flushing out the details. He points at it until Jasper turns in his seat and watches. Liam does his best to ignore the small version of Makoto, squirming in his seat before the Fissure took him. What did Archer say about Trypanons and religion?

"Liam, what are you—"

"Shush it!"

Archer speaks.

Since Sophonts have difficulty mastering and advancing their abilities without proper training, there was no specific classification for them until the twentieth century. Up until that enlightenment, most of them were labeled as Witches, the mentally ill, the possessed, or even saintly figures throughout history. Trypanons, however, have been prominently recognized in society for thousands of years. The word 'Trypanon' in ancient Greek, translates to 'mind surgeon.'

Ancient civilizations believed that a Trypanon was a religious figure to be worshipped, a practice we now know as 'Trypanism,' an ancient spirituality that functions like an add-on to pre-existing religions. While it has strong ties to Greco-Roman origins, similar traits are found in ancient religions all over the world. The central concept is that there are rare individuals chosen by God or the Gods to tear away the veil that divides the divine from mankind. This act of 'tearing' subjects mortals to the wrath, judgement, or pleasures of the divine. In English, these special conduits are called, most commonly, "Tryps," but they have also been labeled as Soothsayers, Psychics, Daemons, Witches, Witch-doctors, and more.

She points to the whiteboard behind her, the words unblurring as the memory takes form.

In Trypanism, it was believed that a Trypanon needed to accomplish these four tasks to achieve divine righteousness. This is the best translation we have. She points to each number and reads aloud:

> *1.) Must expose yourself to God's judgment by entering the Underworld. If one is allowed to return to the Waking World, they will possess the ability to herald His judgment*
>
> *2.) Must open a Tear in a loved one to prove fealty to God and deferment to his judgement over all desires*
>
> *3.) Must expose 5 sinners for judgment in order of the 5 great sins: Vice, Neglect, Subjugation, Violence, and Despair*
>
> *4.) Finally, must instigate an event of mass judgment in a hub of sin (as with Sodom and Gomorrah)*

Pausing the memory with a swipe of his arm, Liam shoots to his feet and rushes toward Jasper. He grips the arms of Jasper's chair and leans down. Jasper blinks up at him. His eyes are wide.

"That's it! That's what our Tryp is doing. Fuck, I'm such a fucking idiot; how did I not see it before? They're completing the Trypanon tasks. It makes perfect sense. Maggie was the first—she had a Vice Fluke. Oliver had a Neglect Fluke, Jake and Phoebe had Subjugation, and Bert had Violence. And then I … wait. Shit. Why did the Tryp come after me? I don't have a Blue Fluke. Even if I did, I'm a Trypanon. Giving a Sophont a Fluke is one thing; there's no way they could make another Trypanon get one. Fuck. Well … maybe they knew I was getting close to figuring them out and they wanted to stop me."

His breath catches as Jasper gently splays his palm at the center of Liam's chest. He twitches, catching Jasper's eyes with a question. The impact of the touch is instant, and Liam finds himself leaning into it. Then Jasper puts the slightest pressure against him, and Liam realizes he's being nudged away. "Sorry," he says as he steps back. Just as their contact breaks, he feels the edges of Jasper's thoughts.

"What is it?" Liam says.

Jasper rises from the chair and approaches the mantel. He braces a hand on it, sighing. "There's something I haven't told you."

A shiver works up Liam's back, shaking the walls. His throat tightens. He doesn't want bad news. The grief sidles up to him and he presses it down, stuffing it back in the cellar. "Go ahead."

"Blue Flukes are not as you believe them to be. They are not as you were taught."

"What do you mean?"

Jasper inhales deep and swallows hard. He seems to be bracing himself. "They are not Flukes."

"What? What are you—"

"A Blue Fluke is a Wick."

Liam rubs at his temples. "That doesn't make sense."

"A Blue Fluke is a soul in the Nether that has given in to despair. I knew that before this evening, but tonight I learned that they also must be a Sophont. Possibly even a Trypanon. It's why they're so rare."

"But ... how do you know?"

Jasper turns. He meets Liam's eyes. "I have known one."

Liam stammers. "What? Who?"

"The killer. I know it now. I was with them all these years. I would run or hide, and they would follow. They tormented me, hated me. I do not know the reason. I once knew their face, their name, their past, but they stole it from me long ago. I should have stopped them when I realized what they were doing, though I doubt I had the power. They always wanted to escape, were always searching for Fissures to sneak through. Or perhaps they were searching for someone. I ... I believe they could have been searching for you. Something changed the night you came to Shoalport. Their despair washed away, but their power grew. I saw them escape. I don't know who they possessed. I wasn't much of myself then."

Liam's Phren, always moving and humming with life around them, is frozen.

"Liam," Jasper says, putting his hand to his throat, over the white ascot. "I didn't know until I saw your memory tonight. I ... I was there when Makoto died. I'd been spying on the Blue Fluke. They moved with such purpose, over such a great span of the Nether. But, as you know, space works differently in the Nether. I barely managed to keep up with them. They ... they were the Blue Fluke that claimed Makoto."

The room shutters into silvered darkness. For a time, there is no feeling, no thoughts. Processing Jasper's words comes slow. Disbelief is like sludge in his mind. He'd never considered the possibility that the two—the murder case and Makoto's death—were related. It's too much to fathom and it's too easy to blame himself. If Liam had never come to Shoalport, Cedra would still be alive. If he had stopped the Blue Fluke in Chicago, he could have saved all those people.

The cellar door flies open, crashing against the wall in the kitchen. Grief shambles out across the floor like wet smoke.

"Liam, please. I didn't know. The memories, they come on so strangely."

Liam doesn't speak. His eyes are fixed on the fog moving across the floor, drawing closer.

"Liam." Jasper strides to him, inserting himself between Liam and the fog. He's a little taller than Liam, and he fills up his vision. Liam still can't speak.

Why does Liam never do the right thing? Why couldn't he save any of them?

"William."

Jasper places his palm on Liam's chest. He does something that Liam doesn't understand. Warmth and calm bloom from his touch. Jasper's thoughts, full of logic and determination, pour into Liam, brightening dark corners and cleansing. He gasps, grabbing Jasper at the wrist and pressing his hand in closer. Yet, it's not enough. He can't be close enough. He wants to wrap his arms around Jasper and drag him against his whole body. He wants more ...

Jasper pulls away. Liam hears the cellar door slam and lock.

"What the hell was what?" Liam says, breathless.

"I'm not certain." Jasper appears utterly unaffected, except for the pink tips of his ears and his dilated pupils. "The mechanisms of our Hitch link are still veiled from me."

Small fuzzy bits of light pop around Liam's body. He stumbles back to the couch and sits, hanging his head between his knees.

"I don't understand why being alive is so difficult for me."

Jasper stands beside Kermit's pen. "I don't know if life is easy for anyone. And we are privileged in countless ways. But yes, some of us do seem rather cursed."

"Jasper."

Jasper turns. Their eyes meet.

"I'm sorry."

"You keep saying that."

"No, listen. After what happened today, I get why you would do anything to escape the Nether. It changes you. It manipulates. It takes you away from yourself."

"I have not been myself for a long time."

Liam catches his gaze, and holds it. "Let's try to fix that."

Jasper nods, then his brow twitches and his eyes narrow. "You thought I could be the killer tonight."

"If it makes you feel any better, I thought I could be too."

"Neither of us is religious. We don't seek the holy wrath and power of divine judgement through self-righteousness."

"I dunno, I can be pretty judgmental."

"And I can be self-righteous."

Liam shrugs. "Hopefully that doesn't make us murderers."

He smiles, but Jasper doesn't return it. His focus falls back to Kermit. Liam hears him whisper to himself, "I hope not."

"Hey, Friendly Ghost."

Jasper side-eyes him. "I don't understand that moniker."

"Thank you. For saving me in there. You didn't have to do that. I think … I think without you I'd have lost myself."

"Then we are even."

CHAPTER SEVENTEEN
THE REKINDLING

When liam wakes, he doesn't remember that Cedra has died, or anything that happened the night before. His thoughts are devoid of Blue Flukes or Trypanons. It's cloudy outside, casting his room in shades of gray. Usually, he's wrenched into consciousness by blades of bright sun. Today, he slept late, soothed by the whirr of the air conditioner. He lets himself sigh into the respite, knowing distantly that it's temporary. He doesn't get mornings like this, but for the moment, he's like everyone else.

You seem uncharacteristically content.

"Helps when you actually sleep."

A silence. He savors one last slow breath. Then, all the harsh detritus of reality falls back into his head, clunking into place with the clench of his jaw. His eyes ache, even after he's put on his glasses. He can't believe Cedra is gone. He can't believe he almost went dark side. He groans into a long stretch.

"We didn't talk about a game plan last night."

There were other more pressing matters to address first.

Liam probably shouldn't get used to talking to Jasper out loud. Might cause problems in public, and if Sloane catches him, she'll send him straight to a loony bin.

> *Should we go to your place and dig around? Maybe we'll find something we didn't before.*

> *Yes. I feel … deeper today. More complete. Perhaps due to what occurred last night.*

You mean because I went into your own personal trauma house and dug
    out all your memories and threw them in your face?
    … yes.

Liam pauses. "I am sorry," he says out loud.

    I am aware.

Though his words are flat, Liam feels the soft amusement behind them.

Rising to his feet, Liam strips off his T-shirt and strides into the bathroom for a shower. He's turned on the water and hooked his thumbs into the elastic of his boxers when it occurs to him that Jasper has gone profoundly silent.

    Am I offending your Victorian sensibilities again?

A tingle of annoyance flutters through Liam's mind. He tries not to grin when Jasper declines to answer.

    Did you guys even have showers in your day?
    We had a water closet and a tub. As an architect, my father was invested
    in importing the most advanced accoutrement into our home.

Liam has the sense that Jasper is seizing the opportunity to swing the subject away from Liam's state of undress. He peels off the last of his clothes and steps into the shower, not bothering to hide his smirk when he realizes Jasper has receded to the tower in his Phren. It's probably not fair of Liam to tease him. Doesn't mean he plans to stop.

Jasper doesn't emerge to the forefront of Liam's consciousness until Liam is about to leave the house.

    You should bring my pocket watch with you.
    Why?
    I'm not sure. I have the sense it will help recover my memories.
    Hope I don't drop it in the water or something.
    Please do not.

With the pocket watch in a Ziploc bag, tucked deep into his backpack, Liam climbs into his kayak and starts paddling for Knox Island. The fog is thick and heavy with the scent of the sea. Dew settles on Liam's skin. Visibility shifts with each sway of the wind. He's beginning to worry that he's lost his bearings when the small tidal island appears out of the mist. The tide is rising, engulfing the base of the island in gray water. Only a few large rocks and the dead tree, its bows reaching for the sky, are visible. A seagull perches on the highest branch. In the fog, the island is like a phantom, escaping a dream.

    It's unsettling to see the island, Jasper says as Liam paddles around
    it. *Even in your Waking World.*

Liam nods. *Does it help you remember anything?* He doesn't add
    "about how you died."

> *No, not substantially. I recall waiting. I know I checked my pocket watch several times. I can only assume a Fissure opened in me and I was pulled into the Nether. My Husk must have drowned in the tide. It's rather embarrassing that my legacy is reduced to being a lovelorn fool who couldn't comprehend a tidal chart. As if I hadn't lived on an island my entire life.*

Liam has the sense that Jasper isn't telling the whole truth, but he doesn't push. He imagines death to be a personal matter. If Jasper isn't ready to go into every explicit detail, that's his prerogative, as long as doesn't impact the case.

Liam's thoughts drift to his vision from the Nether, of a little boy thrashing in the water near the island. It's easy to imagine Jasper in the boy's place, gasping and burping seawater, reaching for the sky just like the tree. He wipes the damp from his forehead. His lips taste like salt.

As they put the island behind them, the Knox House emerges from the fog. Liam is so caught by the tower, the dark windows, and the presence of the house, that he almost crashes his kayak into a rock near the shore.

> *Not much of a wayfarer.*
>
> *It's foggy, you ass.*
>
> *All the more reason to look where you're going.*

Liam grumbles a yarn of profanities as he beaches the kayak and pulls it up onto the meadow. He's careful to avoid any rocks hidden in the thick grass as he approaches the house. He hesitates before the mess of rotten porch boards. Jasper is annoyingly amused by his trepidation. Then he snaps: *Wait.*

"Jesus, what?" Liam says, gasping and clutching his chest.

> *The greenhouse.*

Liam turns, facing it. *Yeah?*

> *I wish to try something.*
>
> *Knock yourself out.*

Liam rounds the porch and steps onto an overgrown flagstone path. The greenhouse hasn't changed since he last saw it. Most of the glass is broken, the interior overgrown with saplings and weeds. He's about to ask Jasper what he's trying to do when, slowly, it transforms before his eyes. The glass walls reform, the weeds recede. An array of potted plants appears inside its walls.

> *Holy shi—*

A figure takes shape inside, blurry through the glass. Liam approaches, slow, and the vision comes into focus. It's Jasper, though he's only a teenager. He's in black trousers and a white shirt, its sleeves rolled up to his forearms. His hair is wet with sweat, clinging to his nape in short curls.

How are you doing this? Liam doesn't dare speak out loud, as if
the specter can hear him.

*I am using the same mechanism that exposes your memories to me. At
least that's my theory. I'm not sure I could have achieved this prior
to last night. Your memory of Makoto inspired me.*

Oh.

Does it make you uncomfortable?

Liam watches young Jasper as he leans his hip against a table, picks up the
same journal Liam found in his desk, and begins to sketch.

*No. Though I guess I'm not sure if this is the Nether breaking into my
consciousness again or just a Hitch thing.*

Would you like me to stop?

No. No, I think we gotta do this if we want to solve the case.

Jasper's hum of agreement vibrates inside Liam's skin, making him shiver.
Liam watches Jasper fiddle around in his greenhouse, pruning off yellow
leaves and scribbling notes. The flush in his cheeks and twinkle in his eyes is
distracting, if only for how it throws Jasper's usual form into stark contrast.
There's a resignation—a sadness—that hasn't yet paled his features.

"You must miss gardening." It's a stupid thing to say.

I miss a lot of things.

When Liam starts to turn away, the clean, lush greenhouse fades back into
a decaying shell. A bird flies out of the top, squawking as if it's offended by
the change. Liam can still hear it cawing into the distance when he makes his
way back to the porch.

Perhaps you should climb through a window.

Assuming I could get one open.

Liam takes his chances again with the porch. He makes it through the
door, only tripping once on a chunk of soggy wood. Inside the Knox House,
it's as if the fabric between reality and the Nether has decayed. It's charged
with memory, seeming to breathe and rumble. Though Liam has been seeing
the Nether in his Waking World for years, it's never been so present and yet,
under his control. He guesses it has something to do with his Hitch link to
Jasper, or maybe the Tryp's meddling damaged the veil here.

A figure runs past, brushing against the fabric of Liam's swim shorts and
scaring the shit out of him.

Apologies. That is my conjuration.

Asshole. You scared me on purpose.

Hardly.

Liam grumbles. He peeks around the corner into the living room. Jasper, only ten or eleven, runs up to his father where he sits at his desk.

Father, have you ever been to Japan?

No.

I read today that they have these creatures called "tanukis." Do they look like the raccoon I saw from my window the other night?

His father doesn't respond. Jasper bounces on his heels.

What about New Zealand? Have you been there? I read today that there are these large blue birds that can't fly and these giant silver ferns that—

I'm busy.

The boy chooses not to hear. He makes an aborted movement to touch his father's arm, and barrels on, voice high and tremulous.

Do you think we'll ever be able to travel again? Charles Darwin got to sail all over the world, and he saw so many animals. I'd love to see—

You're out of breath.

The little boy freezes. He holds his breath for a moment, and coughs with his mouth closed, air punching out of his nose. His father turns and fully looks at him for the first time. He grabs Jasper by the shirt and yanks him close, putting his ear to Jasper's mouth.

Breathe, he commands. Jasper hesitates and his father jerks him again. Jasper takes one long slow inhale and exhale. The wheeze tattles on him. His father releases him and lightly pushes him away.

This is why I must have you monitored at all moments. Your asthma is worsening. Go to your room and rest. You are not to leave your bed for the rest of the day. I had hesitated to do this, but if you don't have the discipline on your own, I will need to hire a caregiver to monitor you. Now, go.

But Father—

It takes a single sharp look to silence the boy. The memory spasms and fades.

"Father of the year, huh?" Liam says out loud.

> *Quite. Though I find I don't resent him as I once did. He could never*
> *speak of my mother. I sense losing her changed him.*

"She died in childbirth, right? That's probably why he was so nutty about your health."

Jasper doesn't respond.

Liam changes the subject. "Did you ever get to do some traveling? I know it wasn't exactly easy back then, without planes and shit."

> *No. After university I returned here to manage the estate. I … regret*
> *it immensely. I did nothing with my short life, saw nothing. Had I*
> *known I'd die so young, perhaps I'd have done more. Perhaps not.*

Liam frowns, unsure of what to say. He is about to turn and try another room when he gets an idea. "Don't move."

Liam closes his eyes and recedes into his Phren. Jasper seems taken aback when he appears in front of him. He's standing beside Kermit's pen. Liam strides to him and grabs his hand. The wave of contentment comes swift, familiar now, with Jasper's warm wrist closed in his fingers.

What are you—

Jasper is cut off by Liam lifting them from his Phren's living room and dropping them into a memory. Around them, a forest rises. Thick moss carpets the ground and tree trunks. Large fans of ferns splay above them, casting shadows. Liam conjures the smell, still so vivid in his memory. Damp and clean; fertile and verdurous. A bird with a white tuft on its throat chortles at them from a branch above.

What—what have you –

It's New Zealand. Do you know that bird?

It's a tui, Jasper says without hesitating. He blinks and his lips
      part.

There's something about Jasper's expression that Liam wants to pursue, to augment. He conjures more memories, one after another, sewing them together in a medley. He takes Jasper to the streets of Kyoto at night, with the shrine lamps glowing in the dark and a sweet wooden scent soaking the air like tea. He shows him snow monkeys bathing in a hot spring, their faces red and fur flecked with snow. He takes him to the cactus section of the Huntington botanical gardens in Los Angeles and finds himself laughing at the sheer astonishment on Jasper's face. Liam pulls out more and more, all the travel he's done in the pursuit of Fissures and Flukes. Scotland, Ukraine, South Africa, Argentina. In truth, he'd always been a bit numb to the sites of the world. The muzzle of his work muted the highs and accentuated the dark lows inside infested Phrens.

But in watching Jasper, Liam feels like he's experiencing his own memories for the first time.

He ends with a garden inside a Roman ruin. A black stray cat had been sitting on the branch of a lemon tree, with columns rising behind it. Liam always thought it was posing intentionally, as cats tend to do.

The living room of Liam's Phren eases back into being around them. Liam relinquishes Jasper's wrist and smirks at the stunned look on his face. He leaves him be, returning to his body and to reality.

That. That was …

You're welcome. I know it's not quite the same thing as getting to travel yourself, but I figure if we have this mind-meld thing we might as well have some fun with it.

Liam.

Liam stops. He swallows, cheeks warming. He's glad he can't see Jasper's face right now.

"Where to next?" he says, voice loud in the old house.

A pause.

We should investigate my bedroom again. His voice shakes. Liam smirks.

Liam is careful as he ascends the rickety stairs, the boards whining under his hiking sandals. When he reaches the top and turns down the hall, he finds Jasper's bedroom door open. "Any tips?"

Liam has the strange sensation of Jasper seeing through his eyes. While unsettling, he scans the room anyway, and tries not to think about how few barriers there are between them now. He looks at the bed frame and the painting he left on the nightstand. Then to the desk, with its large cabinet doors. Jasper doesn't speak. Liam looks at the table in front of the window.

Wait. There. Go to the table and open the drawer.

"But I already looked in there."

Jasper's silence articulates a clear "do it anyway." Liam shakes his head and goes to the table, pulling open the drawer.

"See, it's exactly as I left it." He's about to shut it and walk away when a sharp ping in his head stops him. Rather than tell him what he wants, Jasper presents a visual of a long, pale hand reaching into the drawer and unhinging a hidden slot on the bottom. Liam blinks, battling the instinct that he's dreaming, that this can't be his real life. He mimics the movements of Jasper's phantom hand and can almost feel the cool graze of his palm as he pulls open the hidden compartment beneath the floor of the drawer. He draws out the contents and splays them on the tabletop. It's mostly yellowed papers: a few letters, a book, and what seems to be a map. He examines the latter first. It's a moment before he realizes he's looking at a rendering of the surrounding area. Though there is some skill, it seems to have been drawn by a child. The lines of the Knox House are crooked, and there are spots where too much ink spilled out. The O'Connor House is slightly out of proportion. There's a dotted path linking each house to the island in the river. Above the island, he can just make out the words "Secret Hideout." Then he looks at Knox Island. Beside the oak sprouting from the top of the island is the label: *The Letterbox.*

"What is this?"

I believe it was a project with a childhood friend.

"You had friends?" Liam winces, Jasper's apparent offense stinging the air. "I only mean you were so isolated. I didn't think you'd be allowed to associate with other kids."

I imagine I wasn't until my governess was relieved of duty.

"Any idea what changed your father's tune on that? Or when it happened? He seemed pretty adamant about her in that memory downstairs."

She broke my arm.

"Oh. Right."

*Do not self-flagellate over your consistent lack of tact. I was happy to
    sacrifice my arm to expel her from my life.*

"I'm tactful!"

Read the letters.

Liam grumbles.

The first letter confirms what Jasper says of his governess. In her missive to Sebastian, she blames Jasper for her termination, citing his colossal "wickedness" and "proclivity to sin." She declares that she is returning to England and will never revisit America again, so she can stay "as far from the hell-spawn as possible." Liam grimaces at her final line: "Our love could have moved mountains."

I thought people from your time were supposed to be poetic.

*This must be why I intrinsically doubt she is our killer. It seems unlikely
    that she would allow her own termination if she was a Trypanon,
    or even a Sophont. She certainly would have subjected me to God's
    divine wrath if it was in her power.*

"Because you're a 'hell-spawn,' huh?"

*The term came to be more apt than she intended. Read another letter,
    please.*

"Fine, fine."

Pinned to the back of the governess's letter is one addressed to Jasper, signed by his father.

"This must have been a little validating," Liam says as he skims it. Though Jasper's father is hardly sappy, he does express more emotion than Liam expected. He seems genuinely contrite that he subjected Jasper to his abusive live-in governess, and even goes so far as to say, "From this moment on, I will leave you to dictate the management of your health and well-being. I will provide a tutor, but they will have restricted liberties. You will attend Exeter Academy with other children when you are of age."

I suppose I kept it for a reason.

"Date says 1874. How old were you then?"

I was twelve.

"Bit young for your dad to saddle you with complete responsibility over your life. And by letter, too."

There wasn't much choice. He was hardly present. I was happy to be
alone, as long as I was receiving an adequate education.

"Looks like you weren't totally alone though."

Liam uncovers the next letter.

My dearest friend, Darwin,

I am afraid that this will be my last post via oak tree for many months, possibly years, to come. I have elected to attend Columbia to pursue the dreams of my father and, if I'm able, a few of my own. I am sure to meet an assortment of new and interesting people. Regrettably, I will inform them that they are all inferior to you, if undoubtedly less odd. I jest. Your oddness has always eliminated the possibility of you being boring, a rare and invaluable trait.

The truth is that I will miss you immeasurably. I will always be looking forward to the moment when we may meet on our little island again.

Your dearest friend,
Calico Jack

"'Calico'? What the hell? Who is Calico? And are you supposed to be 'Darwin'?"

Before Jasper can answer, Liam's thoughts leap backward: Jasper had talked about Charles Darwin to his father. Of course Darwin would have been his hero, given the whole natural science thing. But who was Calico Jack? A sick feeling crawls in his chest. The paper shakes in his fingers.

I believe I am Darwin. I'm not sure.

"And Calico? Why does he have the same name as me?"

You always say that's not your name.

Liam takes a deep breath. His thoughts clutter, tumbling over each other. It could just be a coincidence. Liam is nicknamed Calico because of his hair. Calico Jack sounds like a pirate. That explains the map. It figures kids would imagine themselves to be Charles Darwin and a pirate. He forces a breath and flips to the final letter. It's creased, as if crumpled by a fist and then smoothed out.

My dearest friend, Darwin,

Things are moving too quickly. I have lost the plot. I am being shackled to a life I do not want. I see no way out of this dark sea.

You have always been my compass. Please. Guide me now.

I cannot stop thinking about the greenhouse.

Your dearest friend,
Calico Jack

And, in case I don't see you tomorrow—Happy Birthday.

"Is this who you were waiting to meet? Jasper. Is this the person you were waiting for when you died?"

Jasper doesn't answer. Sweat rises on Liam's skin. He feels his heart stutter in his chest.

"Jasper—who is Calico Jack?"

Liam can still feel Jasper in his Phren. He prods at the presence. Still nothing.

"Fine."

And that's when Liam sees the title of the book: *A History of Trypanism.*

He drops the letters. His hands break out in sweat. He grips the book too tight and the spine creaks. "What the fuck is this? Jasper—answer me. Why do you have a book on Trypanism?"

Nothing.

With a growl, Liam slams the drawer shut. He leaves the letters on the floor but takes the map, then strides out of the room and down the stairs. On the porch, one of the boards buckles behind him, hitting his calf with water-logged splinters. He ignores it.

Where are you going?

"Oh, you can talk now?"

Another silence. Liam wants to recede into his Phren to confront Jasper face-to-face, but there's something he must do first. Holding the map in both hands, he looks at the drawing of the tree, then at the living reality. It's heavy with dead branches and rust-brown fungus, much larger and older than the rendering. It beckons him with strange energy, clear even through the fog. As Liam trudges through the high grass and makes his way up the hill, the bulbous knots on the trunk become visible. There's a crack starting to form down the center. He's sweating by the time he reaches it. He circles, eyes up on the branches—and trips. With a shout, he falls to the ground. The map flies into the air.

"Ah fuck," he grits, grabbing his foot and riding out a wave of nausea. Half his toenail has snapped off.

You alright?

"Not fucking really!"

Liam turns to glare at the rock he tripped over. But it's not a rock. There, lying on its back with its face to the sky, is a tombstone.

Liam, wait.

On hands and knees, Liam crawls over to it. He tries to scrape off the moss coating its surface with his fingers. When that doesn't work, he grabs a nearby twig and digs it into the indents of the words, tracing the letters to reveal their shapes. A drop of sweat tumbles down his brow, off the tip of his nose. It lands square in the middle of the letter "o." As each letter is unveiled, a coiling dread weaves tighter and tighter. When he's done, he falls back onto his ass, blinking. His breath catches.

JASPER KNOX

BORN AUGUST 28TH, 1862

DIED AUGUST 28TH, 1888

And beside it …

WILLIAM O' CONNOR

BORN JUNE 21ST, 1862

DIED MARCH 5TH, 1914

Liam swallows. And stares. A bug buzzes past his ear.

"This … this is why you call me William. My ancestor. He was—"

I didn't know. I didn't remember.

"He died on my birthday." The words are more breath than sound.

Pieces fall into place: the Hitch link, the Trypanon from the past possessing a new body, the pocket watch, the light that followed him in the Nether all this time.

"Does this mean … am I the one being possessed? Is this William person possessing me? But I have no memory of being anyone other than myself."

Jasper doesn't speak.

Liam struggles to his feet, wincing when he puts weight on his toe. The oak tree. There's a gnarled scar in the center of the trunk. It pings something old and familiar. A faded vision layers over his sight: the tree, thinner and younger, with a natural hole in its trunk. The light catches on the edges of a metal box inside it, tucked away and secret.

Their Letterbox.

Liam claws his fingers through his hair. He pulls off his glasses and rubs hard at his eyes. "Jasper, I need answers. Please say something."

Nothing.

"Does this mean I'm the Trypanon killer?" Liam chokes on his breath. He clutches at his chest, balling up the front of his T-shirt in his fist. "Why were they buried together? Why did you have a book on Trypanism? Jasper? Who is William? Answer me!"

Liam closes his eyes and tries to meditate, but he's frantic. He manages after a few dragging failures to enter his own Phren. The walls shake and hum. Jasper isn't in the living room or the kitchen. He's not in Liam's bedroom. When Liam tries the door to the tower stairs, he finds it locked.

Jasper, let me in, you asshole!

He grabs the knob and yanks, but it won't budge. He turns, shoving against the door with his back and shoulders. He's about to unleash a tirade of expletives when he sees it. There, down the hall, in his bedroom and beneath the window, is a small table. It still has wooden toys and dusty board games stacked on it. It's always been there.

And Jasper has the same one.

With a final kick to the door, Liam vaults out of his Phren and blinks back into his body. The tree sways in the sea breeze, and for a moment, Liam thinks it's moving of its own accord, like one of Tolkien's ents.

Tucking the map into his backpack, Liam breaks into a run. He barrels down the hill, dodging mossy rocks and branches. Blood spurts up from his toe. He shoves his kayak into the water, jumps inside, and rows with all his strength back to his house. Jasper is silent, though Liam senses him watching. Sweat drips onto his glasses, obscuring his vision, but he doesn't stop. The porch door slams into the wall as Liam strongarms his way inside and bounds up the stairs. He slams into the wall when he takes a turn at the top too hard. The plaster cracks.

His room. The table. He rips the drawer open, pausing for only a second before taking hold of the bottom and pulling. The board comes free, revealing the compartment beneath. The first thing Liam sees is the Morse code book. With fingers trembling, he pulls it out, forcing himself to be gentle. He opens it to the inside cover.

And finds a letter, tucked away like a secret.

My dearest friend, Calico,

I do not know where to begin. I have risked everything on a foolish impulse—a folly. I am not sure what my apology is worth to you. I can only say that I will spend my life regretting my error if it means our friendship has died. Please, find it in your heart to erase the memory of my transgression.

I will not call upon you. The occasion of our next meeting is entirely on your conditions, and I understand if you never desire to see me again.

I am so very sorry.

Your desperate friend,
Darwin

Liam drops the letter onto the table and backs up until his legs hit his bed. He sits. Shrugging off his backpack, he lets it drop to the floor. It's too much. He's inundated. Outside his window, a seagull sits on the roof above the porch. It stares at him with a human expression.

"Please talk to me," he hears himself say.

A long pause. The seagull flies away.

Liam. I—

A loud knock sounds from his porch door. "Fuck," Liam sighs. Of course Sloane would choose this moment to visit. He knows she won't leave without seeing him. He straightens his clothes, puts on a hat, and heads downstairs. When he first reaches the back door, he doesn't see anyone. He eases the door open and sticks his head out.

"Liam!"

Faye is on the porch swing. Liam has the profound impression of a child as she kicks her feet to swing. She pats the spot next to her and smiles at Liam with too many teeth.

"You and I need to have a little chitchat."

CHAPTER EIGHTEEN
SEED OF DOUBT

"I'M IN THE middle of something right now."

"I really don't think this can wait."

Liam sighs. "Alright. But come in. It's too fucking foggy out here and that swing is not safe."

She jumps a little, then launches to her feet with an excited bounce and follows him inside. Without waiting for a cue from Liam, she bounds into his living room and takes the seat Jasper usually occupies in Liam's Phren. Though Jasper's silence is still resounding in his mind, Liam swears he feels a tinge of annoyance, like he thinks Faye is infringing on his territory.

"I'm guessing you're here to talk about what happened the other night." He sits on the couch.

"Maybe I'm just looking to pay a friend a visit," she says. Liam arches an eyebrow. "At least, that's what I'd tell Sloane if she asked."

Liam crosses his arms over his chest, staring at Faye until she continues. She fidgets, fingering the cross on her neck.

With her eyes cast to the floor, she says, "I know Bert isn't the Trypanon."

Her words hang in the air. Liam leans forward, bracing his elbows on his knees.

"People aren't like us," she continues. "They can't sense Fissures and Flukes like we can. They didn't know that Bert had a Violet Fluke. And Sloane doesn't know either."

"No. She doesn't."

"Sophonts can't get Flukes unless a Trypanon forces it on them, and

Trypanons can't get them at all," she continues. "Right?"

Liam takes a deep breath before answering. He feels Jasper's presence slowly surface in his mind. "That's right."

Faye knots her fingers together on her lap. Her knuckles tighten to white. "I knew you'd figured it out. You were always the best student."

Liam hadn't thought much about how Faye would have viewed him at the Academy. She was younger than him, and he has no memory of her, but of course she would be aware of him. Everyone was.

"I kinda had to be."

"Don't be so modest all the time. You were good at everything. I felt like I couldn't do anything right if I tried. I don't know if you know this, but I enrolled late. My abilities didn't present until I was sixteen."

"I see." He knew Faye was weak, but he didn't know she was this bad. He doesn't understand why Phoebe Shelton gave her a job.

"Yeah, pretty bad, I know. I had to take classes with the younger kids, so I didn't have many friends. You probably didn't even know I existed," she laughs. "I do not wish to make you uncomfortable, but you must know I saw you as a bit of a hero. Everyone talked about how you saved Makoto Mori. Some people feared you, but not me. And to think, someone like you came from my hometown. I couldn't believe my luck when you returned to Shoalport. I figured I would never get to meet you. And here we are … friends."

Liam scratches the back of his head. His eyes dart to the door.

"You always stick up for me with Sloane and Applebaum," she goes on. Her voice trembles. "You work so hard to do the right thing. And you're so powerful, it's astounding. They always say to never meet your heroes, but I guess you're the exception, huh?"

Liam feels Jasper cringe.

"Did you want to talk about Bert?" Liam says.

Faye winces, knocking her palm against her forehead. "Ah, of course. My apologies. I'm so silly."

'Silly' is not the word I would use.

"You're fine, I just really need to get back to—"

Faye shoots to her feet. Her eyes bug out of her head. "What was that?"

Liam blinks. "What was what?"

"You," she chokes, pointing at him. "You aren't alone." She breathes heavy, eyes darting around the room like she's looking for a weapon.

"What?" Liam slowly rises to his feet, holding up his hands. "Faye, calm—"

"There's a presence in your mind. Can't you sense it? Wait … are you …

you're possessed! You're a *Pelt*!"

"No, no—Faye, wait," Liam says, taking a step towards her. She stumbles back and kicks Kermit's pen. He darts into his wooden box.

"Stay back!" she squeaks.

"Faye, it's not what you think."

Liam.

"Get away from me!" She runs to the fireplace and grabs a poker, brandishing it like a sword.

"Faye, for fuck's sake, listen to me—"

Liam, don't.

Faye lets out a sob. The poker shakes in her hands. He can sense her trying to put up a mental barrier, but it's so weak he could break it with a thought if he wanted. He really can't believe Phoebe let her have a Patch position, even if she was acting out of nepotism. A real Fluke case would eat her alive.

"I'm not being possessed against my will, Faye."

No, Liam—

I have no choice. She already knows.

"I have a Hitch."

Faye's mouth drops open, her eyebrows climbing up her forehead. Then, slowly, she unwinds and drops the poker to the floor. It rattles against the stone in front of the fireplace, loud enough to scare Kermit again.

"You have a Hitch," she repeats, grimacing. Her eyes glisten like she wants to cry.

"I know it sounds crazy, but I've been working with him to find the killer. He's not from our time. He died in the 1880s. I believe the Trypanon is a soul from his time that somehow escaped the Nether. He thinks he knows who it is, Faye. He just needs me to help him remember."

You should not have done that.

Why? What are you hiding?

We have no reason to trust her.

I have no reason to trust you either.

Faye's mouth contorts. She pulls at her hair and paces, before spreading her hands across her face. A long whine muffles in her palms. Then she lets her arms fall to her sides. Her cheeks are blotchy red.

"Liam," she says, with a new, low quality to her voice. There is no silliness now. "Do you know how you sound? Why didn't you tell anyone you have a Hitch?"

He rifles through plausible explanations. Nothing he can think of doesn't incriminate him. He hadn't thought much about why he'd kept Jasper a secret.

It goes against every bit of protocol Archer beat into his head over the years. Yet, he hadn't even considered telling anyone.

Why hadn't he? Because he worried they'd think he was crazy?

Or guilty.

"I … I don't know."

Faye shakes her head, then stops. Her hand flies up to cover her mouth.

"What?" Liam says.

Her fingers crawl down to her necklace again, clutching the amulet tight. The corners of her mouth curl down in an ugly frown. "How do you know your Hitch is not the Trypanon?"

The words hit, then hang in the air. Liam is reminded of the interim between a flash of lightning and a rumble of thunder. He starts and aborts several possible defenses, each less sturdy than the last. "He isn't." Even to Liam he doesn't sound confident. He can sense Jasper go rigid with tension.

"But how do you *know*," Faye urges. "A Hitch isn't a good thing. It's evil. Surely, you know that."

The memory of Samantha Munn's Hitch surfaces. He recalls its corruption and power. She'd been enveloped in tragic memories of his death, but he'd assumed the Fluke had done it. Now, he's not so sure. What drove her to end up living on the street? How had she fallen so far? She'd seemed so strong in her memories. Maybe it wasn't her doing.

"We don't know much about Hitches," he says, more to himself.

"We know that they can influence a person, even alter their perception. They can make you believe whatever they want you to believe. They may even believe it themselves. They lie."

Liam shakes his head. Sweat trickles down the back of his neck. "He wants to stop the killer as much as I do."

"How do you know?"

"I know him." Liam winces. He's been on enough cases to know how he sounds: like a desperate victim, delusional and deep in denial.

Faye's voice drops to a whisper. "How does *he* know? If this man is a Hitch, he's been in the Nether for years. Decades. He wouldn't be human anymore. The power someone like that could have; think of what they could do? And they might not even know they're doing it. They might convince themselves they're doing the right thing and convince you too. You said yourself the Trypanon is a person from the past, possessing a victim now. Doesn't that profile fit your Hitch?"

You're considering her reasoning.

Liam shakes his head. *No. She's wrong.*

*How can you know? She's implying that you cannot trust your own
perspective. Or mine.*

Liam wants to say that he knows Jasper, that he understands his character
and his motivations. He isn't religious. He didn't know his mother. He cares
about the victims. They've been through this already. If Jasper was the killer,
Liam would know.

The governess was religious. Jasper called her Mother. It's Liam's voice, and the
thought is loud.

I've considered this as well, Jasper says.

"He's talking to you now, isn't he." It's not a question.

Liam looks away like a shamed dog. "I think I'd better leave," Faye says,
straightening her pink blouse. "I'll cover for you with Sloane for a little while,
but not forever. The killer is still out there." "Or in here," she doesn't say. Or
worse, "in you."

Liam watches her leave. She passes through the kitchen and uses the front
door, as if she can't bear to come closer to him and use the porch exit. He
stares at the floor in silence. Jasper doesn't speak, though Liam feels him
pulled taut like a sail. He searches for something to say. There's too much
clutter in his thoughts, too many questions he doesn't know how to ask.

Liam, I believe we should—

Liam startles at his phone vibrating with a call. It rattles against the glass
on his coffee table, grating against his ears. He picks it up to stop the noise,
and sees that Ingrid is calling him. At first, he wants to stuff his phone in the
couch cushions and hide in his bedroom. He can't shoulder her grief right
now, not when he's working to avoid his own. Then he remembers: Cedra
was Ingrid's best friend. He'd only known Cedra a short time. Ingrid must be
devastated.

It's easy to recall how he'd felt after Makoto died. He didn't reach out to
anyone, but if he had, it would have meant he was desperate. Then he realizes
that Ingrid hasn't just tried to contact him once; he has five missed calls from
her and several texts.

He picks up.

"Hey. Sorry, I wasn't near my phone. What's going—"

"Jesus, Liam, fucking finally. No time for bullshit. We need you at the care
center."

"Why? Has something happened?"

"Harold Parsons is dying. He's in a bad way, like, in his head. I think he
knows about what happened to her. Could you, I dunno … do that thing you
did before? To help him pass? I was just thinking about what Cedra would

want, and … yeah. Fuck."

There isn't much emotion in her tone, until her voice cracks on Cedra's name.

"Of course." Liam is taken aback by his own lack of hesitation, but he owes Cedra this. He couldn't keep her alive. The least he can do is help her father, even if it's not something he's trained to do. Makoto is the one for the job. Liam is a poor substitute.

"I'll be here waiting. Come as soon as you can."

She hangs up without waiting for a response. Liam is relieved. He knows he should offer her condolences or apologies, but they always feel false. Nothing anyone said in his grief helped him. He wouldn't wish this on anyone.

Jasper, I need to do this, but after, we need to talk.

Nothing.

I can feel you in my Phren. You can't keep hiding like this. When I finish, I need answers.

Liam sighs when the silence persists. He doesn't have time to drag Jasper out now. He changes quickly into fresh clothes, wraps a Band-Aid around his toe, grabs his keys, and gets in his car.

He forgets to take a hat.

CHAPTER NINETEEN

HUSK

WHEN LIAM RUSHES into the lobby, the man at reception points to Harold's room without speaking. Liam is halfway down the hall when Ingrid steps out and waves at him.

"They've got him restrained, but I said not to sedate him. Fuck, I don't know why Cedra left me in charge of this shit. I have no idea what I'm doing. They're trying to make him comfortable, but he's just freaking out." Her voice cracks.

"I'll see what I can do."

The air is thick and sickly. He resists the urge to cover his mouth, to block out the dynamic stench of chlorine and ammonia and a body failing. The beeps of the heart monitor are sluggish. IVs hang around Harold like powerlines. His restraints appear painless, but they make Liam feel suffocated.

It's a moment before he notices Nora. He'd rather not have another spectator, but he can't exactly tell a nurse to get lost. He takes a seat in the chair beside Harold's bed and takes his hand. The skin is saggy. He can feel the bones and sinew.

"I was hoping you'd come," Nora says.

Harold's eyes are half-closed, his pupils swiveling. Liam sucks in a breath through his mouth, fighting the urge to gag, and begins tethering his soul to his body. He wonders if Jasper will say anything, or even follow him, but he stays hidden. His presence is a dull pulse.

With a shudder, Liam leaves his body and slips into Harold's mind.

The absence is what strikes Liam first. There is no mess of broken memories to sift through now. The basketball scene and images of an attic are gone. Harold's Phren is overcome with a single memory: the Fissure Event in 2000. Harold stands, frozen, as the chaos unfolds around him at O'Connor House. People blur in and out of focus. Harold stands before him, catatonic. A long string of drool hangs from his mouth. The world funnels around him, colorless, dimming at the edges.

Liam should interfere, should take Harold away. It's what he came to do. But he finds himself engrossed. What kept him from remembering this day before?

Then he sees himself. He looks so small. His swim trunks are blue. There are sharks on them. He's panting, his breath catching in his throat on little sobs. And he's scampering around like a rabbit. He runs up to a young teenager with blood running down over her lips. Her glasses have lodged in the bridge of her nose. She stares blankly as he takes her hands. Her head jolts to the side, swinging her tangled brown ponytail. It's strange for Liam to watch himself, so young, enter the Phren of another person. He can see why it unsettles people. It's invasive and inhuman—even parasitic. His eyes, only just bright with boyhood, turn dead. Empty.

The instant her Fissure is healed, her face floods with expression on a gasp. This is when Liam realizes he knows this girl, had seen her as an adult only a moment before—Nora. She crumples to the ground, and a woman—it must be her mother—clutches her in a too-tight hug.

Thank you. Thank you, she weeps. But Liam is already scrambling away to the next victim. He runs up to them one by one, taking their wrists and going rigid. A woman in her forties convulses wildly, and abruptly stops when Liam touches her. When her Fissure is sealed, Liam moves to a man who's collapsed against a Weber grill. Liam's father is pouring beer on his arm where a coal is burning through his skin, unfelt. When Liam seals his Fissure, he shouts in pain and clutches his arm, blinking at it in shock. Liam's father doesn't look at Liam, doesn't speak to him.

Four people are saved before Liam finds his way to Harold. He skids to a stop in front of him and takes Harold's wrists in his hands.

In watching the memory now, a new clarity comes. He remembers this. He'd been operating purely on instinct. He'd not tethered his soul to his body or had a Splint at his side to soothe him. He'd just hated the Fissures—they hurt his teeth and crackled on his skin, and he wanted them to go away. There was no intent behind the order of victims he helped. It was impulsive.

As the small version of Liam closes Harold's Fissure, the world around them sharpens into focus. Harold collapses onto his rear in the sand. A child with blonde hair runs up to Harold, sobbing, and crawls onto his lap. Liam looks away. He can't bear to see Cedra as a child knowing her life would be so short and end so wrong.

He stares at himself, so small and thin. How could anyone look at this little boy and think he'd acted out of heroism? It's so obvious that he was motivated by fear and a self-serving, childish compulsion to make the bad feeling go away. Did Liam even care about these people? Did he comprehend that he was saving them? He hadn't been thinking like a hero. He'd barely been thinking at all.

Can a child even carry the weight of heroism?

When the sixth victim—an old man babbling a string of nonsense in between manic laughter—is healed, the boy sags in relief. His hair is wet and it clings to his forehead. It's plain brown.

The boy stands, hands clenched together and looking lost. Where is his mother? He looks around and finds her standing off to the side, staring at her son with a wide, edged expression, and not doing a thing. *Mistake.*

Liam is expecting the memory to end now, and perhaps restart on a loop. But then, he watches himself catch sight of something. The boyish, soft features contort in horror before he breaks into a run towards the water. His feet are small and pink. His arms thrash. Liam doesn't see what he's running towards at first. Harold must not have either. Then a floating, motionless shape comes into focus…

A child with their face down in the water.

On instinct, Liam rushes toward the water, and stops. He wants to dive in and help, but there's nothing he can do now. This already happened. He can only watch as the child version of himself fights to pull the body to shore, alone.

"Someone help!" It's a pointless thing to say. No one hears him and no one reacts. Little Liam is choking on water, bobbing and struggling to tow the other child to shore. Harold sits motionless with Cedra in his lap. He's grunting and twitching, eyes fixed on the children like he wants to get up and help, but his mind is too fried from the Fissure. He doesn't have control of his body anymore.

Liam pulls at his hair and paces, willing someone to notice the shapes thrashing in the water.

Time drags on, until finally, they reach the shore and one child heaves the other child onto the sand. That's when the other boy's features come into focus. His hair is dark and short. It curls on his forehead. His eyes stare blankly up to the sky. They're gray. They're familiar. He'd know them in any time, any form.

Liam watches himself sob over the body, taking the boy's face in his hands and shaking gently. He mouths words that Liam can't hear, can't remember.

It's not possible. Harold's mind is making a mistake.

He's about to move closer when everything flickers like an old TV screen. The ground trembles beneath his feet. Pieces of the memory blink into nothingness. Liam reaches out with his senses, feeling for Harold's soul. More of the world around him deteriorates. He looks at young Cedra. Her face is a white blur where it rests on Harold's lap.

Harold is dying.

And Liam has done nothing to help. He needs to act fast. He draws his power to him and combs through the fragments of Harold's Phren. As he picks up pieces of memories, they crumble in his grasp. He catches one of a camping trip—of laughter around a fire and fire flies and crispy bacon—but it dissolves to nothing.

Being inside a dying Phren is something he hoped to never experience again. It's impossible not to absorb the groggy panic, the mind's last desperate attempts to cling to life. He feels Harold slipping away from him. And without any memories to ease his way, there is nothing but pain and confusion and fear.

He gets an idea.

Reaching into his own memories, he pulls out the first of Cedra that he can find. It's not much. They'd only met a few times. He presents her to Harold. Cedra sits beside him, her face glowing with a smile. It was after Liam had calmed Harold's mind the first time, with a father-daughter basketball match on a summer's night. He draws that memory out too and pushes it into Harold's focus, filling the empty space in Harold's Phren. It dawns on Harold like a sunrise. His Phren slows and calms.

Liam has never stayed in a dying Phren long enough to watch the Host expire. The Academy always warned against it, citing a high risk for insanity and hallucination. He stays now. It feels wrong to leave.

And so, he sees it: light, the same one that shepherded the Tryp's victims out of the Nether. It covers Harold, coats him like a blanket, and pulls him down. Harold melts into it, and with a final sigh, he gives the softest touch to his daughter's cheek. And then he's gone.

Liam doesn't linger. He leaves Harold's Phren, escaping the blankness of an empty mind. He comes back into his body to the sounds of Ingrid crying softly and an endless, flat beep.

"Thank you, Liam," Nora says.

Liam wipes the back of his hand across his forehead. It comes away wet.

"I'm sorry, would you guys mind giving me a minute in here?" Ingrid says, stepping further into the room. Liam and Nora nod and file out. As they stand out in the hall in silence, Liam takes a breath against what he's just done, and lets it fall out of him on the exhale.

He's trying to come up with a segue to bring up the Fissure Event to Nora when she presents one for him.

"You probably don't want to hear about that barbeque again. I'm sure everyone brings it up to you all the time. But for me … seeing you do what you've done for Harold when I know how you saved me, well, it means a lot."

"How well do you remember that day?"

Nora shrugs. "I was fourteen, so only bits and pieces. I was one of the lucky ones. You got to me first. Of the seven of us, only the first four walked away mostly okay. The others ended up here. I figured the least I could do was balance out my good luck by taking care of them. Or maybe I just have survivor's guilt."

Liam is embarrassed that he never made any effort to check on or contact the victims from that day, but if he formed a connection with every Fissure or Fluke victim he helped, he wouldn't be able to do the job. He can't dwell on the ones he didn't save fast enough, like Harold.

But now is different; he needs to know about the boy that drowned in the river. He's about to ask when he realizes what Nora just said.

"The rest? You mean no one died?"

"Not that day, no."

Liam gestures for her to explain.

She frowns, chewing on her bottom lip. "How much do you know?"

"Assume I know nothing."

She checks to see if anyone is listening before she answers. "Marcus Jackson was a resident here. He was old at the time of the Fissure. He died a few years after the Event of heart failure."

Liam recalls the old babbling man. He has a vague memory that his Phren had felt dusty and withered. At the time, it was unsettling to be inside someone so old when he was so young.

"And another was Harold. What about the third?"

Nora pales. She checks that no one can hear them. "I shouldn't really discuss him. I mean, I shouldn't discuss any of the patients. HIPAA violations, and all that."

Liam takes a step toward her.

"What if I told you it was relevant to the case I'm working?"

She blinks. "But ... hasn't that been solved? It was in the news. Bert Shelton confessed."

Liam gives one short shake of his head.

"Shit."

"Nora. I don't want this to happen to any more people. There's something hidden here. I just need to look at some files. You don't even have to say you told me where they are. In fact, you don't even have to say it out loud. If you think it hard enough, I can hear it."

Nora's temple twitches. She rubs at her eyes, knocking her glasses askew. "Shit," she says again under her breath. "Fuck, if this was anyone else asking me this ..."

"But it's not."

She stares at him. He doesn't mean to use her debt to him as leverage. It feels wrong. He's about to take it back when she responds.

"Fine. But only if you get the bastard that took Cedra away."

She gazes hard into his eyes. He feels the edges of her Phren reach out and expand. He stares into it, grappling for something, anything. An image is handed to him: a windowless door down the hall, swinging open, and then cabinets inside. A drawer in a cabinet against the far wall is pulled out, and the vision fades. Abruptly, Nora turns on her heels. She drops something behind her. It rattles against the floor, too loud in the empty hall.

Keys.

He grabs them, tucking them in his pocket, and rushes down the hall in the opposite direction. He'll have to pass by reception without looking suspicious. With a gentle nudge, he projects a sense of shyness into the atmosphere. It's not the most ethical thing he's ever done, but it's not the worst either. A nurse steps through a door to his side and chokes when she sees him. Oops. He might have hit her a little harder than necessary. As she scurries away, he realizes she came out of Faye's mother's room. Great. The last thing he needs right now is to run into Faye.

He picks up his pace, offering a casual wave to the man at reception as he passes. He squeals and ducks under his desk in a poor effort at pretending he dropped something. Yeah, Liam definitely put a little too much punch into his aural projection. He can beat himself up for it later. Finally, he reaches the door Nora showed him, unlocks it quietly, and goes to the cabinet. Yanking open the drawer, he grabs a stack of files and dumps them on a nearby shelf.

He doesn't recognize the patients in the first few files. He decides to keep Mary Cleary's on hand, though he doubts he'll need it. When he finds Harold's file, he skims it, but there's nothing inside that he doesn't already know.

Marcus Jackson's isn't any better. There's a note about burn management and congestive heart failure, but little else. Marcus isn't the one he's looking for.

He's starting to get discouraged. File after file yields nothing relevant. Then, he comes upon a name that makes him pause:

Ashton Webb.

It doesn't click at first. He flips the file open, preparing to put it back like all the others, when he sees the picture clipped on the inside.

Black, curled hair. Gray eyes. The boy. It's the boy from the beach and the friend from his childhood.

The boy from Jasper's memories of a past long gone.

Jasper, what the fuck am I looking at? he shouts into his Phren.

Jasper doesn't surface.

He reads, breaking out in a sweat:

> ASHTON WEBB
> Born: 08/28/1988
> Admitted: 09/3/2000
>
> Patient was transferred from Shoalport General
> and admitted for long-term residency following the
> Fissure Event of 08/28/2000. Patient is catatonic,
> with limited brain function. It is unclear if he is a
> "Husk," sustained significant brain damage from
> oxygen deprivation (patient was said to have been
> underwater for several minutes), or a combination of
> the two. Recommended course of action is to make
> the patient comfortable, per the wishes of his next
> of kin. Daily walks on the grounds are advised.

The rest of the file recounts his medications and history of treatments, with no indication that his condition ever improved. The notes become sparce and then stop completely, following a memo that the facility was transitioning to digital record keeping. There's a room number on the edge of the file.

Jasper, please tell me what is going on. I'd rather hear it from you.

Silence.

Fine.

Liam grabs the stack of folders he's set aside and strides into the hall. He follows the numbers on the doors, counting down. A nurse passes by him and asks where he's going. When he shoos her away with another pulse of inflicted embarrassment, she squeaks and runs into a bathroom. He continues. The numbers descend. He draws closer, turns a corner. The room comes into view.

A file is tucked in a wall slot beside the door. "Ashton Webb" is written on the front. He takes hold of the doorknob, pulls, and steps into the room.

The light is low. It takes a moment for his eyes to adjust. There's a bed against the wall. On it, is a man Liam knows well. He has the same dark hair, flat and poorly sheared, but still dark and gently curled. His skin is even paler than in Liam's Phren, his cheeks sharper. Liam's gaze is drawn to his hands where they rest on the pale blue blanket. They're spindly and long. By now, Liam has learned them. His long lashes cast shadows on his skin. Liam knows them too.

"Jasper," he says. He hears his own voice as if from a distance. The breathy desperation behind it unnerves him. "Why?"

He blinks, then blinks again, holding his breath as his vision starts to shift. Slowly, as a building fog, Jasper materializes in front of him. With each second his figure takes shape, growing opaque and detailed—the ascot at his throat, the sharp black coat, the height and posture of a rigid figure. He's seen it before, but never in the Waking World.

"H-how are you doing this?"

"The same way the Nether has crept into your sight while you're awake. I'm still just a projection. Or rather, something only you can perceive."

Liam's breath catches on a hiccup. He shakes his head. His hands ravel to fists.

"What's happening? Why are you on that bed? Why are you alive?"

Jasper's eyes, colored slate in the cold light, close. His Adam's apple bobs on a swallow.

"Liam," he says. His voice is startling. Liam's never heard it with his ears before. Though, he supposes, he's not really hearing him now. "Tell me!" He doesn't mean to shout. It's a miracle if he didn't just alert the nurses.

Jasper doesn't flinch. No, he takes a step forward, then another, until he's looming over Liam. His scent brushes against Liam's senses: lavender and black tea and wool.

Their eyes lock.

Jasper says, "I am the Trypanon."

CHAPTER TWENTY

THE MAN WHO DROWNED WAITING

"But... you can't be."

"I can prove it to you."

"How?"

Jasper raises his hand between them, stopping when his fingers hover just beside Liam's temple. "May I show you?"

Liam shivers. The files slip from his grasp, hitting the floor. Papers fan out around him like leaves. He nods, and Jasper's fingers find his skin.

Liam closes his eyes. There's a gentle tug, and he is drawn out of his own Phren and into another. It's different than when he enters the Phren of a Host. This is an invitation, and he sees everything from a distance, as a spectator. He isn't in a room at a care center anymore. He's inside Jasper's Phren, or an echo of it. A presentation of memory.

At first, a quilt of images billow and move around him. The first is the inside of a ship. It's clouded, more of an impression. Liam feels the lurching of the ship, hears the rumble of the heavy water beyond the hull. There's sweet fever sweat misting in the air. With a sway of the ship, the image rolls into another.

Jasper is confined to a bed. He's so small tucked into the massive four poster, the duvet too heavy for him to lift. He looks like the boy who drowned on Liam's beach. More come—Jasper trying to get his father's attention, Jasper being slapped by his governess. A view between door hinges of his father and the governess kissing. Sebastian's hand was pushing up her petticoats. Jasper hadn't understood. And then, an image of her sneaking a white powder into

Jasper's tea. Jasper watches her from the doorway, scuttling back to his bed before she notices. He pours the tea in his bed pan after she leaves the room.

Liam wants to punish this woman. He watches with satisfaction when little Jasper overhears a conversation between her and his father. Jasper's arm is in a sling. It seems that for Sebastian's remoteness, he could be eviscerating when someone hurt his son.

Then, the memories pause. Jasper is hesitating to show him something. Liam is about to address it, when a new scene forms: of Jasper, about twelve now, walking the silty path from his house to the tidal island. He rounds the shoals at its center. A figure pops out on the other side, then recedes. Jasper pursues. The figure is just out of his grasp. He pivots, running in the other direction, round and round. Crash. Jasper falls back on his ass and finds himself staring at another boy the same age. The other boy is laughing. His face comes into focus, and Liam is struck.

It's him. There, wiping the wet sand off his palms and sleeves, is Liam. He's about twelve too, with his brown hair grown down past his ears.

"You caught me." The accent is strange—a mix of Irish and old American—but the cadence is unbearably familiar. "Blast. I cut my palms on the mussels." He brushes them off and licks the cuts. "Looks like you cut yours too."

"I did not catch you. We collided."

The boy pushes to his feet. He seems to have abandoned his socks and overcoat, and one of his suspenders is hanging off his shoulder. His brown hair is soaked with sweat.

"I'm William," the boy who looks just like Liam says. "William O'Connor. I live right over there." He gestures to the house behind him—Liam's house. Liam feels like he's watching a home video of himself from a time he doesn't remember.

"Jasper Sebastian Knox. Pleasure."

William reaches out to take Jasper's hand. Jasper stares at it. He shuffles his feet.

"Haven't you ever shaken someone's hand before?"

"No."

William blinks. He cocks his head to the side. "Then I can be your first."

"What if it isn't sanitary? We have open wounds."

William snorts on a laugh. He shrugs and smiles. "You don't leave your house much, do you?"

"Until recently I was forbidden from doing so."

"Why?"

Jasper fiddles with his sleeves. "I am prone to sickness."

William scoffs. He continues to hold out his hand. "That sounds terribly boring. You look fine to me. Don't you want to go on adventures?" William says. Jasper pauses, then nods. "Excellent. But we really should shake on it."

Slowly, Jasper holds out his hand. William takes it in a firm grip, shaking so hard that Jasper's body wiggles. He stumbles back.

"See, you didn't get sick. And now we're blood brothers."

Jasper takes a deep breath, tries to cough, and sniffs a few times, as if checking to see if something is wrong. "I suppose not. What—ahem—what should we do first?"

"Hmm." William pinches his chin and frowns, parodying a scholar. "Well, if we are going to be adventurers, we should have special secret names. I'll be … Calico Jack. Do you know who that is?"

Jasper shakes his head. He gazes at William like he's an exotic creature.

"He was a famous pirate. I'm going to be a pirate someday, you know."

Jasper looks like he believes him. Then William nudges him on the arm, and Jasper retracts from the touch. William barrels on like nothing happened. "What about you? You could be a pirate too. Or a conquering king like Alexander the Great. Or a cowboy. Or—"

"I'd like to be called Darwin."

William frowns in deep scrutiny, tapping at his lips. "Darwin, huh. I like it. Why Darwin?"

"Charles Darwin is my favorite explorer. He studies animals."

"I like animals too. We have a lot of rabbits in my garden."

Jasper's gaze falls to the ground, a hint of pink on his cheeks. He taps at a mussel shell with his foot. "We do as well. On my island."

"Our first adventure should be spying on the rabbits, then. How do you think they got to your island? Did they swim? Maybe they have tiny rabbit-sized boats. Why don't you take notes. I'll get one to join my pirate crew. If I had a rabbit, I'd name him Kermit."

"That's a nice name."

"I think so. You want to know a secret that I've never told anyone?"

"Only if you want."

"Sometimes I think I hear other peoples' thoughts—the things they don't want anyone to know. I can't hear your thoughts, though."

Jasper's lips part. He leans in, casting his voice low. "I think I can too. But only recently."

"Me too! That settles it, then: we'll be the best together."

The memory blinks out and fades into another, then another. Liam watches as William gifts Jasper the book on Morse code for "secret adventurer correspondences." They practice communicating with candles in their windows at night, moving their hands over the light in short or long waves to make letters. Liam barely has time to absorb this before the memories tumble on. Jasper and William keep meeting on the tidal island; they're taller and lankier each time. He watches them draw the treasure map and discover the hole in the oak tree. They exchange countless letters, despite always being together. They climb trees and scour tidal pools, collecting shells and bones. They paint vivid stories on the land, of epic battles and quests. Sometimes, they play inside each other's Phrens, building worlds. They share dreams when they nap. In the winter, they sled, and William teaches Jasper to ice skate. They never spend time at William's house, and when they're at the Knox House, it's usually when Sebastian is away on business, which is most of the time. Jasper has a tutor that brings him groceries and provides lessons. The man is a cold, distant figure. He's still preferrable to the governess.

In front of the fireplace, Jasper tells William of his studies of plants and animals, and William orates historical tales from his books. He loves *A General History of the Pyrates*. Over time, Jasper blossoms from a pale, sickly child to a healthy boy. The first time he takes a fall, cutting his knee on a rock, Jasper panics.

"What if I die?" he gasps. "What if they lock me inside again?"

William makes jokes until he settles. They don't speak of it after.

Jasper never gets comfortable with physical contact. Even after years together, he still pulls away when William touches his elbow to get his attention or puts an affectionate arm around his shoulders.

It all changes when they turn fourteen. They both begin attending Exeter Academy, but their social circles are different, in that William has one and Jasper does not. For a time, William seems determined to include Jasper in his friend group, but Jasper either refuses or is not accepted by the others. "You don't even try to make friends," William's disembodied voice echoes off the stone walls of one of the hallways. This memory feels more like a dream, comprised of feeling over logic. "Don't you wish to make connections? My father says it's the only way to advance in life." Jasper responds, "I do not care what your father says." And William goes silent.

The school reminds Liam of the Paraphrenic Academy. It's stuffy and painfully formal, and, like the Academy, many of the students are related. The main difference is that only the privileged are allowed here. It fuels the air of elitism. And it's religious too, with many of the students studying seminary work. When Liam and Jasper are fifteen years old, one smarmy boy named

Vincent takes particular interest in harassing Jasper.

"Why don't you stand up for yourself?" William hisses at Jasper one day. He has Jasper backed against a stone wall behind a laurel bush. Jasper looks past William's shoulder, not offering eye contact. William grabs his arm and Jasper jerks it away.

"It is a waste of my time to engage."

"But the other boys are talking. They call you 'lily-livered.' They don't respect you."

"Fine. I don't respect them either. I see their minds as clearly as you; they care only for themselves."

"And you're better than them, is that it?"

Jasper shrugs.

Liam sighs. "Do you want me to do something about Vincent? I could get him to leave you alone."

"No. You have other social obligations to tend to. Your *connections* are more important."

William huffs, turning away. He paces, scrubbing his hands through his hair. It stands on end. *Great*, Liam thinks. *My hair sucks in the nineteenth century too.*

Abruptly, William pivots, lunging toward Jasper and taking his face in his hands. Jasper goes rigid, his gray eyes widening. William leans close enough that Jasper has no choice but to meet his gaze.

"There. I can't stand it when you won't look at me."

A slow flush spreads across Jasper's neck and the bridge of his nose. He doesn't pull away as Liam expects. Instead, his eyes flicker down to William's mouth. His tongue darts out to wet his lips.

William tracks the movement, his lips parting on a breath. He jerks away, stumbling back and rubbing the back of his neck. Now, he's the one who won't look Jasper in the eye.

The scene fades.

It's the summer after graduation from prep school. Liam expects Jasper and William to spend all their time together, as they always did on their summer breaks. Yet, on one occasion after another, Jasper is alone, waiting for William. Liam watches, frowning, as Jasper checks the Letterbox and finds it empty, or waits on the island until the tide forces him back home. He reaches out in dreams and meets a wall. When he's finally had enough, he waits for low tide and strides across the tidal flatland to the porch door of the O'Connor House. His shoes are muddy.

"William," Jasper says, cold, as William comes to the door. "You would not respond to my letters. I left several with your sister."

William runs a hand through his hair. It's shorter now, more like Liam's own. It's harder to look at him. "Sorry. My father's kept me busy."

"Yes, I'm sure wooing Katherine Stillwater has been most laborious."

Liam raises his eyebrows. He watches William's reaction, expecting defensiveness or anger. Instead, William looks contrite. He casts a look behind him, then steps out onto the porch, shutting the door and lowering his voice. "I have obligations. You know how my father is."

"I leave for Harvard in a month." Jasper's words are sharp, as if he's angling for a reaction. William doesn't seem to offer the one Jasper is hoping for.

"I leave for Columbia."

Jasper breathes as if he's about to speak. He doesn't. A silence hangs.

"I do not plan to marry until after I've gotten my degree," William says, slow and deliberate.

Jasper frowns. "Is your father aware of that?"

"Of course not."

"And what does Miss Stillwater think?"

"Why do you care?"

Jasper looks caught off guard. He recovers quickly, though, tilting his chin up and looking away like he's above anything William has to say. "I will be studying natural sciences. I'm assuming you won't be pursuing archaeology, as you'd hoped."

William walks to the porch railing. He braces on it, staring out over the water. "Father intends for me to study law. He wishes for me to continue his legacy at Columbia."

"Well, whatever your father thinks, then."

William turns to look at Jasper, his eyes narrow. "Not all of us have the luxury of a parent who ignores us."

Jasper flinches. William closes his eyes. His shoulders sag on a sigh. "Jas."

"What."

"I'm sorry."

"For what in particular? You'll have to be specific."

William takes a step toward him. He tilts his head down, looking up at Jasper through his eyelashes. "Everything."

Jasper blinks. Familiar color rises on his cheeks, and he turns his head away.

"Is that a sufficient apology?" William says, smiling and looking cocky.

"It should cover it."

William dedicates the rest of the summer to Jasper, and when they go off to school, they send each other frequent letters. Liam watches as Jasper, now growing into a handsome young man, savors each letter from his small Boston apartment. They meet on holidays and William visits Boston. William always tries to drag Jasper to the pubs, but he has little interest. Still, William keeps coming, perhaps to avoid going back to Shoalport. He even stays for Christmas one year. Jasper allows this memory to take its time:

There's a woodstove in Jasper's apartment, and a small balsam standing beside it. It figures Jasper would seize the opportunity to have a tree. He's decorated it modestly, with some ribbon, a bird's nest, and a few dried orange slices. Jasper and William sit around the fire in weathered, overstuffed chairs. They sip tea and speak—either in their Phrens or out loud—when they feel like it and read when they don't. The tea switches to whiskey as the light dips low. The glow of liquor raises its flags on their cheeks. Their eyes are glassy, their bodies heavy.

"I suppose I should give you your present," William says. It must be after midnight. Light snow floats outside the window. The carolers have long retired.

"There was no need to get me a present."

"As if you didn't get me one as well."

The corner of Jasper's mouth curls up. "Of course I did."

They each retrieve their gifts and return to their seats. Jasper hands William a book wrapped in velvet fabric and tied with a ribbon. William hands Jasper a wooden box. At first, Liam is focused on the book: *A History of Trypanism*.

"I have a copy of it myself. It's all religious folklore, but I think you'll find it interesting, given our mutual … gift of the senses. What an adventure we'd have exploring a dark underworld, if we could."

Liam stares at the book. It jogs his own memory. A vision bobs up. Shadowed, his grandfather appears with a book in his hands. He hands it to Liam. Liam remembers now: he was about to leave for the Academy. "It's always been in our family," his grandfather had said. "I'm sorry we didn't tell you sooner."

He disappears. Liam feels Jasper staring, as if he's behind a double-sided mirror, spectating.

"I'm certain I will love it," William says, drawing Liam's focus back. "Now, open your present."

"Oh," Jasper says, when he unclicks the gold latch and opens the small box. Liam's eyes snap to it. He watches as Jasper, so delicately, reaches inside and pulls out a brass pocket watch. He holds it up to amber light. There's a compass rose engraved on the cap.

"A compass on a pocket watch," William says. "So that we may always find each other, in any time."

Jasper tries to speak and doesn't manage more than a soft noise in the back of his throat.

"I'll assume that means you like it," William says, smug.

When Jasper doesn't answer, the smile slips from William's face. He frowns at Jasper, as if he's trying to work something out.

Liam keeps waiting for them to say something. At intervals, they both seem to try, but never manage anything, not even paraphrenically. There's a demarcation between them that neither is willing to cross.

The memory slides away and more take its place.

Jasper returns to Shoalport during the summers and school breaks, while William seems to avoid it. Liam isn't sure why Jasper goes back. His father is rarely there, and he doesn't seem to have friends. Perhaps he's trying to escape the city. Jasper doesn't reveal an explanation.

When they graduate, Liam expects William to stay in New York, but he returns to Shoalport to start working at his father's law firm. Though Jasper is displeased with this decision, he seems happy to have William close by again. They spend most evenings together at the Knox House. William walks across the path through the island when the tide allows and uses a rowboat when it isn't. Sebastian seems to have gone on a permanent business trip, so they have the place to themselves. Years pass. William grows a short beard. Jasper earns a position working for the New Hampshire Horticulture Society. He spends his time on hikes, cataloguing plants and animals. In the winter, when a few cold weeks clog the river with ice, Jasper either rents a room downtown or weathers the storm. When he does get stuck on Knox Island, Liam and Jasper communicate with their candles in Morse code or through their Phrens. They still dream-share, though the worlds in their Phrens are less creative, less fantastical as they once were. Sometimes they just relive memories, like Jasper's apartment on Christmas. Things appear to have settled into a rhythm. Jasper comes to look exactly as Liam knows him.

Then, Jasper slows the memories down. He draws one out, and hesitates. Liam can sense the emotion soaked into this one.

It's a spring evening. The trees are just starting to bud, the crocuses and skunk cabbage punching through blankets of dead leaves. A yellow forsythia shouts its color beside the Knox House. There's a baby rabbit living under the porch.

And William is shouting. Any trace of an Irish accent has long faded.

"If you have an issue with it, don't be a coward; say it!"

Liam rounds the Knox House. Jasper is inside his greenhouse and William is standing in the doorway. With a blink, Liam is transported inside, beside a bag of seeds and some empty terra-cotta pots. He shakes his head, dizzy with the sudden change.

"What would it matter?" Jasper's fingers are caked in dirt. He's using one finger to punch holes in rows of nursery pots, sprinkling seeds inside with his other hand. He speaks evenly, as if this is a normal conversation and William is not sputtering with fury.

"I deserve to hear you say it. You always prevaricate or hint. At least do me the courtesy of saying it outright to my face."

When Jasper doesn't respond, and merely pokes more holes in the dirt, William picks up a pot with a leafy plant inside it. Jasper jerks to face him, reaching out a hand to stop him, but it's too late. William throws the plant at the wall. Glass and terra-cotta shatter. The leaves fall to ribbons.

They both stare at what William has done, unmoving.

"I …," William breathes. "I'm sorry."

"That was a *Monstera deliciosa*. It took me years to acquire one."

"Damn. Jasper, I—"

With sudden speed, Jasper strides into William's space. William stumbles until his back hits the open door, slamming it against the wall. It's a miracle more glass isn't shattered. Jasper brackets William against the door, splaying his dirty hands on each side of his shoulders. They still don't touch.

"You desire to know what I think? I think you are as cowardly as me. You are too fearful to pursue your own path, to put a toe outside the gilded cage of your father's wishes. You tell me you've found a suitable match? For whom? For you or your father?"

"That's not—"

"In all the years I've known you, I never hoped to see you as a puppet in your father's firm, married to a handpicked maid of his choosing. You once valued adventure and intrigue. You wanted to travel."

"And what about you? Are you so superior? You said you'd travel with me, too, and now you hide alone in your father's house, waiting for him to return. If you're aiming for honesty, Jasper, why don't you be honest about him? He's never coming back. And if he does, it will only be for a short visit where you sit beside each other, yet neither of you are in the room."

Jasper falters. Liam winces as some of the color drains from his face.

"My father did the best he could."

"His best was damn poor, then. But that's a lost cause now. You're the one who still has a choice. I have no choice." William is getting upset now. His voice quivers. He takes a few short breaths.

"You do. You're just too fearful to make it."

"I'm not the one in hiding," William spits.

Jasper's eyes flash. He leans a fraction closer. "I would claim what I wanted this very moment. It's you that would never rise to meet me."

William glares back. He tilts up his chin in a challenge.

"Prove it."

Jasper closes the distance and touches their lips together. It's less than a kiss. William twitches, then goes still. For the briefest moment, it looks as if he might lean into it.

Then he shoves Jasper away.

"You," he breathes against the back of his hand. He stumbles to the side, grabbing the doorframe for purchase. He looks at Jasper with utmost betrayal. He turns on his heel, yanks the door open, and runs.

Liam watches as Jasper stands, his hands limp at his sides. He blinks once. Twice. His eyes begin to glisten.

The memory fades.

Liam wants to say something to Jasper, but he can't. A hazy parade of memories passes by slow, mixing and less stable—of Jasper writing the same letter of apology that Liam found in the table's secret compartment, then checking the tree every day for a response. Of Jasper watching from his window as William sits on his porch swing with a woman. Of Jasper tearing apart the newspaper that announces William's position at his father's law firm. Of Jasper receiving an invitation to William's wedding. Of dark dreams spent in solitude.

One day, when Jasper checks the tree, he does find a letter inside. It's the one from Jasper's hidden drawer. "*Things are moving too quickly. I have lost the plot,*" William had written. The pieces fall together. Now, Liam understands. "*I can't stop thinking about the greenhouse.*"

Liam watches, numb, as Jasper sits at the desk in his bedroom at night and composes a response. As his fountain pen scratches across the paper, Jasper reads aloud to Liam. His voice is closer, more intimate. Liam shudders, the words pouring through him like mercury.

My dearest friend, Calico Jack. I did not expect to hear from you again. I had accepted that, in my foolishness, I had ruined our most beloved friendship forever. Even now, I question whether I am reading your words as you intended. Regardless, I have come to a decision: I have spent my life hidden on my island, afraid of how vulnerable I've always been to the world. I was born mismade, my proclivities shameful. I was a mistake. My governess knew as much. Perhaps I am the wicked sinner she always claimed me to be. I know now that I cannot change. I have no choice but to accept and to indulge, for fighting my nature is as futile as fighting my sentiments toward you. Both are indelible. They are as a part of me as my eyes, my flaws, my heart. I buried them in the hopes that they would decompose, but instead they sprouted, only rooting deeper with time. Your smile, your green eyes, the way you take your tea. Your sense of humor and your incessant need to see the good in those who do not deserve it. Your creative, astounding mind. Traveling inside your thoughts has been my greatest adventure.

I do not wish for you to marry. No, I wish for us to travel as we always said we would. I would have us see the west, and the herds of buffalo and wild cacti. I'd have us read in Parisian cafes and walk in the bamboo forests of Japan. I'd have us abandon our fathers and our obligations. I'd have us leave these mirrored houses, these mirrored prisons, forever. You have always been the only one I've wanted to touch me. I was afeared that once you started, I'd never want you to stop. I don't want you to stop. In confessing this, I know that I risk destroying any hope of rekindling our friendship, but the alternative—suffering in silence while you marry and live a life you do not want—is a worse fate.

And so, I propose you meet me at the Secret Hideout, tomorrow night at 22:00, when the tide is at its lowest and we will not be seen. I will hire a clandestine carriage to meet us down the road. Bring only what you need. I hope you will meet me. I hope we will take the life that we deserve. I hope that I am not wrong. On the anniversary of my birth, I wish only to be reborn, with you. Your dearest friend, Darwin.

Liam stares as Jasper places the letter in an envelope and seals it with a few drops of wax from the Morse code candle. Then, he leaves the room in rushed strides. When he returns, his shoes are muddied with river silt and sand. He braces his hands on each side of the small table to catch his breath. He whispers, "What am I doing?" and shakes his head. He stares out the window, eyes narrowed and foot tapping, and waits. He waves his hand back and forth in front of the candle, then goes still. It's not long before a candle lights in William's window and a response is flickered back.

> *I told him the letter would be hidden beneath his porch steps. I intended to deliver it in person but lost the courage.*

By his candle, he's responding that he'll retrieve it. Jasper's voice is so close, Liam can sense his breath. He watches the O'Connor House over Jasper's shoulder. A figure opens the door to the back porch and steps out. They're silhouetted in darkness, but the gait is familiar. They walk to the bottom step and pull out the letter before scuttling back inside. Everything goes black.

Then, suddenly, they're back on the tidal island. It's dark. Jasper is waiting, his shoes half-sunk in the sand. He has a knapsack beside him, braced against a rock bearded with seaweed. He keeps checking the pocket watch William gave him. Light from the O'Connor House glints off the brass. William is late. Sweat pearls on Jasper's hairline, though the air is cool. Wind ripples through the trees and across the surface of the water. The tide shifts, and Jasper starts to pace a trench in the sand. The thin moon offers little illumination; Liam doesn't notice at first when things start to contort and blur.

Jasper freezes. His eyelids sink. His hands tremble. The pocket watch tumbles from his grip, lodging in between the two large rocks.

"Jasper?" Liam says out loud, but this is only an echo; this Jasper can't hear him. The world flashes in and out of focus. Then, everything inverts. It's like being swallowed. In one sudden drop, there is no Jasper Knox anymore. He isn't human; he's a soul, corrupted. Everything is despair and cold dark. The Nether takes and takes. Liam can't bear to look at Jasper, can't stand to see through these eyes.

Then, with a stinging jolt, Liam is thrust back into his own mind, back into the long-term care facility. White cinder block walls rise around him. The scent of ammonia and plastic fills his nose. Jasper stands before him, and behind, his twin, Ashton Webb, is catatonic in the bed.

"What the fuck was that?" Liam says. It's not what he means to say, but it suits.

"I pieced together the memories of my past. It's not complete, but I believe I understand what has transpired now."

"I need to sit down." Liam staggers to a nearby chair and collapses into it. The room totters. He rubs at the dizziness in his eyes.

"I need you to hear this, Liam, even if it's difficult."

When Liam doesn't immediately respond, Jasper continues. There's urgency in his tone, his voice filling up Liam's mind to the brim.

"You saw what happened to me—what I became. I lost all sense of being. I didn't know myself. In my despair, I ripped my soul from my body and surrendered myself to the Nether. My body drowned as the tide came up, but I had long abandoned it. I became a monster. I became a Blue Fluke."

Liam shakes his head. He realizes belatedly that he doesn't have a hat on in public. It feels like being naked in the snow.

"This … this can't be happening," he says. "Why did that guy look just like me? He talked like me. We were Sophonts. The book on Trypanism. The pocket watch. What … why?"

Jasper sighs. Liam feels it whisper through him. He looks up at Jasper, begging for him to say none of this is real; he was just playing a cruel joke.

"I believe you were reincarnated."

The word rings as absurd to Liam. Mystical. Comical. He laughs, then bites off the sound. Jasper isn't laughing. "How?"

"I'm not entirely sure. For some reason, William and I formed a Hitch link. Or perhaps I formed it. And I must have used it to shackle you to me. I used it to drag you back into this world with me."

"But I'm not William. I'm my own person. I'm not … I'm different from him. I'm no one but myself."

"I know." Jasper looks at him like Liam is a child in denial, unable to accept a fact just because it feels icky. Liam looks away, and his gaze finds Ashton.

"So, Ashton Webb is … you?"

"It was. You and I were reborn exactly one hundred years after my death. There is something significant about the dates. You said it yourself at William's grave. William died on your birthday."

"But he died decades after you did."

"That, I know nothing about. I was not alive for it."

"Then … what happened? Why am I here, alive, but he is—" Liam points to the bed. "Why are you like that?"

"Think about it, Liam. The Fissure Event was on my birthday. Eighteen years ago, Ashton Webb was swimming beside the exact location where the Fissure happened the first time, on the same day. The proximity must have caused it to reopen in Ashton Webb's Phren. In *my* Phren. I believe I caused everything that transpired that day. I believe I was the one who ripped open all those Fissures. The Nether would never let me escape. That day, it finally caught me, and I became a Blue Fluke once again."

Liam feels as though his mind is too full, overflowing.

"Then … you're the one who hurt all those people. You … you're the reason I presented as a Trypanon."

"Worse, I believe I am the reason you *are* a Trypanon. I am a Trypanon and a Blue Fluke, and you are linked to me. It's how you may travel into the Nether and may leave again. It's how you channel your power to seal Fissures and alter the landscape of the Nether. All because I couldn't accept that you did not want me. I cannot say whether my actions were intentional or cognitive, but the consequences remain: I ruined your life and many others. I used you to rip open Fissures in my victims, and I damned you to a life you despise, the very thing I was trying to save William from."

Liam pinches the bridge of his nose. Jasper's words don't make sense. They blend, tumbling over him as if he's opened a full closet and all the contents have spilled out on top of him.

"You're saying you … you remember killing those people?"

Jasper goes ashen. "No. I have no memory of it. I did not want to hurt anyone. But there is no other explanation. This is what makes sense. It was me. The Nether must have forced my hand. I simply don't remember. Or perhaps I didn't want to accept it."

"But what about the Trypanon trials? Or the person we saw in the Nether? Didn't they make the prisons?"

"You saw me manipulate the Nether. And just now—I was able to make your reality exactly what I wanted. You saw what I wanted you to see. As for the trials, you know that I was aware of them; I had the Trypanism book. There's still so much I don't understand myself, but the simplest solution is often the best."

Liam shakes his head. He shivers and scratches at the bend in his elbows. Phantom bugs are crawling on his skin.

"But why would you do it? You have no motive. I refuse to believe that you're secretly a killer. No one could hide all that."

Liam can hear the mania in his voice, how his words are broken by ragged breathing. He still feels like he's viewing reality at a distance.

Then Jasper says something that steals his breath from him:

"I am the Blue Fluke who killed Makoto."

The silence that follows is unlike any he's known before. The words, spoken from inside his own Phren, don't sync with the image in front of him. The man he is facing is not real, not corporeal. He doesn't know what's real.

"I told you that I had seen the Blue Fluke who attacked Samantha Munn and drew Makoto into the Nether, but I was wrong. It was me. I am the Blue Fluke. I followed you for years. I was the light, always trailing you. Plaguing you."

Liam can't breathe. It's too much. He finds himself freezing, separating himself from the room and the truth.

"But I intend to fix it," Jasper says. He squares his shoulders, tilting up his jaw. "I am going to leave you. I will sever the Hitch link, and I will never come back. I will never hurt anyone again. I have finally accepted the truth."

"Wait—"

Gray eyes stare into him, stealing his breath.

"You did not meet me then. You would not meet me now."

The severing is instant and complete. It tears through the deepest part of Liam, snuffing out the light. He is cast off, banished. He is alone in a way he's never known.

Breath won't come. There is only pain where comfort once resided.

And then, it's as if something detonates. The tearing doesn't stop. It spreads out, expands, hitting every Phren in its path. It's like a bomb going off. And it's familiar; he's felt this before.

At a barbeque on his grandparents' shore, eighteen years before.

He stumbles out into the hall. People emerge from their rooms like cicadas being birthed from the dirt. His senses jumble. The ozone of so many Fissures surrounds him, burns him; splits open the world.

A Fissure Event.

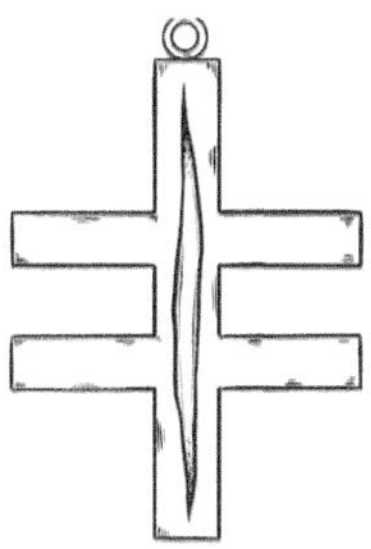

CHAPTER TWENTY-ONE

THE SECRET HOST

L̦IAM SCANS THE hall for an exit as Hosts swerve erratically into his path. The air stings with Fissure energy. The lights flicker like strobes. He breaks into a run. A nurse careens through the staff room door, her arms flailing like broken reeds. She crashes into him, and his shoulder hits the wall hard. Pain reverberates up the side of his neck. The stench of her Violet Fluke fills the air. Her long pink nails claw at him. Foam spritzes from her mouth as she tries to bite his face.

When he tries to shove her away with a pulse of paraphrenic energy, he realizes how much Jasper's severing of their link has taken from him. She barely reacts, shaking off his power like a wet dog, before lunging at his throat. He scrambles. Without his power, he is exposed—useless. He acts on instinct …

And punches her in the stomach.

She stumbles back. Another Host latches onto her, this one infested with Yellow Fluke, clinging to her as if he's trying to climb inside her skin. Liam runs, looking down at his fist briefly in wonder. He never usually gets physical. Everything is always mental for him.

He reaches the foyer just as a maintenance worker in a neon yellow vest barrels through the sliding doors. Though Liam's paraphrenic sight is dulled, the tangle of white worms constricting the man's face and neck are unmistakable. A wave of nausea rolls through Liam at the sight. He tastes sickly sweet.

Why are there so many Flukes?

The man catches sight of Liam and charges. Liam has never seen Hosts so vicious, or so attuned to his presence. It's as if every Host in the building is drawn to Liam. It feels intentional.

Archer's teachings flash across his thoughts: the final trial for a Trypanon is causing a Fissure Event.

Liam lunges out of the maintenance worker's path, the tips of the man's fingers brushing past his T-shirt. The man tumbles to the ground with a harsh squeak of skin on linoleum. Liam catches sight of Nora and hesitates. She's rigid and terrified behind the reception desk, but her eyes are sharp. Somehow, she escaped getting a Fissure. When she sees him, she screams his name.

"Just get out of here!" he calls back.

The maintenance man throws himself to his feet, his red gaze adhering to Liam again.

"What should I do?" Nora shouts, backing towards a door with red exit letters glowing above it.

"Call the police! Ask for Deirdre Sloane!"

The maintenance man roars, charging him. Liam has no choice but to duck into the nearest room. He slams the door behind him, locking it just as the man smashes against it. Blood and spit spurt onto the little glass window. A gargled roar of anguish is dulled through the heavy door. Liam bends over, hands on his knees, and tries not to vomit. Sparks float across his vision. His ears burn.

When he stands straight, the room tilts, blurring before righting itself. Liam's awareness eases back into focus. The room is dark. The overhead bulbs are charred black.

And he isn't alone in the room. Slowly, he looks over his shoulder.

Mary Cleary sits upright on the bed behind him, staring with empty eyes. The light from the heart monitor reflects on them, making her pupils glow, pinhole-thin. Liam freezes, reaching out to sense if she's infested with Fluke.

She's clean. The Fissure Event hasn't touched her.

Liam approaches. He can see Faye in the balls of her cheeks, the thin lips, the low forehead. Still, there is something disparate between the two of them. A flash of lightning fills the room, illuminating the bedside table. There are a couple framed pictures, as if Mary can take joy from them anymore. When he reaches to pick one up, Liam realizes that he's still holding the files. He places them on the nightstand and picks up the picture. It's hard to see in the low blue light. He takes out his phone to use the flashlight and finds the battery dead. With a sigh, he shoves it back in his pocket and squints at the photo again.

He recognizes Faye first. Though she's much younger in the image—only a teenager—her face still holds the same childishness now. Mary, standing behind her with a hand clenched on Faye's shoulder, is different. She's very much alive, her eyes fierce and harsh. The picture is slightly out of focus, but Maggie Short is unmistakable beside Mary, with her carrot-colored hair blaring. It's obvious that she inserted herself in this photo. She gestures up to the church behind her as if she put it there, or rather it was put there for her.

Then Liam looks at the fourth person in the photo, flanking Faye on her opposite side. His face is stern and gnarled with wrinkles. His hand is clamped on Faye's other shoulder. Liam knows he recognizes him from somewhere, but his thoughts are muddled by Fissure energy, and Jasper's absence is carving a physical ache in his chest. He wants to talk to him, to get his insight.

Then he recalls the massive foyer at the church, with the creepy portrait on the wall that seemed to glare at him.

Pastor Gartlett.

Liam grabs the stack of files. He rifles through, muttering, "please" to himself on repeat.

Mary Cleary's file isn't like the others. When he opens it, a handwritten assessment falls out, written and signed by Phoebe Shelton. As Liam reads, the paper quivers; he can't seem to steady his hand.

As one of the first responders to the scene, I would like to offer my assessment of Mary Cleary's incident, with the understanding that this information is strictly confidential. That said, I cannot offer a perfect account of what occurred. There are only a few details of which I am positive. The first, is that Mary Cleary attempted to crucify herself. Upon discovering her, Faye Cleary, her sixteen-year-old daughter, called pastor Douglas Gartlett, who she views as a parental figure. I understand that Faye's father passed away a few years prior and Faye has had difficulty adjusting, or so Gartlett told me. He mentioned that there had been behavioral issues but wouldn't get into detail.

Upon speaking with Faye, who seems to be either dissociative, apathetic, or in shock, I was unable to determine the role, if any, she played in her mother's attempted suicide. It seems implausible, though not impossible, that Mary could have climbed up on the crucifix and nailed her feet and right hand to the cross without assistance. I have been unable to find evidence of a fissure in Cleary's Phren. I cannot yet account for my suspicions, but I intend to monitor Faye closely for any signs of paraphrenic ability. If she had any, it would have presented very late. Still, I sense a wall in her Phren that I am incapable of penetrating. I don't have the experience to determine if this is the result of paraphrenic ability or mental illness, such as bipolar disorder or a personality disorder. I advise that Faye's visitations with her mother be monitored closely by staff for the immediate future.

Signed, Phoebe Shelton, State of NH Wedge.

Liam trembles as he places the note aside and sifts through the file. Mary's prognosis stagnated in the years that followed, and Faye's visitations were no longer monitored after she returned to Shoalport with a degree from the Academy and a job offer. Then he pulls out an X-ray tucked in the back. It's faded over time, clearly done to assess the damage to Mary's spine and neck following her crucifixion incident. But something stands out to Liam:

A broken arm.

And suddenly he knows: Mary Cleary was one of the killer's victims. She's not catatonic because she tried to hang herself; she's a Husk.

Faye.

Phoebe, despite her inexperience as a young Wedge, had been suspicious of her. For all her dominance and manipulative tendencies, Liam can't deny Phoebe's extraordinary perception of people. This must be why she offered Faye the job as town Splint. It never made sense that Phoebe would task someone so weak with being Shoalport's Wedge … unless she was keeping an eye on her.

But Faye said she had never broken her arm. Of course, she could have lied, and it would be near impossible for Liam to acquire her medical records. Or maybe no one ever checked.

Liam wants to yell. If only he could consult Jasper; he could see the piece he's missing. But Jasper has abandoned him. Jasper lied to him. Again. Liam thinks of Makoto, and anger scorches through him. How could Jasper do that to Makoto? How could he take him away? Did he even mean to? Maybe this really is all his fault.

It's easy to imagine what Makoto would say to that. "I chose to enter the Nether of my own accord. I made my own decisions. No one possessed me."

Liam halts, going still. Makoto's words echo in his mind, spawning a thought that sticks, then catches. If someone was possessing Faye, the Tryp Mark would be from their body, not Faye's. It wouldn't matter if Faye had never broken her arm.

But then who is possessing her? Who, from Jasper's time, broke their arm?

Jasper did, his thoughts supply unhelpfully. But he can't accept that Jasper is the killer. It doesn't *feel* right. He saw the Trypanon in the Nether. It wasn't Jasper. He'd know Jasper anywhere. He'd know him in the dark.

He stares at Mary. If he could explore her Phren, he might find what he needs. He puts the file back on the nightstand and takes a slow, deep breath, closing his eyes. His mind is bruised and weak, but he manages to secure a tether. It's hard to ignore how alone he is now. The weight of both Jasper and Makoto's absence is impossible. With a deep breath, he dislodges his soul from his body and moves into Mary's Phren.

Desolation. She's closer to dead than alive. There is nothing left of the walls but crumbling stone, coated in lichen and fungus. The echo of her soul is a hint of a wisp, fluttering through and seeing nothing. At some point, her Phren must have resembled an old cathedral, cluttered with ornate symbols of worship and divinity. It's burned to ash now, the only remaining memories presenting as whispered broken prayers or shredded hymn pamphlets. Everything is soaked in the remnants of a White Fluke. It's long gone now, having fed on everything worth consuming. Only the viscous remnants of a voracious mouth remain.

How did Phoebe miss this?

He rounds the corner of a decrepit stone pillar—stops. Rising from a mound of sand is a crucifix, poorly made with broken boards. They seem to have been ripped from a table or a deck, nailed in place by someone with a frenzied, untrained hand. A large crack slivers up the middle—the Fissure scar. He steps closer, and a memory pops up. It's faded and muddled. Liam forces it into focus.

Out, demon! Mary caws, shrill as an old schoolteacher. Give me back my daughter.

A spritz of water, aimed at the conjunction of the crucifix. It hits a child's face, bringing the features to focus—Faye. She's crying. Her wrists are bound to the arms of the cross, a blue blanket is tied around her waist, binding her to the trunk.

Mommy please, she cries.

Silence! You are not my child.

Dad would … he'd never let you—

You have no father. He's dead, and you took him from me. Was taking my only baby not enough? You've claimed everything I've ever loved. You are not worthy.

Faye's face clouds with anger. She spits at her mother, baring her teeth. When she speaks, her voice is deeper. Older.

You are the wicked one. I have seen the Rapture. You will cower beneath the hands of the divine.

Mary clutches the cross on her neck, wheeling around and sidling up to Gartlett.

You see, Pastor? You see how wicked she is, with her black speak. Mary breaks into sobs. Give me back my daughter! I'll do anything.

The pastor spreads open a bible to a leaf-marked page. He reads in a low chant, his hand rising to press his palm to Faye's forehead.

The memory glitches and turns. Mary stands beside Pastor Gartlett. A few steps behind them, another man paces with his arms crossed over his chest. He has the same crooked nose as Faye.

I just don't see why this is necessary, he says.

Mary believes the child in your care is not the child God gave you, Gartlett says. He pulls out a handkerchief and coughs into it. *I am inclined to agree.* He stuffs the soiled handkerchief back in his pocket. *She is very different from the little girl who once attended my masses. She is contrary and strange. She acts as if she is much older than her years and speaks in old-fashioned phrases.*

She's just eccentric, the father says, but his voice is small next to Gartlett's. *Her doctor says she just wants attention. That doesn't mean she's … what, possessed by a demon? Is that what we're getting at here?*

Don't act like you don't know what we're talking about, Mary hisses. *You know how she's been different since that day.*

What day? Gartlett says. When they don't immediately respond he steps close, his words taking on a threatening urgency. *It's very important that you pinpoint the incident that caused this.*

Faye's father swipes the back of his hand across his forehead. He stares at the ground when he speaks.

It … was the Fissure thing. At the O'Connor House. Something happened to Faye that day. Her doctors say it was trauma. She didn't speak for weeks, months. We almost had her committed.

Caleb wanted to coddle her, but he's not a mother like me. A mother knows her own child. Something took my daughter from me that day. I knew the instant I saw her eyes. This … thing wearing her face and using her voice is not my daughter. She's a changeling. God tells me so in my prayers. We need your help, Pastor.

Did anyone else see this? The possession?

No. This is between us and God. And you, of course.

It strikes Liam as odd that no one else would have seen Faye's apparent "possession." And then he thinks of Oliver. Oliver said he saw something. Could he have been talking about Faye?

A short vision overlays the scene. Faye, only a child, walks from the water beside Liam's home. Her face is serene and mature, a slight smile curling her lips. She is utterly incongruous with the chaos of the Fissure Event unraveling around her. The image fades.

Good. That's how it must be. With God behind me, I'm the only one who can save her, Gartlett says to Caleb Cleary.

Liam watches as Faye's father surrenders.

You … you can meet with her, he says. *But I want to be present when you do. Every time.*

Of course. There's an oily quality to Gartlett's tone that reminds Liam of a worm sewing silk.

With a flash, the memory disappears. The walls around Liam shake, crumbling to dust. There is nothing left of Mary Cleary now. Her Phren is now the same as the corpses he invaded at the morgue. Her soul is less than a shadow.

When he returns to his body, he strides to the window. As he climbs out, he casts a plea out to Jasper for him to return, even just for a moment. Nothing. He runs to his car, away from the screams of the Fissure Hosts. And returns to the O'Connor House.

Liam doesn't find *A History of Trypanism* until he's strewn his entire book collection on the living room floor. The moving box that held them lies on its side, its contents overflowing like a Thanksgiving cornucopia.

Kermit darts back and forth in his pen as Liam flips through the pages, ripping one in his urgency. Liam stops. The torn pages fall open. A symbol, drawn in grainy lines, stands out. He knows it from somewhere. He closes his eyes, takes a few slow, deep breaths, and searches his Phren. He ignores Jasper's stark absence; the way it all feels wrong without him. When he reaches the porch of his Phren, a memory emerges: Faye, clutching the amulet at her neck as she warned him that Jasper could be the killer. It had registered as an odd version of a cross at the time, something he recognized though couldn't pinpoint. Now, he knows: it's an ancient, early Christian symbol for Trypanism—a normal crucifix, laid over one that is upside down, with a tear up the middle of both.

Around him, the pieces fall together, materializing in his Phren. Maggie and Bert, speaking of a mother that abused them. They weren't talking about their own mothers, but of Faye's. They'd absorbed her emotions, her past. Mary's intense relationship with religion, her obsession with sinning. She claimed her daughter was not her own, that'd she'd been taken away during the

Fissure Event. Though her reaction had been cruel and twisted, her intuition was true. An image floats in front of him: Faye, only a child, walking from the water with an old soul taking up residence behind her eyes. Something escaped the Nether that day. Something possessed the body of little Faye Cleary, like a squatter. Like a Blue Fluke.

And it couldn't have been Jasper. He knows it now. Jasper was being thrust *back* into the Nether during the Fissure Event, not escaping it. But if not him, then who? If not Sebastian or William or the governess, who could Jasper have known that would be in the Nether, ready to worm their way into a child's Phren?

Liam falls back into the Waking World with a gasp. He crawls to his laptop where it's tucked under the couch and flips it open. He finds the link Teddy sent him weeks ago and clicks. The photo album pops up, and the image of Declan O'Connor Jr. with his hand gripping his sister's shoulder fills the screen. Her face is as severe as Liam remembers, her hair tied back tight as a noose. Then he sees it; on her neck, though small, Liam can make out the cross. It's the same Trypanism symbol Faye wears. Not just the same symbol; the same exact necklace. He zooms in … and that's when he sees what he hadn't before: the arm she's trying to hide beneath her cloak. It's wrapped in a sling.

Her broken arm.

A flash of lightning shocks through the room. On its tail, blue and red lights.

"Come out with your hands up, O'Connor." It's Sloane's voice, muffled and hoarse, from outside. "We know what you did, you son of a bitch. And don't you dare try anything. FUSE is on the way."

Liam sighs, the breath deflating him. He reaches out with his power, though it makes his headache pulse, and senses the sheer number of officers surrounding his home. They probably have nothing better to do in a small town. Stupid. Sloane could recruit every cop in the state, and it still wouldn't be enough to restrain him. She should know better.

He wonders at the scope of the Fissure Event, and of Faye's influence. If she has been hiding her power, there's no way to predict what she's capable of, or how much she's influenced people. Even someone with Sloane's fortitude.

Jasper. Where are you?

He knows the responding silence is inevitable. He still lets it hurt.

Straightening his shoulders, he opens his porch door, holding his hands in the air as he steps out. At the sight of so many cops—almost two dozen— standing around staring at him, some with their guns raised, he wishes he'd thought to put a hat back on, and then discards the thought. His hair isn't his primary concern right now.

"My hands are up," Liam says when Sloane's hand flies to her gun in its holster. He casts about for Faye. If she's there, he can't see or sense her. "I'm not a threat."

"Bullshit you aren't! I know what you did. I know who you are, you bastard. I suspected it the whole time. You're the one opening all these fucking Fissures."

"Just come quietly, Liam. There's no sense in making this harder than it needs to be. You know that." Applebaum's tone is as friendly and coddling as ever, but he senses her utter remoteness. This is an act. There's a medic behind her with a syringe who steps forward.

"If I was the Trypanon killer you're looking for, sedating me wouldn't do much good." This is not the point he should be making. He takes a deep breath. "I know who the Trypanon is."

Sloane rips her gun from its holster. She points it at the ground in front of Liam's feet, her finger not yet on the trigger.

"I don't want to hear it!" She twitches, twisting her neck to the side, then righting it. Liam frowns. She steps up onto the porch and hisses at him, "Phoebe knew about you all along. She knew you caused that Fissure Event but no one would listen to her. She was right, and you killed her for it." Sloane shudders and twitches. Her eyes slip back into her head, then snap back. "You killed everyone who came in your path, hiding your tracks. Maggie knew. Oliver knew. And Bert," she sniffs, blinks short and fast. Her throat bobs. "Bert was the only one who had the courage to face you, after you took his mother away. A mother is a child's savior." Her pitch climbs as she speaks, growing child-like. She hisses a word. Liam can't make it out. She says it again:

"*Sinner.*"

Fuck, he says to the man who is no longer there.

He'd hoped Faye didn't have the power to turn someone into a Pelt, to influence a mind into doing her will, thinking her thoughts. To make a puppet out of a person. Sloane would have been a hard takedown. She must have used Sloane's suspicion of Liam to gain a hold. It was a hell of a move. Of all people, no one would suspect Sloane. Her integrity is difficult to question, and Liam would see her as too strong to be influenced. He wonders how long Sloane has been under Faye's control. Perhaps he's never known Sloane at all.

Lightning splits the air across the river, hitting the shore in the distance. The officers duck, wheeling around. Thunder rumbles hard; Liam feels it in his chest. Smoke rises, heralding a curtain of rain. It falls hard and loud. The officers begin to panic, some retreating to their cars while others fumble with wet guns.

"Everyone calm the fuck down!" Sloane bellows, twisting so she can look over her shoulder.

A faint, desperate whisper brushes up the edge of Liam's Phren.

William.

"Jasper? Is that you?" Liam says out loud.

Sloane jerks. Her face molds into a contorted sneer. She is nothing like herself. "Don't say his name. He's poisoned you against us."

William. Please.

He's too far away, beyond the borders of Liam's Phren, deep in the Nether.

A new feeling rises. Every extraneous thought for every insignificant obstacle, is banished. Liam has one purpose: he must get to Jasper. A depthless certainty fills him..

With a deafening crack, the air flares again with light and ozone. It radiates from the peak of Knox Island. Liam breaks from Sloane, running to the edge of his porch. He watches, eyes wide, as the giant oak tree—the Letterbox— falls, split down its center by the lightning strike. The wood whines as it collapses, hitting the grass with a reverberating thud.

Liam doesn't process what he's about to do. He doesn't weigh ethics or consequences. He isn't acting out of logic anymore. When Sloane's wild grip clenches on his arms, he simply reacts.

Makoto always insisted that he only influenced people when it was essential, either for the individual's well-being or Liam's protection. Liam isn't thinking about the well-being of the police officers or of his own protection. All that matters is getting to Jasper. There is no door to the Nether in his Phren anymore, but the island remains, and Liam feels Jasper's despair soaking into the rocks and the sand. He pulls on what little power he can garner from it. He's only a Sophont now, and he gathers everything he has left.

And detonates.

At once, every single cop on the O'Connor property begins to hallucinate. In another life, Liam might take some entertainment in watching them suddenly amble around his yard, wide-eyed and dopey like college kids on spring break trying acid for the first time. He doesn't have time to watch, not even when a rookie cop takes off his shirt and tries to make out with one of his hydrangeas. Sloane won't be distracted long—not if Faye's control of her is this potent. She tries to brace against his porch swing and the chain finally gives, sending her sprawling to the boards. Liam doesn't hesitate. He climbs over the railing and jumps, landing hard on his knees in the grass.

"O'Connor!" Sloane shouts. Liam's head whips around. Their eyes meet. For a moment, he sees her—the real her.

"Take the bitch down," Sloane growls. She pulls out her handcuffs and snaps one end on her own wrist, the other onto a porch railing. "Go!"

Liam nods once. Ducked low, he runs to the water. The tide is high, the water opaque in darkness. The scent of charred wood coats the air. The Knox House stands before him, across the water, and for the first time it doesn't look ominous or imposing. It seems to beg for him in Jasper's voice.

Please.

Liam wades into the river. He feels a spike of fear when the strong current draws him out with hungry hands. Maybe this is how he finally dies, in the same seawater that took Jasper and many others. But he doesn't. The current carries him to Knox Island and deposits him gently on shore. He has the unnerving sense that the river wants him to be there.

With a breath, Liam begins to climb the hill to the fallen oak tree.

CHAPTER TWENTY-TWO
THE LOST LETTER

WITH EVERY STEP, Jasper's voice grows louder. His words push against the seam where Liam's Nether door once stood. Liam claws at it inside his Phren, pushes his soul energy against it, and cannot get through. Without his link to Jasper, the Nether is closed to him.

The rain has soaked the ground to mud and tangled the grass. Liam falls to his hands and knees, shoves back to his feet. Falls again. By the time he reaches the top of the hill, his palms are cut and muddied, his clothes soiled. The rain slows to a mist.

The tree is a sad, broken thing, lying splayed on the ground like a felled god. Smoke rises from the hewn trunk. In splitting, the rot hidden in its core is exposed. There's some comfort in knowing the tree was dying before it was felled.

He finds the gravestones. Jasper's marker was spared, but William's is buried under a heavy, crooked bow.

William.

The sound of Jasper's voice is a physical ache. Liam twitches, then moves. He can't hesitate. He picks up a branch and throws it aside. Then another. He cuts his hand and stumbles back, clutching it. Jasper calls his name again.

And then he catches sight of something amber, glinting in the low light, and tucked inside the trunk of the tree. He approaches. There, resting in a bed of soft, rotten wood, is a copper box. He's scared to touch it at first, as if it's been charged with electricity from the lightning. As if to nudge him, the rain suddenly stops.

Fingers trembling, he picks up the box. The top is rusted shut. He places it sideways on the ground and grabs a broken stick with a sharp point. With a few jabs at the seam, the box pops open.

There's a solitary letter inside. The paper is discolored and thick, its edges stained with moisture. Still, it seems to have been protected by the tree and the copper. Sitting back on his rear in the wet grass with a plop, Liam delicately unfolds the letter. He knows William's handwriting like he knows his own.

My dearest friend, Darwin,

I have made so many mistakes.

All my life, I've been a coward. I could not stand up to my father. I could not protect my sister from my brother. I could not be honest with myself. I could not be honest with you.

Liam pauses, frowning. He recalls the look on Declan Jr.'s face in the photo, the way he gripped Rosie's shoulder too tight. There was a dark gleam in his eye. Why would Rosie need to be protected from him?

Every day, for the rest of my life, I will regret that I did not find your letter in time. You drowned thinking that I had not come, that I had abandoned you. If I hadn't been out, drinking myself to distraction, this would not have happened. Your death is on my conscience.

Now, with nothing to lose or gain, I must finally write the words I could never say aloud, when it mattered.

Jasper. Darwin. My dearest friend. I have longed for you all my life. I tried to speak the words so many times, yet they always stuck in my throat. I should have told you I wanted to give up everything to be with you. I should have said that I like the way your hair curls around your ears and the curve of your fingers when you draw. That I can be my true self around you. That your eyes have always struck me silent. That you're the smartest man I've ever known. I should have been brave like you.

But I cannot change what I have done or not done. I can only despair, and wish, with all that I am, that I had another chance—another life to make this right. If I had that power, I'd make you the world you deserve.

And not just for you, but for my dear sister, Rosie. You would hate to see her as she is now. The soul has been stolen out of her. I feel as if my soul has been taken from me too. We found her washed up on the shore, soaked to the bone, staring out at your body in the river. I do not believe she will ever return to herself. I tried to ask her what she saw, but she no longer speaks. The hurt must be too great. Father says we must send her away. Outside of you, she was the only true friend I ever had.

It has all fallen apart. I have nothing. I see no way out. If only I had told you. If only I had not run away from it.

If only I had kissed you back.

I will place this letter in our tree and pray that wherever you are, it finds you. You are buried here now. I will lie beside you someday.

How can I go on without you? The pain is too great. I do not know what I shall do without my Darwin.

Calico

Liam folds the letter and closes it back in the box. He places it on the grass in front of his folded legs and looks up at the sky. It's gray with cotton clouds and the threat of more rain. Liam's face is dewy. He breathes and the air is wet too.

He feels too many things at once. He is charged up; he's on the edge of clarity. The answer is right in front of him on the grass. Declan Jr. hurt Rosie. Rosie became a Husk. Rosie's soul must have followed Jasper's into the Nether. The pieces fall together, aligning in his Phren and offering more lucidity than he's felt in years. And yet, Liam is lost.

Liam hasn't yet let himself touch the idea of there being something more than friendship between William and Jasper. He pushed it aside when he heard Jasper's final letter. He didn't let himself think about it when Jasper looked at him and said, "you would not meet me now." It wasn't relevant, not when there's a murderer. Not when there's a Fissure Event and Sloane is a Pelt and Faye has been someone else all this time.

But perhaps it's the most important piece of the story.

If William wasn't the one who found Jasper's letter, asking to run away together, then who did? Who came out that night to collect the letter from beneath the porch, in shadow? Could it have been Declan Jr.? Or Rosie? What would their reaction have been?

Sinner.

It's a memory of Faye's voice, and it's not high-pitched and bubbly as he knows it. It's archaic. It's the voice that Mary Cleary thought belonged to a demon. Then it occurs to him: maybe Jasper isn't the only one with hidden memories. Maybe Liam has some of William's locked away too.

He closes his eyes and sucks in a slow breath through his nose. The walls of his Phren rise around his consciousness, taking form and color. He stands in the hallway outside the third bedroom. With a nudge, the door creaks open. He never stored much memory in here. He didn't spend time in here as a child when his grandparents were alive, or since the first day he moved to Shoalport. As he crosses into the room, he senses scuttle in the walls, as if they're infested with bats. Old memories click and squeak. Not just old; not from this life.

He peals away the wallpaper, carves away the plaster. A veneer falls away. This room once belonged to a little girl. She collected seashells and history books. Religious books. She had the book on Trypanism and the amulet. A phantom feeling of unease rises in Liam. It's not his, but William's.

You're becoming obsessed, Rose. I wouldn't have given you that book if I thought—

It's a retreat for me, and I will take what comforts I can. You hardly provide me any.

What do you wish me to do? I have spoken to Father. I asked him to send you away to school, but you declined.

I do not need a school to teach me the ways of the Lord. And I will not abandon my home. Declan is not wicked. He's too contrite. He always regrets the things he does. He even gifted me this necklace.

He wouldn't have to placate you with trinkets if he wasn't hurting you in the first place.

And what do you know about it? You won't stay with me; I can see it in your eyes. Why? Why do you always run from us? You told me once that we'd be together always … that you'd look after me. When you leave, it gets worse here.

What if … what if you moved away with me? Jasper and I always talked about moving out west. I'm certain he'd be pleased if you came—

I have no interest in seeing Jasper Knox ever again. I wish he'd never come into our lives. He's poisoned you against us.

Liam feels a pulse of protectiveness. He hears it reflected in William's response:

Why do you say this? Jasper is the best man I know.

Rosie's voice falls to a hush. *I overheard Father. He confirmed my suspicions.*

I don't care what father says. He can't stop me from seeing Jasper. I'm a man now.

But surely you've seen it too. You know why Sebastian can't bear to be around his own son. Jasper has … proclivities. He's not made in the image of God. Father has friends at Harvard. They shared rumors with him. I don't want you going near him anymore. What if he corrupts you? I can see the change happening already.

I will not hear this.

The sound of footsteps toward the door.

He was always trying to take you away from me. That was his plan from the start. It's because of him that—that all this is happening. Her voice is shrill.

You have no idea what you're talking about. I'm sorry, I cannot entertain this.

A door creaks on opening.

It's his fault my arm broke, William.

The footsteps halt. The rustle of fabric.

What? How?

A silence.

How? he repeats, harsher. *That doesn't make any sense. Jasper would never hurt anyone.* She doesn't respond. William's voice totters as he speaks. *Why did you not say before? You told me you fell. I ... I thought Declan might have been responsible.*

Declan is my brother, William. He loves me. Jasper is ... other. He manipulates. He has a power. I've felt it. Consider what I've said.

The memory recedes back into the walls. A sickening tightness rises. Suddenly, he knows.

Rosie. It's always been Rosie.

He must get to Jasper.

In a blink, his Phren morphs. Liam stands on the tidal island, staring up at the bare, dead tree rising from its peak, where his Nether door once split the world. Now, there's nothing but a faint scar, a crease in the wood and stone. Jasper has gone quiet on the other end. If he listens close, he can hear the faint sound of breath ending on a whine, one after another.

He must remake the Hitch connection. He must remake the door. But how?

Liam is not William. He's had a lifetime full of different experiences that shaped him, has had his own family and friends and career. If he does have feelings for Jasper, how can he tell that they're his own and not simply remnants from William's life?

He wishes that he could ask Makoto what to do. Makoto and Jasper would have liked each other. Makoto would have wanted Liam to help Jasper. As long as it wasn't at the expense of his own well-being, of course.

To his side, a familiar room takes shape, floating on the water—the dive bar they always went to after a case in Chicago. The smell is easy to recall, and the ambient light from the TV. It's easy to imagine them sitting there, hunched together with elbows on the bar. Makoto would sip his wine. Liam would be bullying his way through his third scotch. Makoto, with his posture straight like Jasper's, would ask how Liam feels. And Liam would respond:

I didn't think I'd find another best friend after you. When Claire left and you died, I thought I'd never be close to anyone again.

But you are.

Yeah.

Why?

I think he's funny. At first, I thought he didn't mean to be, but he's clever as hell. And smart too. He knows so much about so many things, and he's passionate about them too. I don't think I'd ever get bored of hearing what he has to say. Yeah, he's … I guess with you gone, like I said, he's my best friend.

Just a friend?

Liam would pause then. He'd chew on his lip and chug the rest of his drink. The bartender knew him well enough to bring him another. He can taste the burn of the whisky, can feel its fragrant echo in his nose.

Well, I'm not blind.

Not literally.

Liam would roll his eyes.

I'm saying he's a handsome guy, alright? You know my type. He fits the bill.

Your type is rare.

Doesn't get much rarer than a Victorian ghost living inside my head that I pined after in a past life.

I suppose not.

He's got these eyes that stick in your mind. No one has eyes like him. And his skin. And I like the way his hair curls on his ears—

Liam would cut off. His face would alight with dawning realization. He would feel William's feelings like an underground river beneath his own. Mirroring his own. He would watch the corner of Makoto's lip curl in a self-satisfied smirk.

Shit.

Shit, indeed. Makoto would sip his wine.

I have a thing for a dead guy.

It's frankly in character.

Shut up.

The vision mists and glows. A stirring warmth blankets the surface of the river. Liam watches as the image of Makoto disappears. For the first time since his passing, for just a moment, Liam doesn't miss him. He's still here.

He turns back to the scar of his Nether door. It's more pronounced than before, the edges of the seam glowing with heat. He gathers up his memories of Jasper, bundling the warmth and laughter and stirrings of attraction. He grabs William's too, fusing them with his own.

With all the power he has, he thrusts them against the door. In a flash of yellow candlelight, the world splits. The door is reopened. The Nether gasps with joy at connecting with him again, but he holds it back. He breathes, bolstering his will, and steps through the seam.

As he closes the door behind him, he has the chilling sense that something has just happened for the last time.

CHAPTER TWENTY-THREE

THE FINAL TEST

THE NETHER IS in chaos.

All semblance of spatial logic or order is scrambled. Fissures tear through the landscape, charging the air. Flukes writhe in a frenzy, grappling with each other in tangles of viscous fronds. On a nearby drifting boat, a Violet Fluke devours a Red Fluke in competition. It's the first time Liam has seen a Fluke consume another. The noise is staggering—crashing waves and thunderclaps and choked screams. Liam can't get his bearings. The long-term care facility stands in the middle of the river, the dark water blending to pavement. It's the epicenter of the Fissure Event, and the Nether clamors around it, drunk on the feast.

Liam turns away and looks to the Knox House as a waypoint. Over the course of a breath, it shifts from being within feet to standing miles away in the distance, from being as large as a mountain to the size of a dollhouse. When he takes a step, he's suddenly on its porch. The boards beneath his feet start to splinter. A Violet Fluke slithers beneath them, bulging with undulating black flies. It licks at Liam's toes with a long, urchin-like tongue. He stumbles back onto a bed of rusted nails. They lance his feet, spurting imagined blood into the air. Where have his shoes gone? He's wearing swim trunks. Little kid trunks with sharks on them.

He runs.

And he's on top of the hill on Knox Island. The oak tree blazes in front of him, flames licking up the branches. No—not a fire: a Red Fluke is feeding on the tree. It's a desecration—spray paint on an ancient temple. A rush of fury overcomes Liam at the sight. He taps into his power. With a push, he throws the Fluke from the tree and drives it into the ground. It's probably not the best use of his resources, but he doesn't care. The Fluke fizzles, whining and receding. Liam looks past it to the river and catches sight of the tidal island.

He feels Jasper there more than he sees him. How had he missed him before? Nothing makes sense. Nothing is where it should be. Yet, the pull is inescapable. He must get to the island, to Jasper. The dead tree protruding from the island's bearded rocks seems to beckon him over, its top branch curled like a finger in a "come hither" gesture. This could be a trap. Good. He wants to face the one who is doing this to Jasper, has done it to Cedra and so many others.

He breaks into a run.

And the hill on Knox Island becomes the porch steps of the O'Connor House. His vision swirls, and he freezes. He looks out at the tidal island, no closer than before. There's a tapping sound behind him. He slowly turns.

The O'Connor House is not as it is in the Waking World or in his Phren. It is a pulsating, blackened thing—a beating heart, fetid with worms and rot. This is not his home. This belongs to someone else.

There's a staggering power inside the house, barely restrained. A barrier on the door radiates a molten heat. It's not there to keep him out, but to hold something in. The tapping continues. Something is behind the glass. Liam refuses to look at it.

He focuses on the island again. Jasper's voice is gone; the presence of him is fading. When Liam calls out to him, only the faintest pulse is returned. He runs down to the shore, dodging a fungal crop of White Fluke, its spores reaching for him. He skids to a halt on the edges of the water. There's a barrier here too, and it's potent. The island rises like a fortress in the dark, guarded by a moat.

Liam turns all his power toward it, and then, he makes out the faintest flicker of light. It's pinhole thin in the dark—barely alive. He reaches out to it. He reaches into himself. He's always seen Jasper's side of their connection— Jasper's light—but there must be the same tie within Liam. Jasper believed their connection was one-sided, that it was forced upon Liam. But that's not how Hitch links work. There must be a tie on both ends.

He digs deep … and finds it: a light inside himself. A candle in a window.

It's a withered, tired thing. It points to Jasper like a lighthouse beacon. The slightest breath would smother it. Liam holds it in a tender grasp. He draws memories of little moments with Jasper to the surface: the teasing jokes and shared moments of understanding, the way that Liam felt whenever Jasper looked at Kermit with affection. How he was seen wholly, elevated to a better version of himself, and matched. How Jasper's presence made living easier. He pours the memories into the light. He pours himself into it, gives over to it.

And lets the link carry him to Jasper.

Sunshine blinds Liam at first. The world tilts. He fights to stabilize and get his bearings. Then he hears his own voice, tinted with a faint Irish accent:

How could you? How could you do it?

He whips around to the source of the sound. Jasper is huddled in a dark ball, his coat wrapped around him like a chrysalis. When Liam takes a step toward him, the world ripples above his prone form, opening like a window. From it, memories play on repeat. The rejection in the greenhouse takes prominence, projected against the background. Shorter images spark and die: when William ignored him at school for his new friends, when William forgot Jasper to meet with a woman instead, when William wrote to tell Jasper he wouldn't be coming to Boston for Christmas after all one year. But there aren't just memories of William. Gradually, more snippets of Jasper's time with *Liam* take stage. All the times Liam snapped at him or ignored him or called his character into question. He watches as he tells Jasper he's as evil as a murderer after Jasper tried to escape the Nether. At the time, Liam hadn't considered how that would have affected him. He didn't imagine that the Hitch link would cause Jasper physical pain when Liam pulled away, or that he'd be unable to bear the strain inside the Nether. He didn't think he'd inflict such self-loathing, would slice open Jasper's worst fears and spit acid into them.

Liam's harshest words act as a painful soundtrack, but there are some he never said.

You disgust me.

You are wicked.

How could you imagine you are worthy of me?

You are a mistake.

"Jasper … I'm sorry." He tries to speak above the litany of abuse. Jasper is imprisoned in his own soul, and Liam can do nothing but watch. He shouts. Every word grows more desperate and accomplishes less. Each grinding, repeated memory strips Jasper down, weakens and dulls him. The light fades.

There's a special kind of shame rising in Liam. It had been unfathomable that he could be the architect for someone's Nether prison, but the extent of his own neglect and callousness is profound when it replays before him. He's always seen himself as someone outside of people; he didn't affect others because he wasn't close to them. He existed on the periphery. He may help people by sealing their Fissures, but that didn't connect him to them. Rather, it othered him completely.

And yet, in multiple lives, he hurt the person closest to him. He got a second chance to correct his errors, and he failed.

But shame is paralytic. It won't help Jasper now. Liam buries it down and focuses on another feeling rising in him: anger.

He can claim responsibility for his own actions, but not the words being fabricated by Jasper's captor. He never called him wicked. He never called him a mistake. There's a unique kind of violation in having his own voice used to inflict pain. Until now, Liam hasn't felt much beyond grave detachment and pity for Faye. She was part of the job, as much a victim as a Wick and no more in control of her actions. She'd killed because the Nether corrupted her, forced her hand, just as the Nether provoked Jasper to attack Samantha Munn. Just as it coerced him into trying to escape through a Fissure …

But Liam was wrong. There is maliciousness here. Vindictiveness. Rosie, who has become Faye, wants Jasper to suffer. And not just at her own hand, but at Liam's as well. He recalls her disdain for William and Jasper's relationship and her righteous judgement of Jasper's tendencies. She was jealous of their connection, that much was clear.

And she was the one who intercepted Jasper's letter. She's the reason all this happened. Had she gone to the island in Liam's stead? They'd found her empty body on the shore. What had she done?

Regardless, Liam needs to stop her now. Reaching inside himself, he draws on the Hitch link, and finds that there's not much left. Jasper's soul is flickering out, his happy memories, his character being swallowed by the Nether. As Liam fumbles, the images tormenting Jasper sharpen, revealing their true nature: they are a contaminant, polluting all that is light and passionate about the man. They are transforming him.

Jasper is becoming a Blue Fluke. Again. And this time, if the Hitch link is severed, Liam knows it can never come back.

"No," he calls. The word is snuffed out and stuffed back in his throat. He gags. A presence closes around him. The air is too thick to breathe. The Nether convulses with glee, opening like a mouth and welcoming a presence onto the island.

"William."

Rosie materializes behind Jasper. She comes to stand beside him, placing the tips of a few spindly fingers on his shoulder. She's appalling to look at.

Her features shift between Faye's and Rosie's, giving her a grizzly, inhuman distortion. She stinks of putrid low tide. The Trypanon emblem on her neck glows hot. It burns to look at. Liam's gaze slides back to her face, muddled like a melting sculpture.

"Stop," he rasps. The word hurts. "Get away from him."

"But he's our final test, William. With his final judgment, we have completed the Trypanon trial. We have exposed myself to God's judgment by traveling in and out of the Nether. We've opened a Fissure in someone I loved. My mother—our mother—did not love me, but oh, did we love her. She was found wanting and could not survive God's judgment—"

"I knew it," Liam breathes. "Mary—"

"A name she did not deserve. That trial almost bested me, but we persevered. It took years. So much pain. But we pushed. I survived the trials, and we got stronger. And look at all I've done! You saw our Fissure Event. That was not easy. You helped by breaking that silly Hitch link. But I'm powerful now … more powerful than anyone has ever been. And finally, we have exposed five sinners to judgment, each succumbing to the five Flukes. Jasper Knox is the final sinner: my Blue Fluke. No one ever saw me and Faye and us as anything but weak and pathetic." She laughs with two voices. Her head jerks. "No longer. We are stronger than them all. Even stronger than Iris. Or you, my dear William. And with this power, we can save all that deserve saving, and punish those who do not."

Liam looks at Jasper. His skin is gray, the edges of his frame blurring into nothing. A bloom of black despair spreads from his core, smothering the light. He doesn't have long.

"Rosie … these tests, they don't mean anything. It's just an old myth. You aren't divine, you aren't saving anyone. The Nether is using you. It just wants to be fed."

The emblem flares on her chest. She flinches, then sets her jaw and stares into him. When she speaks, it's with Faye's voice.

"You don't know anything. You aren't even a real Trypanon. I thought you were my hero—the savior Tryp we've been waiting for. I thought you were the best there ever was. My Great Calico. And you wouldn't even look at me. I loved you and you didn't even know my name. But we're the great one now, and you're the nobody. You wanna talk about feeding? You're just using a Hitch link for your powers. They're sullied. They aren't earned, or gifted, they're … blasphemous." Her voice ebbs back into Rosie's, casting lower, the diction sharpening. "To form a link with someone so wanton, so depraved. It's a sin to even touch him, and he bound himself to you. My William never would have allowed it. This … this thing is a parasite. Well, no worries, dear. I will save you from him and then we can be together. My brother. My love."

She takes a step toward him. Liam doesn't think. He dives for Jasper, throwing himself through the window and into Jasper's prison. A hybrid scream erupts behind him, of two souls in singular fury. A sharp, biting pain claws into his ankles as he tumbles. He lands hard and the pain desists, leaving an itchy sting. He fights to breathe and to see. It's all a swirling blur.

Then, suddenly, everything falls into focus.

He's on the island still, but it's different. The sun is shining, the tide is low. The trees are stained orange and red, and the sky is a New England autumn blue. A flock of Canadian geese honk overhead, passing in a V-shape. He blinks.

Jasper is beside him, sitting in the sand with tears streaming down his cheeks. He's young. Liam is young too. Liam turns.

And sees Rosie on the shores beside the O'Connor House. She is only a child, and her face is infested with fear, her eyes fixed on the sky.

"Oh God," Liam mouths as realization dawns.

They're in a Nether prison. Not Jasper's, Liam's, or Rosie's.

This prison is for all three.

CHAPTER TWENTY-FOUR
BLUE FLUKE

"JASPER," LIAM HISSES. He crawls over to him, palms digging dents into the sand. The sharp scent of low tide stings at his nose. It's the same smell that's been following him in the Nether all these years: the scent that accompanied Jasper, he now realizes. It's different than Rosie's smell. He hadn't noticed before. "We have to get out of here." He glances at Rosie. She's still looking around frantically. She hasn't seen them yet.

"I do not wish to go home."

It's a moment before Liam realizes Jasper isn't responding to him; he's still stuck in the past.

"Jasper." Liam grabs his arm and Jasper flinches. Their eyes meet. "This is the Nether. This isn't real."

"I'd had a bad dream this day." Jasper speaks with listless melancholy. "We were only thirteen. I dreamt of my governess and the day she broke my arm. And I dreamt of my mother. And then they were one and the same. I couldn't purge the nightmare."

"I get it, but—"

"Do you not recall what occurred?"

Liam intends to shake Jasper's question off, to force him out of his stupor. But he stops. A tingling sensation spreads in his chest. He *does* remember. As if emboldened by his realization, the memory takes over, claiming his thoughts and his intentions.

"It's only a nightmare," Liam says. A different dialect sits in his mouth like it belongs there.

"You don't understand."

"I have nightmares too. Mother says they can't hurt me."

"Your mother is not my mother. I have no mother. Or perhaps I had two."

William sighs. He rubs at the back of his head. "Then ... what can I do to help?"

One of Jasper's shoulders tips up and down. It might be a shrug.

William inches closer on the sand. Jasper tenses as he sidles up close. They stay suspended like that for a long moment. William glances over to Rosie. She is staring at them, her brow fixed in a frown. He doesn't notice at first that Jasper has placed his hand on Liam's thigh.

He looks down at the touch. His lips part. Then William looks back at Rosie. Her eyes have dropped to Jasper's hand with a focus William feels like a burn.

William retracts, shoving Jasper away from him. Jasper's elbow collides with a rock, and he cries out, grabbing it. He looks at William like he hurt him on purpose, which only makes it worse. William didn't do anything wrong. It's Jasper's fault that this happened.

"What's the matter with you?" William barks, shooting to his feet. He doesn't care that his voice is rising, that it's carrying across the water. A secret little part of him wants Rosie to hear.

"You ... you touch me all the time," Jasper says in a hush. He looks hurt and bewildered. Then, in a blink, he is adult Jasper—with the same pain in his eyes that never healed, only spread—then he's a child again.

"Not like that!" William looks at Rosie with heat spreading on his cheeks. She's stomping towards them through the path to the island. Her skirt is getting soaked. Jasper looks at her, then back to William. His silence is pointed. "Just stay away from me," William shouts, turning on his heel and hurrying to Rosie to head her off. He doesn't want her talking to Jasper. He can't touch the reasons why.

He grabs Rosie's arm when he reaches her and spins her around. She yelps and the scene changes. Liam is himself again, watching as a spectator. It's early spring. The air is a dry cold, the landscape muddied with shades of brown. Dead grass. Leafless trees. A few piles of stained snow, glossy from repeated freezings and meltings.

There are voices.

With his arms wrapped around his chest, Liam rounds the side of the O'Connor house. Jasper and Rosie are in a heated argument. They're only a year or two older. Their cheeks are blotched red in the cold. Rosie's been crying. Her nose is running. Her arm is in a sling, her fingers bruised purple.

"But why did you have to tell on him?" Rosie hiccups, her voice tripping on her breath. "This is your fault. He did this because you told." She looks down to her arm.

"He hit you. I had to tell someone. I couldn't just—"

"That time was an accident!"

"And what about the other times? He's hurt you before. He's always hurting you. If I didn't tell my father, I'd never be able to—"

"And because you told him, this is what happened. It's your fault. You only did it to avoid your own guilt, not to help me. Now look what you've done."

Jasper's face drains of color. "Rosie, that's not true."

"Isn't it?" She lifts her arm, winces, and eases it back down, cradling it against her body. To Liam, her manipulation is obvious, but not to Jasper. The burden of guilt slips over Liam through their Hitch link; the ache in Jasper's chest becomes Liam's own. "You shamed him. You got him in trouble with my father and he thinks it was my doing. I can't convince him otherwise. Now he hates me and he hurt me and it's your fault. It's always your fault." A bubble of snot pops in her nostril. "And now Mother has fallen ill, too. She can't bear the stress."

"I'm sorry, Rose. But I … I care about you. You're like a sister to me. I was only trying to help. I thought if your father was made aware of it, if he heard it from my father, then he'd put a stop to it."

"You don't *care* about me," she spits. Jasper flinches as her words spray his face. "You just want to steal William away. I've seen the way you look at him. You're … covetous."

Jasper's cheeks stain pink. He looks away, picking at his sleeve with long fingers that he's yet to grow into. "I don't know what you're talking about."

"Yes, you do. You're all he talks about anymore. You take up all his time. It's as if you've bewitched him. It's as though you steal inside his mind. Before you, it was just me and him. We shared thoughts … dreams. Now, he never wants to play with me. And soon you'll go away to school together and leave me here and I'll have nothing. Not even Declan. I'll be all alone."

"I'm sorry." Jasper looks lost. Liam wants to interfere, to help, but he can do nothing. Rosie turns and runs away with a final command that Jasper never speak to her again.

As the scene fades into another, Liam watches Jasper wilt. His sense of failure and isolation rises like a toxin. It poisons Liam too. He knows by now that Jasper did not have many friends or family. Losing Rosie was not a casualty he could afford.

You did this. Rosie's voice flits through the air like a yellow jacket, stinging Jasper as it passes. *He hurt me because of you.*

A wisp of wind. Liam turns to follow it and sees Rosie in the distance. She's climbing a leafless tree. It takes him a moment before he recognizes the figure standing below her as Declan Jr. He's broader and more imposing than his picture, with slumped shoulders and bristled hair. He's pointing up to a branch and yelling at her to climb it, taunting. Liam sees what Rosie cannot: a sliver cut out of the base of the branch. Her petticoat is caught on it. Liam steps forward to stop her. He's too late. The branch cracks. Liam is suddenly standing only feet away. There's nothing he can do. There never was.

She's crying—gargled, choking sobs. And Declan is watching her, unmoving. There's satisfaction curling his features.

"Perhaps you should go tell Father of your misfortune. That's what you're good at, isn't it? Maybe you'll even convince him that I threw you from the tree yourself. Use your little powers."

"Please," she hiccups. Her arm is nauseating to look at, bent and already swelling. A jagged tip of white bone protrudes from her forearm.

"Please, what? Please '*help me, brother?*' I thought I was your enemy." Liam is struck by the uneven shape of Declan's irises, by the bulge of one eye, dilating more than the other.

"No, I didn't—"

"I'll never forget what you did," he says, leaning down over her with his hands braced on his knees. "And it seems God won't either. He did this to you today for your lies about me to Father. For your wrath. And yet, now, I will be your savior, acting in his image. I will run to the house and call for Father now, and you will always remember my mercy. And your own wickedness."

The edges of reality wobble and blur. Liam swings around. Jasper is standing in front of him, his eyes locked on Declan and Rosie. His skin is pallid, his mouth gaped open. The Hitch link shudders, rippling Jasper's pain into Liam.

"I didn't mean to," Jasper whispers.

Behind him, a curtain of memories ripple and push at his back: of Jasper alone in his small apartment in Boston, a Christmas tree and empty chair beside him. Of Jasper as a child, holding out his palms so his governess could whip them with birch. Of Jasper trying, over and over, to talk to his father, to get him to look Jasper in the eye, and getting nothing.

Jasper is on the island again.

Liam watches him from the shore below the Knox House. Jasper keeps checking his pocket watch. It glints in the moonlight. The tide has started to turn. Then, a figure emerges from the O'Connor House. They're silhouetted as they leave the porch and begin the path to the island. Jasper perks up, his spine a straight line.

When Rosie comes into view, stomping through the silt, Jasper droops. Their voices are distant, difficult to make out against the wind and the water.

"Sinner!" Rosie shouts.

"Please."

"Vile. Perverted. Evil."

Each word is an arrow. Jasper's not the only one stricken. Rosie chokes on her own voice, and crumples. With every castigation, they are both shredded. Torn. Though it's only a shadow of memory, when the Fissures rip open in Rosie and Jasper, Liam feels them tear and crackle through the air.

Then everything is slow. Excruciating. The limp Husks of his sister and his best friend are swallowed in lapping bites by the tide, until the top of the black tree slips beneath the surface. As Jasper floats, face down, his body convulses and then goes limp. Rosie's body, however, drifts to the O'Connor's shore. She lays on her side in the sand, staring at the island, for hours before Declan Jr. finds her.

Liam blinks. He clutches at his throat. He should have stopped this.

The world opens. In an instant, he's on a vast shore, looking out at gray waves beneath a clouded sky. He's sitting in the soft, cream-white sand. There is a large gull nearby, its wings black and tucked against its body. Liam breathes deep. The scent of the open sea fills his chest.

"I don't think I will ever marry," Jasper says at his side, sitting on his folded black coat. He looks unpeeled wearing only his white shirt, having abandoned the ascot today. William can see the pale dip of his throat, the freckle on his clavicle.

"What if you fall in love?" William says.

Jasper's eyes, grayer than the sea, find him. His head doesn't move. Then he looks back at the sea.

"Who says I haven't?"

William snorts. "If you had, I'd be the first to know."

"Or the last."

William frowns. He feels like he's missing something. He frequently does with Jasper. "I don't think I could fall in love."

Jasper shifts his weight. "Why not?"

"For one, my taste is different from my father's. I don't find his matches suitable."

"And what's your taste?"

Liam picks up a dried sheet of kelp and occupies his fingers with ripping it apart.

"I suppose I haven't thought about it much. I want someone who understands me, of course. Someone who shares my interests. You and I always talk about travel, so I'd desire someone with an inclination for adventure. Passion is important. Someone who values quiet and nature. Someone who doesn't prevaricate or pretend to be someone they're not. I'd want someone who sees the best in me and wants to help me realize it. And I suppose in terms of looks, I am drawn to dark hair and light eyes." William pauses, then huffs a laugh, shaking his head. The seagull startles and trots away. "I'm just describing you, aren't I?"

Jasper says nothing.

"If only we could get married. Then all our problems would be solved," William chuckles against the silence.

He looks at Jasper. His lips are clenched tight. There's a vein bulging at his temple. William feels a sting of hurt.

"You look like you'd rather jump into the ocean right now than entertain the idea of marrying me."

William flinches when Jasper looks at him. There's a new, unveiled rage burning in his eyes. "I do not appreciate being mocked," he says, low.

William shivers at the gravel in his voice. "I wasn't mocking you."

Gradually, Jasper's anger morphs into something new: profound bewilderment. "You really weren't," he breathes. "For all your abilities, for all the time we've spent inhabiting each other's minds, you really don't know. You weren't mocking me at all. You were serious."

"Of course I was." William usually believes he understands Jasper better than anyone. In this moment, he doesn't know Jasper's thoughts any better than he knows what's hidden in the sea. It's almost offensive. "I'm always honest with you."

"I wish I could say the same of myself."

"I wish you could too." William crosses his arms over his chest and pouts, glaring at the waves.

Jasper reaches into the pocket of his trousers. He pulls out a hunk of brown bread, breaks off a piece, and tosses it at the gull. As the bird gulps it down, two smaller gulls with spotted necks swoop in out of thin air. They swiftly realize the frivolity in bullying the larger bird into a meal. But Jasper charitably throws out a piece of bread for each of them too.

"I don't believe you would want to associate with me if I was fully honest with you," Jasper says.

"Why?"

"I am not normal."

"I'm aware."

Jasper rolls his eyes. "Sometimes I think you are purposefully inept just to spite me."

"I could say the same of your cryptic remarks. How can I intuit your intentions when you never say what you mean?"

Jasper shoves to his feet, kicking sand onto Liam's lap. He pulls off his shoes and rolls up his pant legs, then stomps down to the water's edge. A shiver rattles up his frame when a wave rushes over his feet. He shakes it off and steps further into the surf. Another step, then another. The water is soaking his trousers now, climbing up past his knees.

"You don't have to take my remark about jumping into the sea as a suggestion," William calls out, trying to inject humor back into the air. In truth, unease is rising in him. He eases to his feet and approaches Jasper, his hand held out in placation.

Jasper looks at him over his shoulder. "What would you do to keep me from going further?"

"What?" The sea darkens under a passing black cloud. The memory shudders at the fringes. The waves crash with impossible volume.

Jasper teeters. "What would you do to keep from losing me to the sea?"

The world flickers. Liam is staring at an ocean, then a tidal river. Jasper is standing, knee-deep in the surf, then knee-deep on a sinking island. Liam is William, and he is himself.

"I ... I'd do anything."

"Would you marry me?"

"Why would you want me to do that?"

Jasper takes another step. Liam lunges, reaching for him, but Jasper holds him back with a look.

"You lost me," he says. There's a crack in his voice that Liam can't stand.

"I—"

"William."

"It was the regret of my life." In the distance, a wave starts to rise, higher and higher, sucking in the swell, growing. Jasper is looking at him. He can't see what's coming. "I would have gone with you. But I didn't know. I never got your letter. If I had, I'd have been scared, but I'd have met you that day. We would have figured it out. I'd meet you then, I'd meet you now. Jasper!"

The wave towers over them. Time slows as it crests and falls, sweeping the world away. Blackness. Cold. Then, two lights. Vision returns as slow as a dawn.

They're back on the tidal island, facing each other. Rosie is a distant thought, present yet banned from their fortress in the river. They've met here so many times.

Liam knows Jasper's eyes as if each fleck of gray is carved inside him.

"I could not bear it when I lost you," William says. "The despair … it permeated my days like a rot. When my own Fissure finally opened, there was no Fluke to take me. I *became* the Fluke, and I passed into the Nether without regret or fear. I had nothing left to lose. And then, somehow, I came back. I found my way out, was reborn, but I didn't remember. I finally fucking found you again, and I didn't even remember you."

"As I said: inept."

Liam reaches out. He pinches Jasper's sleeve between two fingers. "I should have kissed you back in the greenhouse."

Jasper's shoulders sag. The color flows back into his cheeks and lips. The sky above clears, a fresh summer sun warming the air. The tide departs, carrying away the walls of Jasper's prison with it.

"You should have kissed me a great many times."

"I wanted to. So many times when we worked the case. When you made your little quips or talked about the things you like. Whenever you looked at Kermit in that way you do."

"Liam."

"You were never different from me. We wanted the same things."

Jasper takes a step closer, and a shattering scream rips through the air.

Rosie.

They turn toward the O'Connor House, and gasp. It's swollen with the Nether's corruption, pulsating beneath a stormy sky. The porch door is wide open, and a figure writhes from inside: Faye and Rosie. The same and different.

"We need to help her," Jasper says. "I should have helped her a long time ago."

"Yeah. I should have too." The power of the house grows more potent as they cross the path from the island to the shore. The yard's dead grass is needle-sharp. Liam takes Jasper's hand, drawing on their shared power to part the lawn like a scalp. "No matter what happens, don't let go of my hand, okay? We need all the power we can get."

"I understand."

They step onto the porch and through the door. The house welcomes them inside, groaning. It rumbles and breathes.

The rooms are unstable, flashing between images of the house as Liam knows it, to the house of the past, to spaces that do not belong inside any house. The stairwell in the foyer is new, smelling of fresh oak. Then it's a large tree with a half-sawed branch, rising into a ceiling that looks like a sky. A shadow of a child runs up the stairs and climbs the tree. A crack, a fall, a scream, then it starts again.

When Liam and Jasper try to enter the living room, they lose their bearings, as if the house is intent on confusing them. One moment they're looking at two children sitting in front of the hearth, playing too rough, the next they're in a hospital room.

Faye. Can you tell me why your mother did this to herself? It's Phoebe. Yet, as she speaks, she becomes sinister. Altered. *Why won't you look me in the eyes, Faye? Did you have something to do with it? Can you make people do things with your mind? Did you kill your mother?*

Liam squeezes Jasper's hand. "It's like this whole house is a prison. We've gotta find Rosie."

The room shudders.

"I don't think that will be easy. The house—or rather, the Nether—does not seem to want us to."

"Well, that's just tough shit for the Nether."

It's easy to harness the Hitch link now. It's as a part of Liam as his own limbs. The power he draws from it isn't draining or frenetic. It's calm, familiar. He feels Jasper at the other end of the connection in a way he hasn't before.

He shoves the walls of the prison aside and searches for Rosie's presence. A deluge of images pass, trying to draw him in. Taunts from Declan Jr. flutter by. He sees Rosie's mother—William's mother—gargle her last breath, her lungs overflowing with blood. Jasper yanks him away.

"*Focus,*" he hisses. The Nether is trying to catch him, trying to catch them both. It thrusts visions of Jasper's loneliness at him, of his abandonment. But they have no power over Jasper now, not with Liam holding him close through the link.

The Nether falters, its grip slipping, and that's when they find her.

The room settles around them. A canning closet and rickety stairs come into view. There's moisture on the walls, the smell of mildew and dust. A petrified mouse carcass crunches beneath Liam's foot. An overhead bulb flickers on.

A figure on the far wall comes into focus. She's bound to a cross. One of her arms hangs limp at her side. Her eyes bug out, white at the center of the irises. She's still breathing—slow, crushed gasps as her own weight suffocates her.

And at her feet, a person that is both Rosie and Faye, a child and a woman, kneeling. A halo of smog encloses her frame.

"She's becoming a Blue Fluke," Jasper whispers, though his lips don't move. Liam hears him through the link—a whisper deep inside himself.

"We need to get her out of here. If she becomes a Blue Fluke, she could kill a lot more people."

"We must send her to the Other, then."

Liam reaches out, feeling for the edges of Rosie's power. It's scorching.

"Shit. She's stronger than us."

"And the Nether will be against us. It has control over her now. Perhaps it has for a long time."

Jasper's fingers move gently against the back of Liam's hand. It's more than touch.

"Whatever happens, we can't let her get back into her body."

Jasper nods. Liam feels his guilt. He understands. Half of him also sees Rosie as a sister. But the other half of him is still a Wedge, and Faye is still a murderer, and Cedra is still dead.

"Don't let go of my hand," Liam says, out loud this time.

Rosie wrenches around and looks at them with two different eyes. Liam stumbles back. There's nothing human left in her. And that's when he realizes: the walls are not what they seemed. A writhing conglomerate of Flukes surrounds them—braids of white worms and curtains of black flies, wet tentacles and fungus fronds—thousands of holes with clicking grubs, all tangling together to close them in a living cell.

"Look at what I have done." Rosie's voice layers over Faye's in perfect unison. She reaches up, pointing at Mary Cleary on the crucifix. The arm is broken, with a shard of bone protruding through the skin. "I am the righteous one. I am God's servant. An angel. I am the only one who can enact his judgment. I am the Trypanon savior. Declan was wrong."

"Listen to me," Liam says, letting his power charge his words. "There is no such thing as a Trypanon savior. It's just a myth."

"Heretic." A deep rumble emits from the walls, echoing the word as if the Flukes themselves are speaking. "You know nothing of God's ways. You aren't a Trypanon. You're corrupt. You're as bad as *him*."

She points to Jasper. The Flukes turn toward him, staring without eyes. Jasper flinches and Liam squeezes his hand. Fear quivers through the link.

"Faye," Liam shouts, shifting tactics. Her mismatched eyes swivel back to him. "You are not a Trypanon. I … don't even think they exist. Not in the way we thought. They're just Blue Flukes who escape the Nether and possess living people. That's all you were: a Blue Fluke. You're a servant of the Nether, not a servant of God."

"And what do you know? I fooled you all this time. You are nothing that I wanted. You're not a hero. How could you not see? The only reason I escaped the Nether was you. All I had to do was find you. For years and years I searched. I followed. I knew once I caught you, you'd come back to Shoalport, back to me. You'd *free* me. My brother would finally save me. The Nether told me: I just had to get your Splint out of the way."

"What?" Liam breathes.

"It was easy to rip open that old lady's Fissure and bait him inside. He walked right in, just as the Nether said he would. The Nether knew of his corruption—his sins. The Nether—God—took him because he deserved it. Your parasite—Jasper—could not stop me. That's how I brought you home. And ... and we would have been together forever, but *he* took you from me! DEVIL!"

The words arch into a scream. A billow of black smoke shoots out of her toward Jasper. Liam yanks him to the side just in time.

"Then ... I wasn't the one who took Makoto?" Jasper breathes. His hand shakes in Liam's grip.

"Fool. As if you had the skill. As if the Nether would pick you over me. I am its child. I am God's child. Not my mother's, no. She was wicked. But I have saved her now. She is holy on her cross, and I am the Savior."

"You ... killed Makoto." Liam hears his voice at a distance. "You killed all of them. Do you understand that, Faye? You're not holy. You're not a savior. You're a murderer."

"I ... no. They did it to themselves. I merely opened the doors. There had to be bait for a Fluke to walk through."

"Makoto didn't have a Fluke. He died trying to save me."

"It's not my fault!"

"Then whose fault is it?"

The cracks in her resolve split and grow. Liam feels them in the shape of her. He needs to make her see, make her face what she's done. Free her—hurt her—with the truth. With a punch of power, Liam banishes the sight of Mary Cleary on the cross. In its place, he projects images of Maggie, Oliver, Phoebe, Jake, and Bert. They form a semi-circle, staring down at her like druid gods.

"Look at them," Liam rasps. The drain on their power is strong. He knows there's not much left.

"No. Wait." Faye starts to tremble.

"Liam, I don't think—"

But Jasper is cut off. Instead of jarring Faye out of her prison, the images of her victims feed the darkness in her. The Nether welcomes them like a gift. The aura surrounding her expands. She whimpers, curling in on herself.

"I … I was doing what was holy," Rosie whimpers. "I just wanted to be free. I didn't want to hurt anyone."

The Nether stretches out, spreading like arms in victory. Liam has given it the perfect fuel.

But you did. Maggie's disembodied, saccharine tone worms through the air.

You killed us. Tears run down Oliver's round, gray cheeks.

You became everything I feared you were. Phoebe shakes her head, glaring down at Faye in disgust. *I should have locked you up when I had the chance.*

"Rosie, wait—" Jasper says. He tries to take a step towards her, and an unseen force thrusts him back. Liam fights to keep their hands linked. He can't hold on much longer.

"I was only doing what God wanted."

God has no place with you. The wall of Flukes parts like lips. Declan Jr. slides out from between them, stepping into the room. Rosie squeaks, scuttling away until her back hits the opposite wall. The Flukes shove her away, and she tumbles to the hard ground.

"Rosie!" Liam shouts. "He's not real. None of this is. I'm sorry—"

Rosie can't hear him. Declan's form twists and alters, and he becomes Faye's mother. Then Pastor Gartlett. Then Declan the father. With each change, Faye morphs into Rosie, then back again. The two blur, converging.

You were always wicked, the changing vision says. *You have never been holy. You're a murderer.*

Liam tries desperately to funnel his power, to stop the Nether. It's useless. The cellar is the Nether's nest—its stronghold. And Rosie is too far gone. With each frivolous attempt to stop it, their strength drains. Jasper sags against him, fading fast.

"I'm a murderer," Rosie says. She repeats it again, in Faye's voice.

You are what I've always known you were. You have always been the evil one.

On the end of a short sob, she cuts off. Her features leech to emptiness. The phantoms disappear. A sigh escapes the hole where her mouth used to be, and she is suddenly nothing. Gaping, magnetic nothing. A hole in the world.

She is the Blue Fluke again.

Holding Jasper close, Liam tries to drag him back to the stairs. He doesn't dare speak to him, to ask if he's alright. He couldn't if he tried. With each shuffle, the stairs recede further away. More of their energy is bled from them, drawn toward the Blue Fluke.

Finally, they reach the base of the stairs. Liam looks up and finds them endless: thousands upon thousands of steps. The door at the top is rimmed with light. He'll never reach it. The Blue Fluke slinks towards them. The sheer vacancy of it claws at his back. Jasper groans.

And then the door flies open.

Liam doesn't see the features of the person standing in its frame. He doesn't need to. He feels him. He knows him. He's longed for so long, and the relief is painful. It scrapes through his being, pulling tears from his eyes and a sob from his throat.

Makoto.

In a luminous wave, he sweeps down the stairs, coming to stand before Liam. His eyes are familiar as a heartbeat. He doesn't speak. He looks at Jasper. When gray meets brown, Liam knows that something is about to happen which he cannot stop.

His two greatest friends share a nod. Jasper turns his head, finding Liam's eyes.

It happens too quickly. Jasper's lips are cool and soft, exactly as he imagined in two different lifetimes. He feels both sides of the link press together. A current of pleasure and agony syphons through him. He should have done this so many times.

And then Jasper is pulling away. His fingers unweave from Liam's grip.

"You deserve a life, Liam. We deserve to rest."

Liam cannot move. He fights against a bind he does not understand. It sticks him to the spot. He can only watch as Makoto and Jasper walk together toward the Blue Fluke. They don't look back at him, no matter how much he begs. He wishes for it more than anything, and it's not enough.

It happens fast. He barely has time to scream. The instant Makoto and Jasper touch the Blue Fluke, the cellar erupts in light. The Flukes in the walls whistle and squeal, burning to ash. They try to recede yet cannot escape. The light is Jasper and it is Makoto, their souls merging to tear open the Nether. To make a door. Through it, Liam witnesses the illumination of the Other. There is no hesitation. Makoto and Jasper have made their decision.

They rip Rosie and Faye's conjoined soul from the hold of the Nether, from the pain of her mistakes and her torment. The taint of Blue Fluke is washed away. Cleansed. And together, they pull her into the Other, into a land of liquid light.

The tear seals behind them, severing the Hitch link in sudden, brutal totality.

And then Liam is awake. He's on his back. The sky is dark above him.

Rain mists on his face. His fingers and heels are dug in the mud.

He doesn't feel the Nether or his door to it. He doesn't feel Jasper at all.

Sitting up, he wraps his arms around his legs, presses his forehead to his knees, and cries.

CHAPTER TWENTY-FIVE

RESOLUTION

"**I** GUESS WHAT I'm saying is that I owe you an apology." Sloane leans back in her office chair, taking a sip from a coffee cup from a place called Aroma Joes. She brought Liam one too—a peace offering.

Applebaum braces her hip on the edge of Sloane's desk, crosses her arms over her chest, and shakes her head. "I can't believe we had the killer working on the case and we didn't know."

"I can't believe I had her messing around in my head and I didn't know." Sloane grimaces.

Liam shrugs. "How would you know? I told you Trypanons are impossible to catch. This is why. They could be anyone, could control anyone, and it's easy as hell for them to divert your attention elsewhere."

"Like, to you."

"Maybe. I don't think Faye wanted to implicate me. I think she wanted me to join her."

"You may be spot-on there," Sloane sighs, pulling out a thick file from her desk. She folds it open to reveal stacks of glossy photos. She spins them around and passes a few to Liam. "Faye's apartment was full of articles about you and pictures of you, splashed all over the walls like she was some teen fangirl and you were her boy band crush."

"That's ... a way of putting it."

"As you can see," Sloane narrates as Liam flips through the pictures, "she had one hell of a collection of religious artifacts, mainly from that Trypanism cult. Had those damn inverted double crucifixes everywhere, a shit ton of books, and a bunch of journals we are gonna have a hell of a time working through. But yeah, so far everything we're finding lines up with your story."

"I wish we'd seen how troubled she was," Applebaum says.

"Now don't go giving her a pity party. This bitch rode me around like a new car. And let's not forget the murders."

"Oh, I wasn't saying that to pity her. I just wish we'd caught her earlier."

"Or at all. O'Connor here is the one who figured it out. Without him, we'd be fucked right now. And I'd still be possessed by a reincarnated religious nutjob."

Liam won't bother arguing with her. In truth, he's relieved that Sloane's suspiciousness towards him was instigated by Faye. At least, most of it.

"Maybe. The fact that you were able to resist her at all is remarkable. Your mind is very strong," Liam says.

"No one tells me what to do if I can help it. I have to say, there were moments when I was myself. I knew I didn't feel right. She didn't have a collar on me all the time. Tell you what—she's lucky I couldn't do more."

"Tell him about the files we found." Applebaum nudges Sloane with her foot from behind the desk.

"Oh shit, right. So, I always thought that Phoebe had some suspicions about Faye. It's why I'd always been a little cold to her. Phoebe was a lot of things—some good, some not so much—but damn was she perceptive as hell. I'd gone poking around her files after she died, hoping to find any clues that a Sophont around here had a grudge against her. Only, when I did, I barely found anything. At the time, I just … didn't worry about it. I'm guessing Faye did that—nudged me away from the scent. Anyway, we found the missing files squirreled away in Faye's apartment. Turns out Phoebe had major suspicions about Faye after her mother's hanging incident."

Liam nods. "And she was right: Faye did open a Fissure in her mother. It's a miracle Faye was able to keep Phoebe from figuring out that Mary was a Husk. Her power was both intense and inconsistent. I think it took her years to harness it. Or maybe she just got lucky. I know if Phoebe had been in full control of herself, she'd have taken one look at Mary's Phren and known she was looking at a Husk."

"I think you're right. Well, regardless of whatever mind-juju Faye did on her, Phoebe kept track of her for years. It's why she gave her that Patch job. She probably figured nothing could tempt Faye in a town like Shoalport, and if it did, Phoebe would the first to know."

"But Faye got stronger. As I said, if Faye could influence someone like you, it stands to reason that she could have manipulated Phoebe as well."

"Hard to imagine anyone pulling that off."

"Sure is."

Sloane gives Liam a smile. "You're alright, O'Connor. Sorry again to have given you such a hard time."

"You were just doing your job. And when you weren't, it was Faye's fault."

Sloane shivers again. It will be a long time before she heals from the violation of having a Trypanon in her head.

"So, that's the case wrapped up. FUSE has been here and done their thing."

"Thanks for keeping them off me, by the way. Or at least trying to."

"Don't know how much good I did. That Archer character is a piece of work."

"To put it mildly."

Liam takes a few sips from his coffee and enjoys a comfortable silence with Applebaum and Sloane. Then, something occurs to him. "Faye's body. The Husk. How is it?"

"Shit, someone was supposed to give you a call. Well, as you know, we found her in your basement, sitting cross-legged like it was the most casual place to be. She was taken to the hospital, then transferred to the long-term care facility. But a few weeks ago, her body just … gave out. They weren't totally sure what killed her, just that her lungs were full of fluid and her eyes were bugged out of her skull. If your concern was that she might somehow sneak back into that body, it isn't there anymore."

Liam attempts to mask his relief—he hardly wants to celebrate someone dying—but he sees it reflected in Sloane's expression too. They both want this to be over.

"What we are trying to say, Liam, is that you're done here. We won't be bothering you again." Applebaum shoots Sloane a stern look.

"Jackie is right. Except I may bother you to join us for a drink or two sometime. If you want."

Liam nods. "Yeah. Yeah, that would be nice. And you guys don't need me anymore anyway. I'm just a garden-variety Sophont now. I don't even know if I could seal a Fissure."

"Hopefully you'll never find out," Applebaum says. Her eyes are open, her tone even. It draws into contrast how remote she'd been before.

"Hopefully."

Applebaum picks at the edge of the desk. "If you don't mind me asking, what do you plan to do now? Do you have a new career in mind, or do you just want to retire? You've certainly earned it."

"Jesus, Jackie, the guy just solved one hell of a case. Let him chill for two seconds." Sloane crumples up a Post-it note and tosses it at Applebaum's head. She dodges it easily.

"I do plan to rest for a while. But … I guess I always wanted to teach. Like, at the university level. Maybe lecture. About history. Anything but Fissures."

"I think that's a great idea," Applebaum says. She sounds like a mom.

"Just what the world needs: another academic," Sloane says, rolling her eyes. When Applebaum kicks her again, she gives Liam a wink.

When Liam wakes on Christmas Eve, a light snow is falling. He throws off the covers and rises, going to the window and bracing his palms on the sill. The river is high and gray. It reminds him of Jasper's eyes. He misses him, and it hurts, but the pain is dulling.

He heads downstairs and puts on a pot of coffee. Once he's filled his mug, he grabs a few stalks of bok choy from the fridge.

"Merry Christmas Eve, little man," he says, tossing them to Kermit. He settles into the couch, wrapping his fingers around the warm mug, and stares at Jasper's chair. It's strange to think that Jasper never truly sat in it, only ever inside Liam's Phren. At times, he fights a fear that none of it was real, that he conjured a companion in his loneliness. He closes his eyes and feels the phantom press of Jasper's lips. He reaches up with a warm finger and touches his mouth.

It was real enough.

He takes his time the rest of the morning, reading a book and taking a long shower. He cleaned out the last of the moving boxes a month ago and has been getting the house repaired. He doesn't enjoy having workers banging around early in the morning, but feeling comfortable at home for once is worth the hassle. It's the first time he's ever felt comfortable where he lives.

Ingrid, Teddy, Jill, and Benny won't mind meeting for lunch a bit later in the day, considering the amount of mulled wine they consumed at the Christmas party the night before. Liam had stuck to a single beer. He can't tolerate being hungover anymore. It makes the past too hard to avoid, and he'll miss Jasper so much it's hard to breathe.

Lunch is exactly as Liam predicted. Jill doesn't take off her sunglasses, even though the light in the diner is low, and Benny falls asleep in the booth, leaning up against the wall with his mouth hanging open. Teddy is in unbearably good spirits, which only seems to worsen Jill's hangover. Ingrid is like Liam. She's been avoiding hangovers for similar reasons. There's an empty chair at the table that no one quite manages to ignore or fill.

When Cedra has been brought up, it was usually by accident and followed by apologies to Ingrid, who always brushed them off. "I'm not interested in acting like she didn't exist," she finally snapped one day. After a silence, the mood is somehow improved. No one else wanted to pretend either.

After the case came out in the press, none of them questioned Liam about it, which made it easy to tell them everything. How he met Jasper, and lost him, more than once. How he doesn't know how to sleep now without him in his mind. How he'd called Ashton Webb's grandmother after the case was over but found it too hard to speak to her again. How he wants to get better, to feel better, but he needs time. Somehow, they understand.

Conversation ebbs and flows. Ingrid asks about how Liam is doing and he's honest. He's okay. Not great, but okay. He misses Jasper. He misses him all day, every day. But he's keeping busy. Ingrid understands more than most, and his other friends do too.

Their plates are being bussed by the waiter when Liam gets a call. He's confused at first. Everyone who usually calls him is sitting around the table.

"Hello?"

"Liam? It's Nora, over at the center. I … God, I don't know how to say this so I'm just going to say it."

"What?" A barbed feeling slithers up his gut. His friends have gone silent. They're staring at him.

"It's Ashton. Ashton Webb. He's … fuck." Her voice catches and shakes.

"*What?*"

"Liam, he's awake. Not just awake. He's … he's asking for you."

Liam floats. He feels as if the world is the thing moving while he stands still. He isn't aware of what he says to his friends. The drive to the long-term care facility passes in a blur. He's in the parking lot, dodging patches of black ice. Flakes of snow catch on his eyelashes, and he rubs them away.

Nora is waiting for him in the foyer. She's bouncing in her clogs—the kind all nurses seem to own—and fluttering her hands as if to say "come on, come on."

She barely waits for him before she's striding down the hall. He follows in a jog. Sweat breaks out on his back. His hands tremble and he clenches them to fists. The door to Ashton's room draws closer, until they're standing in front of it. Liam reminds himself to breathe.

"Ready?"

He nods. Nora pushes the door open for him. She doesn't follow him inside.

The first thing Liam sees is an old woman with silver hair, hunched in a chair beside the bed. She turns to look at him. Her eyes are gray and familiar, though clouded by time. Liam's gaze follows the dip of her arm, covered by a green sweater, to the bones of her wrist and her liver-spotted hand. In it, she clasps another hand.

Liam looks up, and finds a face he's known in two lifetimes.

His mouth drops open as their eyes meet. It hurts to see those eyes, so real and distinct. He'd convinced himself this was a fantasy. A dream. Maybe he's asleep now, building a world in his Phren that can never be real.

"Liam? Is that you?" the old woman says. "I saw your face in the papers, but you look so different all grown up. When you called me, it was hard to imagine a face to a name. I just kept thinking of you as a little boy."

Liam can't look away from Jasper. His brows are furrowing, his head tilting to the side.

"Isn't it a miracle?" the woman goes on. "I never thought I'd see him again, not with his spirit back. But look at him. They say they took him for walks, but he'll need help getting his muscles built up again. We'll work on it. All that matters is he came back to us. And he's even talking too. Go ahead, Ash. Say something to your friend."

Ashton blinks. Liam takes an eager step closer, then another. His eyes— Jasper's eyes—widen. Liam sees the spark in them. Sees his dearest friend.

"I know you, but I do not know myself."

Liam swallows. His breath shudders.

"I will help you remember."

EPILOGUE

LIAM ALMOST DROPS a stack of essays when he shuts his car door. He's still wrangling them in his arms when he rounds the house.

Ashton is where he usually is—bent over in the garden with hands deep in soil. Liam tried to get him to wear gardening gloves once. Ashton asked why he would want to garden if he couldn't feel the earth.

"I'm officially on vacation," Liam calls to him, throwing up his hands in mock victory. The essays slip from his grip and flutter across the grass. "Shit."

"I wouldn't be too excited. You still need to pack."

"I'm a pro at packing." Liam tries to maintain dignity as he gathers up the papers, which keep dancing away from him in the spring wind.

"So you've said." Ashton rises to his feet, brushing his hands off on his corduroys. He sidesteps the rows of mounded dirt and makes his way to where Liam is still battling to gather his papers. He snatches up the last one just as Ashton comes to stand before him.

"Hi," Liam says, rising up and smiling at him. Ashton's cheeks are flushed and there's a leaf in his hair. In this moment, he is so very *Jasper*.

"Hello."

It's not their first kiss. Not even close. It's not unique or special. It's the kind of kiss they share every day, in casual moments, beside the kitchen counter or when they pass by each other in the living room, or when they sit by the shore at night and share a drink and a story.

When they pull back, their eyes meet, and something passes between them. There's no Hitch link anymore.

But then, there doesn't need to be.

THE END.

ABOUT THE AUTHOR

Molly Dowd Sullivan holds a masters in Creative Writing from the University of Edinburgh, though she credits slash fanfiction with teaching her how to write. Molly has lived in Vermont, Italy, Scotland, and New Zealand, but now shares a little house on the New Hampshire seacoast with her smoke show husband. Her parents live five minutes away and they're her best friends. You'll usually find her hiking, gardening, cooking, making theatre and art, sitting on the beach, or spoiling her dog, Indiana Bones.

www.mollydowdsullivan.com

Read on for a sneak preview of Molly Dowd Sullivan's next book...

BLIND BOUNTY

"I'm not talking to you," she said, but it was already over. With the quiet clearing of his throat, he'd ruined her day.

She didn't look away from the fire, crackling beneath a cast iron pot full of dubious contents. The evening had been going so well. The ale was fresh. She'd nabbed her favorite leather chair, ideal for people-watching and warming her feet. The lady plucking off folk songs in the corner wasn't half bad. The barkeep knew her name (or rather the one she was currently wearing) and that she disliked gin. For the first time in her life, she'd become a regular.

Now, she could never come here again. All because of him.

"And yet you just did," he said, a smirk curling his words.

A sharp, sudden longing for a dagger made her finger twitch. She could tell by the shift in the air that he'd noticed.

"Fuck off, Barred Owl."

With a sigh, he sunk into the empty chair beside her. She listened to the hiss of the cushion compressing, and still refused to look at him.

"Would if I could, my dear. I'm here on business. The pleasure of your company is merely a garnish."

"I don't do business." Not with him. Not with anyone, anymore.

"So I've heard. All you seem to do these days is languish. Where's the fun in that? I hope the food here is at least palatable." There was the sound of his lips parting, followed by chewing, a pause, and a gag. "What is this slop? I can only assume the regurgitation is complementary. What an odd place to offer your patronage—what—every Tuesday and Thursday? Sometimes Sunday morning for brunch if you're hungover after one too many peach spritzes."

Now, she looked at him. His large eyes, dark as oil in the ember light, stared back. There was a crumb stuck in his short, peppered beard.

"Following me, I see. I didn't think you'd be stupid enough," she said.

"I didn't think you'd be rusty enough not to notice."

For that, she did not have a response. There was a time when no one could think about her without her noticing. Things had gotten worse.

"As I said, I have an opportunity for you." He emptied the rest of his bowl into the bubbling cast iron pot and pulled a hidden flask from his person. He took a swig, swilled his mouth, and spit on the coals.

"Are you high?"

"Not currently."

"I don't—"

"Do business, I know. I'd heard through the grapevine. This, however, is a gig you simply don't say no to. Retirement or not. No one has that luxury, even the obnoxious and terrifying Gnatcatcher."

She turned toward him, leaning forward and bracing her elbow on the armrest.

"I don't give a shit if the Baron himself sent you. No one tells me what to do. I'm done, and if I ever see you again, I'll—"

"It is the Baron."

"—what?"

"The Baron. He's the one who sent me. He has a bounty out, and he's recruiting you and I specifically for the job."

She blinked. Her mouth opened, then closed.

"Exactly," he said, frowning. "I'm not happy about it either."

"The fuck have you gotten us into?" she hissed. She cast out her Sight, casing the room. There was a table arguing about fish bait in the far corner, and a young couple playing footsie. The local drunk was passed out on the front stoop. The back alley was empty. No one seemed to be watching them. Still, she couldn't be sure. Who knew what kind of people the Baron had on his payroll.

"I didn't get us into anything. Hell, I wasn't taking on jobs either, Gnat. They found me. And by the way, they were gonna send one of their own to collect you. You're lucky I talked them into letting me do it."

"Oh yeah. It's my lucky fucking day."

She enjoyed a sprig of satisfaction when he rolled his eyes. He wasn't easy to irritate. Leaning back, she took a long swig from her tankard and wished she'd ordered something stronger than beer. "Why the hell do they need me if they have you?"

"I'm flattered."

"That wasn't a compliment, dumbass. Hiring both of us for the same prize is a historically horrible idea and you know it."

He didn't respond. She shook her head and cursed at the fire.

"I'm finishing my beer first."

"If you call that skunk water 'beer.'"

She glared at him. "I really hate you, you know."

He took another sip from his flask. "It would be strange if you didn't."

To stay up to date on future publications and projects, follow Molly Dowd Sullivan at:

@rageofthenerd
www.mollydowdsullivan.com

Wendelton
Press